AND
All the
SAINTS

Also by Michael Walsh

Exchange Alley

As Time Goes By

AND
ALL the
SAINTS

Michael Walsh

WARNER BOOKS

An AOL Time Warner Company

Photographs from the private collection of the late Agnes Madden provided courtesy of Kathern Kinsey.

Copyright © 2003 by Michael Walsh

An AOL Time Warner Company

Printed in the United States of America

First Printing: February 2003
10   9   8   7   6   5   4   3   2   1

Library of Congress Cataloging-in-Publication Data

Walsh, Michael
    And all the saints / Michael Walsh.
      p. cm.
    ISBN 0-446-51815-8
    1. Madden, Owney, 1891–1980—Fiction.   2. Irish American criminals—Fiction.
  3. Hot Springs (Ark)—Fiction.   4. New York (N.Y.)—Fiction.   5. Criminals—Fiction.
I. Title.

   PS3573.A472242 A86 2003
813'.54—dc21   2002031123

For

Patrick Joseph Walsh (1867–1931)

Joseph Patrick Walsh (1902–1979)

and

John Joseph Walsh (b. 1926)

I put for a general inclination of all mankind a perpetual and restless desire of power after power, that ceaseth only in death.

—Thomas Hobbes, *Leviathan*

If you ever have to cock a gun in a man's face, kill him. If you walk away without killing him after doing that, he'll kill you the next day.

—Murray "the Camel" Humphreys

There are now no gangs in New York and no gangsters in the sense that the word has come into common use . . . merely young hoodlums who seek to take advantage of ancient reputations. They [have] nothing in common with such great brawling, thieving gangs as the Dead Rabbits, Bowery Boys, Eastmans, Gophers and Five Pointers.

—Herbert Asbury, *The Gangs of New York* (1929)

AND
All the
SAINTS

Hot Springs, Arkansas
April 1965

LATELY I'VE BEEN THINKING about the Mad Mick and how he died bloody in the London call box on 23rd Street, and about Little Patsy and his gunsels, Granny and his damsels and Texas and her brassy lungs, and about how we shot the Dutchman in the Palace john in Jersey along with his dear boy Lulu.

The Cotton Club has crossed my mind more than once, which was after it was Jack's Club Deluxe, although if you ask me, it was never the same after they moved it from darktown to midtown and Hymie Arluck went Hollywood and turned into the Wizard of Oz. So has the Duke, for that matter, although nobody ever called him that when I was around, because I was always the real Duke, if you ask anybody who knows. Like Walter and Damon and Jimmy Hines and Joe the Boss and Arnold and Lucky and Meyer, and Estes the Senator from Tennessee and John the Senator from Arkansas, and Joe's kids Jack and Bobby and all the rest of them who made my life so remunerative and difficult more or less at the same time. Not to mention the Kitchen gang, One Lung, Razor, Happy Jack, Art and Hoppo, but also Legs, Lucky and the Bug, the Big Fella and the Little Man.

Gone now, most of them long gone, except for old friends like Mae and Georgie, big stars now, four-letter household words. And here I sit in Bubbles, alone with Agnes and my pigeons, gazing out on North Mountain and West Mountain and the rest of the Ouachitas, which remind me of Ireland, at least the Ireland my mother used to tell me about, which was probably mostly a lie. Whereas they've all been plugged, fried, planted and otherwise disposed of.

When I think about them other mugs, I suppose I got off lucky, luckier than Luciano, although I never went for a ride like him, although he never got it from the Hudson Dusters like I did. Lucky ran dames, I ran after 'em, which may be the basic difference between us, when you come to think of it. And right now, who would you rather be? Me, sitting here pretty if semi-ventilated in Hot Springs, or Salvatore Lucania, dead on the tarmac in wop-land, his nasty heart bursted wide open and his last view the phiz of a Hollywood producer, there to seek his life story? Me, I never did much worry about immortality.

Except now, when mortality's as close as a barber's blade. If you ask me, you could learn a thing or two about life from yours truly, if learning there is to be had from the ruminations of an old English Irishman, if you call 73 old, which I guess you have to, especially in my profession.

As far as this truthfulness stuff goes, though, I have to tell you that in my opinion truthfulness is vastly overrated, especially in a court of law, where lying is always much more efficacious, not to mention safer, not to mention profitable. Besides, lying's something I've known since I was a kid, something I've tried to teach all my boys, on account of in our business that's what you do if you want to stay in business. When somebody tells me how that's different from what other businessmen do, then maybe I'll stop. But first I'll laugh in his face and tote up my swag one last time.

They say that every man is a hero to his dog, of which I've had plenty and each one of 'em a Jack Russell, but no man is a hero to his valet, of which I've had only one, because you can replace a mutt but not a man. I guess if I have a purpose these days, it's to get people to remember us, our gang and our girls, recollection right and proper, givin' the divvil his due as it were, which is why I'm summoning memories and conjuring the dead. Because when everything else has departed, slipped aside, fallen away or been blown asunder, what do we have left except remembrance? Old and fading, mayhaps, but alive and whole and full of life's coursing blood as long as we are.

There isn't a day that goes by that I don't think about them all, and what we did and how we did it and sometimes even why. Most of all I think about them that died and those what lived, whether any of them deserved it or not, and wonder how it all turned out the way it did and why I'm still here, with five bullets in my gut and six gone but God it hurts, still hurts, fifty years on and more.

And most of all, in this month of April I think of May.

PART I

Chapter

One

ME AND MARTY was up on the roof puttin' down a sick pigeon when Ma called us in for supper.

Some folks will tell you to use an ice pick, but me I prefer to use a knife. A nice sharp knife, it has to be: real sharp, otherwise you might not kill your bird straightaway, and I always believed in being both quick and sure.

"Martin Aloysius Madden!" she shouted, and Marty's head swiveled on his shoulders like a lazy Susan that just got spun but good. Marty was more afraid of Ma than he was of getting hit by a locomotive on Death Avenue, which was to say pretty damn afraid, because Martin never had no taste for violence or any of that sort of thing, which is also why he wasn't helping me much with the pigeon. "Owen Vincent Madden! Both of ya get in here right this minute!"

We could tell Ma was mad because that's what her using our two Christian names signified. In this she was pretty much like all the other Mas in the neighborhood, who would shout out the litany of given names of their miserable broods at full blast up and down the Avenue when they was especially peeved or put out.

Still and all, I didn't much like my full moniker in them days. My dear departed Da had always called me Owney, right up to the end on the dock in Liverpool. But since Da's death, no one else had called me that, and so it was by the name of Owen Vincent that I was first known in the great City of New York, although that was one of the things I determined to change as soon as I could, since I felt that a new land called for a new identity of my own choosing and the time to start was now.

"I'm not Owen Vincent, Ma. I'm Owney Madden of Tenth Avenue! And this here fella is me brother and sidekick, Marty." I glanced over at Martin, who was still wrestling with the pigeon, and the pigeon was getting the upper hand.

"I don't care who you're after callin' yourselves, you boys get down here right away," ordered Ma, and so now Marty and I had a problem, which was to kill this bird in jig time or let him go, which was hardly bein' merciful. Marty was all for freeing him because the bird was flopping around something fierce and trying to peck his hand, which was making it difficult for me to get the point of the knife into his mouth.

I, on the other hand, was for sending him on to the other side, because Ma was always complaining about how the pigeon shite on the windowsills looked disgusting, and here was I, trying to do her a favor, not to mention put this bird out of his misery, because that's the kind and moral thing to do. "Hold him tight, for sweet Jesus' sake," I said, but Marty was having his hands full and I could see he was about to lose control.

The bird didn't like the idea of going over to the other side any better than the rest of us, and it fought like hell, beating its wings and trying to bite my brother's fingers off, so I grabbed it away, figuring to do the job myself. I could hear Ma's heavy tread in the stairwell that led up to the roof from our flat on the top floor. Ma was a short woman who since our Da's death always dressed in black and wore her hair, which was already turning white, pulled back in a bun. She seemed old to us kids, but when I think back on it, she couldn't have been but a couple of years beyond thirty. People got older younger back then.

She poked her head through the door that led to the roof and was searching for us in the twilight, although luckily for us, her eyes were having trouble focusing in the dark. "What are you boys doin'?" she yelled. "Get down here and wash up before your supper gets cold. It's rude to keep me and May waitin'." Across the North River, I could see the sun setting behind Jersey and I might have enjoyed the view if only the damn bird would keep still, cooperate and die.

"We're over here, Ma," piped up Marty just as that pigeon sank its beak into the heel of my thumb. I let out a yelp and dropped the knife, the knife my Da bequeathed me, which damn near flew over the edge of the roof and down the grimy ventilation shaft that must have seemed like a good idea to the reformers who built the dumbbell New Law tenements, but were mostly used as swill slops and garbage dumps by us tenants. That's goo-goos for you:

always tryin' to fix one problem and creating two or three others. Which of course just gives them more to fix.

So there I was, one hand around the bird's neck, the other reaching for my knife, and my brother, Marty, just standin' there stupid.

Story of my life.

Just before the dreaded hand could clamp my ear and hoist me to my feet I managed to bring pigeon and knife together and that was the end of the job.

"Jesus, Mary and Joseph and all t'e saints," said Ma, looking down at the mess. "What in t'e name of God are ya doin'?"

"Nothin', Ma," says Marty.

Story of his life.

Then I was gone too, bein' dragged downstairs by my Ma and into the kitchen, which is where we took all our meals and where, truth to tell, we mostly lived on account of there wasn't much room on the top floor of 352 Tenth Avenue, New York, New York, just a tiny parlor with a stick or two of furniture; a bedroom, where Ma and my sister, May, slept alongside Ma's steamer trunk brought over from Ireland, which doubled as her hope chest; and a little kitchen where the bathtub lived along with the rest of the family. On cold winter's days we slept there, me, Marty, May and our Ma, boys with boys and girls with girls, wrapped up in blankets like penthouse Eskimos, which is pretty much what we felt like in the morning after the stove fire had gone out.

Now, Tenth in those days wasn't anything like it is today, what with the West Side Highway, the Lincoln Tunnel and Dyer Avenue and all. Tenth in those days—when it really was Tenth Avenue—was lined with five-story red-brick tenements, the kind where nobody felt superior to nobody else, on account of everybody was the same, which was to say poor, except for the landlords. There was a streetcar line running down the middle of it, and the rail yards were just across the way, which maybe wasn't so scenic, but the fact that there were fewer buildings on the west side of the avenue meant that there was a lot of light in the afternoon, and when you've lived in New York for a while, you realize that light is something that money can't buy, and here we were getting it for free.

I was still thinking about that bird as Ma yanked me downstairs. "Owen," she said, "you ought to be ashamed of yourself torturin' t'at poor t'ing. Tomorrow you'll go to church and say ten Hail Marys for the repose of its soul."

"But, Ma," I protested, "it's free now."

"Free as a boid, Ma," added Marty. He had already adopted the pronunciation of the neighborhood. I never saw anybody become an American as fast as Marty did. Me, I was hedging my bets. I figured it was better if the Americans thought I was English and the Irish knew I was Irish. Safer too.

"It don't matter whether it's hurt or not," replied Ma, who was never anything but Irish, even though she'd lived in England for a third of her life; like most real Irish, she never did learn to pronounce her *th*'s. "You was after hurtin' t'at bird, and in God's mind t'at's all t'at matters."

That didn't make no sense to me then and it still don't. "But if nothin' happens, then you ain't guilty," I retorted as politely as I could, given that she still had me by the ear. "I mean the coppers gotta catch ya before they can arrest ya, right? Plus ya gotta've actually done it. Otherwise it's just—" I looked to Marty to help me out, the dumb cluck.

"Hearsay," says he.

"Somethin' like that," says I.

Ma settled this fine point of legal understanding by giving me a sharp yank on the lobe and letting me go. "Don't talk back to your mother, boy," she said. "God's listenin'. And so's Mary."

By now we were in the kitchen, where May was slicing a potato into the soup. Like Ma her name was Mary, but we called her May, because that's what the Irish did. "Owen, are you in trouble again?" she asked, smiling, and I guess if you asked me who was the first girl I ever loved, I would have to answer May—not in any filthy-dirty way, mind you, but purely because she was my six-year-old sister.

"I was just takin' the air, May," says me with a wink, and I knew that she knew I wasn't. There was this kind of secret communication between us, which I never had with Marty. Whenever there was trouble between me and Ma, May always stuck up for me, which was more than could be said for Marty.

"Liar," said Marty.

I threw a mock left at his head like I was the Black Prince, Peter Jackson himself, the Australian colored boy what could put down a white man with one punch. Even back then I loved the fight game, like my Da had, and couldn't help be a little bit proud that in the very year I was born Gentleman Jim had fought Black Peter to a sixty-one-round draw on his way to the heavyweight championship of the world.

Marty tried to duck but he never could duck very well and I caught him flush on the cauliflower. I couldn't help but follow through with a right to the old steak and chips, which dropped his jaw as he gasped for breath, and I woulda clipped him one right on the jaw, just like my Da had taught me, when . . .

"Ow!"

May's hand was bleeding. The peeler had slipped as she turned to look at us, and had nicked her finger. I was at her side in a flash, squeezing the wound and holding it tight under some fresh water. May never said nothin', just stood there very calm, letting me take care of her.

"I hope she don't get no blood in the spuds," said Marty, "or start into bawlin'. You know dames."

I was about to take another poke at him when Ma said, "No more fighting, you two." She had that tone in her voice that even the dumbest kid could understand, and I wasn't the dumbest.

"You know what Da made us promise," May said, her own pain forgotten.

At the mention of Da's name, Ma's anger was suddenly replaced by sorrow. "You know how I hate fighting," she said softly. "You know why I hate fighting."

We knew. Even though it was fighting what had got the Maddens, most of us, to America. And it was fighting that, I knew, was going to keep us here and help us make our way in the world. That was what I had already learned in England, and me I never had to learn things twice that really needed learning.

So we stood there, the four Maddens, a girl between me and my brother and our Ma standing off to one side, observing. Somebody had to lead and it might as well be me. "Let's eat," I said. The spud soup went down warm as we finished grace and we finished dinner, almost in that order.

We pushed our bowls away in anticipation of what we called the sermon, which was our mother's post-supper words of wisdom. Mary O'Neill Madden looked every bit of her thirty-two years, an unimaginable age to us then, as she addressed us.

"Children," she said.

It's funny how everyone considers his life to be unique and unusual, when in fact it's usually pretty much of the same old malarkey—absent husband, abundant alcohol, unruly offspring, bad companions, irresistible temptations, ugly sins. Then you live a few years and realize that every man jack of us is pretty much the same, with pretty much the same story, and somehow they came through it and somehow you did too, except of course for them what didn't. But it's the living that writes the stories.

So looking back on things, I guess Ma was no different from any of the boat women who came to America to raise their children, most often by themselves. Sure, there was kids that had fathers on our block, but most of the time the old man was either working or drinking, or both, in which case sure as shooting there would come a day when he would not come home, having fallen off a beam or drowned diggin' a ditch. So the point of whether you had a Da or not was moot. Which meant that it was up to the Mas of our world to try and keep the kids on the straight and narrow, and not lose them to the streets, which was next to impossible. For Ma—every kid's Ma—was Ireland, or Italy, or Germany; Ma was the old ways that had done the likes of us such dirt that we had to flee them. So we fled her, because what else could we do?

"You, Martin," she began, as she always did, with the oldest. "You're all of thirteen years now, and it's time you were after t'inkin' about what you'll be doin' for a livin'."

"Yes, Ma," said Marty, shuffling his feet, the way he always did when he was nervous, which he always was in the presence of our Ma. "A fireman or somethin'."

Now, that I knew for a fact was a dirty lie, for sure wasn't Marty already starting into mixing it up with some of the boys on Tenth Avenue and the surrounding streets, and hadn't he already got himself into some sort of trouble or other. This trouble was principally caused by various tough lads resident on 30th Street and the environs who, seein' what they thought was a soft touch, would request of my brother various loans and remittances pursuant to his passage along 30th Street and environs. Which example he was after following, much as I tried to dissuade him—not for any moral reason, like the kind they taught you down 34th Street at St. Mike's, but for the most practical of reasons, which was that he lacked the talent for it.

Anyway, a paddy could always be a fireman, and at least he had the decency not to lie to her face and say a copper.

"A fireman," she repeated. Ma had nothing against firemen; in her book a fireman was the third rung of the career ladder, right after priest and policeman or maybe navvy or sandhog because there was always paying work for the Irish digging the tunnels for the aqueducts from upstate or the subways that were borin' in over on Seventh Avenue or both.

"You, May?" she said, out of courtesy. May hated to be left out of this kind of discussion, even though she was a girl and it didn't much matter. Her answer never changed.

"Married, Ma," she said, "to a rich man who'll live on Fifth Avenue and always treat me swell."

Now it was my turn. I don't know why it was always my turn last, except that I suppose Ma knew I was smarter than my brother and that when I set my cap for something, I generally did it. I knew that Ma was hoping I'd shoot high, all the way for priest, because the job was steady and the pay was regular. But I'd somethin' else in mind, something better than priest. Something that would combine the toughness of a fighter, like my Da had been, with the cannon-enhanced authority of the cop and the suasion of the padre, although morality had nothing to do with it.

"And you, Owen," she said. "What might you be after becomin'?"

I didn't have to think either long or hard. "A Gopher," says I, ducking.

Chapter

Two

THE REASON I WANTED to be a Gopher was simple: them gangsters never had to work for a living, because there was no percentage in such nonsense, plus nobody took no guff off 'em either. Even after just a few months in New York, I had already figured out that my parents had been right, that there really was golden coins raining down from the heavens and running down the gutters: you just had to reach down and then pick them up, if only you had the sense to know where to look, the courage to take them and the moxie to keep 'em.

It was in precisely this area that I intended to distinguish myself from my own dear Da and all the Maddens that had gone before us. That of taking what Fortune offered, even if it meant grabbing it, instead of waiting for St. Nick to leave it on your doorstep. Born on the birthday of our Lord and Savior, 1891, or perhaps even a week earlier, I might have been inclined to wait for Himself to favor me with signs and signifiers. But even as a lad I was too restless for that.

The name Madden, or so Da used to tell me, means "hound," and indeed of all the animals that made it safely back to the flatlands from Mt. Ararat, I was most fond of dogs. Whether you spell it Ó Madáin, O'Madden, O'Maddane, O'Madigane or Maddigan, it all amounts to the same thing: *Madach*.

My other favorite creature was the lowly pigeon, which my father had taught me to raise on the roof of our flats in Leeds and Wigan. "Sable, a falcon volant seizing a mallaid argent," which is coat-of-arms-speak for our crest, which I can best describe as a vicious bird of prey grasping a hapless duckling with its talons and looking forward to its imminent dinner. Not exactly a pigeon, but aviary enough for me. We had that coat of arms above the dinner table; it was one of the things I brought over on the *Teutonic* with me on that terrible and glorious day that the Maddens proper set out for America, and there never was a day that I didn't identify with the falcon and not the mallard, and swore that would always be the case.

That was my Da's doing. Next to his wife and his children, pigeons were Francis Madden's special passion. The homely homing pigeon, to his eyes, was one of God's finest creatures, nearly infinite in its variety. Why, didn't the Bible record the sacrifice of a pigeon as being pleasing to our Lord way back when?

My Da was not what you would call a reading man, but he had boned up on the lore of the family Columbidae like nobody's business. There were more than 175 different sorts of pigeon—not to mention the majestic variety within each breed—and he could rattle off the names of the different kinds of breeds the way he could recite his evening prayers: Racing Homers, the Colored Homers, Birmingham Rollers. Utility Blue Kings, Gros Mondaines, Giant Homers and Red Carneaux. Fantails, Pouters, Tumblers, Giant Runts.

Da and I spent a lot of time up on those English roofs. Even though he and Ma'd both gone to England shortly after they were married, to look for work in the mills—where more often than not you'd end up losing a finger or a limb before you'd made enough for the Passage—Paddy still wasn't good for much except laying the bricks, and so while Ma worked, Da spent a lot of time at home, takin' care of us kids and keeping himself in shape to fight fists in the local clubs.

Marty never had much interest in birds, but little May did. Da and I were often joined by my sister, who took great childish pleasure in the antics of the pigeons, their flappings and flyings. Sometimes she'd make like a bird and, flapping her baby arms, would try to take flight, runnin' like hell toward the edge of the roof, making chirping noises, getting up a head of steam, and if we didn't look lively and hustle, she'da been over the edge in a second.

"I wanna fly!" she'd say as Da would catch her in his great arms before she could do herself any harm, sheltering her in his shoulders, protecting her with his fists.

"Oh, you'll fly someday, my sweet," Da'd say. "You'll soar. Over across the great wide ocean, to the magic land where the buildings rise higher than the birds, and where a man's reach is limited only by his spirit." As he spoke he'd be holding her tight and wouldn't put her down until he'd carried her safely inside and tucked her back into her wee bed, where he'd stroke her hair and tell her stories of the great Irish heroes, every man jack of which had been a direct Madden ancestor.

A lesson my Da had taught me early was that if you were going to put a bird down, you had to do it quick and subtlelike, so he wouldn't catch on to what you were up to until the knife point was already penetrating his brainpan. Da kept a six-inch knife handy for just such usage, and he could deliver a bird from his misery like nobody I ever saw, with such ease that you got the idea that the bird would have thanked him for it, had the bird lasted long enough to do so. So I was a bit ashamed about the episode on the roof, but I was already learning that's what happened if I let my brother get involved in my business.

My mind was further made up the very next day.

It was one of the hot Indian summer days of the autumn, the kind we didn't have in England, and Ma was on her way back from the market, with Marty, me and May trailing behind her like a bunch of baby ducks, when all of a sudden a gonoph comes running by and just like that snips the strings holding her sack and takes off with our supper in his paws.

It happened so fast that I think it took Ma a moment or two to realize our victuals was gone along with what little money she had left over and she stood there a couple of steps away from our doorway looking after him as if by staring hard enough she could make time stand still and then run backwards until she had got back her haddock and her change. I'll never forget the look on her face, the shock that there could be such horrible little heathens as would steal from a hardworking woman trying to feed her children.

Since this was all so long ago, let me try to give you a clear picture of what this buzzer looked like, because not only was we different back then, we dressed different too. First off, he was wearing a suit and tie, which was the way everybody dressed, whether he was a man or just a punk, and high lace-up shoes. And a cloth cap of course, which was how you could tell how old he was, since a boy didn't graduate to a proper bowler until he was at least sixteen. He mighta been wearing a collar too, I forget, but the point is the light-foot looked exactly like everybody else on the street, except he was running like hell with something that didn't belong to him.

Of course I was mostly looking at his rump, hightailing it up the Avenue, because Marty and me were lying arseways on the sidewalk. When the thief rushed by, he ran right between us, knocking us both for six. I'd like to tell you that I tried to stop him but this boy was good and by the time I realized what he done I was sitting on my duff.

First thing I noticed was that I was okay and so was my brother and the second thing, which by rights ought to have been the first, was that May had been knocked down as well. In them days she couldn't have weighed more than eight stone and there she was, lying sprawled on the pavement like a felled dray horse, and didn't that get me to my feet quick as you can say jackrabbit, and over to her side.

The little lass was already picking herself up, but I could see her lip was bloodied and her brow bruised. This got my blood past the boiling point posthaste, and I didn't know whether to tarry or take out after the miscreant, and in the interval between the two choices he was long gone and so my mind was made up for me. So was my vengeance.

May ran over to Ma and put her arms around her leg. "Don't cry, Ma, we'll get some more food," she bleated, and there was Ma, not having the heart to tell her daughter that no, we wouldn't because it was either that day's meal or the rent money at the end of the week and we may go hungry from time to time but she'd be damned if we were ever going to wander the streets like poor tinkers.

Then Marty was up on his feet, sputtering about how he was going to kill that bum when he caught up to him, etc., although even then I knew Marty didn't have the stomach for killing anybody and never would, which pretty much meant I would have to do it, when the time came.

As for me, I wasn't so much mad as jealous. Sure, I was sore about losing supper. But when I saw how easy it was for him to take the food right out of our mouths without having to work for it even a minute, unless you call stealing work, which I don't, I was confirmed in my belief that that was the kind of living I was going to make. Nobody was ever going to give us nothing, so we would have to take it. Gangsters had things because gangsters took things, and tough gangsters kept things.

I knew. I'd seen them, swaggering around the Kitchen like they owned the place, which they more or less did—and nobody took nothing from them. But I also knew that real gangs didn't take no punks or sissies, so I was going to have to get noticed somehow.

Ma finally tore May away from her leg. Marty was on his feet and I was getting to mine when she said, "Children, let us say a prayer for that poor boy who felt he had no recourse but to steal from us, we who have nearly nothing," and I'll be damned if right then and there on Tenth Avenue we all didn't bless ourselves and say three Our Fathers and three Hail Marys for the eventual salvation of the young thief, although me, I was praying for the repose of his soul because I had already made my vow to God that I was after killing the bastard as soon as I caught up to him. Henceforth, no one was ever going to steal from Owney Madden again and get away with it.

For I alone knew his name, which was William Moore. He called himself Billy but we called him Fats, for he was a chubby boy of about fifteen, the kind that always kept his hair combed and that nobody liked, who lived up on 33rd. Standing there on that dirty Tenth Avenue sidewalk, I swore on the desiccated teats of St. Philomena that I was going to fix Fats's wagon but good and that Ma was going to get her money back with interest before the sun set the next day.

That night in bed I made the mistake of confiding in Marty, whose bravado was evaporating in inverse proportion to his hunger. "Sure, that would be a sin, wouldn't it now?" says he.

I had to tell my brother then and there that it would be a greater sin for me to kill him deader than a rat for being such a coward, but I was perfectly willing to have both sins on my conscience should he so much as breathe a word of my plan to Ma, and I sunk my teeth into one of his dirty toes for emphasis until he hollered uncle and promised to keep his trap shut, come what may.

Fats's Ma—she was even meaner than he was—made him go to St. Michael's School, which was also on 33rd Street, toward Ninth Avenue. I was supposedly attending the same worthy institution as well, but after just a few weeks I realized that prolonged and abstract book learning was only going to slow me down from achieving my life's goals and that therefore there was no percentage in it for yours truly. About the only things I needed to know were how to read and write, which mission had already been accomplished back in Wigan, and how to do sums, not that I had much use for that particular skill yet, but I was counting on it to come in handy down the road, and frankly not so far down the road as all that. A month of sixth-grade classes in arithmetic was more or less all it took for me to get the hang of it, so I was already on the verge of bidding my school years good-bye when Fats came into my life.

I don't think my schoolmate would have been able to distinguish me from Adam or even Adam's rib: I was small, even for my age, and to him I was just another mutt from the neighborhood. So I had the element of surprise on my side when Fats was making his way back home for lunch. I was waiting for him down the stairwell that leads to the tradesmen's entrance of all the buildings, with my cloth cap pulled good and low and holding a rolled-up copy of the *Sun,* or maybe it was the *World,* I forget, in my right hand.

"Hey, Moore," says I as he goes past, and he says, "Who wants to know?" because he can't see me, hiding in the shadows there, and then I says, "Me, I got something for ya," which I knew would get his attention, him being so greedy and all.

As he steps down into the darkness he can just make out my shape but he can't see my face, only my cap. And that's when I bring the newspaper down on his head with a terrible crack, the crack on account of the lead pipe within it that I snatched from the back room of Ginsberg's hardware store when Ginsberg wasn't looking, and down goes Moore like he was shot.

I let him tumble toward me, taking my time. I knew the Maddens' chow was long gone but I also knew the bastard had kept the money. "Lookit at what I brung ya," is what he probably said to that old harlot Mrs. Moore, all the while pocketing Ma's cash. He was mumbling something as I rifled his pants pockets and sure enough, there was Ma's one dollar and twenty-seven cents, which meant Fats had spent sixteen cents on something, although I had certainly got sixteen cents' worth of lump out of his head in return so I figured we were square and everything was jake now that I had the jack back.

Bloody froth was coming out of his mouth, the bubbles popping as he tried to speak, so I put my ear down to his lips, taking care not to get any of his slobber on my lapels, but I couldn't make out no words. And then I, already thinking about my place in history, says, "It's the Killer what done this, you fat bastard," and then I give him another whack, not too hard but just hard enough so that he could appreciate the error of his ways, keep his mouth shut and maybe go to sleep and give me enough time to get away with my hands clean.

He closed his eyes like a good lad and I put the bloody newspaper at the bottom of one of the bins and tossed Ginsberg's length of pipe among the trash that filled the side yard. You think New York is dirty today, you should've seen it then, the yards mostly filled with broken crockery and dog shite, not to mention the shattered glass from the bottles that everything came in in those days, beer bottles and nostrum bottles and pill bottles, each one a different shape and size and all of them useless except for the beer.

Then I walked up the steps as calm as you please and pounded on the door of the Moores' flat and kept pounding until the missus herself opens the door and says what's the matter fer chrissakes, because she could swear something fierce. "Billy's taken an awful tumble," says I, leading her down the stairs to the scene of the crime, at which she lets out a shriek that would have waked the dead and sends myself hustling around the corner to the fire station on 35th Street for help.

"God bless you, boy," was the last thing I could hear her say as I scooted out of earshot. I stopped and got myself a soda at Hutscher's fountain on 34th, drank it down slowly and then strolled up a block farther ten or fifteen minutes later to tell the man on duty what had happened—the truth but not the whole truth and certainly not nothing but the truth.

The soda was so delicious that I felt obliged to treat myself to another on the way back, which is why the firemen had already got to Moore's street by the time I passed by. A small crowd had gathered and before I could get my gob open to ask what was going on I could hear Fats blubbering that a punk named the Killer done it, which was of course me.

Then I saw Moore, propped up by a couple of firemen, talking to a big bottle and stopper named Branagan, who worked our beat when he felt like working. We all knew Branagan: practically every kid in the neighborhood had seen him fooling around with Jenny Gluck, scaring and scattering the pigeons on the rooftop of her family's flat at 380 Tenth Avenue while they did it, and her being underage and all. Fats's eyes were rolling and there was blood all over one side of his face, but he seemed able to talk well enough so I figured he would live. I knew there was no chance he would recognize me, but he would remember my voice for a long time; anytime I wanted to terrify him I would just have to walk up behind him, whisper in his ear and watch him wet his pants.

"Owney," says Eddie Egan, "didja see it?" Eddie lived on Tenth across 30th Street from us and was becoming my best friend. He was a tall, strong kid who was already wearing one of his Da's hand-me-down felt hats, although he never went to school; instead he hung around the rail yards on the west side of Tenth, trying to snatch what he could and either eat it, use it or sell it, and lately he had been taking me along with him because Eddie liked to have some help deciding which was which.

"Wha' happened?" says I, innocent as hell.

"Somebody conked Moore," pipes up Billy Tammany, whose father had a political job downtown, just like his name promised; I never did find out if he was related to Tammany Hall in any meaningful way other than through nomenclature, but everybody figured he was, which was just as good. Every time I saw him, no matter the season, he was wearing the same clothes, which was a gabardine suit with a real collar and long pants; they made me ashamed of my mean knee pants, although my cap was always the best one I could steal. I was just starting to get friendly with Billy, and if he played his cards right, I would probably make him part of my gang, because already back then I knew I would need mugs like him, who were all heart and no head. "Said his name was the Killer." I could feel a shiver of pride run down my spine.

"About time somebody took care of that Moore punk, him what's always stealing from the old ladies, the fook," said Chick Hyland. Chick lived in the same building as Eddie, but Chick was a couple of years older than the rest of us and didn't seem either to work or go to school, so I had him pegged for a gangster for sure. Hyland was almost as big as Branagan although he hadn't yet filled out, the way he did later. I heard Chick hung around with the Gophers, and I was hoping I heard right.

"We've had our eye on him," continued Chick, which I took to mean that they was scouting Moore for membership, but any yertz who would let himself get clobbered like that was obviously not much of a candidate for the gang and so I figured that I had just killed two birds with one pipe: Fats out of the Madden family's hair and out of the Gophers—and me, if I played my cards right, in like Flynn. "But if there's any stealin' going to be going on around here, it's us what'll do it, not this oaf." Chick whistled softly. "A nice piece of work, whoever done this. Could use a fella like him."

Branagan was making his way through the crowd, trying to shoo the people back onto the sidewalks to let the fire wagon with Moore on it get past and on to hospital.

"How is he?" I asks, my mouth full of butter.

"He'll live," says Branagan, brushing past us, "but he'll have a hell of a shiner. Which is nothing compared to what that punk what did it'll get when I catch up with him."

"You and who else?" says I behind his back.

Branagan stopped and turned back to glare at us. "Who said that?" He walked over to us, big as life, waving his nightstick. "Who among you little girls would have the guts to say that to my face? You, Hyland? I hear you're pretty tough." But Chick didn't say nothing, which disappointed me a little, especially with Branagan's booze breath blowing in his pan. Neither did Eddie or Billy, which I guess left it up to me.

"That's for us to know and you to find out, bull," says I.

"Oh, a tough guy," laughed Branagan. I think he was relieved that it wasn't Chick who was giving him the back talk, but me, the littlest fella present; I was so small he didn't even bother to ask my name. "A banty little rooster, aren't you, boyo?" says Branagan, whisking off my cap and ruffling my hair. The whiff of tiger sweat on his breath was so strong I wouldn't need a drink for a month. "Why don't you go home to your milk and cookies, sonny boy?"

"Why don't you go to hell?" says I quietly.

That did it. Branagan straightened up, his eyes flashing above his dirty mustache. He swatted me on the bum with his billy club, hard. "Let me tell you something, buster," he said, but before he could get another word out of his gob and across his food-flecked handlebar, Chick pipes up.

"Hey, watch it, why don't ya, ya big lug, go pick on somebody your own size, fer cryin' out loud."

There they stood, Hyland and Branagan, toe-to-toe, nose-to-paddy-nose, and I guess I was half expectin' the rounder to bring his billy down on Chick's bean, and I'll bet Chick was betting even more than I was. But maybe in some dim recess of his idea-pot Branagan realized that was exactly what Chick wanted, and the rest of us too, and he wasn't about to give any of us the satisfaction.

He jammed his stick back into his belt. "The next time I lay me eyes on you, if you're up to no good, why then you're going to get what's coming to ya." He glared at all of us and then stalked away.

I could feel the lads staring at me, particularly Chick. "That's tellin' that copper," he said, and kicked some dirt my way.

"It was you what told him," I replied.

"I was just backin' you up. You'da done the same."

"Thanks."

"Wasn't you scared?" asks Billy.

"Nah," says I. "Coppers is nothin'."

"Who're you anyway?" asks Chick.

"That's Owney," says helpful Eddie.

"Owney Madden," I said, offering my hand.

"Pleased to meet ya," says Chick, looking me over like I was a full-fledged rooster instead of a peahen. I wasn't no cock of the walk then, but I played bigger than my size, which was the way we did things. "And what have you got to say for yourself, Mr. Owney Madden?"

The crowd was dispersing now, and I could see Mrs. Moore sitting on the stoop, still keening, although it wasn't like her boy was dead or nothing, just learning a little lesson, courtesy of me.

I made up my mind fast and I acted on it. I was going to be twelve at Christmastime. If it was going to happen, it was going to happen now, and me I always believed in making things happen rather than waiting around. "My friends call me the Killer." I jerked my head over to where Fats had fallen. "So will he when he gets back, but he won't be no friend." The pat on the back I got from Chick was the biggest thrill of my life up to that point.

As I gave Ma back most of her money, I told her I had been saving it up for a month by working after school at Ginsberg's store, and what choice did she have except to believe me? May was looking at me with her Sphinx-like gaze, while Marty kept his mouth shut, which was a good thing for him, because what he knowed coulda killed him. Ma's eyes were filling with tears, and I only wished she could have been as proud of me at that moment as I was of myself the next day when Chick asked, real casual-like, if I was after meeting a few of the Gophers.

Chapter

Three

NATURALLY MY BROTHER, MARTY, tried to beat me to the punch as far as the gangster life was concerned.

The dumb cluck had got himself arrested the day after April Fool's Day 1903, which was the spring after we'd arrived in New York, on the charge of bein' an "incorrigible," which got him remanded for a couple of months to the New York Catholic Protectory, Holy Mother Church's alternative to a juvy pen like Elmira upstate. It was a minor attempted half-arsed lush roll of some toff that merited Marty this distinction. Under ordinary circumstances it wouldn'ta got more than a passing nod or mere mention in our neighborhood, but for Ma you woulda thought he had desecrated the Holy Sepulchre itself. So Marty was sent away for a short stretch, which meant I had to look after my sister.

"Is Marty bad?" she asked me one afternoon. We were up on the roof, as usual, her bein' after school and me having played my favorite sport of hooky.

"No worse than the rest of us."

"How's he gonna turn out?" she asked.

"Fair to middlin'," I replied.

"How come?"

"He's dumb."

"That's cruel."

"That's the truth."

About that point old Wagner came up to take the air and that was the end of our conversation. Wagner was the landlord, who'd made a small pile as the master brewer at Bernheimer and Schwartz, way up on Amsterdam Avenue, and had more or less retired to keep an eye on his real estate investment.

"You schildren should be at your homework," he said. Like most Germans, Wagner hated kids.

"Ah, shaddup," I said.

"You're right, Mr. Wagner," said May, pulling me away.

The Kitchen wasn't exclusively a paddy province. There was plenty of Italians, Germans and what have yous there as well: the Reillys, the Brancusis and the landlord Wagners all lived in our building, in various states of familial disrepair. Wagner's German accent was as thick as a piece of the sausage he was always chewing on. Mr. Brancusi appeared to be deceased, because none of us had ever laid eyes on him and Mrs. Brancusi went around wearing mourning black all the day long; there was rumors that the Black Hand had disappeared him for something or other, but there was always rumors about the Mano Nero whenever a wop vanished. Most likely he just got sick of the sight of his fat signora and either hightailed it back to Sicily or took up with one of the flashing-eyed girls he could have met at the Haymarket in Satan's Circus, over on Sixth. As for Mr. Reilly, he was that rarity in our neighborhood, a good, hardworking man—a day laborer who always seemed busy either tearing something down or building something up, oftentimes on the same spot, and that's New York for you.

But if you wanted to be a real gangster, there was only one choice, and that was to be a Gopher, if they'd have you. There'd been gangs in the city since before the riots of '63 and God knows there'd been plenty of them after, most of them Irish, but of all the gangs of New York, it was the Gophers who were the most feared, the most envied and the most desired.

The Gophers were so called because their hideouts were to be found in basements and cellars across the Kitchen, but everybody pronounced the name "Goofers," which they certainly were not. The Gophers were the meanest gang in New York, meaner even than the Five Pointers and the Eastmans, and they could put five hundred lads on the street inside of an hour, every one of them expert in the use of the pipe, the blackjack (which we called a Bessie) and the slungshot, which the old-timers called a Neddy and what the kids today call a slingshot. If you were Irish and were living in the Kitchen, or even on the fringes of the Kitchen, the Gophers was what you wanted to be when either you hadn't quite grown up or weren't quite expecting to, since it was the rare Gopher who managed to attain his twenty-fifth birthday in the vertical position.

Even the Gopher girls was tough. They called themselves the Battle Row Ladies' Social and Athletic Club because their clubhouse was on 39th Street between Tenth and Eleventh Avenues, which was known to all and sundry as Battle Row, but everybody else called them the Lady Gophers, and they'd go into action with the boys, just as good at hurling a brick or a bottle from a rooftop as any man. There was an abattoir at the end of the street, which added to the pungency.

I'd been hearing about the Gophers from the day we got off the boat. Unless you was deaf, dumb and blind, you couldn't help but hear about the Gophers, for they was feared by everybody and that went double for the bulls. The Gophers were the lords of the Kitchen in those days, from 14th Street all the way up to 42nd and beyond, and as I lay in bed and thought about how life would improve when I became one of them, I dreamed of the day when I would not only be chief of the Gophers but the duke of the whole damn West Side, which to me was pretty much the whole world. For already then I was planning how I was going to take over the gang, but if there's one thing I've learned in this life, it's you have to start planning early for anything you really want. With a little luck and a lot of plans, a man can go far and I was sure I had both.

The Gophers was loosely allied to a number of smaller gangs in the area, including the Gorillas, the Rhodes Gang and the Parlor Mob, who lurked to our south, down around 17th Street, where Thirteenth Avenue split off from Eleventh, until somebody got superstitious and the city just made it part of Twelfth. Reinforcements came in handy whenever we were doing battle with the Hudson Dusters, who controlled the turf down the Village way, south of 14th. The Dusters didn't get their name for any bravery or suchlike, but because they were dusted off their noggins with white powder when they went into battle, which as far as us in the Kitchen were concerned was the chicken's way, since in our estimation beer was both a faster and cheaper way to achieve the same effect, which was to smash the noodle of whichever sonofabitch was opposing you, man-to-man, across the field of battle.

The Jewish and Italian gangs was mostly on the East Side, so we didn't see much of them, although about them we heard plenty. Especially about Monk Eastman, the toughest Jew in New York and the leader of the Eastmans, and about his enemy, Paul Kelly, the king of the Five Pointers, who took a mick name but was really an Italian named Paolo Vacarelli who could spout Dante at the drop of a skimmer.

As I've said, the Gophers and the Dusters was mostly Irish, but I don't want you to get the idea that the Irish had a monopoly on criminality. Just about every group but the Germans had its own gang, including the Negroes, the

Italians and the Jews. There were still colored gangs in the Kitchen then, mostly up Little Africa way, over on Eighth and on up to San Juan Hill in the 50s, but they were never the same after the big dustup of 1900, when the Irish gangs and the cops teamed up to beat every woolly head silly, after which the blacks started moving up to Harlem, where they ran into the Irish all over again, only this time they licked them good.

The Jews in our neighborhood were quiet types like Ginsberg whose kids would scoot home as quick as they could after school so as not to get clobbered for killing our Lord and Savior Jesus Christ, while the Italians still lacked the numbers to cause trouble. Why the Germans didn't have a gang of their own was a mystery to everybody, except that back then the Germans were a peaceable sort who talked funny, went to church regular, kept their windows washed and fresh flowers in the flower boxes nine months of the year. You could push them around easy then, not like later.

Now, what the Gophers did mostly was two things: steal and fight with the cops, both of which suited me just fine. There wasn't a peddler, horse cart or New York Central Railroad car on the West Side that was safe from the Gophers, and if and when any of the Metropolitans tried to stop them, a battle royal would ensue, in which the Gophers were usually victorious. You should have seen it back then: bottles, flowerpots, bricks and pipes raining from every rooftop down on the heads of the police, while down on the street the two sides were exchanging body blows and, occasionally, gunshots. Even after Teddy Roosevelt had come and gone, the cops were still as much criminals as any Gopher, and so the fights between them could really be seen as just another gang war, fought as usual over boodle, turf and women. Frankly I couldn't think of anything worth fighting for more.

The other principal occupation of the gangs involved politics, something lost on me at first, but which I came to see later in life as the primary object of all worthy gangland activity. For it seemed that there couldn't be no election without the services of various gangs across the city being enlisted, in order to make sure that the voting men in their district voted in correct and orderly fashion, that is to say for the candidate they were told or paid to vote for. The element of surprise was always unwelcome in a municipal election, since political fortunes rose and fell on predictability.

Chick took me round the summer clubhouse. By summer clubhouse I mean a place under the West Side docks overlooking the North River, which is where the Gophers conducted their business during clement weather. This being a time of relative peace and tranquillity among the various chieftains and subchiefs of both the Gophers and the Dusters, whose shifting alliances were harder to follow than the comings and goings of Democrats and goo-goos down at City Hall, most everybody was in attendance on the day I was presented at court.

The names I'm about to reel off may be hard to believe. It seems impossible that there could be so much talent gathered in one place at the same moment, but so it was during the glorious Indian summer of ought-three. It seemed to my young mind that every famous gangster on the West Side was there, surrounded by henchmen, drabs, mabs, molls, gonophs and what have you. But if you want to know the truth, the first thing that caught my eye wasn't One Lung Curran, sitting like a pasha in his harem, nor the spooky mug of Happy Jack Mulraney, nor even the fearsome Razor Riley, but—a dame. She was a little older than me, but not by so much as would make a difference, and she had just about the prettiest set of ankles I'd seen on a West Side girl yet, not counting my own sister of course.

I gave Chick a shot in the ribs and a stage whisper. "Who's the tomato?"

He looked and saw the object of my interest. "Forget it. She's already been plucked. More than once, if I ain't losing my hearing."

"Yeah but—"

"Yeah but nothin'," said Chick. "Owney Madden—say hi to Mr. Curran."

I'd been so struck by the dame that I'd barely noticed we was standing, Chick and I, right in front of the great man his own good self, setting there amid what looked at first glance to be a sea of New York City coppers.

Uniforms were everywhere. Roundsman's tunics, caps, belts, daysticks, even a pair of shoes or two. All of which adorned not the beefy bodies of the bulls who sometimes patrolled our neighborhood when they were dutch enough to screw up the courage to walk our streets, but the lissome bodies of young lasses, or lasses who were still trying to pretend they were young, each of them sporting some item of a copper's costume, and I must say it did look fetching on them.

"That would be Owney the Killer," I said, amazed at the sight.

One Lung musta seen my look of surprise because instead of greeting me or asking me a question, he rose to his feet with a hacking cough. This was obviously the signal for everybody else to shut the hell up, which they did, turning their attention toward the boss expectantly. The former Duster was the first man I ever saw who had obviously already laid eyes on his own grave site; he had that look, half-scared and half-defiant, that soon-to-be-dead men get when they know they're due for reaping.

"Says Dinny," he begins.

Well, if this had been O'Carolan himself come back to earth to sound the sacred stanzas of Scotia's bards, the effect could not have been greater. Curran's poem—his one and only, as far as I could tell—had been composed on the occasion of his delivering a memorable beating to a copper named Dennis Sullivan of the Charles Street station down the Village, who'd had the temerity to try to put the Dusters out of business. Even worse—Sullivan had called into question the Dusters' effectiveness as a fighting force and election enforcers. Even though the Dusters was the sworn blood enemies of the Gophers, cops were even worse, which is why Curran was celebratin' them.

"Says Dinny," repeats Curran, but that's as far as he gets because he up and hacks a big glob of blood, which one of the uniformed lassies wipes away on the sleeve of her tunic. Nobody else moved, as if this was more or less the ordinary course of things, which it more or less was.

One Lung righted himself, dabbed a few flecks of foam from his lips and gave it another try.

> Says Dinny: "Here's me only chance
> To gain meself a name;
> I'll clean up the Hudson Dusters
> And reach the hall of fame."

A ritual chorus of boos and cries of "damn his eyes, the dirty pig" greeted this arresting opening as the audience settled in to enjoy once again the well-told tale.

> He lost his stick and cannon,
> And his shield they took away.
> It was then that he remembered
> Every dog had got his day.

I can no longer recall all the dozen or so verses, if indeed I ever could, but I never forgot the story, which was as well known in the western precincts of Manhattan as any tale of the Arabian nights. Curran and the Dusters ambushed Dinny on Greenwich Street. First they beat him senseless, then they beat him bloody and then they beat him damn near to death. They beat him with paving stones. They beat him with blackjacks. They stripped him of his tunic, his shield, his stick and his revolver. Finally, they took turns grinding their heels into his gob, until he looked like he'd been run over by all four wheels of a horse cart and left for dead. That was the last time the coppers had challenged the Dusters. One Lung had composed this masterpiece from his hospital bed in Bellevue, where he had landed after the exertion that came with nearly killing Sullivan, and for treatment of his tuberculosis, which was killing him.

Everyone shouted and cheered at the conclusion of Curran's versifying, the happy ending of which proved profoundly satisfying to all and sundry. Me I gave a few perfunctory claps, but my eye was still fixed on the vision I'd seen, who was now coming into better focus on account of she was looking right back at me with the frankest stare I'd ever seen on a girl up to that point. Then I remembered I'd seen her before, over on Ninth. She was a hot-corn girl, one of the last of them, flaunting her wares around the neighborhood as she hawked ears of corn from a pushcart; it was still a girl's job then.

While I was busy remembering, everybody else was busy noticing. "Looks like we got a lover boy on our hands," sneered Razor Riley, who fancied himself hell with the cows and kisses even though he was shorter than me and not half as handsome. He weighed less than a hundred pounds, but it's amazing what a little proficiency with a blackjack, a revolver and your Da's spare shaver will do for a fella's reputation with the distaffs.

"You sure he's a fighter?" asked Happy Jack Mulraney, who spoke out of only one side of his mouth because the muscles of his face were permanently frozen in a grin, and was plenty sore at the world because of it. Some said he got paralyzed in a knife fight, others said it was something his Ma ate when she was carrying him. Nobody knew.

"A right regular Billy Noodle he is for sure," said Goo Goo Knox. Goo Goo was esteemed among the company as the former Gopher who had wandered away to found the Hudson Dusters on account of he had a fight with Mallet Murphy, the Gopher chieftain who ran a saloon in Battle Row where the gang liked to hang out. But when Goo Goo realized what a bunch of rollos he had on his hands south of 14th Street, he came crawling back to the real gang and bringing One Lung with him. There were similar wisecracks from Newburgh Gallagher, Marty Brennan and Stumpy Malarkey and even Battle Annie, the leader of the Lady Gophers, who was the most frightening of them all, and for a moment there I thought I was going to have to fight them all when One Lung Curran himself intervened.

"Ya like it?" he asked, and I had to take my eyes off the dame for a moment so as not to be disrespectful.

"The poem's grand," says I.

"I ain't talkin' about the damn pome," corrects One Lung. "I'm talkin' about this here little filly, Freda Horner. Sure her hot corns'll warm your arse of a cold winter's eve."

Everybody was laughing at me now, and here I am seein' my dreams of Gopher glory goin' up in smoke and my chances with Freda goin' to hell in a handcart when she herself comes to my rescue.

"Aw, leave off," says Freda. "I think he's kinda cute, in a scrawny way."

"Ain't no bigger than a chicken," cracks the Razor.

"Mebbe a rooster," manages Mulraney.

"Copper Branagan called him a banty little rooster," offers Chick, coming to my defense with an adjective.

"If that's true," says I, "then it's a banty little rooster from Hell I am, and damn any man here what says different."

"He means it too," chimes in Freda. "Just look at them eyes. Killer's eyes. Dead man's eyes."

I wasn't sure what I was going to do if any of 'em had taken me up on my offer, but luckily One Lung was still running the meeting. "So you want to fight, do ya?" he asked between hacks.

I nodded, both fists balled tight.

"Then why the hell don't ya get yer new lady friend here a proper piece of wearing apparel, 'stead of these worn-out rags what her old man probably stole off a Jewman?"

Thus it was One Lung his own good self who suggested that, seeing as how I was after being a Gopher and was obviously sweet on Freda, and seeing as how Freda was after becoming a Lady Gopher and was obviously sweet on me, I should evidence my bona fides by handing over the requisite garment in conformity with Gopher tradition, namely, a cop's tunic.

> *If the Killer's the man he sez 'e iz*
> *an' Freda's the gal we thinks she iz,*
> *then Branagan's coat's just her size*
> *and Owney's the best of all her guys*

is how I remember his command, but I could be wrong.

The next thing I remember, everyone's pounding me on the back and telling me to go get 'im, Killer and suchlike, but I hardly noticed the pounding I was taking and sure didn't feel it because Freda had just planted a big one on my kisser that drove almost everything else from my mind.

Chapter

Four

WE WERE TRAILING HIM somewhere along Ninth Avenue late that afternoon, me, Billy, Eddie and Chick, pretending to be just bumming around. The street was full of kids, as it always was: urchins in knee pants and cloth caps, girls in long dresses, hanging around, with nothing to do and nowhere to go except home. Most of their parents were either working, drunk or dead, and so they were left to fend for themselves all day and well into the night. Some of them worked, some of them loafed and some of them even went to school. Nobody looked twice at a boy or girl, not yet six years old, standin' on the street corner begging alms or worse.

Two boys, about ten years old, were having an imaginary gunfight as we passed, shooting at each other with their fingers and dying all sorts of horrible deaths. One of them was beefy and Hunnish; the other was lean, and he hopped around like his pants was on fire.

"Bang! Right between the eyes and Harry goes down!" screamed the first one.

"Pow! Two slugs shred his heart and there's Butch, bleedin' to death on the sidewalk," shouted the other.

We motioned them over and they came on the double.

"What's your name, yegg?" Chick asked the Hun.

"Crazy Butch."

"What about you?"

"Harry the Soldier."

Chick looked at me and the boys. "Who wants to smack these punks around?"

Billy and Eddie each grabbed a kid and pinned his arms back behind his back so hard it almost brought tears to their eyes. Neither of 'em cried, though.

"Where'd you learn names like them?" Chick demanded, for sure weren't Butch and Harry sainted gangsters of the time, and this duo most certainly weren't them.

"Heard 'em in the alley," says the first kid, whose real name turned out to be Art Biedler. "Dint we, Johnny?"

Johnny McArdle, the hoppy one, nodded like his head was going to come off. He had a funny way of parting his hair, way over on the left side of his head a few inches above his ear, then combing the whole thing over his head so it flopped on the other side. It almost made you laugh except there was something about the kid that dared you to, and so probably nobody did.

"So you want to be gangsters, huh?" says I, as if I already was one.

Both punks nodded yes.

"Well, then, you gotta earn your names—you can't just crib 'em. That's like stealing."

Chick joined in. "Just you watch it. Chowderhead goes around pretending to be somebody else, the next thing he knows he gets his noodle conked but good."

"And his stuff stole," added Billy.

"And his dames plucked," said Eddie.

Chick nodded and Art and Johnny were free, but they stood put. "Beat it," I snarled, trying to sound tough.

Johnny was looking at me queer. "You're Owney the Killer," he said.

"Who told you?"

"We seen what you done to Fats," said Art.

"Gave him a hell of a shanty," said Johnny.

This was my second tough moment of the day. I wasn't sure if I was supposed to deep-six the two of them for being material witnesses, or bring 'em both on board.

"Pow!" shouted Johnny, emulating me whacking Fats a good one.

"Right on the bean!" screamed Art.

I looked at Chick. "Whaddya say we let 'em tag along, maybe they learn something?"

"Your call," said Chick, and I realized I'd just made my first gang decision.

"Okay," I says to Art. "You too, Hoppo. But screw up and we'll be feedin' ya to the fish."

And so off we all went, to look for Branagan.

We found him soon enough, and the good news was that he was alone. Now, this was highly unusual in our neck of the woods because normally the coppers was hardly ever seen on our streets unless they was traveling in pairs or packs, which meant Branagan was either planning on cooping, or he was up to something. Which proved to be the explanation, because even back then you had your odd honest copper or two, like poor Dinny Sullivan, and a fat lot of good that done him.

Branagan was shaking down Mollinucci's fruit stand. "I'll be thanking you very much, Signor Milluci," he was saying, for he never could get names quite right, especially Italian ones. Branagan was one of those dumb micks who thought all foreigners were funny, which if you ask me is the English influence on the Irish because limeys really do think all foreigners is funny, especially us.

He left the fruit stand munching on an apple and whistling to himself while the family gave him the evil eye, especially Luigi the son, who was about my age. I would have felt sorry for them except that I didn't like Luigi much because I'd heard he had been making lewd remarks about May at St. Mike's School, and I filed away in the back of my mind that I needed to have a chat with him about that real soon.

We tailed Branagan easily, a block behind, just a bunch of kids walking down the street with time on their hands and him oblivious. Branagan paid us no mind because he had more important things to do, like counting up his wampum.

He turned into a small shaded alley that ran between two of the tenements. We didn't want to chance him seeing us, so we decided that the other fellas should hang back while I, being the smallest and least conspicuous, continued to dog him, and that if I got into trouble, I was to sing out.

He ducked into a backyard, which was as devoid of greenery as ours, except for a small tree that was putting up a good but losing fight against the city. My angle was perfect, for I could see both the tree and the alleyway. I signaled to the others to approach and turned my attention to the yard.

Next to the tree in the dimming light stood a man in a dirty apron, the kind a bartender might wear, who greeted the copper sullenly. "Let's have it, I ain't got all day," I heard Branagan say as I hid in the shade of one of the buildings, tucked in behind a pile of trash. As the man walked toward Branagan, I noticed he had a pronounced limp. "God damn you to hell," he said in thick Irish.

The copper let out one of his big stupid laughs. "Why, Mike," says he, "what kind of an attitude is that to take with an officer of the duly constituted municipal constabulary? You shouldn't begrudge me a little coin to encourage me to ever greater vigilance on your behalf. Surely you'd rather give up some of it to me than all of it to one of them Gopher punks what are scouragin' the neighborhood."

The gimp was still walking toward Branagan, and starting to reach in his pocket, when the cop suddenly leaped forward and struck him a tremendous blow across the shoulders with his daystick. This got my blood boiling, not because of any distaste for violence, but because in my opinion a fight ought to be fair, or at least fixed, and this was neither.

Down went the man named Mike, but not out. As he lay there on the ground, I could hear Branagan saying, "Ya shouldn't have tried to reach for yer weapon, Mike, and sure no one's going to blame me for putting you down." With that he pulled Mr. Mike's hand from his pocket, coming up of course not with a Bessie or a shiv but with a fistful of dough. He pocketed the cash quickly and left the poor fella lying there.

A trash pile is the punk's best friend, for all the tools of the trade can be found there in embryo. You could fashion a club from a old pipe, brass knuckles from discarded metalwork, a shiv from a broken bottle. And of course there was always plenty of paving stones. The glorious thing about New York then was that a weapon was always to hand if only you knew where to look, which I did.

I took out my slungshot and carefully fitted a splendid stone. So intent on counting his loot was Branagan that he probably never heard the whoosh that a rock makes when it's whizzing through the air, never felt the hairs rise up on his neck in anticipation of getting clocked. The stone caught him square in the back of the noggin, which started him to toppling, and then Eddie Egan was on him with the pipe, catching Branagan with a sharp blow right behind the knees, which of course sent him over backward, the spittle flying from his lips. He hit the ground with a thud, and then Chick and Billy were there too, kicking merrily away at his midsection until I put him out cold with a boot right in the teeth. It was a tough job getting his tunic off him, him being so heavy and all, but after a bit of bother the job was done and I had my trophy.

When we looked up from our labors, there was Mr. Mike, struggling to his feet. "You'll forgive me for not helping you out, son," says he. "And may God forgive me for not tryin' to stop ya neither."

I returned most of his potatoes, with me keeping a penny or two for my trouble. He was too polite to count the dough right in front of me. "My thanks to you," he said, shoving it back in his pocket.

I must have looked a tad comical, drawing myself up to my full height, such as it was, but Mr. Mike only smiled. "I hold no brief for violence, but 'tain't right what he's been doing, and to his own people. If you ever need my help, you just ask for Mike Callahan of Callahan's Bar, 'round the corner, and you'll get it, no questions asked." He put out his hand to shake mine, and it was then I realized that I'd never shaken hands man-to-man. It felt good.

So that's how the Gophers got themselves a new member. And that's how I got my first girlfriend.

We got back to the clubhouse after dark, Johnny and Art still tagging along, and there was some minor grumbling about how the gang was goin' to the dogs, what with kids showing up and all, but all the mutterin' stopped right quick enough when we spread Branagan's coat on the ground for all to see and admire, especially One Lung, who was looking more and more like he was hardly going to last through the week.

"Now you gotta give it to one of the girls," says he ceremoniously.

I don't think there was any doubt in anyone's mind which moll was going to receive this particular token of my youthful esteem, but I made a show of looking around just the same. At Drowsy Maggie, and Grace the Virgin, Big Mary, Little Mary and of course Margaret Everdeane, who was already becoming a dish and a half, but in the end it was Freda who got Branagan's uniform and as I wrapped it around her gentle shoulders everybody cheered like hell and somebody handed me a fresh glass of beer straight from the growler but I hardly had a chance to take a single sip because Freda interposed her lips between mine and the beer and the beer lost bad, although it caught up a bit later in the evening.

There was nobody in the flat when Freda and I staggered in around midnight, which meant that Ma and May was sleeping on the roof, and maybe Marty too if he hadn't gone out somewhere. It was still plenty hot out, which meant the temperature in the flat would be like Hell on a bad day, which is why half the building was up on the roof, hoping to catch a drift of air off the river to the west.

Here's something about roofs in them days. Like the yards, they was filled with junk, and you had to watch your step if you didn't want to trip and break an arm, or worse, trip and stumble and go plunging over the side of the building into the courtyard below, which let me tell you happened to more than a few, especially them what had been tipplin'. So we stepped carefully over the fat belly of Mr. Wagner, who was snoring fit to beat the band, and just dodged the head of Mrs. Brancusi. Then Freda stepped right on Marty's hand and he woke up and started in to whining and whimpering. I got my hand over his mug right quick and stifled him.

"Shhh," says I, quietly I thought, but I guess it wasn't that quiet, 'cause May stirred beside my brother and looked me right in the eye. Unlike Marty, when May awoke she was really awake and you could shake her in the middle of the night and ask her to do the seven times tables and she would, and no mistake. "Owen," she said, and smiled at me.

"Hello, May," says I, wobbly. "Say hey to Freda. We're going to be married." Freda just giggled, for truth to tell, in her state talking was not such a good idea.

May took this news without batting an eye. "That's swell," she said, but even in my condition I could tell that she didn't really mean it, that she was just humoring me. "Wait till Ma hears."

May snuggled up tight against her Ma, and even Marty had stopped making noises. Freda and I set ourselves down against the low rooftop wall which, before I put the things of childhood completely behind me, I used to pretend was the crenellated wall of a castle, and me the intrepid defender. Sometimes I was Ivanhoe and sometimes Brian Boru and sometimes just plain Owney Madden of Tenth Avenue, the North River was the moat and the Palisades were the fortifications of the enemy. Freda and I cuddled ourselves up together, pulling Branagan's big coat around us in case it cooled off before sunrise, which was unlikely, but in New York you never knew.

I looked at Freda, her blond hair loose now and tumbling down to her shoulders. Her head had fallen onto her breast and she was breathing slowly and deeply. With her figure covered up she didn't look like a woman anymore, but like the child she still was. Sir Owen of Tenth Avenue, gallantly protecting the youthful Lady Horner from the likes of the wicked Branagan clan. I drew closer to her, and watched the few city lights that I could see glinting and glimmering behind us, like a magic kingdom in which lay vast riches just waiting for the taking, and where anything was possible, even for an Irishman, and right then and there I laid claim to it all. The rail yards were quiet and still, and across the river there was no sign of an invading host, nor even any coppers, just the water lapping gently against the piers, whispering that all was well.

I kissed her once, tenderly, on the cheek, closed my eyes and tried to go to sleep. Then I saw May, looking at me with that look of hers.

"Whaddya want?" I muttered.

"Not much," she said. "Just everything."

Chapter

Five

THE KNOCK ON THE DOOR was followed by Branagan, coming through it in his braces and a big bandage around his head. "Where is he?" says he, barging in, and right away I knew that he could only mean me. Marty's breakfast fell out of his open mouth as he confronted the majesty of the law, and Freda let out a yelp, but May's eyes were shining. Ma tried to get some words out, which I didn't hear because Branagan was already well into the parlor, whereas I was already well out the window and down the fire escape.

I had no idea which crime he was pursuing, but I wasn't taking any chances. I thought I could trust Mr. Callahan, especially after giving him most of his money back and all, and I knew there was no way the copper could have seen me, sneaking up on him from behind like that.

But Fats had got out of hospital a couple of weeks earlier, after being there for about a month. I suppose I had hit him harder than I knew, or perhaps it was just in the right place, thus contradicting the boxing maxim that you never hit an Irishman or a nigger in the head because they don't have any brains to harm. But it didn't take many brains to figure out that the bastard had ratted the Killer out, triggering God knows what sort of suspicions and memories in Branagan's bean, and as I was scrambling down the fire escape, I recalled I'd seen Moore on the street the day before and it must have been the cap he remembered because I was wearing it the same way I had worn it on that day, pulled low and over my left eye, which I was beginning to consider something of a signature look.

I got to the bottom and dropped the last half-story, not knowing quite where to go. I started this way and then that, and thought briefly of trying Ginsberg's but he would be there by now and even blind he couldn't miss me

running in like a demon was chasing me and for sure he couldn't miss Branagan the bull, but that moment of hesitation was my downfall. For here came
Branagan, charging down the stoop stairs like an enraged buffalo, so off I
went in the opposite direction when I run smack into another copper, Branagan's partner he must have been, and then his hand was on my collar and I
found myself hoisted into the air. I took him for a kraut, for he was a big
square-jawed sonofabitch, even bigger than Branagan, and he had my feet
kicking futilely for purchase on the ground as he held me aloft.

"Where might you be going in such a hurry?" he asks.

I twisted around to get a look at him. He had hard brown eyes with a tinge
of green in them. "Out," says me.

"That's where you're wrong. I'd say you were headed *in*."

A small crowd of neighborhood types—kids, punks, drunks, housewives,
fishwives—had already managed to gather, soon to be joined by my Ma and
my sister. I felt acutely embarrassed by my arrest, for the shame of it all, and
although I knew even then it was a feeling I would get used to over the years,
it didn't make it any easier that first time.

"Is this the incorrigible?" asks my captor.

"The very one, Charlie," says Branagan, puffing like one of the locomotive
engines parked across the yard.

The cop called Charlie set me down earthward and with an ease that I
could only admire, and slapped the cuffs on me just like that. "You're in the
soup now for sure." I knew I was in trouble, but I almost didn't mind because
it made me feel dangerous.

They frog-marched me over to Moore's house and up the stairs to their flat.
A pounding on the door soon enough brings the missus front and center and,
right behind her, hanging on to her skirts like the coward he was, comes Fats.

"Is this the mug what hit ya?" asks Branagan, and Moore steps out of his
ma's shadow long enough to nod yes. I could see the humiliation writ large
upon his map, and him a foot taller than me and fifty pounds heavier,
brought low by yours truly, so I made like I was going to clobber him again,
no matter the odds, and he retreated pronto.

"Owney Madden," says the missus, looking daggers at me. "May God have
mercy on your soul, for sure you're a bad one and it's to no good you'll come."

"It's already to no good he's come," chimes in Branagan, giving me a shake.
He turned his ugly puss toward mine, and I could smell garlic on his breath,
like he was an Italian or something. His hair was bloodied and matted and his
clothes were dirty, and I realized he must have spent the night in the alleyway,
unconscious. Which only served to worsen his mood.

"Said his name was the Killer," pipes up Fats in a tinny little voice.

"Well, this is one Killer that won't be doin' much killin' for a while," says the copper named Charlie, whose surname was Becker. "It's the reformatory for him."

For some reason I was more afraid of Becker than of Branagan, perhaps because I had already put Branagan down. Becker looked altogether a more formidable foe, and I knew right away that brute force wasn't going to cut much mustard with him.

After gettin' me positively ID'd, they jigged me up the street. Some of the neighbors turned out to see the all-too-common spectacle of one of the lads being hauled away to face the music, but I kept my head held high and worked up a small smile for Freda's benefit. She squeezed herself between the two bulls and kissed me as I whispered "Callahan." Then she was off, to report the news of my misadventure to the gang.

Whereas we were heading for the West 30th Street station house, in which we soon found ourselves. Those of you who think New York today is the epitome of wickedness must bear with me a bit, for back then the old town was far wickeder than she is today, and even though I've been away for these thirty years, it beggars the imagination to think that any of your modern vices could be worse than what was going on all around us back then: teenage whores, thieves and murderers who couldn't have cared less about the "value" of human life, muggers, sluggers and second-storey men, dusters, gonophs, blowens, bludgets, cows, divers, forks, figure dancers, bingo-boys, danglers, high pads, lush workers, moll buzzers, pigeons, turkey merchants and wires, and worse.

All of them and more were in the station house with yours truly, being monitored by a rotund little man sitting behind a great high desk and scribbling away at a great big book as if his life depended on it. The moniker of this man was recorded on a nameplate to one side: McDougal.

"Name?" asks the man.

"Not guilty, Your Honor," says I.

"I'm not a judge, just the booking sergeant," says he, barely looking up. I wanted to make a good showing at my first arrest, and here I was rushing things. He shuffled some papers on his desk, grabbed a pen and made as if he were starting in to write. "Charge?" he said.

"Mugging wit' a club," says Branagan, gleeful.

"Name and address?"

"Owney Madden of 352 Tenth Avenue," I supplied.

"Native or foreign-born?"

"I was born in England," says I. This intelligence brought the first kindly look from the sergeant my way.

"Then my condolences to you, lad," he said, looking at me over the edges of his spectacles, "for sure there's nothing worse than to be from England, and nothin' better either, for now you're here and not there." He took off his glasses, wiped them on his shirt, perched them back on his nose and stared at me for a nonce.

"Juvenile," says he. "Who speaks for Master Madden, then?"

"I do," says Mr. Mike, coming through the door. I looked over to Branagan and saw him blanch.

"Mr. Callahan," says the desk sergeant, "do you know this here lad?"

"I do, Pete," says Mr. Mike. "He works for me." Now, if that wasn't strictly speaking God's honest truth, it was certainly close enough under the circumstances, considering I had taken a bit of remuneration from Mr. Mike for getting him his money back.

"I'm not saying you're fibbing, Mike, but many's the time I been in your saloon and I never seen this lad before."

"He works out back," says Mike. "Or down cellar."

"Out back," repeats Sergeant McDougal. "And might he have been out back on the afternoon of . . ." and he names the day I slugged Billy Moore.

"He might very well have," says Mr. Mike. "Or down cellar."

This brought forth a derisory guffaw from Branagan. "Well, now, that's a lie and I've got witnesses who can prove it," says he.

"You're out of uniform, Roundsman Branagan," says McDougal, as if he had just noticed.

"That I am, sir," admits Branagan. "But—"

"It's far from the first time," pipes up one of the drabs, a girl named Molly who worked the Circus with her mother and three of her four sisters; the other sister was a nun. "Why, most of the time I've seen him, he don't even have that much on."

Branagan's face started to turn even redder than normal when Black Betty ruffles her skirts and cracks, "I'd recognize that hairy arse anywhere, even in the dark," at which point pretty much pandemonium its own good self breaks loose and McDougal is hammerin' for order, but he's beet-red as well and it's just about this moment when Ma comes bustling in with May by her side, taking in the scene and making the sign of the cross some several times.

"And why might that be?" asks the sergeant, finally regaining control of the situation. He had a little twinkle in his eye the way my Da did when he would slip me a ha'penny back in Leeds, so pleased was he with something I had done.

"Sir, I was set upon by ruffians such as what's been plaguing our streets in these sad and parlous times," interposes Branagan.

That was all Ma needed to hear. "And just who do you t'ink yer callin' a rooffian?" she demanded as May tugged at her hand.

McDougal gaveled Ma into temporary submission and turned back to Branagan. If the copper was looking for sympathy, he got only scorn. "I'm gettin' sick and tired of seeing you officers of the law come trooping in here having let punks like this Madden—"

"And just who do you think yer callin' a punk?" says I, but luckily he ignored me.

"—get the best of you. If you can't maintain the dignity of your uniform, then perhaps you'd be comfortable in some other kind of work clothes."

"Like stripes," a bat named Brown Bess, who was black, cracked wise.

"Makin' little ones outta big ones," perks Black Betty, who was white.

"Wish we could make big ones outta little ones," said Molly, who'd started the whole thing.

Ma clapped her hands over May's ears just as Branagan turned on Molly like he was going to smack her a good one when up pops Mrs. Moore, her pudgy weeping fat boy by her side, and damn if they both don't try to lay the finger on me. "'Twas Owney what hit me," says Fats, "with a piece of lead pipe."

This news seemed to disappoint Sergeant McDougal. "What makes you think so?"

"I know it was him because he's of the same size and build plus he wears his cap exactly the same way, over his eye like that, like he don't wanna see outta one eye or sumpin' I dunno . . ."

"You don't know nothin'," says I. "It coulda been anybody."

"Or nobody at all," says my sister, and I coulda kissed her. "It coulda been an accident."

"You coulda fallen down the stairs," says Molly.

"Or banged your head on the sidewalk," says Black Betty

"Or tumbled down the coal chute," says Brown Bess.

"Happens all the time," says my little May, turning to her Ma.

But that old hoore Moore wasn't buying. She started into brandishing a scrap of stained newsrag. "See, here's the newspaper he wrapped it in," offers the missus, "still stained with the blood of my boy." I didn't see what that ugly old thing, all torn and ripped, proved, but I made a note to myself never to leave evidence lying around again, either that or eliminate all the witnesses one way or another.

The sergeant inspected the paper like it was fish wrap and then tossed it aside. "Are you sure positive this here is the lad who assaulted you?" he asked Fats, who nodded. "I heard his voice," says he, and I knew I was sunk.

This left the sergeant in a confusing position, what with two contradictory stories, not to mention my own denial, so he returned to scribbling in his big book once more. "Unless there are any objections," he said, "and absent any contradictory testimony, defendant is remanded to custody pending a hearing before the magistrate."

I could see my gangland career ending before it had begun, doing ignominious juvy time in the jug before I had got right and proper squared away. "Why don't you ask Fats about stealin' my Ma's money!" I yiped as Branagan made a move for my arm. "Why don't you ask this dirty copper about shaking down Mr. Mike?" I yelped, which pretty much brought the place to a standstill. Sergeant Pete's head whipped up from his ledger and stared at Branagan, who had stopped dead in his traces and was looking daggers at me. "I seen him do it! Tell 'em, Mr. Mike. Tell 'em."

I don't know what would have happened next if what did happen hadn't happened. I was too young then to understand Mr. Mike's reluctance to testify against Branagan, for the same reason that saloon keepers across the city would later not wish to testify against me. The principle of force majeure, so beloved of politicians, was new to me. In any case, Mr. Mike never had to open his gob, for at that moment the front door of the station house flung itself open and in walked the most frightening personage I had ever seen in my life.

Branagan's eyeballs started bulging, and Sergeant McDougal's brow started waggling and his pen stopped moving, and just about the whole of Frog and Toe, which is what real gangsters back then called New York, most of their argot deriving from good old familiar Cockney rhyming slang, don't ask me why, came to a dead stock standstill, the dusters, gonophs, divers, figure dancers, danglers, moll buzzers, pigeons, turkey merchants and wires suddenly as quiet as tombstones, and I alone the center of attention as the hideous creature made a beeline for me.

Now, when I say hideous, I do mean hideous, uglier even than Humpty Jackson was ugly, because Humpty, whose face looked like somebody mashed it with an iron, at least was conversant with Shakespeare, which gave him a certain air and animation. This fella, on the other hand, had a face that when seen from the side looked like his mother had given birth while lying up against a hot stove. His head was mashed flat front and back; if he'da had a third side, he'da been the Flatiron Building of crime.

He was short, like an ape. The biggest thing about him was his stove-in head, which had a flat schnozz and a forehead that stretched all the way up to his receding hairline, where a black oiled thatch defined the top of his skull. His ears were probably his best feature once upon a time, because they didn't stick out like a railroad mail catcher, but now they was thick with cauliflower, as if he were a prizefighter. He also had a weak chin, which sloped down to his Adam's apple like the Inwood cliffs tumbling into the Spuyten Duyvil. To top it all off, his face was criss-crossed by so many scars, nicks, boils, teeth bites, whatnots and what have yous that it looked like the road map to Palookaville, and him the mayor.

The effect this character had on the assemblage was nothing short of remarkable. I've never seen a man dominate a room the way he did, and without doing a damn thing except showing up. Although I had no idea who he might be, I could see the respect he engendered in the eyes of the coppers and of the various personages of low birth or avocation that surrounded yours truly in his time of tribulation. If my complaint against Branagan had stopped the show, it was nothing when set against this ambulatory accusation.

"Tell 'em what?" demanded the apparition. "Anyt'ing Callahoon gotta say 'ready been said to me and he ain't said nottin' or else I'da knowed. In fact," and now he was addressing the entire room, "da least said about anyt'ing da better."

As well as I came to know him later, it's impossible for me to give an accurate impression of the quality of his speech. So I invite you to imagine a sound that rumbled up from somewhere below the new Interborough Rapid Transit lines that were even then undermining our neighborhood and then was crushed through a smelter and finally pushed out of a voice box that may have belonged to an accordion once a long time ago. The accent was Brooklyn Jewman by way of East Side paddy with a touch of colored: the world of our New York in one appalling package, come to life to give nightmares to all those who dwelled above its surface.

He shambled to a halt just before me. "I know what you seen and you ain't seen nothing." All I could manage was a shake of my head, which I hoped he'd interpret that I was agreeing with him, whatever he meant.

Next he turned to Branagan. "And neither has this here copper. Ain't dat right, Breenihan?"

All eyes were on the copper. "If you say so," he said with a quiver in his voice, as if Mr. Gluck had just caught him with the better part of himself in young Miss Jenny, and Mr. Gluck carrying a heater.

"Good," said the troll, setting down on one of the uncomfortable-looking benches that were the room's only furniture. "For a minute I t'ought dere was goin' to be some trouble."

He reached into the recesses of one filthy pocket and produced a pipe, filled with what execrable smoking substance I couldn't imagine, and struck a match against the wall. The phosphor flared to life and dove into the pipe bowl, there to ignite, flame up and flare out. He took a long deep drag of his troost and looked around the room. Everybody thought he was going to say something else, but everybody was wrong. So we all stood there for a minute or two, watching this leprechaun fill his lungs and exhale, until McDougal spoke up.

"No trouble at all, Monk," says he, and I could see that his hand was shaking a little.

"Goot," says the man named Monk. "I gots enuf tribble as is wit'out what I needs more." He puffed on his pipe a while more and inspected his clothing as he sat.

I can't say that he was dressed well, but he seemed to take a certain pride in his appearance. His black suit was worn shiny and his dusty derby was a couple of sizes too small, which meant it perched rather than sat atop his head. But what really caught my eye was the Bessie and the pair of brass knuckles that dangled ornamentally from his belt, like a Red Indian's scalps.

"And how might our friends over Tammany way be today?" ventured McDougal.

I could swear Monk broke wind before answering, which caused a couple of the fallen women to edge away from him, they who were used to almost anything. "Da Wigwam's foine," he said. "What I wants now is for my frien's over dis end of town to be just as fine." He rose and made his way toward the humbling desk of Sergeant McDougal and while he was no taller than I, he cut it right down to size. "Do we have ourselves an understanding here, Sergeant," he asked, "or do I have to consult wit' my cauleegs?"

"I believe we do, sir," said the much-intimidated sarge. "Why, not two minutes ago, Mr. Mike Callahan here was saying that the lad was working out back or down cellar the night in question, whereas our witness, as the boy himself has pointed out, could well be—in fact, most likely is—mistaken."

"Well, now, ain't that interestin'," said the orangutan, patting me on the shoulder like I was a long-lost pal. "Because you see my good frien' Mike must be mistooken as to da day. This here yegg was wit' me the whole time, discussin' the kits and da boids, not knockin' anybody onna head, and he what sayz different is just plumb wrong and that's the end of it." Monk turned to me. "Ya likes boids, don't yuz, kid?" he asks me, and I said sure.

"Any furdah questions?" says my new friend to the sergeant.

"None whatsoever," says McDougal, pounding his gavel down on the desk. "Arrest dismissed for lack of evidence." The room cheered. The Moores were doing a *Pietà* imitation off in the corner, but nobody was paying them any mind. Branagan seethed.

"Mike tole me about you, boy," says my new friend. There was a booger coming out his nose, and rye stains on his tie, and something I took for cat shite on his trousers, but what did I care, he was my new pal, the man who sprung me. "Eastman," he said, sticking a hairy paw in my face. "Pleased to make your acquaintance."

I thought I would fall down right there in a dead faint, for it was only then that I understood that the personage confronting me was none other than the great Monk Eastman his own good Jew self and no mistake, come to save me from my own people and get me started on the proper path to glory, as befitted not my station, which was humble, but my ambition, which was boundless.

Chapter

Six

MONK EASTMAN WAS THE BRAVEST and most violent fellow I ever met. Oh, you can talk about your Legs Diamond and the Dutchman, but in his day, when it came to the rough stuff, Monk had no equal, and that went not only for his tough predecessor Mose the Bowery Boy, homicidal Chinamen like Mock Duck and Gophers like One Lung and Goo Goo but for Paul Kelly most especially as well. It was from Monk that I learned pretty much all the skills that was to stand me in such good stead in my youth, and when I think how close I came to missing the great man entirely, well, no doubt my life would have turned out wholly different.

I was spending a lot of time over on the Lower East Side that late summer and early fall of 1903, so much that the boys back on the West Side had begun to think I had gone over to the other side or something. Now, they knew as well as I did that there was no way I could ever have become an East-man, much less a Five Pointer, but after all I owed my freedom to Monk, and as tough as the Gophers was, there wasn't a man of them, not Goo Goo, One Lung nor Happy Jack—who later killed his friend Paddy the Priest in a bar because the man, drunk, asked him why he didn't laugh out of the other side of his face for a change—was as tough as Monk

And did he ever have the scars to show for it. Once, when he was shaving, which he did religiously, every day, although he seldom washed his hair or the rest of his body, I counted the knife tracks on his torso: at least a dozen from his neck to his belly button, and probably an equal number below the belt. There was also half a dozen or so bullet wounds, some of them with the bullets still inside him, so that when he climbed on the scales for one of his infrequent medical exams (for Monk swore that the doctors killed more innocent men than the gangsters ever had) or when the cops was weighing him for their records, he used to joke that they had to take off a few pounds for the lead. Not once did I ever hear him complain about this pain or that, although sure some of them slugs must have still been causing him anguish. This was another lesson I learned well from Monk, and it stood me in good stead a few years later.

I've said that Monk was ugly, which he was. Monk—or Edward Osterman, to give him his real, although obviously not his Christian, name—came from a respectable Jewish family over Williamsburg way, where his father owned a delicatessen. Monk had a lifelong love for cats and birds, so much so that his Da bought him a pet shop in the hopes that he'd settle down, except that Monk loved his kits and boids so much that he couldn't bear to part with any of them, and so he usually had a number of the former trailing along after him, and at least one of the latter, a big blue-breasted Utility King named Hilda who perched on his shoulder as he went about making his daily rounds.

Physically, Monk may have been the spitting image of Piltdown man, but by God was he useful in all the areas which politicians deem important, although and of course in the end he was betrayed by the brass hats and feathered headdresses down the Wigwam he thought were his friends. And it was perhaps this lesson which Monk taught me that turned out to be the most important one of all: that no matter what they say, no matter how sweetly they name the prizes and no matter the promises they make, the men behind the desks are never really your friends, any more than a cheap whore giving you the come-on from her crib window is. Many was the man I seen in our line of work what fell for their worthless assurances, and many the man who lived to regret it, right up to the moment when he took his seat in Old Sparky and some screw threw the switch.

At the time I met Monk, though, he was the Prince of the Gangsters, the undisputed boss of the East Side from Nigger Mike Salter's Pelham Cafe in Pell Street to Paradise Square, all along the waterfront and as far south as you cared to go before you fell into the harbor. Even the Gophers generally gave the Eastmans a wide berth, although we weren't averse to mixing it up with them now and then, just for the sport of it. As the Sheriff of the New Irving dance hall, Monk clobbered so many men that the ambulance drivers at Bellevue took to calling the hospital's accident ward the Eastman Pavilion.

Monk was a master of all manner of mayhem. He could wield a beer bottle, a lead pipe, a shiv, the knucks, a black Bessie and a barking iron with equal aplomb, and generally patrolled his turf armed with a big club, upon which he had notched a tally of his victims. They say that once, lacking a single notch to bring his total to an even fifty, he turned to the fella sitting next to him on a barstool and laid him out stiff.

Being himself impervious to pain, Monk assumed everybody else was as well and treated them accordingly. One of his favorite fighting tactics, as I soon witnessed, was to break a beer or wine bottle over a man's head and then, while he was still staggering from the force of the blow, gouge one of his eyes out with the shattered neck. Or, if they fell quickly, to stomp out their teeth with one of his heavy steel-toed boots. Monk's handiwork could be viewed on almost any block in the vicinity of the New Irving. "It don't hoit dem none," he explained, "for they's already half-dead when it happens. It only hoits later, when and if dey wakes up." One thing you had to give Monk, though, was that he would never club a mab; oh, he might knock her down, but never in such a way that would mark her, for Monk had the respect for the ladies, he did, whether they deserved it or not, which in his milieu most of them didn't.

Monk's most recent exploit was the Battle of Rivington Street, in August 1903, the year after we arrived in New York, back when gangsters had names like Kid Jigger and Johnny Spanish, Nigger Ruhl, the Lobster Kid and Yakey Yake Brady. There had been trouble brewing between the Eastmans and Kelly's Five Pointers for a long time, mostly over turf, which meant making money, and not, as was so often the case, over dames, which meant spending money.

As I look back on it, and note the confluence of days and dates, I suppose I would say that Rivington Street, and its aftermath in the Bronx, marked the end of old New York as most of the gangsters knew it, and the beginning of a new era, one that offered me the chance that I both seen and took. No matter that the boroughs had only recently been dragged into the municipal fold: the only part of town that mattered was Manhattan, and the part of Manhattan that mattered was still mostly south of 42nd Street. The subways were just getting started then, numbering the days of the els, and the days of the kind of mischief one could get into beneath them, in the city of shadows that belonged to the gangs.

I missed Rivington Street, but a number of the Gopher brethren happened to be passing by the intersection of Rivington and Allen, under the Second Avenue el, on that fateful day and of course Monk later told me all about it, and thus I've heard the tales pretty much straight from the various horse's mouths or arses, as the case may be. There had been trouble brewing between the Eastmans and the Five Pointers for a couple of years, but this particular fight started when some Pointers decided to stick up one of Monk's stuss games. Stuss was a card game, a variation of faro. Nobody plays faro anymore, but back then it was so popular that half its terms joined up with the English language, like keeping tabs, being a piker or a stool pigeon, breaking even, landing in hock, stringing somebody along, getting a square deal and so forth.

Faro was also a betting game, a kind of cross between blackjack, roulette and craps, in which the players laid wagers on which card or combination of cards would turn up as the dealer dealt them two at a time and placed them on a big layout. It was supposed to be fair, with the house having only a slight advantage over the players, except that it wasn't the way they played it in the brace houses down around the Bowery. There was different versions of faro, like skin faro, short faro and rolling faro, but east of the Bowery the one most people played was stuss, or Jewish faro, which was a simplified version that gave the bank a huge advantage, and of course the stuss games were often fixed too, which gave the bank an even bigger advantage. There's nothing as sure as a sure thing, which is the only kind of thing to wager on.

On the night in question, this particular stuss game was taking place under the arch of the el when some Eastmans and some Pointers got into it and gats got drawn and all of a sudden a full-scale donnybrook was under way. The boys was blasting away at each other, and soon others came running, and before you knew it there was more than a hundred gangsters mixing it up, including some Gophers who just happened to be passing by and decided to join in the fun. Which continued until the cops showed up, firing, and three guys was killed and a bunch was arrested, including Monk, who gave his name as Joseph Morris and was released the next day, as usual.

The boys from Tammany decided they'd had enough and so they forced both sides to smoke the peace pipe, although everyone agreed that the East-mans had gotten the better of it, and I think that must have rankled Kelly, who for all his book learning and his airs was after all a hot-blooded Italian and just how hot his blood was we would all discover soon enough.

What the politicians said was this fighting stuff was bad for business and, worse, it was bad for politics. The damn reformers, Republicans mostly, was always holding up the gangs as an example of all that was wrong with New York in general and Tammany in particular, and truth to tell they had a point, for in them days the politicians owned the gangs lock, stock and barrel, which meant there wasn't a hell of a lot of difference between the goose and gander. Meanwhile, the newspapers were sounding the alarm about crime in the streets and how the young folks in the rum wards was nothing but affectless animals who'd kill a man for three cents, then buy a glass of whiskey. So Tom Foley, a Tammany man to his toenails and the fella that they always sent when a diplomatic hand was needed, got into the act and personally made the peace between Monk and Kelly at a dive called the Palm Cafe.

But in this lull between two storms, as it were, I had Monk all to myself, and I put it to good advantage. The man had a positive genius for avoiding arrest, which was due to his Tammany connections, for Monk was an extremely useful field commander in the Tammany Tiger's ongoing wars against the toffs and swells, because who was less swell than Monk? This of course was how he managed to get McDougal to give me the air on just his say-so, which was Tammany big shots like Tim Sullivan's and George Washington Plunkitt's say-so as well. It was the gangster Monk Eastman who introduced me to politics and right from the start I knew which group I preferred.

Monk's minions were among the most effective sluggers—shtarkers, Monk called them in his Hebrew way—the Tiger had, and nobody could take out a pesky poll watcher like Monk; he regulated Tammany elections on the East Side like Theodore Thomas waving his wand in front of an orchestra. There wasn't hardly a soul who would admit to even thinking about voting the wrong way when Monk and his boys showed up, and them that did succumb to error soon found themselves sleeping it off under a park bench somewhere.

"Ya needs guys wit' whiskers," Monk explained to me one afternoon. "Them's da guys what you vote t'ree or four times and nobody da wiser." You could always tell when an election was coming up, because beards sprouted like weeds in sandlots. Men with beards were ideal Tammany voters, because you could vote them once, then shave off part of their whiskers and vote them again, and then shave off everything but the mustache and vote 'em again, and finally shave them clean and vote them once more and there you had it, four votes for the price of one. After which everybody repaired to one of Monk's blind pigs or tigers because defending democracy is thirsty work.

I don't want you to get the notion that during my apprenticeship I was neglecting my duties on the home front. I reported in to Tenth Avenue most every night, and when Ma went off to work each day, I was always sober enough to assure her that I would be in school later that day. The way I had worked out the school problem was by simply having a couple of Monk's lieutenants named Kid Twist and Richie Fitzpatrick show up there one day and explain to the padre in charge that young Master Madden would hence-forth be pursuing his studies informally across town, and that all concerned would be very grateful if the school might carry me as active on its rolls, from time to time indicating the exemplary nature of my attendance, academic achievement and so forth, in exchange for which a certain personage of import was prepared to offer financial emoluments to the parish, which I do believe came from some of Kelly's stuss games that Monk's gang held up, which meant that the poor Jews were indirectly supporting the poor Catholics, at least in my case.

God love her, May would always cover for me, even if she frowned at sleeping until almost noon or even one in the P.M. each day and then leisurely rising and going about my ablutions as best one could in our flat. I kept Marty in line by virtue of my standing in the gang, so that he never dared squeal on me. By the time she got home each night Ma would be too tired to inquire how our days had gone and even if on the off chance she had been alert, I was hardly ever there anyway, so my activities were pretty much a mystery to her, although she must have deep in her heart known, because mothers are rarely as dumb as they pretend to be.

On the afternoons I didn't spend with Monk I was usually to be found over at one or the other of the Gopher clubhouses, where despite my conquest of Branagan and my obvious professional ability, I would still often be set to such menial tasks as fetching the beer growlers from the nearby saloons to slake the fearsome thirsts of the gang. There may have been laws against underage drinking back then, but if there were, we didn't know about them, and no self-respecting barkeep would have paid them any mind, so it was not uncommon in the slightest to see children aged six or seven making the hourly treks from home to pub, passing through the family entrance on their way to fetch Da another beer or, late in the day, to fetch Da himself

The gangsters were basically no different than your average Da. They too lay about all afternoon drinking beer, but unlike your Da, who drank to get drunk and forget all about his fat wife and his cruel foreman, the gangsters was busy fortifying themselves for their next job or battle with the cops. I would not care to impute any degree of cowardice to them in this respect, but the fact remains that for more than a few of them a little dutch courage was no bad thing when it came to punching, eye-blackening, jaw-breaking, blackjacking, ear-chawing, arm-shattering, limb-winging, back-stabbing or even the Big Job itself.

But calculating the profits thereof, that was something about which you needed to be sober as a judge. Since the time of the sainted Whyos there had been a more or less fixed rate for various services, ranging from two dollars for a simple punch-out to a hundred simoleons and up for murder. There was another racket that in my eyes held out even grander possibilities, namely, protection, for sure weren't the streets of New York overrun with criminals looking to take advantage of the helplessness of a businessman? Hadn't the Branagan–Mr. Mike dustup proved that? Why let the police have all the action and all the profit when you could take care of your own? The beauty of protection was that everybody needed it, even when they didn't, and it was during this period that the Gophers got into the taxi-stand protection game, chasing off other drivers with bottles, bricks and pipes, in favor of one or two local companies.

There was even more money to be made from simple robbing and stealing, and the Gophers were the acknowledged masters of being able to heist your aunt Sally off the back of your cart or out of her railroad car and yourself never the wiser. Said heisting mostly had to do with thieving from the New York Central Railroad, whose yards—and here was our gang's stroke of geographic genius—lay conveniently across Tenth Avenue, tantalizing in their proximity and lightly defended by a corps of flatfoots who were mostly the bedraggled and drunken Das about whom I spoke above, who couldn't get no other kind of work. In our poor Kitchen the wealth of nations lay just out of reach for most of the citizenry, locked in rail cars that stood parked and idle within sight of the most miserable widows and orphans. And yet the goods they contained may as well have been in Jerusalem for all the chance the average honest John had to get at them.

We had the keys to the kingdom, though, and made use of them whenever we could. Our problem, in my opinion, was that we didn't make use of them enough. As tough as the Gophers was, when sober they most preferred the easy target, like clobbering a peddler wearily pushing his cart up one of our streets, instead of planning how to take the big prizes. That was something I intended to work on, once I had fully learned my trade.

Monk and I exchanged all manner of confidences that late summer and into the fall and winter. "Own," he would say as we stood together on the roof of his pet shop on Broome Street, where his roost was. He always called me Own, as if he couldn't decide between "Owen" and "Owney" and didn't care to.

"Own, sufferin's a terr'ble t'ing." Monk had a nasty habit of swallowing hard then belching after almost every sentence, the eructation punctuating his sentences like a cymbal crash at a band concert. I think this was because talking was so difficult for him, that it took the cooperation of practically his whole body in order for him to communicate in a nonviolent way. "Tha's why I's tries to end da sufferin' quicklike, and so should you. When you kills a man," and here he looked at me with those blackpool eyes of his, "make sure ya kills him dead right then and there, for ya don't wan' him ta come back ta haunt ya or, worse, kill ya."

Monk took it upon himself to drill me in the arts of war, and I quickly became an ambidextrous virtuoso of the Bessie, the pipe and the slungshot. My tactical mistakes with Moore and Branagan were made clear as the dawn over the East River to me, and I resolved not to repeat them. Monk taught me the proper technique of lush-rolling: how you spotted the toper from his distinctive weaving walk, like a sailor without his land legs; how you cased him for backup, in case he was being followed by a police decoy; the words you used to lure him into an alleyway or blind pig; the way you brained him with a pipe or rock; and how you slipped your hand into his pockets in order to relieve him of his purse and other valuables.

Already, though, I could see other possibilities. The automobile was just beginning to come into popular use, and it seemed to me that when we combined larceny with motion, a whole new way of doing business would suddenly be opened up to us.

I think it was the gangster who made the motorcar really popular, for very quickly we realized that the auto enabled us to strike at our enemies without much fear of getting struck back, at least right away. Whereas before one had to step up to one's enemy and confront him, with all the risk that entailed, with the auto you could simply drive on by and shoot him right there in the street. It wouldn't surprise me a bit if statistics showed that half the cars that was bought in the first decade of this century was bought by gangsters.

All at once, I felt glad to be as young as I was, for as much as I loved Monk, even then I knew that he was a man of the nineteenth century while I was fated to be a man of the twentieth and I intended to take full advantage of it.

And then one fine day he reached into his pocket and presented me with a splendid .38-caliber Smith & Wesson pistol that I would henceforth be proud to call me own. "Own," he says, "I wants ya ta have dis."

Now, granted I was just a kid in them days, but kids is people too, and I had certainly been around enough by then to know the difference between a fine piece of armament and a piece of junk and this was most certainly the former.

"Folla me, kid," says he, and with that off we go, ambling along a path under the Second Avenue el that looks like all the life that had ever been beneath it had withered up and died. It is true we had a wide variety of els to choose from, for back then there was els practically everywhere you looked: the Gilbert lines on Second and Sixth Avenues, the New York Elevated lines on Third and Ninth, running in various spurs and addenda every which way from there.

What the el did was smooth the flow of traffic up and down the avenues, more or less, although there was always jams on the el the same way there is

today on the streets, but what the el also did was cast the streets into permanent shadow, blighting the ground floors and affording the passengers the
added sport of spying on the intimate doings of the folks living on the third
floors of every building the el passed by. You don't hear much about it today,
but this afforded the traveling public a good deal of edification and entertainment, and many's the youngster who first learned the facts of life from the
simple act of riding the el.

If I was to have gone off banging away indiscriminately at any old target on
the West Side, the coppers would have had me in the calaboose sure as shooting. But under the Second Avenue el I was in Monk's territory, as safe as if
I was in the Wigwam itself.

We ended up in the dirty backyard of a tenement on DeLancey Street
whose owner, wouldn't you know it, was an Irishman named O'Donnell from
Connemara. The Irish still had a presence on the Lower East Side then,
although most of the boat paddies were heading for the West Side. But this
O'Donnell had bought the Old Law tenement back when the micks still had
some say in those wards, and damn me if he wasn't gouging them Jews for
dear life. He knew they would pay it too, for what choice did they have? It
was pay, work, beggar your neighbor by selling your goods cheaper than he
could sell his, and either get up and out or fail and die. Life was simple in our
neighborhoods.

We were firing at beer bottles that had been collecting in the yard, and I
had just put down fourteen bottles in a row, seven with each hand, which
Monk had set up for me on the top of the backyard fence. "Own," says Monk
to me, "you knows I thinks you got talent." That was the nicest thing Monk
had ever said to me, and I accepted the compliment with the dignity and
gravity it warranted. "There ain't a one of my boys what can shoot like you."

I squeezed off a couple more shots, shattering the last of the bottles and
scaring the bejesus out of an old lady who'd peeked her head out a back window to see which Gentile was disturbing the peace of the Sabbath. "Thanks,
Monk," says I. "But it ain't really nothing."

Monk belched and farted simultaneously. "Yeah, well," he says, "just be
glad them coppers can't do the same."

"No copper's ever going to put any lead into me," I promised him.

That got a laugh from the expert. "It ain't the coppers you got to worry
about, Own," he said. "They couldn't hit ya if there was a dozen of them, got
ya surrounded point-blank. No, it's your fellow gangster what's dangerous,
them guys what have a reason to learn to shoot straight. Watch out fa dem."

I said I would. Monk had been around for a lot longer than I had, and I always assumed he knew what he was talking about. Already I trusted my life to Monk and would do anything he asked me.

Which he was about to do. "Own," he said, "dis t'ing wit' Kelly, it ain't gonna last."

I had learned Monkspeak well enough by now to know what he was talking about. Kelly, as I've said, was the wop leader of the Five Pointers. Both Monk and Kelly had the protection of Tammany, but latterly the uneasy truce between the gangs that had followed the Battle of Rivington Street and the Peace of the Palm had begun to break down. As a Gopher, I was officially neutral, but my love for Monk was such that if and when the shooting again started, I had already determined to be there, and damn Paul Kelly's dago hide to hell.

"What's up, Monk?" I asked, toying with my .38. I already loved this gun so much that I would rather sleep with it than with Freda.

"Big fight comin'," said Monk, puffing on his pipe and stroking one of his cats. "Him and me. Inna Bronx."

"I want in." At that point in my life, I still wasn't quite sure where the Bronx was, but I already knew I didn't like it. I waited for some response, but he just pulled his bowler down over his eyes and began petting two cats at once, and didn't say nothing for a while.

When Monk got like this, I knew better than to interrupt him. Once we were in the New Irving of an evening when a couple of his boys came along with their frails. Generally the boys would tip their hats to their chief and mutter something respectful, but on this occasion one of them got an attack of fool's courage and said something out of the side of his mouth to his girl about Monk's toilet that I didn't quite catch, but Monk sure did. Nobody had quicker ears than Monk when he wanted to.

He up and felled that bravo, just laid him out there in the saloon, right in front of his girl. First a beer bottle over the head, brought down with such force that pieces of the fella's scalp went flying, followed closely by a couple of the guy's choppers when Monk caught him right in the jaw with one brass-knuckled fist; how he had slipped the knucks on I never quite saw, for Monk was quick as lightning when he felt like it. Monk hustled the bum through the doors of the saloon and right straight into the street. And then he was lying in the gutter, looking up at the stars and not seein' a thing.

The cats was meowing prettily, so content that they didn't give a damn about Hilda perched on Monk's shoulder, nor she them. I had never seen the man sleep, but I would swear before a magistrate that that's the way he probably lay abed, with a seegar in his mouth, his hands calming his pussies and his birds rooking somewhere between his neck and his shoulders or maybe in his hat; and God knows there was enough food specks on Monk's shirtwaist to keep a pride of lions well fed for a month.

"Okay, Own," he said, his voice issuing from somewhere deep in his belly, though his eyes never opened and his lips never moved. "You can come. But if youse gets in da way, I'll kill yas." As much as he loved me, I knew he would too.

Chapter

Seven

I was never quite sure why Monk adopted me the way he did, us bein' of two different professions and all, he of the Hebrew and me of the Roman, but some things in life ain't worth questioning and Monk Eastman most certainly was one of them. If Mr. Mike hadn'ta sent word to him about the precariousness of my situation, if I hadn'ta helped out Mr. Mike in the Branagan department, if Monk had been busy clobberin' some poor sonofabitch instead of attending to Hilda and six of his cats at the pet shop . . . if and what if and I'll be damned if I know.

One of the reasons I took to Monk so quick was that in many ways he reminded me of my own Da, gone but still very much missed, not only by me and my brother and sister but most especially by my Ma, who dressed all in the black, the way a proper Irish widow should.

Not that my own Da in any way resembled the great Eastman in face or form. Francis Madden was of the Galway Maddens, the handsomest and bravest of all the Maddens, dark-haired and blue-eyed, like my own good self. No, the way in which the one recalled the other had more to do with the way each man carried himself, surefooted and confident and not about to take no guff off of no one.

Which are the selfsame qualities that endeared him to Ma, and which made the Madden brood possible. The story, which Ma was wont to tell encouraged merely by a cool evening and a small libation, was that he'd made the journey from Clifden to Galway City in a donkey cart, and then, realizing it was nearing harvest time and he'd not yet found a wife, continued on to the town of Lisdoonvarna in the County of Clare, there to seek a bride among the many young women who flocked to the Burren spa for the selfsame reason, except in reverse.

When, where and how exactly he first spotted Miss Mary Agnes O'Neill is the stuff of familial myth and legend. Da used to tell me 'twas at a dance, while Ma recollects it somewhat otherwise: that a rude but fine-looking young lad bumped into her in the street and then stared after her thunderstruck as she moved away, straightening herself. The next day she found him standing in the doorway of her father's cottage, cap in hand, and this time she got a good long gander at him back, and that pretty much was that.

Back home in Connemara, objections were raised about the O'Neills of Lisdoonvarna, discussions were had about the superiority of civilized Galway folk to Clare poor wretches, etc., whereupon Francis and his old man stepped outside to settle things in the Irish manner. This may have been error on the old man's part, for Francis was regarded far and wide, the length of Connaught in fact, as the finest young pugilist in the province. And indeed, after a few rounds in the little plot of land sandwiched between the farmhouse and shitehouse, his Da saw the strength of his son's argument, and so grudgingly relented. "Jesus, Mary and Joseph and all the saints," said Grandma upon witnessing the results of the discussion. This was the September of 1888.

And so Francis Madden and Mary O'Neill were married, in Corpus Christi Church in Lisdoonvarna, with the bride all of eighteen years old. Corpus Christi was not a grand church, having been built bereft and bare of any superfluous ornament, in the true Calvinist tradition of Irish Catholicism. Christ Himself glared down from the cross with a particularly pained expression on His face as He regarded the miserable sinners in His flock.

Folks flocked to the wedding, from all over the baronies of Corcomroe and Burren, from the towns of Lisdoonvarna, Ballyvaughan, Kilfenora, and Ennistymon, from the hamlets of Carrowney Cleary and Cloughaun and Ballinalacken, and by God even some passing tinkers, having observed the festive commotion, tried to stop in and pay their respects to the newly wedded couple, but the parishioners of course shooed the dirty gypsies away in the spirit of true Christian charity.

Immediately following the blessed ministrations, the newly minted Mr. and Mrs. Madden and the entire wedding party made their way west for a mile or two to the O'Neill home, which sat astride the Slieve Elva, with a fine prospect of the Cliffs of Moher and the Aran Islands and the Bens of Connemara. On a clear day, or at least a clear ten minutes or so—so quickly did the clouds scoot in from the ocean, like footballs aimed at a hapless goalkeeper's head—you could practically see the Madden homestead across

Galway Bay. Or so the former Mary O'Neill had whispered during their courtship, the wish and the reality being for the Irish more or less the same thing.

Such music and dancing as then followed can only be imagined, and indeed is still spoken of in those precincts today: "Mna na Eireann," "Clare's Dragoons," "An Cuilfhoinn" and the Sligo song "A Chuaicín Bhinn Dílis" were among the most requested. The pipers let the music ring forth with great vigor, much vim and passable skill. But surely the highlight of the event was provided by Francis and his older brother, Daniel, who, as tenor and baritone, sang the pathetic and beautiful duet "Au fond du Temple Saint," from Bizet's opera *The Pearl Fishers,* which brought tears to everyone's eyes, so poignant and pathetic was the rendition.

Now, the thing about this party was it was not only a celebration but also a wake, for the Maddens were bound for the English Midlands, where they planned to tarry just long enough to earn their passage to and find their fortune in America. First to Leeds, where Francis had a cousin who knew a man who knew a brother of a mill owner, who might be able to give him a job as a cloth dresser, and which paid eighteen shillings sixpence a week, not to mention whatever Mary could take in from the washing. And thence to the great City of New York, whence Mary's sister, Elizabeth, had already departed.

"We're bound for greatness now, Mary, and make no mistake," he said to her as they crossed the Irish Sea, staring as hard as he could into the future and seeing only the Liverpool shoreline in the gloaming, rising up to meet them faster than he had ever expected it would.

Or so the story goes, the story we got from Ma between drinks and tears back in them early years. Bein' that it was before my time, I cannot vouch for its accuracy, but can only observe that that's the way I would have written it, if I could have.

Chapter

Eight

THE FIVE POINTS was where Cross, Anthony, Little Water, Orange and Mulberry Streets all crashed together. Everybody knew one thing about the Five Points and that was that it was the worst neighborhood in New York, even with goo-goos like Jacob Riis whaling away at it as they'd been doing for some time. Several of its choice locales were known far and wide: Mulberry Bend, Bandit's Roost, Bottle Alley—from the way some New Yorkers talked about these places it was as if they'd actually been there. No wonder the Tombs prison was just over on Centre Street.

The center of both the Five Points and the trouble between the Pointers and the Eastmans was a little park called Paradise Square, which believe me it wasn't. It was a little dump of a place that had a paling fence around it, which the neighborhood folks used as a clothesline, so that when you walked by, you would see everybody's wash hanging out in plain public view like it was in their own backyard, and a tribe of boys armed with brickbats and staves, there to keep away thieves from stealing the washing or getting fresh with the knickers.

Everybody who didn't live there, and most of those who did, hated the Five Points, said it was worse than Whitechapel or the Seven Dials in London, which is saying something and which is also why it doesn't exist anymore, because the difference between the Americans and the English is we get rid of our problems and they call them history. Anthony Street later became Worth, Orange bloomed into Baxter and Cross turned into Park Street, and the Five Points vanished unmourned. But that was later, after what happened . . .

The thing about the Points is whereas it had once been pretty much paddy, at this point it was mostly wop, with some chinks lurking off to the side on

Mott Street. Like most Irish lads, I had nothing but contempt for the Italians, who were flooding into New York hard on the heels of the Jews and were, as far as we were concerned, even worse. The guineas were cowardly sorts, as quick with a razor as any Negro as long as your back was to them, and we made fun of them, the way they looked, the way they smelled and the food they ate, not to mention their womenfolk. They weren't even good and proper Catholics, at least not by the lights of the Irish, who practically invented the holy faith, after all.

Paul Kelly was a different kind of dago. He looked more like a professor, and not the whorehouse kind, always dressed to the nines, soft-spoken, and with a kind and gentle manner about him that belied an innate ferocity. He could speak French, Spanish and Italian as well as English and was never to be seen without some sort of reading material to go along with his brace of pistols—maybe not Kant and Hegel like Humpty Jackson, but high-toned stuff nonetheless, such as literature. Kelly had also been a tough bantam-weight boxer who was now the Sheriff of the New Brighton dance hall, just as Monk was the Sheriff of the New Irving.

The function of the sheriffs like Monk and Kelly and Eat 'Em Up Jack McManus and the others was, in addition to keeping the peace in the dance halls, which never stayed peaceful for long, to make sure that the Tiger stayed sleek and well fed, which fodder consisted of the votes of the multitudes who were more likely to be found in the Paresis, Suicide Hall, the Pelham Cafe or the meanest black and tan than up Astor Place way. And with the shores and inlands of Europe emptying out of Irish, Jews and Italians, most of whom had no choice but to dwell with us in the lower wards, where Rum was bishop, pope and rabbi rolled into one, sure weren't there more votes to be found down our way than uptown with the swells. Which is why, if you read your history books, Tammany won more elections than it lost, and I mean well after Boss Tweed, when began the parade of paddies who ran the Tiger with such distinction for so long a time.

Tammany Hall understood something that the *Times* or the *Tribune* most certainly did not, which was that when you had nothing, you also had nothing to lose, and therefore everything to gain, unlike them. When someone gives you a hand up, instead of a handout, you're naturally going to be grateful. And if a vote—or two, or four—is all he asks in return, well, sir, then that's a small enough price to pay. The reformers was always worried about the people's souls, which was more properly the people's own business, whereas Tammany was concerned with their corporal selves, which is much to be preferred when you're hungry.

Still, it seemed to me that the balance of power was the wrong way 'round. Much better for the gangs to own the politicos than to have them runnin' us. For who, after all, was really running things? This was the first and central political question of my young years, and as things turned out, it never changed very much. As much as he was feared, Monk still took the backseat to the likes of Tom Foley, whereas I had already made up my mind that when I was in charge, them bowlers was going to do as I told them, and not vice versa.

Be that as it may, Plunkitt and the bosses had decreed that there was to be no more trouble between the two sheriffs, on account of it was bad for the electoral business, and for a time there wasn't. Because trouble begot headlines in the papers and headlines begat headaches, and nothing was more inimical to the smooth running of the political system. For politics, like crime and sex, does its best and most effective work in the dark. After the Palm Cafe truce, the Tiger even threw a party for both gangs, where Eastmans and Five Pointers alike drank to each other's health and danced, and more, with each other's girls, for sure there's never been a lady who didn't love a gangster, no matter his stripe.

But Monk and Kelly, they just couldn't help from mixing it up. This business of a no-man's-land grated on both sides; the nightly stickups of each other's stuss games, the routine beatings of each other's streetwalkers and the regular killings of each other's soldiers soon enough brought things back to a boil, and there was nothing for it but to go to war once more. But the Tiger had its spies everywhere, and word filtered northwards there was trouble once more in the low-life precincts and all of a sudden there was not Foley but the great George Washington Plunkitt his own good self come around to lay down the law, and we could tell from his exasperated manner that it would be the last time, for sure Tammany had had it.

Plunkitt was neither a tall man nor a grand one; he dressed neatly but simply in a dark suit and derby hat. Back then politicians often put on airs and went about town sporting a high silk topper, but Plunkitt looked more like one of us than a big shot. Which helped when he had to pay a visit to the precincts, such as now. He sat at a table at Nigger Mike's, accompanied by an Irish kid in a cloth cap, about my age, who looked up at him like he was God His own good Self, whom Plunkitt called Jimmy.

Mike himself stood off to one side, polishing some glasses. Like everybody named Nigger something or other in them days, he was a Jewman of swarthy hue, which I'm only telling you so you can picture the scene right and proper.

"Lads," says Plunkitt, creamy as butter, "sure if Big Tim Sullivan and I are not hearin' turr'ble t'ings." For George Washington liked to talk real Irish, even though he was merely shanty, having been born in a sty where Central Park now stands, and many's the time my fancy has turned to wondering how the Fifth Avenue toffs would feel if they knew that where they was walking of a fine summer's day once was home to the poorest and most miserable of the bog-trotters, but then again they would probably feel just fine, thank you, and better's the place for having got rid of its paddies along with the pigs.

Monk and Paul just shuffled their feet and said nothing, for neither had been invited to sit. I stood over in the corner, trying to dodge the fresh hands of the drabs and molls, whose philosophy it was that hardly a lad was too young to make the acquaintance of their custom. "You both know that this here fightin', reports of which are even now being shouted from the rooftops along 14th Street, has got to be concluded in both an expeditious and equitable manner." Plunkitt was scrupulous about not taking sides, for politics is about one thing and one thing only, and that is power and the keeping of same, and therefore it didn't matter a tinker's damn to him which side won as long as one side did, and with a minimum of public disruption and outcry, so that business as usual might continue in peace, with profit for all.

"And conclude it will," he continues. "Since you two lads is feeling the need for havin' t'ings out, I wants ya to settle it between your own good selves man-to-man-like, alone and lacking weapons other than those that the Good Lord above has already give ya, by which I mean yer two fists and your thirty-some-odd teeth." In case anyone present had not quite understood what he meant—and, given Monk's presence, the chances of that were exactly even money—Plunkitt continued. "Therefore," he said, "it'll be just the two of ya, in a place and at a time to be determined by yours truly. Do I make meself clear?"

Kelly nodded like the gentleman he wished he was, while Monk merely clapped his bowler back on his bean. I thought that was the end of it, so I started to approach Monk, but G.W., as I was to learn, never missed introducing himself to a new or unfamiliar face, because a new friend was another marked ballot for Tammany, or perhaps more, and no matter that I was still a ways off from being of legal voting age. "And who might this foine-lookin' young lad be?" says himself to me.

"Owney Madden," says I.

"Owney Madden!" exclaims Plunkitt, as if he had known me all my life. "Another young Irishman come to America to seek his fortune, eh?"

"Born in England, sir," says I, "but Irish through and through."

This seemed to please Plunkitt. "Well, now, son," he says, "there's one t'ing you must always remember and that is that the Irish are born to rule, and with a little bit o' the luck that the Good Lord has proverbially and providentially given dose of us of t'e Hibernian race, it's rulin' that you'll be doin', if only you'll follow the example provided by me and other stout Tammany men."

At this moment a picture of my poor Da in our flat in Wigan came to my mind. The Irish back home didn't seem to be born to rule much of anything except jails and cemeteries, but things here were obviously different. "I know that for a fact, sir," I replied.

"Good lad!" exclaimed Plunkitt. "A born optimist! I t'ank you not to forget that if it's anyt'ing you're ever after needin', why, boy, Tammany's the place for you and yours, whether it's a position, some eatin' money or expenses for a funeral. Just tell 'em George Washington Plunkitt sent ya, and that'll be t'e end of 't, Mr. Owney Madden."

"Owney the Killer, sir," I added, trying to look as tough as I could.

Most folks, taking only my age and my size into account, would laugh when they heard this self-description for the first time, but not Plunkitt. He gave me a serious evaluation head-to-toe. "Well, young Owney the Killer," he said, "I don't know who you're after killin', but I'm forced to assume that the sonofabitch's likely to deserve it." He patted me on the head and ruffled my hair. "And when the time comes when you're old enough to cast your first ballot, I'll be proud were it cast in the Wigwam's humble direction."

He glanced 'round the place to make sure that everyone had got the message: whatever happened between Monk and Kelly, Tammany wanted it settled; and that henceforth Mr. Owney Madden was under G.W.'s personal protection.

He pointed me at the lad with him. "Killer, shake hands with Jimmy Hines. Jimmy used to be a blacksmith till the Tiger raised his sights, and he's goin' places that don't involve a horse's arse. I've a feelin' you two's gonna git along splendidly."

"As long as he don't get in my way," says I.

"As long as you ain't runnin' for anything," says Jimmy, who clearly was going to be.

That settled, we shook hands. And that's how all of us, Eastman, Five Pointer and Gopher alike, and in the company of Mr. Plunkitt, happened to be gathering a few weeks later in a drafty barn somewhere in the vicinity of Fordham Road in the winter of 1903–4 to witness Monk and Kelly go at it with bare knuckles, just like the great John L. himself, and may the best man win. It was the boxer against the puncher, the ring general against the slugger, with Monk cast in the latter roles. For this was well before the era of gloved fighters; in them days a man fought the way God intended, until either he or his opponent was felled by a blow or exhaustion, whichever came first.

My money was on Monk of course, not that I had much. Even in the short time I had known him I had never seen him lose a fight of any kind, be it with fists, Bessies, brassers, pipes or pistols. But Monk in the ring was no Mendoza, who won the championship of England by beating Bill Warr on Bexley Commons in 1794. I know this because, in Irish boxing circles, Mendoza is a hero, him being the one who founded the first boxing school in Eire, and of course as a lad in England I had heard all about him from the tough Jewboys who ran in the gangs in Leeds and Liverpool and used to taunt the Irish kids that everything we knew about boxing we had learned from a Jew, which was true. Still, Monk was quicker and smarter than he looked, which was another lesson he taught me: never let your enemies gauge your true skills, for a tendency to underestimate one's opponent always worked to your disadvantage.

Monk and Kelly came out brawling, which signaled to me a Monk victory. Kelly darted in, looking to land a hard punch, and Monk caught him with a right to the head that split his ear and nearly floored him. Immediately, a great cheer went up from the Eastmans, for they could foresee a Monk blitz, but Kelly just shook it off and got on his horse, backpedaling as if his life depended on it, which it did.

Monk wasn't averse to killing Kelly then and there. I had already seen him put any number of men in the ground without benefit of clergy, and I knew that this blood feud between him and Paul had become more than simply business. Monk wanted to kill the wop—not because he hated him, which I do believe he did not, but because Kelly was all that was standing between him and being the number one fella on the muscle rolls of Tammany. Monk didn't have much ambition, but that was it and God help any man who came between him and it.

Kelly came in again, bobbing and weaving. The only question was whether he'd be able to dance away from Monk's roundhouses until Monk dropped from exhaustion, or whether Monk would catch him, coming in, flush on the button, and put an end to it.

The dance continued like this for some time, Kelly ducking and Monk flailing, and I was just about to succumb to the temptation to take my eyes off the combatants for a moment to see how Plunkitt was reacting when Kelly caught Monk one flush on the chin and put him down.

Even today, sixty years and more after the event, I can scarcely credit my eyes or my memory, for sure didn't Monk hit the deck, down like a sack of Erin's own praties. I forget whether his bum or his head hit the canvas first, but in any case they both landed soon enough, one after the other, and a great cry arose forthwith from the Pointers, as if their man had just felled the Antichrist himself.

The shock this blow engendered in my breast can only be imagined. I had never seen Monk down, not once, and in the most vicious barroom fights; for Kelly to have laid him low seemed almost inconceivable. I don't think there was an Eastman there who doubted for a moment that Monk would make short work of the bookworm and that we would be out of that Bronx barn and on our way back to civilization pronto, instead of lookin' on in shock at our man in the prone position.

When Monk went down, as I say, a great roar went up from the Pointers, but soon enough he was back on his feet, with a new respect for his foe visible in his eyes. Kelly's ring experience was obviously going to be of far greater utility than any one of us had hitherto thought, and now Monk must have come to the same realization. So when Kelly rushed him, which he began to do with regularity, hoping to land another lucky one, Monk would simply lean on him, using his superior weight and strength, until the dago managed to wriggle away.

Matters settled in like this for some time. After the first knockdowns, neither man was able to get the better of the other. Had the battle taken place thirty years on at the Garden, when the Mecca of Boxing was in its glory at Eighth Avenue and 50th Street, I suppose the fans would have been booing and throwing chairs into the ring, but this was a limited audience, present by invitation only, and every man jack of them had a rooting interest that went beyond a mere wager with a turf accountant, for the fate of the city rested on the shoulders of the fella that would come out still standing, and their fates along with it.

Most particularly mine. Plunkitt's benediction meant I had already stepped up a notch or two in class as far as protection was concerned, and I had already decided that whatever the outcome, both Monk and Kelly would never be the same. There had been a tone in the voice of Plunkitt that belied the stage-harp smile, and watching his indifferent reaction to the course of the bout, it seemed pretty clear to me, even if it didn't to the others, that this whole idea of fisticuffs was meant to signal that Tammany wished both chieftains away, and wouldn't they be kind enough to do the Wigwam a favor and kill each other, nice and cleanlike, so that the politicians could get on with the business of stealing.

Therefore, I had also decided that someone was going to have to be around to pick up the pieces when both Monk and Kelly finally fell, and furthermore, I had determined that someone was going to be me. The old ways were not my ways, and at the rate things was changing, what gangland needed was someone with youth and vision, both of which I possessed in abundance.

My philosophizing was interrupted by a spatter of blood and a piece of tongue, which I noted came from Monk's jaw. Kelly had caught him coming in, trying to duck under a left jab but getting caught flush with a right uppercut, and one of Monk's teeth went flying, not that he was likely to miss it or that it would alter his appearance to his disadvantage. By my reckoning, the two men had been fighting for nearly an hour and while it was pretty clear they were both tiring they had plenty of gumption left and they flailed away at each other like a couple of madmen. It wasn't exactly a Marquis of Queensberry bout, and so there was a great deal of hair-pulling, nose-tugging, eye-gouging, kidney-slugging, ear-slapping and so forth, in addition to the punching and pummeling. This was where Monk was in his element, and every time he managed to get his mitts on Kelly's formerly elegant person, the damage done was considerable.

It was about this time that Eat 'Em Up Jack and Razor Riley jumped into the makeshift ring, which was mostly delimited by cow pies and some straw. For a moment I thought they was going to go at it, but they was only calling a temporary halt to the proceedings, to allow the combatants a breather. Although it was damn cold in that barn, both Monk and Kelly were stripped to the waist and sweating like pigs. Somebody dumped a bucket of water over each of them, although where they found water that wasn't frozen I have no idea. Each man was given five minutes to catch his breath and to have his second provide what little medical attention was possible, and then someone else clapped his hands and shouted, "Fight on, lads!" and fought on they did.

Among the many things I learned from watching this spectacle was that having a few rules makes for a better fight, which is why nobody pays to see a barroom brawl, but millions are willing to fork over some dough for a proper heavyweight duel. The spectator quickly tires when there's no way to tell who's winning, for not even the amount of blood on each man is a true indicator of advantage, since it can just as easily be the other fella's. Well into the second hour, I found myself wishing that one or the other of them would end it, and while I was rooting for Monk, at this point a Kelly victory would also mean getting back to the city and a cozy evening with Freda.

At this very moment weren't my prayers answered: With a last great roar of pain and anger and anguish and pride the two enemies threw themselves upon one another, tearing and biting. Monk had sunk his teeth into one of Kelly's ears (tearing ears off was a great sport back then, especially when women was fighting each other) and was fumbling with his fingers for Kelly's eyeballs, while Kelly had Monk's jewels in one hand and was punching him in the liver with the other. Everybody present knew that this was it, that either Monk or Kelly would have to fall, and there wasn't a sound in the barn, other than the noises that men make when they're animals.

Well, they both fell, Kelly with his eyes still in his head and Monk with his bollocks still attached to his groin. I don't know whether it was the wounds or the exhaustion that finally brought them both low, but suddenly there they were, flat on the floor. For a moment nobody could say nothing, just the sounds of collective hearts beating and sinking.

Then Plunkitt stepped forward, looming over the fallen Hectors like a victorious Achilles, which in a sense he was.

"That'll be all for today, boys!" he exclaimed, very merrylike, as if he'd just been to the circus, or out to Coney of a summer's afternoon. "'Twas a fine account you both give of yourselves, and now's the time to bury the hatchet all around." To be sure, Monk and Kelly were insensible to this plea but their gangs weren't, and I could see in all their faces the dawning realization that the real chief in the room was neither Osterman nor Vacarelli but Plunkitt and, behind him, Big Tim and the Tiger, licking their lips and smacking their chops, with the whole town spread out before them like one great hot meal ready to be devoured.

Still unconscious, Monk and Kelly were bundled into waiting transports, whose horses lugged them away. Plunkitt was saying something to the rest of the gangsters, about how it was now going to be business as usual once more, only different, but I paid him no mind, for the growl in my belly reminded me I was hungry.

Chapter

Nine

I WAS AT MONK'S BEDSIDE when he finally woke up. The big blue pigeon named Hilda was roosting on his shoulder, as if her master had just decided to take a nap and the bird didn't know what else to do except remain in place and wait for developments. Two or three cats curled at his feet, their meowing muffled by the bedclothes. We were in his flat, above the pet shop on Broome Street, and I could faintly hear the sounds coming from the street, although they were hardly loud enough to wake a sleeper, much less the dead, since it was a cold day and the windows were shut tight, as tight as such windows could be shut, against the elements. I thought he might die, or perhaps was already dead, when he suddenly lurched bolt upright, tossed over the covers and started shouting.

"Ya yeller bastard," exclaimed Monk, swinging wildly with his right. "Fight like a man."

When Monk suddenly started awake, I had been busy taking inventory of his newly missing body parts. His left earlobe was gone, as well as a good chunk of his right nostril. Clumps of his hair were also absent and I think he was missing a fingernail or two, but they may have been a casualty of earlier frays. This of course was in addition to all the razor scars, bullet holes, knife wounds, bite marks and other manifold disfigurements that marked him like a Red Indian brave.

I was about to tend to him, to try and do something to ease his condition, when the door to his bedchamber swung open and who should be standing there but Plunkitt. "Leave him be, lad," he counseled. "For sure, after such strenuation, he's just venting it out, and who wouldn't?"

After sweeping away a pair of turtles, George Washington P. took a befouled cane chair and lit his pipe in the airless room, the better to contemplate what was left of the great Monk Eastman. I couldn't figure out why he was there, since he had taken so little interest in the outcome of the fight. Later on I learned that the art of saying almost nothing was the hallmark of a Tammany man, and that was another lesson I took to heart.

"Who do you think won, sir?" I ventured to inquire after a decent interval. Monk had flopped back with a groan and was snoring soundly once more.

"Won, lad?" asked Plunkitt, as unmoved and indifferent as Sitting Bull, smoking his Virginia and thinking his thoughts, whatever they happened to be. Finally he sent a plume of smoke my way. As I was coming out of the fog, I heard him say: "Why, nobody, that's who won. You seen it with your own eyes."

"What do you mean?"

Plunkitt looks at me, exasperated. "I mean it don't matter. Monk didn't emerge victorious, nor did Kelly, and dat's da end of it. If you're as smart as I suppose you to be, Mr. Owney Madden of Tenth Avenue, you'll soon enough see the wisdom of my sentiments."

This remark set me to pondering, which I did as best I could over the racket that the sleeping Monk was setting up in his combative slumber.

Plunkitt took a deep breath of whatever fresh air was left in the room. "In this great city of ours, there's Democrats, God bless 'em, and unfortunately Republicans. Come election time, there's not a man on this here island second to GWP in ardor for the rightness of the Democratic cause in general and Tammany's way with it in partic'lar. But once da fightin' is done, why then, lad, business has got to go on, win or lose, and as stupid as the Republicans may be, them's that made a profession of the political calling understand this as well as I do. Me and the Republicans are enemies just one day in the year—election day. Then we fight tooth and nail, and all's fair, even what ain't. Whatever it takes is what we do, be it compromising a married fella or rattin' out a stooge what thinks he's high-and-mighty and holier than the pope in Rome."

"Rattin's never right," I interrupted.

"It ain't rattin' when you rat on a rat, and don't you forget it," says Plunkitt. "Meanwhile, the rest of the time, it's live and let live with us, because sure don't ya know there's plenty to go around if nobody gets greedy."

This went against everything I had learned thus far from the Gophers and from Monk: that you fight your enemies and hate them; beat them and thump them and kill them if necessary, and never let them get the best of you. That what they said of the patron saint of the old Five Points, Fatty Walsh—"He never knew when he was beat"—should be said of all of us. That it was humiliation beyond all understanding should a man of the opposite and contrary persuasion get the drop on you, or steal your gal, or rob your stuss game, or insult you in a thousand ways for which the code of honor of the streets demanded satisfaction. And now here was this grand muckety-muck from 14th Street come to say that all of that didn't matter a jot or a tittle. I couldn't accept what he was saying. "That ain't right," I squeaked.

"It's better than right. It's politics." The great man's pipe had finally gone out, and he was searching for his pouch and plug. "On election day I try to pile up as big a majority as I can against Wanamaker in the fifteenth. Any other day, George and I are the best of friends. You see, we differ on tariffs and currencies and all them t'ings, but we agree on the main proposition that when a man works in politics, he should get something out of it. Politicians have got to stand together this way or there wouldn't be any political parties in a short time. Then where would we be?"

Plunkitt gave up his search for a refill, rose and stood over the body of the fallen Monk and tousled his hair, as if Eastman were a child. "Just like him, is where," he said. "Beaten, bloodied, friendless and alone."

Now, I may have been inexperienced, but I could sense the man's meaning as plain as if he had just spoken his mind bluntly: as far as Tammany was concerned, Monk and the Eastmans was finished, and Kelly too, because if there's one thing politicians cannot abide, it's a draw. Someone has got to win and someone has got to lose, and the public has got to see, appreciate and respect the difference. Monk and Kelly each had lost by not winning, and by not losing either.

"You're a bright lad, Owney the Killer," said Plunkitt by way of a valedictory. "And I hope and trust you've learned a lesson or two tonight." He donned his hat and drew his cloak tightly about his person, ready to venture out into the cold night. "Now forget about this one and go home to your mother and your brother and your sister. Take care of them, boy; it's the calling the Good Lord above has give ya, and on that you'll surely be judged. For by the looks of ya, rendering unto Caesar is not going to be a problem; it's the rendering unto God that may give ya some small difficulty along the way."

I sat there alone, in contemplation. I knew that Monk's henchmen—Kid Twist, who had sprung him from the Jersey jail in Freehold the year before, and Richie Fitzpatrick—were probably already tending to details on the street and plotting how to succeed the boss. There's nothing as ineffective and useless as a leaderless gang.

Which was the same problem with the Gophers. It was all very well for Plunkitt to proclaim that the Irish was born to lead, and maybe that was true over at the Wigwam. But on the West Side, leaders was in damn short supply no matter what race they was. You could rely on Razor or Goo Goo or One Lung or Happy Jack to fight like the very devil when they were battling the coppers or the railroad pigs, but the big picture, the long range, eluded them entirely. And it was for this reason, I felt, that there were splinter gangs all over the West Side—not just our rivals the Dusters but the Marginals and the Pearl Buttons, not to mention the gangs that was mostly on our side, like the Gorillas, the Rhodes Gang and Parlor Mob. Whereas, with strong leadership and five hundred guns to back it up, the Gophers by rights should be running the entire West Side and after that who knew?

At that moment I decided that Razor had to go, and with him Happy Jack, Goo Goo, One Lung and whoever else got in my way. I knew Chick, Billy and Eddie would back me up, plus I had made friends with another tough kid named Tanner Smith, who was starting to run with the Marginals, sworn enemies of the Hudson Dusters and therefore one I felt was on my side.

Dawn was gloaming through the dirty panes when Monk finally awoke from his long enforced slumber. I could see him looking around, strangely calm, figuring out where he was and then, when he had satisfied himself on that score, who he was with and who was with him. Which was only me.

"Own," he finally croaked, and raised his right hand as if to pat me on the head.

"Right here, Monk," says I, bright-eyed and smiling. I knew that Monk, who had survived worse than this, didn't want no tears or weaklings in his presence. "You licked that dirty dago but good."

And then I did something I never would admit to a living soul for all these long years, not to Freda, nor Marty nor Ma nor even May: I threw myself on his breast and cried like a baby, for sure wasn't Monk a Da to me and more. I'd seen one Da die and had no hankerin' to witness another, so to tell you the truth, I'm not sure who I was crying more for that morning, not that it much mattered. My tears were occasioned not only by my memories and his condition but by his prospects, which I hadn't the heart to tell him, not then and not later, figuring that deep in his heart he must have known them as well as I.

Monk said nothing more as the light illuminated his ravaged phiz, but lay there, staring at the ceiling, trying as hard as he could to stare into his future and seeing nothing but the darkness looking back at him.

Chapter

Ten

I watched over Monk that morning, the false winter sun as perfidious as ever, promising light and warmth and only half coming across through the dingy panes. He heaved and rolled and flopped like the *Teutonic* in rough seas, now shouting and now quiescent as the mood took him. There was nothing much to do but sit and wait and watch and wonder, and I did plenty of all four.

Flopping, I came to know, and in fact already had reason to know, was the sign of the dead man: the collapse, the bounce of the head, the jerk of the body, the spine twitching, the mouth agape, the breath seized and labored, grasped and expelled, a fixed fight to the finish and everybody betting the wrong way except God. I'd seen this act before, which didn't make me like it any the better, and once again viewing Monk I beheld my Da . . .

Liverpool was no fit place to take a young bride. The town was full of rough and resentful laborers whose job it was to service the great ocean liners which plied the Atlantic trade from France to England to Ireland to America, and all other manner of dockside life, which as you may know is not always of the highest quality. Liverpool was a place from which to escape as quickly as possible—so you could get back even quicker, board the ship and whither away.

It was here that Francis and Mary Madden got their first taste of life abroad, when Francis's pocket was picked just moments after they disembarked from the packet boat. He had turned to assist Mary with her steamer trunk, bending forward at the waist, when along came a fellow whose fingers found their way into and out of Francis's waistcoat with a speed that could hardly be credited.

Now, there were few young men who could run faster than Francis Madden, especially when he had the wind up. Mary had spotted the reprobate almost at once and was pointing furiously in his direction. For aside from the few shillings she had in her pocket, all the money they had in the world had been in Francis's purse, which even then was fast disappearing along the quay.

Francis took out after his quarry like a man possessed. He was not about to let some miserable little sod put paid to his glorious dreams at such an early stage, and soon enough had taken the light-fingered wire down. It was with more than a bit of surprise that he heard the lad cry out in the accents of west Ireland.

Listening to my mother recount this tale more than a decade later, I was astonished to hear in her voice some trace of sympathy for the gonoph, just because he was Irish. To me, he deserved not understanding but a good hiding, his race be damned.

The lad was not about to submit to the tender mercies of Francis Madden without a struggle, which commotion soon enough attracted the attention of a policeman, who had been trolling dockside looking for newcomers to shake down. His solution was to lay about with his truncheon more or less indiscriminately, which gave the thief an opening to duck away from my Da, which left him to face the wrath of the law alone.

Now, given that in Ireland the law was pretty much always your enemy, Francis harbored little hope of being able to explain things to a British copper in a civil way. Nevertheless he tried, dodging the blows from the daystick and attempting to get a word in edgewise. The copper, however, was having none of it, and kept flailing away, which left Da to approach the problem as one of fisticuffs and not discourse; and when an opening in the policeman's guard presented itself, he decked his man with one well-aimed blow.

That was the signal for a general melee. The English side being in the majority, the Anglo-Saxons quickly began to carry the day over the Celts, as history informs us.

So it was that Mr. and Mrs. Madden spent their first night in England as guests of the Liverpool magistrate's court and then, after a bit of legal business that neither of them fully understood, of the central receiving gaol, to which each was remanded for the night for the crimes of vagrancy and disturbance of the peace.

The next morning Mr. and Mrs. Madden were informed that, having been convicted of a crime, they must pay a fine before being permitted to go about their business. Which misdeed carried with it a financial penalty that, by an amazing coincidence, nearly totaled to the penny the small sum of money that they had left in their possession. They were allowed to retain just enough scratch for two fares to Leeds on a train leaving that very hour.

This is why Mother never much liked fighting, even though it was fighting that had won her hand, for it was also fighting that first got my Da into trouble there in Liverpool, and it was fighting that transformed him in Leeds, where he took up the noble art of self-defense in any tavern or alley where men gathered for sport and blood and money. It was fighting that propelled the five of us—Marty, born in 1890, myself in '91 and May a few years later—from Leeds to Wigan, not much of an improvement, mind you, but still moving in the right direction, which was more or less west, back toward Liverpool, back toward those docks, back toward the ocean, which led away from England and to America, where the Maddens' bout with God would be decided once and for all.

The dreaming Monk let out a snort that woke me from my reverie and as I fixed my eyes I saw that he was looking at me with that stare that the living imagine is the gaze of the dead. He reached out, half swinging, all reflex, but he wasn't trying to clip me. At the end of the punch he did something I'd never seen him do before: he opened his fist and made a hand. I took it and he held me tight, his great paw crushing my little mitt, but I didn't care because he was not trying to take my strength from me. He was trying to give me what was left of his.

Chapter

Eleven

THE COVE WHAT KILLED MY FATHER was named Iron Tom Jefferson, a strapping Welshman undefeated in forty-two fights and more or less uninjured in same, not counting the occasional gouge or tooth mark from an unscrupulous yet nevertheless defeated opponent. Jefferson stood taller than six foot and weighed on the order of fourteen stone. The muscles in his forearms rippled as he grasped the rope to step into the makeshift ring, and a gasp went up from the crowd at this specimen of adult manhood.

In the other corner was the fine figure of Francis Madden. In contradistinction to his rival, Francis did not ripple, but was as sleek as a tiger, and before the opening bell rang he danced a little Irish jig, just to show the paying customers a thing or two and also to give the last-minute punters a chance to get their bets down, Jefferson having gone off at a 5 to 3 favorite.

This is not story now, but fact. I remember, because I was there. "Jeez, that Jefferson is a big sonofabitch!" I exclaimed.

The reason my Da was fighting Jefferson was threefold. The first was simple improvement in working conditions, for work in the mills was fierce. The incoming wool, whether pure merino or mongrel crossbreed, most of it still bloody, had to be sorted, graded and scoured down before it could be sent for processing into yarn. The scouring with alkaline soap was to remove not only the blood but the yolk, which is the name the woolen manufacturers give to the dried sheep sweat, made of lanolin and suint, that sticks to the wool. On the looms the warp and the weft had to be threaded intricately through the bobbins, and it made a great deal of difference whether the finished product was to be woolen or worsted, the distinction having to do with whether the fibers were carded or combed, and so on to the roving. A man or a woman could easily lose a finger or a hand in the carding machine, and worse misadventures awaited the unwary. I learned enough about wool to know that I never wanted to have anything to do with it.

The second was Irish pride. My Da was never one to let a fight pass him by, even those he should have, and when the challenge came from a local promoter named McCafferty to take on the champ, he couldn't pass it up, no matter that his fellows at the mill told him he had no chance against the bigger man, that he'd be pounded into submission in no time flat. But the challenge was too great and the prize too dear.

Which brings me to the last and best reason: money. Da had placed our entire savings with the turf accountant, to be wagered on his own good self, for a week before, he and I had done the sums and realized that a win against the local champ would get us all out of Wigan and England forever.

The bell sounded and the two men came dashing out of their corners. Francis shot out a series of jabs, testing his man, but Jefferson laughed them off and, without preamble, swung from his heels with a roundhouse right. Da danced easily out of the way, for only a careless fool would get clipped by a punch like that, delivered from a mile away; now that he knew how Jefferson telegraphed his big swing, he could render it harmless by skittering along the edge of the ropes like a water bug, always alert for the incipient haymaker.

A more pressing issue for my father, as round one melted into rounds two, three, four and then five, was how to do some damage to his opposition. The jabs may have scored points with the aficionados of the fight game, but they were doing precious little damage to Jefferson. Crisp punches rolled off his cheek, nose and jaw like water off a duck's arse. Da was contemplating the problem when he stupidly walked into a Jefferson right. It was as if his legs had been suddenly kicked out from underneath him.

"Get up, Da, and give it to the dirty bastard but good!" I cried, because what boy likes to see his Da lying flat on his back, blood gushing from his nose, and a monster standing over him, ready to clobber him again the minute he got to his feet, or even before.

"Is Da all right?" asked Marty.

"Don't you worry," I said. "Da'll lick 'im."

He got to his feet as the bell sounded. The roar from the crowd was something I'll never forget, fear mixed with bloodlust. I liked it.

Just before he went out for the next round, Francis was able to turn quickly and shoot a quick wink at Mother, and I know for a fact she carried that wink with her for the rest of her days.

The following twenty-one rounds unfolded more or less in the manner of the first five, Jefferson swinging and Madden dancing, until the crowd began to whistle in derision. The good folks of Wigan were not used to seeing a bout go on so long without some significant level of mayhem. "Whatizis, a waltz?" wondered one souse, who had a fiver down on Jefferson and who in his own mind had not only already spent his winnings but explained their absence to the lady of the house.

By the twenty-eighth round it was clear to me that this frame was going to be the measure of both men. The previous round had ended with Da and Jefferson draped over each other like a couple of drunks. Jefferson was beginning to wear down, whether from the effects of Francis's punches or the effort of his own, it didn't matter. And Da was knackered.

Still, he came out battling. For the first time, he took the fight to Jefferson, catching him on the side of the ear and staggering him.

Right away, the crowd was on its feet, shouting for blood in the way that crowds do when they sense that something is up. Jefferson, enraged but gratified that his opponent was finally beginning to fight like a man, snorted and charged. Da tried to fend him off by throwing his arms around him, but Jefferson's momentum was too great, and down they both went, Jefferson on top and Francis on the bottom. This Jefferson had not become champ without fighting dirty, and so he took this opportunity to sink his teeth into Da's left cheek.

The ref pulled them apart and both men got unsteadily to their feet. The howling of the mob had now risen to painful levels: jungle excitement in the English Midlands.

Jefferson was confident that the finish was near. He stopped to play to the crowd for a moment and that proved to be his undoing, for Da had cleverly positioned himself just behind him, so that when Jefferson turned back, he caught the full force of a Madden punch smack on his nose, which exploded in a rain of blood. He shook his head, showering sweat and blood over the spectators who were crowding the ropes, then counterattacked with a swing of his own, which blow, however, caught only the breeze and spent its force upon the currents of air.

According to the laws of physics, the body of Jefferson now followed his fist over and past his adversary, which gave Da the opening he had been so long seeking. Crouching down and then coming up with terrible force, he landed a right squarely to the point of the Welshman's chin—a perfect pigeon-killer—and down went Jefferson; as his head flashed by on its way to the canvas, I could see the blankness in his eyes, and before the referee had reached the number 4, I knew Jefferson was out, maybe even before he did.

Da seemed no less in a daze, and stood over his fallen rival mutely, gazing down at his handiwork and swaying from side to side. Then all at once Da's fight arm was lifted high in the air by the ref, and then, for his own safety, he was quickly hustled out of the ring and back into his makeshift dressing room in one of the mill's storage rooms.

We found him midst warp and woof, lying on a cutting table. "How do I look?" he croaked. His nose was smashed, his cheek was torn, his eyes were swollen shut and his right hand, which had shattered on Jefferson's chin, was useless. Mother could hardly bear to look at her husband.

"As fine as the day I married you," replied Ma.

"Yer Ma always was a good liar," he said, just before he passed out.

McCafferty entered with the cash. Da was unconscious and Ma was weeping, so he looked us children over and instinctively handed it to me. I counted it quickly—I'd never seen that much money in one place at one time before. "Now beat it," I commanded.

He glanced at our broken Da. "I hope it was worth it to him," he said, half out the door. "I hope it was worth it to you all." Then he left.

No one said a word. I guess it was in that moment that I became boss in the family. Ma looked at me, and I could tell she didn't know whether to be proud of me or afraid.

A week later we were all bound for Liverpool.

Chapter

Twelve

WE STAYED SOME SEVERAL MONTHS in the port city while my father recuperated. To all who asked, he'd been hurt in a mill accident, which was more or less true. His healing was coming along very slowly, though, which meant we were spending part of the winnings. So one evening in the spring of 1902, when I was ten years old, Da looked at Mother and said, "I think it's best that you go on first without us."

He might as well have asked her to leap to the moon. "Out of the question," she said.

But Da wasn't listening. "Get settled with your sister Lizzie. Find us lodgings, learn the territory, and then sure as the sun comes up in the morning, why we'll be aboard the next ship with bells and bows on."

"What about the children?"

"Don't worry about the little ones, love," he assured her. "Even flat on me back I can still handle them. And besides, Marty is all of eleven now."

"It ain't Martin I'm worried about," said Mother. Meaning me.

Da coughed up some blood, and she wiped his mouth clean with a rag. "The only trouble Owney's gonna get into is with me if he don't obey," he promised.

"But, Francis, he's so—"

Da's head flopped back onto his pillow. "Just do this thing for me, Mary," he murmured. "Just do this and I swear to you that everything will turn out right."

And so it was that our mother, Mary O'Neill Madden, set off for America alone on board the *Oceanic* in May of 1902. The *Oceanic* was no coffin ship, but the pride of Robert Ismay and J. P. Morgan's White Star line: 704 feet long, 63 feet wide, weighing more than seventeen thousand tons, and, powered by steam-driven twin screws, she could make up to twenty knots. There were one thousand third-class passengers, and Mother was one of them.

She bid us good-bye quayside in Liverpool, accompanied only by the steamer trunk she'd lugged over from Ireland. Da stood there, a cap pulled tightly down over his forehead to conceal his bruises; his right hand was splinted and bandaged tightly; and he walked with a cane, which helped him to fend off the dizzy spells.

"Good-bye, Mary," he said quietly, shaking hands with her in deference to decorum. "We'll be along presently."

"Good-bye, Mama," said Marty, his eyes downcast and teary.

"Your mother wants no tears today, Martin."

"I love you, Mama," said little May serenely. To look at her face, you might have sworn she was proud of her Ma, who was undertaking this great adventure on behalf of the entire Madden family.

Then it was my turn. "Won't you kiss your Ma before she goes?" asked Mother, reaching down to me. "Or will you always be my darlin' problem child?"

I threw my arms around her and hugged her tight, for sure wasn't I both sorry and happy to see her go. Sorry to lose her company and happy that she was staking our claim in the New World. "Don't you worry none, Ma. I'll take care of everybody. You just do your part and everyt'ing'll work out fine."

Mother started bravely up the gangplank and then stopped. "Oh, Francis!" she cried. "Kiss me once, quick, before I go! For God help me I do love you so!"

I reached out to help him but Da shook me off and stumbled forward. "Mary," he whispered, kissing her hard. "Did we have enough time?"

"Don't be stupid, husband," she said, crying now. "Sure, we've got all the time in the world."

He was still clutching her tightly when the porters herded her along and away. Ma's last view of her family was of Francis standing erect on the platform, his good arm held out to her, and her three children waving good-bye, handkerchiefs held in each hand like small semaphores whose message was unmistakable in any language.

By and by, Da was beginning to feel like his old self, if not exactly to look it. He still walked with an aid, and his eyesight meant he wouldn't be dodging many blind-side blows, but at least we could see in him a semblance of our old man. That summer was spent awaiting her letters, the first of which arrived by post some six weeks after her departure. It was chockablock with information about the wondrous City of New York.

My darlings,

You will all be pleased to know that I have found a place for us to live. It is located in the Tenth Avenue of New York, which is on the West Side of Manhattan, not far from the North River. The Flat is located on the top floor of a splendid Building and while the area is perhaps not the most refined—there is a large railroad Yard across the street, although I am told we will not be overly disturbed by the noise of the trains—it is more than adequate for our Needs. New Yorkers ride on Railroads in the sky they call Els, which is short for Elevateds, and there is one nearby us, in the Ninth Avenue to the east. There are many Irish People here, but also many Germans and Italians and Jewmen and even African negroes, which I have never seen the likes of before, but do not be alarmed because they are all here, except the black people, for the same Reason that we are, to make a new Life, and even if it proves to be a hard one, it must of necessity be better than the one we are leaving behind.

"I think yer Ma's gone daft," was Da's reaction.

"It ain't like Ma to make up tall tales," said Marty.

I hit him hard on the shoulder. "You callin' Ma a liar?" I demanded.

"I think it's wonderful," said May. "Trains that fly."

Came the time when Da was able to get about well enough for us to think about traveling. We'd hit that point of no return where our remaining funds were just about equal to the price of the crossing, so Martin wrote to Ma that we'd be coming along by and by, and May and I went down to the Cook's office and booked ourselves third-class passage on the *Teutonic,* the newest ship of the White Star line. That just about tapped us out, but I knew that it was only a short matter of time after we landed in New York that my lucky stars would be smilin' down on me.

We spent our last evening in Liverpool down the public house, the King's Arms, where Da could get a proper whiskey, which he hadn't had since before the fight.

"No more kings now, lads," says he, savoring the water of life. He always called the three of us "lads," which plural formation included May, because I think he was always leery of singling her out on account of her sex, the very basic idea of which made him uncomfortable. "Just presidents, of which I'm told every lad can hope to grow up to be one, providin' he's right and proper American-born."

"Guess that leaves me out," said Marty, thumping his fist on the scarred lounge table. I loved my brother, because I had to, but damn his eyes if he didn't always see the dark side of things, the debit side of the ledger, whereas I felt that positive numbers were the only kind to hanker after, and therefore the only kind to admit.

My father ordered another whiskey—two in fact. One for himself and one for Marty and me to split, us bein' so young and all. For my Da was of the opinion that it was better for him to introduce us to the Creature in a controlled setting, as it were, rather than the Creature to introduce itself to us, on its own terms and in a place of its own malignant choosing. I scooped the whiskey away from Marty with my right hand and downed it in one go.

"There's better things than bein' president," I said, and meant it.

We set out for the quay early on an overcast morning in June of 1902. A huge crowd was milling about, awaiting the signal that all was in order to board. Paddies, limeys, lascars, Polacks and Roosians mingled, only too happy to see off England at last, and me foremost among 'em.

I looked up at the great ship that was to bear us to America. Displacing more than twenty thousand tons, she stood taller than St. George's Hall, and her three stacks proclaimed her membership in the ranks of the swiftest ships of the line. "God bless this ship," exclaimed Father, leaning on me and Marty, waving his good arm in her direction and beholding her with awe. "It's a honor to be quitting these shores aboard such a fine lady!"

The ropes blocking entryway to the gangplank had been loosened, and the passengers were pushing forward. I was doing my best to support my Da and hang on to my sister when Pop paused, almost halfway up, and began to mop his brow. "My God is it hot," he said. I didn't have the heart to tell him that, on the contrary, there was a brisk wind blowing and that, if anything, it was a bit on the chilly side.

"So hot have I never been," he cried, tugging at his collar and stumbling. He righted himself briefly, then leaned, swayed. "Give me water quick!"

His legs buckled and he started to topple backwards.

"Da's ill," said May.

Marty and I caught him as he fell and not only tried to prop him up but to push him forward, for at that moment the only thing I could think about was getting on that ship and away.

"Come on, Da," I said. "Coupla more steps. One foot in front of the other. You can do it."

He tried to move forward, but the pitch of the plank was exerting a more powerful pressure than his legs could overcome and to our horror he sank back into our arms.

I was damned if I was going to let his head bounce on that hard wood, and I managed to cushion his fall just enough that he wound up lying in my arms like a little child, as if we had reversed roles in an eyeblink.

"Owney," gasped Da, his breath short and harsh. He was doing his best to focus his eyes on mine, to be able to look into my soul, and I wished for just about the first and last time in my life that there was a priest handy, to administer extreme unction, because I knew what this look meant, and it meant the end. "Don't let me down."

"I won't, Da," I promised. "Bank on it."

"Good lad," he said, squeezing my hand. "Give New York a licking for me."

And then all of a sudden the anxiety went out of his gaze and I felt his body relax, the muscles go slack, the frantic desperation to get his last words out exhausted, for to him was suddenly given the insight, given to so few, that when your time comes, you embrace it happily and without regret, for what else can you do?

He shuddered one last time, taking one last swing at Death before it felled him for good. "Mary!" cried Da as he gulped his last breath. "God, why is there no air in the world?"

He died with his eyes wide open, as if they would devour and consume the great vast planet one final time, so he could take the sight with him to Heaven.

The doctor determined that Francis Madden had died from brain injuries sustained from a beating, and demanded that the police put forth their best efforts to discover who had done this. This being Liverpool, the doctor naturally assumed that Father had died from one of the usual causes of death—a barroom brawl being the most likely. When no report of a fight meeting the vague description and hazarded time emerged, the case was filed quietly away, just another paddy demise, with no known relatives to care or mourn.

This we learned later, from the post. With only two hours to go before the *Teutonic* sailed, the authorities decided on the spot to honor the surviving Maddens' fares, in order that three fatherless and bereaved Irish children would not become an English public trust, and to unite them with their soon-to-be-grieving mother in New York.

The voyage lasted six days. I kept my brother and May in my sights the whole time, my cap pulled down firmly on my head and Da's old pigeon-killing knife at the ready, clasped tightly alongside my leg, ready to kill the first sonofabitch who looked at us cross-eyed.

Chapter

Thirteen

THE END OF MONK EASTMAN came sooner than I would have thought. That's the way demises are; otherwise, nobody would talk about them. The worst thing that can happen to you, in my opinion, is that you die and everybody says, well, he did his time and about time too.

On the frozen, snowy evening of February 2, 1904, as we were making our way by foot across town, who should cross our path near the Croton Reservoir but one Llewellyn K. Massey (as I learned later), pie-eyed and puke-bibbed, staggering east on 42nd heading for his home over on Fifth. He was dressed swell, in silk topper and tails, and clearly just came from an evening of women and libation at Satan's Circus, which lurked in the gloom of the Sixth Avenue el. Like most rich drunks, he was being trailed at a discreet distance as he rounded the reservoir by a tough-looking customer that Monk's expert eye right away picked out as a rival for the man's purse.

"C'mon, Own," says he, "let's roll da lush before da udder guy does."

I was against this, for I didn't think Monk was in any shape for combat, no matter how mild, but Monk was already scuttling through the snow toward Mr. Massey. "If you please, kind sir," I could hear Monk saying as he approached. "Could you tell me the way to Bishop Doane's domicile?"

This was always the prelude with Monk, for the bishop was a standing joke in the repeat-voter precincts such as ours, and a question about him always took a drunk aback enough to let Monk slip in underneath whatever guard he might have left. Sure enough, in no time flat Monk had his pistol out and under the young man's nose, and not a copper in sight. I was standing impatiently off to one side, awaiting only the inevitably successful outcome of this operation.

The gunshots that followed caught me with my pants down. Monk rarely killed civilians unless they deserved it, and almost never in the course of a simple robbery, which was something Tammany frowned upon, and my first thought was that the lush had said something untoward about Monk's appearance or parentage, about both of which he was quite sensitive. But a second later I realized that the shooting was not coming from Monk but from the fella who had been following Massey.

"Stop, thief!" he shouted, all the while continuing to fire.

Monk ducked and called out to me: "Pinkertons!"

I'm second to no man in my dislike for the coppers, but Pinkertons is another and lower order of life altogether. There's not an Irishman in America who can hear the name without wanting to vomit, after what they did to the Molly Maguires down in Pa., and if I'd had my gun, I would have shot my first man then and there. Monk was running madly down 42nd and firing wildly back in the direction of the Pinkerton man, who was blazing away himself. A fella coulda got hurt with all that lead in the air.

I don't know whether Monk was feeling safe when he hit Broadway, or whether he was just getting tired, but he slowed as he rounded the corner and ran smack into the arms of a roundsman by the name of Corcoran, a Broadway Squad bull from county Westmeath called Happy John on account of the smile that always played across his lips, who was by happenstance standing just outside the Hotel Knickerbocker. I guess the Pinky man was still shouting about thieves, and Monk looked as guilty as sin, for no sooner had Monk entered the periphery of the copper—a giant of a man standing well over six feet tall and weighing 250 pounds—when said fellow unholstered his nightstick and delivered Monk a tremendous blow to the head, one that felled him as sure as an oak under the saw of an Oregon logger. I pulled up short, half a block away, and for the second time in a couple of months, contemplated the wreck of my chief and best friend.

To all of you who are caterwauling about the brutality of the police in our day and age, let me say that in my youth the coppers pretty much abided by the law of the nightstick, and whenever a criminal came within shouting distance, they were sure to take advantage of it, which is why Monk went down. In short order, there was a couple of more cops on the scene and without so much as a how-do-you-do, they dragged Monk's carcass off to the 30th Street station and there he was booked on robbery and felonious assault and remanded to jail.

Monk was no more after accepting this than the pope was likely to credit the existence of Jehovah, except in a past-tense kind of way, and just bellowed all the louder, rattling his cage like a monkey at the Bronx Zoo. I saw an opening here, having slipped into the precinct house.

"Please, sir," says I, "I need to see me Da." It was not unusual to see kids wandering through the holding cells in those days, so plentiful were the Das who were brought in on drunk and disorderly or vagrancy charges.

The pig looked at me querulous-like, but let me pass.

"Monk," says I.

"Own," says he. "Get over to Plunkitt's right away and tell him what's up."

I didn't have the heart to tell him it was no use. Not no use because it was four o'clock in the morning but no use because, like Pontius Pilate, Plunkitt had already washed his hands of Monk Eastman. "Sure, Monk," says I.

I guess there must have been something in my tone of voice that told the great gangster that whatever intercession Plunkitt might have been willing to offer, which was none, would be useless. He took his bedraggled hat, which was still too small for him, in his hands and wrung it like a wet towel. "I'm sorry I let ya down." Another twist and that was pretty much it for the derby.

I almost cried again as I left his cell, heading for home, for sure didn't I know that there would be no use in waking Plunkitt, and thus riling him up, when there were no further votes to be had from the bailing of Monk Eastman. Indeed, there was more votes to be had from keeping Monk behind bars, and down deep I knew that nobody knew that better than Monk. He was as finished as his hat.

The next morning I was to be found down the bootblack stand at the New York County Courthouse, where G.W. normally held court. As soon as Plunkitt had finished speechifyin' he caught sight of me, and greeted me as warmly as if I could vote Democratic three or four times in the next election when in fact at my age I could only vote once or maybe twice.

"Oh, if it ain't the Killer himself!" he exclaimed while a colored boy named Hiram Watkins shined his shoes.

"Say, Mr. Owney," said Hiram without missing a beat. He coughed up a glob and planted it square on Plunkitt's high-tops. "How you been?"

I'd met Hiram, who lived up Little Africa way on the West Side, a couple of times before and had found him to be a fine fellow. Just like in the old Five Points, the coloreds and the Irish lived side by side, and more or less hated each other, except that Hiram and I got along just fine. As far as I was concerned, paddies and jigs was passengers on the same coffin ship, foundering or coming safely ashore as God's whim took us. Half the colored I knew had Irish names anyway, which ought to tell you something.

One of the things that still strikes me is how well dressed we all were in those days. Back then everybody looked pretty swell and I do mean everybody, even colored boys like Hiram. I can see him now, a good-looking little Negro in a three-piece suit with a high starched white collar and a tie, a cloth cap and brown button shoes. Nowadays you see a boy looks like that and it strikes you funny, like he's on his way to church or something, but back then even a shoeshine boy like Hiram dressed almost as sharp as the mayor.

"And what brings this bright lad to these humble precincts?" That was G.W., not Hiram, speaking. "Don't tell me you're thinking of entering the seminary."

This reference to the seminary was one of our ways of referring to the Eastmans' territory on the East Side.

"No, sir," says I, "for the seminary's a bit too strict for the likes of me these days," which was another of our agreed-upon exchanges, meaning of course that Monk was in the kind of trouble that only Tammany could fix, if it felt like it.

"Now, ain't that too bad," said Plunkitt, this time addressing the multitudes that was always gathered around the bootblack stand. "A young Irish lad what don't want to encounter head-on the challenges of our Lord's sacred priesthood. What is this country comin' to?"

My heart sank, for what we had to discuss was not for public consumption unless himself wanted it that way, which he did, and which signaled the end of Monk Eastman, as he had foretold. Because didn't Plunkitt already know the news before I told it.

"Ladies and gents," announced Plunkitt grandiloquently. I noticed the scribbler Bill Riordan scribbling furiously in his notebook as he took down the great man's words verbatim, as he always did. "This fine upstanding God-fearin' boy has just brung me news of the most joyful sort," continued Plunkitt. "It seems that the notorious gangster Monk Eastman, who has been the scourge of the lives of so many in these parts, not the least of which have been our Hebrew brethren, has at last been apprehended by the forces of the law, red-handed in the act of robbin' one of our fair city's foinest citizens."

There was a smattering of cheers, and some boos, from those who knew how things really stood between Monk and Tammany.

"So now," continued Plunkitt, "this ruffian will finally face his comeuppance before the bar of justice and, an honest judge willing, be sent up the river where he can do no further harm to the likes of a daycent citizenry!"

With that, Plunkitt turned his back on the crowd and walked away. I chased after him as he ducked into the Tweed Courthouse and into the gents'. "Ain't ya gonna do nothin'?"

Plunkitt smiled at me warmly as he snuggled his private parts up against the porcelain. His bowler hat fitted him like a nightcap on a miser. "What's done is done, lad," he said, shaking himself dry, "and what's goin' ta be done is done as well."

Plunkitt was at the washbasin now, performing his ablutions. My hands were wet as well, from preventing the tears. I was no tough guy anymore, just a kid who was about to lose his best friend forever.

Plunkitt took a towel from the colored attendant who sat silently nearby. I never did get his name. "'Tain't t'e end udda world, boy," he said. "There's plenty more where Monk come from, and plenty smarter too. A bit more growin' and bit more learnin' and then you come back and see old George Washington Plunkitt and wouldn't I be surprised if there isn't some business that you and I, or my noble successors, can't be doin' together." He tossed the towel back to the invisible colored man, who caught it without glancing his way. "Now get along home wit' ya."

I walked out of the courthouse with my head low and my heart lower, making my way slowly across town back to the 30th Street station house. The weather had turned even colder, as frosty as my spirits. By the time I had slogged through the snow to the precinct house it was early afternoon. With a wink at the sarge, I slipped in the front door and headed back to the holding pen.

But when I got to where I had last seen Monk, the cell was empty. I must have stood there for a minute or two, gaping in confusion, and then a strong hand gripped me by the shoulder. I looked up and wouldn't you know it, it was my old friend, the copper Becker.

"I thought I kenned you," he said.

The force of the blow, which I never saw coming, knocked me against the iron bars, and as I rebounded, Becker caught me square in the breadbasket, a neat right cross, the artistry of which I would have admired had I had the time. As the air went out of my lungs my chin went down, which gave him an opportunity to catch me just under the button with his knee, and then the lights went out, and all I can remember was the sound of his laughter as he mocked me for my pretentions and my presumptions.

Becker told everybody I'd had an accident, which was true.

Chapter

Fourteen

THE CHARGE WAS "MUGGING WITH A CLUB," for which I spent some several months as a guest of the Protectory, just like my older brother had. I was never quite sure whether they nailed me for Fats or for Branagan or just bein' an accessory to the Massey fiasco, because the Tiger stepped in before things got out of hand and made sure I was treated with the deference and mercy my youth deserved.

Ma of course got all weepy at the thought of her darling middle child being sent off to pay his debt to society. May simply gave me one of her grave looks. "Good-bye, Owen," she said. "I'm sure you'll come back a better man for all this." Now, let me tell you that got to me far more than Ma's more or less obligatory tears. For to look at May you would have thought that she was bidding me farewell as if I was going on a journey to some far-off place like Hindoostan or Wyoming instead of just up the road a piece.

"Good-bye, May," says I, kissing her on the cheek.

Aside from family, I had only one visitor during my time and wouldn't you know it was old George Washington P. himself. He came up to me all of a sudden, as I was weeding a bed of azaleas in the greenhouse garden. One thing churches always need is flowers and plenty of 'em, so the padres were teaching me something about horticulture, which I rather liked.

"How they treatin' ya, boy?" he asked with a smile. Plunkitt wore the same thing season in and season out: a wool suit with a waistcoat, foulard and derby, and I never once saw him sweat.

"Can't complain," I said, wiping my brow. It was true: I didn't have to do no hard work, and got to spend most of my time working with the flowers.

"Didn't think so," remarked G.W. "Nobody likes a complainer."

"I'm grateful to you, sir," I said.

He pulled out his pipe and lit it. "Everyone appreciates gratitude."

He smoked for a moment, sending plumes of tobacco wreathing through the air. "You mayn't've heard," he said, "that former roundsman Branagan is no longer with the Metropolitan Police."

My eyes widened at this news of my enemy's professional discomfiture. "Indeed, he is not," continued G.W. "Didn't a little investigatin' into the loss of his tunic reveal the nefarious activities to which he was up, thanks to the privately presented testimony of your colleagues and cohort, and a bunch of fine upstandin' young men they is too. The upshot of which is that he's been stripped of his rank and his position, and is now nothin' more than a common day laborer, albeit in the vineyards of Tammany, for sure we always take care of our own, just as we're takin' care of you."

I had to admire the way the Tiger always hedged its bets, always took the vigorish on any wager it laid, so that it could not lose. I was about to say something when Plunkitt pulled out his pocket watch and made a great show of consulting it.

"Just look at the time, lad," he said, placing it back in his waistcoat. "I was just passing by, makin' the rounds of my constituents you might say, and I thought I'd look in on ya, to see how you was makin' out. And now that I've satisfied meself on that account, I'll be takin' my leave."

We shook hands gravely, and then he was gone. That night, I dined on steak, and snuck a schluck of sacramental wine. They let me out not long after.

I'm skipping over the next few years not because I didn't do nothing of note during that period, but because I've never been much interested in reading accounts of anybody's hod-carrying. No matter whether the trade is rags, carting, transport or mischief, the experience is pretty much the same: long hard hours of drudgery, accompanied by growing skills and equally growing resentment at the fellas in front of you who won't get out of the way gracefully and let you assume your rightful place at the table. So there's not much more to say than that I went from boy to man. We all grow up, unless we don't.

Monk got ten years in college—Sing Sing—for his attempted Massey mugging, of which he served five. They let him out in June of 1909, when Ma was thirty-nine and I was seventeen and still ungainful by the lights of the City of New York, but very much on track in my own system of self-employment.

Monk made straightaway for his old East Side haunts. I'd heard that he was back in town but so far I had made no effort to see him. I suppose I could plead that I was busy establishing my career independent of him, trying to take charge of the Gophers and of course attending to my Ma and May and trying to keep Marty.

The sad fact of the matter was that, much as I loved him, there was nothing Monk could do for me anymore. The Eastmans, discouraged by their chief's unaccustomed incarceration, had more or less drifted apart, which taught me something right then and there. Namely, that there was more likely to be a leader with no gang than a gang with no leader.

Indeed, all of gangland was more or less of a mess at this time. What with reformers like Riis, the Reverend Parkhurst and his busybody Committee of Fourteen meddling about, some of the smaller gangs had disappeared altogether. Eat 'Em Up Jack McManus had taken a lead pipe to the skull during a brawl and One Lung Curran had finally croaked owing to his condition. Even Paul Kelly was gone, having moved up to 111th Street in East Harlem, north wopland, after he shot it out with Razor Riley at the New Brighton.

As for Monk's boys Kid Twist and Richie Fitzpatrick, that rivalry had been briefly settled in favor of the Kid, who had put a hard one between Richie's eyes in a dump on Chrystie Street just after Monk went up the river. The Kid finally got his in 1908 out at Coney Island, fighting with a Five Pointer named Louis the Lump over some dame.

All of which left only Goo Goo Knox standing between me and the unquestioned leadership of the Gophers. For if not me, then who? My boys Billy, Chick and Eddie were smart enough to know they weren't smart enough to be the boss—and if they weren't, Art and Hoppo Johnny, who'd grown into sizable boyos entirely loyal to yours truly, were on hand to remind 'em. Down the Village, I had my pal Tanner Smith of the Marginals keeping tabs on the Dusters for me. Then there was Jimmy Hines, the pol I'd met with Plunkitt, who was rising fast within the Wigwam.

I'd even found a friend up in Harlem in the person of Hiram, the shoeshine boy who'd moved uptown with his family and the rest of the colored people from the West Side after the Jews started selling and the Irish and the Germans started moving. He wasn't shining shoes no more either, thanks to a singularly large pair of feet that came his way one day. They belonged to Mr. Jack Johnson, the heavyweight champion of the world, who plunked his doggies down on Hiram's stand one afternoon and was so pleased with the results that just like that he offered him a job in his entourage as a valet. Mr. Jack always liked to look swell, which drove the white people crazy, especially when he stepped out on the town with one of his white wives.

Hiram had been with the champ in Australia when he snatched the title from Tommy Burns in Sydney in 1908 and, in the summer I'm talking about here, had gone out to Reno to witness Jack give a washed-up Jim Jeffries the beating of his life.

"You should see him, Mr. Owney. When he hit a man, the man done stay hit, don' matter whether he white or colored, he got to go down. He got a will of iron, Mr. Jack. He got pride. He a man."

"He's the champ." My attitude toward coloreds was that they weren't no worse than anybody else.

"Mr. Jack'd like you."

"I'd like to meet him someday."

"Sure you will. Jes' let me know."

Everything was rounding into place. It was time to make my move, for sure at nearly eighteen I wasn't getting any younger.

Chapter

Fifteen

WHAT FINALLY MADE UP MY MIND was a conversation I had with my sister one hot night that summer. We were up on the roof, trying to find the oxygen in the air.

"You don't need Monk no more," she said, sensing what was on my mind. That was the thing about me and May—she always knew what I was thinkin', half the time before I did myself. "You're Owney Madden of Tenth Avenue. It's like what the nuns said about . . ."

I looked over her way and realized that, at fifteen, she wasn't no kid no more. How she'd grown up so fast, when I wasn't looking, puzzled me. I didn't want nobody gawking at my kid sister, certainly none of the lowlifes in the gang, and the thought of somebody's paws on her made me hopping mad just thinking about it.

"Hey! Ain't you listenin' to a word I'm saying?" She brought me back to earth with a shove.

"About nuns?"

"No, silly—Moses."

"I thought we were talking about Monk."

She made like she was going to hit me again. "Moses could lead his people to the Promised Land, but he couldn't get there his own self."

I guess I just didn't get it.

"Come on," she said. "I'll show ya."

We rose, she took my hand and we walked toward the city, not the river. The river was dark, as always. New Jersey was dark, as mostly. But New York wasn't.

"See that?" says she, standing near the edge of the rooftop, facing east. I held her arm tight so she wouldn't fall.

Lights. In the pitch-dark, lights. Electricity was all the rage then. I kenned the whole town, 14th to 50th, aglow. Gopher territory. My territory. Home.

"The Promised Land."

She said it in a voice that, like her body, was making the transition from girl to woman, plunging from high little-girlish to something lower, throatier. You still had to lean in close to hear her properly, though, which I didn't mind. She smelled like fresh soap.

We stood there for a while, watching the lights flicker and wink. The only sounds were those our breathing made as we turned and walked back.

As we passed by my coop we could hear the birds, gurgling in their sleep, dreaming their avian dreams. If we dreamed of flying, did they dream of walking?

"Is it true they mate for life?" May asked.

I wasn't much in the mood for a discussion of the mating habits of pigeons, but she persisted. I wondered how much she knew about the birds and the bees and who told her, but decided not to ask.

"Is it?"

I thought for a moment. "Pretty much."

"Tell me."

"What do you care?"

"I just care, is all."

There was no way out of it. "Okay, here's the deal. Seventeen days in the egg, five or six weeks of childhood, and then they're on their own. Married for life at six months. They'll go fifteen, twenty years together, if nothing happens. Hell of a thing, huh?"

"Aw, that's sweet." She appraised the sleeping squabs. "How can you tell if they're old enough? You know, for marriage?"

I reached in and took out one of my prize cocks, a Hollander I'd named after Monk. He was nesting with his mate, a hen called Hilda of course, and a couple of their brood. He stirred a little in my hands, but I soothed him with a couple of strokes and he took to snoozing again. "Here's how you tell."

Gently I lifted up his right wing and exposed the full feathers beneath. "See that? Them feathers means he's at least four weeks old." I put his wing back in place. "In Monk's case you know he's at least six months old on account of he got Hilda and they got babies."

I replaced Monk in his cote and picked up one of the hens. "Look." I raised her wing, and her pinfeathers were clearly visible. "Sissy's too young for much of anything. But this cock, Arthur"—I took another bird, a brother, a few days older—"he's never flown."

"I wish I was married," says May out of the blue. Even though it wasn't cold she was shivering just a bit, so I put my arm around her as she looked at the lights, which were starting to pass in Manhattan for stars.

I pretended to look out over the rooftops, Arthur asleep in my grip. "Why would you want to go and do something silly like that? You know how much Ma needs you. Marty too." I gave myself a mental pat on the back. "I'm the only one who's got a future around here."

Right away I wished I hadn't said that, and that goes double for right now, but one of the things about life is what's done is done and there's no taking it back.

"I'm almost sixteen. All the other girls got fellas. You want I should be an old maid?" She looked sad. "Besides, why shouldn't I? You got plenty a girl-friends. You got Freda—"

"She ain't no real girlfriend." Pretty much true.

"—and I seen you making goo-goo eyes at her chum Margaret Everdeane—"

"You have not."

"Have too. And I hear that Loretta Rogers is sweet on you."

"That cow?"

"That's what she's been saying to some of the girls."

"You're dreamin'."

"I hear things."

"You hear too much."

"I listen. Try it sometime, why don't you?"

I decided to change the subject. "See that?" I said, gesturing at the city. May nodded and pulled a little closer to me. "They got rules, same as us, only better than us. 'Cause their rules make sense and ours don't."

"What kinda rules?"

"About how to behave. What to do, and suchlike. You know—a code."

May's eyes searched my face by the faraway glow of Broadway. "Every-body's gotta have rules. Otherwise, it's nothin' but a jungle."

Arthur's gray head was nestled against my left thumb. I liked the way my birds trusted me.

"It is a jungle," says I. "But even jungles got rules, and we don't know 'em." I swept my free hand out over the city, the way I sometimes did when I was alone and could pretend it all belonged to me. "I mean, why are they out there, having fun, and we're stuck up here?"

"'Cause they're somebody."

That made me mad. "At my age I oughtta be somebody. I mean, look at that dope Goo Goo what runs the Gophers. I'm smarter than him."

"That's what I'm trying to tell ya," May said, like I was the dopey one. "With the Moses stuff. You're the fella who can lead the Gophers to the Promised Land. Not just the Gophers either."

Maybe I *was* a little dopey right then, because I still didn't get what she was saying. "They'll never let us off Tenth Avenue if they can help it."

"So we get off ourselves."

Now I was getting it. "We fight our way off."

"Just takes a little cooperation is all. Teamwork."

"And a few rules. Like treat everybody on your side square."

"The golden rule is what the nuns call it."

"Never tell the coppers nothin'."

"Makes sense."

"If they bust you, deny everything."

"You might be innocent," said May. "Or at least not too guilty."

"If they've got proof, say it don't prove nothing."

"Tough to really prove things."

"If they've got a witness, persuade him otherwise, or make a monkey out of him."

"It's him or you."

"If they try to get you on the stand, refuse."

"What if they make ya?"

"Say you can't remember nothin'."

We were really having a good time now. "What if the judge or jury ain't seein' things your way?" asked May.

"Find out where they live."

"A bribe or a beating?"

"Whichever works best."

"And if somebody double-crosses you?"

"Cut him dead," I said.

"Without a second thought," she said. "Just one more thing. Never, ever—"

"Rat," I said, finishing.

She smiled at me. "Maybe if you'da gone to St. Mike's School every day, the way you pretended to, you'da thought of this before."

"The Catholic jug was plenty school for me. But you know things."

She nodded. "Plenty of things. That's why . . ." Her voice got tiny, like her. She took a deep breath, which even in the dark I could see made her pretty little bosom swell. "You need me."

"Of course I need you. Everybody knows that."

"Then why don't you—"

She started to say something, then stopped. In the distance, way beyond the city and the East River, I could see the first faint glimmering of dawn over Queens. I watched it come up, with Arthur in one hand and May in the other.

"You sure do love them birds," she said after a time. "Sometimes I think you love them more than you love me or Ma or Marty."

"How can you say a thing like that? They're just dumb animals."

May squeezed my hand. "Sometimes, when you ain't looking, I creep up here while you're over at the coop, and I watch you with them. I watch you as you let them fly. I see the look on your face as you watch them take off, flutter a moment and then speed up into the air." She paused. "Fly away, from this. I see how much you envy them their freedom."

I looked at her. She'd obviously been planning to say this for some time, and me none the wiser until now. "But they always come back."

"That's why they call 'em dumb animals. Me, I'd never come back."

She started tugging at me, leading me back inside. I realized I still had Arthur in my hand.

"Ain't you gonna put him back to bed?" she asked.

I took Da's knife out of my pocket. "I wanna show you something," I said.

Very tenderly I forced Arthur's mouth open with the tip of the blade. "When a cock's crazy about a hen, he opens his beak. If she puts her beak inside his, that's how he knows it's true love."

"Sorta like smooching."

"They bob back and forth together for a while, getting a taste of each other."

"I hear they call that French."

"Whadda you know? Anyways, once they're good and ready, the hen crouches down and the cock mounts her and that's that . . . Ma'd wash my mouth out with soap if she knew I was tellin' ya this stuff."

She seemed offended I'd think her ignorant. "I hear things. I listen. I learn."

"Okay, here's all you really need to know."

I smacked the heel of my hand against the base of the knife, through the bird's mouth and clear into his brain. Arthur never knew what hit him.

"That's what I'd do to any mug what tries to get fresh with you," I said.

For a moment we stood there on the roof of 352, looking at each other and knowing that we'd just made a covenant. I'd half expected her to cry out and weep for the dead bird, who after all never did nobody any harm, but she stood there silent. I held out my hand to her and she slipped hers inside mine.

"What are you going to do with him?" she asked at last.

I threw the body over the roof, down the air shaft, to take its place with the rest of the refuse. "The hell with him," I said.

Chapter

Sixteen

"Goo Goo," says I the next day, addressing himself. His boys, Newburgh Gallagher and Marty Brennan, were sitting right beside him, doing nothing in particular. "I got an idea."

"Yeah, whuh?" burped Goo Goo, downing the last of his morning beer. Goo Goo was not what you would call a fine specimen of a man. He had sandy blond hair and nonexistent eyebrows, which gave him the look of a circus freak, although no one would have said that to his face, such as it was. For Goo Goo, like most of us in those days, would beat a man to death as soon as look at him, so hair-trigger was his temper. I had always looked upon him as Happy Jack without the grin and minus the brains.

Gallagher and Brennan, who were as matched a set of Irish dumbbells as ever was, were giving me the fisheye as I spoke. Their job was to prevent any attack upon the person of the chief, but I always had the impression that neither would mind very much if some misfortune befell the boss.

I poured some more beer for all of them. It was warm, but it didn't seem to matter. "Yeah," says I, "a real good one."

Loretta reached out and squeezed my hand as I started to talk. May was right: she was my new girl. I had grown tired of Freda, who was always after me to get her more swag, and Freda had grown tired of me, on account of my getting her best friend, Margaret Everdeane, into a compromising position or two, which meant that both Freda and Margaret were now mad at me. A whole fleet of gangsters mad at you was preferable to a dame or two, to which wisdom I should have listened.

"Owney's ideas is always good," chirped Loretta, whose real name was Dorothy, which she never used, and her last name was Rogers, which she was more or less stuck with. Why she was called Loretta I hadn't the slightest idea and never asked. Loretta was quick-eyed, dark-haired, with dainty wrists, ruby lips and, even at sixteen, a full bosom, which I was always fond of. She lived over on Eighth. "You mugs oughta listen to him."

I figured my forthcoming motion stood a pretty good chance of success even before I made it.

"Whadda we done lately?" I asked by way of preamble. Brennan scratched his bollocks and Gallagher cut one, which was about as eloquent as either of them ever got. "Nothin' is what," answers myself. "And sure if it isn't time we did."

Goo Goo cast one of the eyes that wasn't on Loretta's headlights in my direction. As undisputed lords of the West Side, the Gophers were ready for some action and any chief that didn't give it to them, and right quick, wasn't going to be chief for very long. Because there's nothing a gangster hates worse than boredom, just as there's nothing he'd rather do than lie around unless there was a fight brewing. Which is exactly what I was counting on. "You got sumpin' in mind?" asked Knox, widening one rheumy eye.

I pointed across the avenue, at the Central Yards, as I outlined my plan. Over the past few months I had noticed the Centrals taking on extra men as guards. As I mentioned before, these men was mostly poor drunks, fathers of some of the lads in the neighborhood to be exact, probably even the paters of some of the members of the gang, although the lads would be ashamed to admit it, and first I had figured this was simply the Tiger's way of finding jobs for the poor harps who voted right but drank wrong. But when more and more of them kept coming—not just Das now, but young men full of fight— I figured something else was up. So I'd sent my little pal Georgie Ranft over to investigate.

Georgie was half-pretzel, half-spaghetti, about four years younger than me, who lived with his family on 41st between Ninth and Tenth. There were ten kids in the Ranft family, nine boys and one girl. I never did learn the rest of their names. Georgie was the oldest. His father was one of those stern krauts who liked to use a strap, so Georgie spent most of his time hanging out with me. Maybe it was because we were both about the same size, maybe it was because he liked me. Whatever the case, whatever I did, so did little Georgie.

I gotta say one thing for Georgie. He wasn't much of a gangster, but that boy had a way with dames that had to be seen to be believed. There wasn't a female of age between Eighth and Tenth Avenues who wouldn't have will-ingly dropped her drawers for little Georgie. It was like some kind of magic spell or somethin', the effect he had on women. As I was no slouch in the broads department myself, I made a mental note that perhaps little Georgie could be helpful if, during a run of bad luck or a disfigurin' accident or something, I was in need of some assistance.

Georgie also had one advantage that I didn't have, namely, no juvenile arrest record and no reputation in the neighborhood as an incorrigible. Everybody knew that George Ranft wanted to be a gangster in the worst way, but for some reason this was looked upon as a charming foible rather than a lust for a pact with the devil, and so Georgie was able to have it both ways, except at home, where his father beat him unmercifully whenever he returned late from one of our gang meetings, which was often.

It seems that the Centrals had had it up to their keisters with the depredations of us Gophers and had decided to smash our gang once and for all. For the bait, they was countin' on our being interested in a particularly peachy shipment that was coming into the city from some rich fella's estate upstate. To hear Georgie tell it, there'd be riches that woulda made a king blush, and every one of them, I knew, ill gotten and thus fair game for the likes of us. Packed up neat and ready to ship out.

The bait set, the Centrals were planning to meet the next Gopher raid with a force three times as large as ever before, and for the gang to stage a raid would be the height of folly. So here was my plan . . .

"You bet I do, Goo Goo. Let's take a walk over the rail yards. Somethin' there I wants to show ya."

Chapter

Seventeen

BEFORE I GET TO DESCRIBING WHAT HAPPENED, it's incumbent upon my own good self to tell you what transpired a little earlier, and that would be my little visit to G. W. Plunkitt down the Wigwam. I know I shoulda told you this before, but you have to be in the dark, like Goo Goo, to fully appreciate what I was up to.

I'd gone looking for Plunkitt down at City Hall. Hiram was long gone from the shoeshine stand but other colored boys had taken his place, well mannered and eager to please. I grabbed a shine from one of them and tipped him plenty, because if there was one way I had already parted company from the shanty Irish, it was that I was a damn good tipper, even when I didn't have to be. A man what stiffs a shine or a serving girl, at least if they're tryin' and even if they ain't very good, why he ain't much of a man in my book.

Inside, they told me GWP was up at the Wigwam. There was plenty of ways to get uptown back then, more than today: You could go by streetcar or el or horse or horseless carriage. You could also go by the new Interborough Rapid Transit, if it was going where you was going. The only problem was, with all the competition in the streets, you couldn't go anywhere very quickly by conveyance, which is why I was aboard shank's mare.

I picked my way carefully through what was left of the Five Points. Nothing had been the same here since the big fight between Kelly's gang and the forces of Monk; so close to City Hall it was that whenever one of the damn reform mayors got in, they was always after making noise about cleanin' it up or tearin' it down or simply removing the whole bloody thing out, root and branch. Paradise Square had turned into a little park where the few decent people in the neighborhood could go (I think they called it Mulberry Bend

Park, or maybe Columbus), and many of the old tenements had been torn down.

I jigged my way up the Bowery and cut over to Chrystie Street heading north and admiring the storefronts along the way. But it wasn't only the storefronts that tempted you; everywhere you looked, there was advertisements for this, that and the other thing. I sometimes almost wished Ma hadn't taught me to read, because every time you turned around there was a big sign trying to sell you something, until it got so's you'd feel guilty about not having any interest in having the good people at Floyd Grant & Co. buying and selling your furniture, or drinking C&C ginger ale for fifteen cents the split, or staying at the Hotel Cadillac, or admiring the wares of E. Booss and Bros. Furriers. It was still something of a wonderland to me, this great City of New York, and I loved it the way I loved my mother and my brother and my sister. It was the place I shoulda been born in, to do the things I was born to do.

I made Houston Street in less than half an hour. The el went rumbling over my head as I crossed into Kleindeutschland, or what was left of it after the *General Slocum* disaster and a thousand people went down the drain. A lot of the kraut families had lost a relative or two when the steamboat burned and sank in the East River a few years earlier, and many of them had already moved out. As I passed what had been a Lutheran church, I noticed some Jews in their *payes* and their beanies scooting in and out of the building, and some heebie-jeebie writing on the wall. That was the thing about New York neighborhoods: the neighbors was always changing. Church today, shul tomorrow, and the Tiger standing there with a great big grin on its face, ready to greet and eat every one.

A few minutes later I was in front of the Wigwam. Braves in cloth caps and sachems in high-button waistcoats and bowler hats came and went, bustling, for sure somebody had to run the city, and it wasn't going to happen with a dope like Gaynor in City Hall, so it fell to Charlie Murphy and his boy, Big Tim Sullivan, who although in his dotage was even then collecting a paycheck from the suckers as a state senator, the better to keep an eye on the mischief in Albany.

Monk may have been on the outs with the Tiger, but himself still had a soft spot for me. And so the next thing you knew, there was I, face-to-face with the great man. As I hoped, Jimmy Hines was there with him.

"They'll jig tomorrow sunset, after the lockdown," I was saying.

"Sure about that?" asked Hines, pursing his lips and landing one square in a brass spittoon. I always admired the way that lad could spit.

"As a bishop layin' a bet at Belmont."

P. and Hines looked at each other, real pleased. "So how come you're rattin'?" said Jimmy.

Now, if there's one word that's sure to provoke the cutting off of an ear, or the gouging out of a eyeball, it's "rat." Words don't come no dirtier than that. The way most of the gangsters saw it, we had enough rats around us as it was, crawling through our clubhouses and scurrying across our floors while we slept, so the last thing we needed was the two-legged variety.

But what's worse, a rat meant you couldn't trust nobody. And how was New York supposed to function without trust? The way I saw it, the entire town was perched like a million angels on the head of a pin, and the pinhead was trust. New York City in them days was a magical place, where barbers and bootblacks could become specialists in roadwork, and sure didn't everyone think the better of them if they did their road inspectin' from the comfort of their parlor chairs and a couple of pints to the good already. Where a lad whose only professional interest in oysters and shellfish came in the eating of 'em could become head of the Fisheries Department of New York State. Where every man, no matter how humble his trade, could be a political scientist of the first order so long as he was a Democrat.

"It ain't rattin' to rat on a rat." I looked G.W. right in the kisser. "Didn't you tell me that yourself?"

Plunkitt picked up a seegar. "Too-shay," says he. "Indeed I did. But I do believe that was in the general context of an electoral contest, when the livelihood of many a man is riding on the outcome. Ain't that right, Mr. Hines?"

Jimmy had already struck tinder and was proffering same to G.W., who sucked in the flame through his weed like it was the breath of life itself. Himself took a few puffs. "But this is different. This ain't politics."

I stood up on my hind legs. "That's where you're wrong, sir," says I. "Unless the theft of Boss Croker's own personal goods ain't political."

The magic name of Croker got everyone's attention toot-sweet. Richard Croker, a Dublin man, had been the grand sachem of all sachems, until the meddling Lexow Committee queered the pitch for everybody by criminalizing the honest graft that had made men like the Boss and G.W. exemplary success stories. Tammany's man lost the election in '95, and then again in '01, at which point the Boss quit the ungrateful town and returned to Ireland to enjoy the fruits of his public service. Even at a distance of some several thousand miles, however, it wasn't good for life nor limb to be stealin' from Boss Croker, as any fool could plainly see, although not Goo Goo Knox, thank God.

"I mean, after all the Boss done for the Gophers, it just don't seem fair that a bunch of glorified gonophs like Goo Goo Knox and Newburgh Gallagher should swipe it," I pointed out.

Hines quit spitting and spoke up. "The Boss is expecting a shipment of . . . furnishings . . . from his place in the Adirondacks over to Glencairn." Hines looked at me to see if I understood. "His horse farm in Ireland."

"And should they somehow go missing . . . ," muttered G.W. He wandered over to one of his windows and smoked for a while in silence. Most of his windows commanded 14th, from Third Avenue all the way west, but this group looked both north and west, toward the river and, in the distance, Central Park.

"The Boss always said Charter'd be the ruination of New York," he mused. "That once we let them hayseeds from Brooklyn into the workings of our fair city, well, then, I got two words for you: Seth Low. A Brooklyn Republican become mayor of the consolidated City of New York, if you please. Come here, Mr. Madden."

Still in his mouth, the seegar pointed the way north. "Ever been to Central Park?"

I couldn't say as how I had been, not properly, and so I didn't.

"You got just as much right to be there as any of Mrs. Astor's Four Hundred. Nice place now. Grass, trees and such. Not when G.W. was born. Nothing but pigs and Irishmen in a shantytown of shite, and it was damn hard to distinguish between 'em."

He glanced over his shoulder to make sure I was following. "Pigs and Irishmen, sir," I said.

"Porkers and paddies indeed, and make no mistake—there wasn't a one of them high-and-mighty episcopals and presbyters who bothered to make the distinction. We thought we was coming to a new land, and we was, except that they got here first."

"We're here now," said Hines. "Whether they fookin' like it or not."

Plunkitt turned on Jimmy. "Watch yer mout', boy," says he. "It don't prove nothin' when a man what ain't no stevedore starts into talkin' like one."

I shot Jimmy a glance but he was too embarrassed to look my way.

"Along come Tammany," continued Plunkitt like there'd been no interruption. "Tweed, Honest John Kelly, the Boss. To give the little fella a chance, when no one else would even give 'im the time of day. Went to their christenings and their funerals and their bar mitzvahs, celebrated with 'em, married 'em, buried 'em without regard to whether they was dago or sheeny or chink, spic, mick or even nigger."

"Didn't matter a bit," said Jimmy, learning.

"Nor a whit, jot or tittle," continues Plunkitt, fully declamatory. "Sure, there's no crime so great as ingratitude in politics, and don't the great unwashed know it. Them morning-glory goos-goos and reformers always forget that, and aren't they surprised when, after a term's flirtation or two, the voters throwed 'em out on their arse and put a good solid Tammany man back in City Hall, the way God in His wisdom's ordained it. Why? Because we care about people here at the Wigwam—and the people care about us. And if one or two of us sees an advantage to do well here or there by doin' good—well, I ask you, where's the harm?"

That was a question I sure didn't have an answer to then, and still don't.

"It's a *dunkel* day when rats like the Gophers stoop so low as to take from him what give 'em everything they got," Plunkitt perorated, turning to Jimmy. "Lad, inform the Centrals this very hour. Have 'em throw enough coppers around them cars to discourage the Turks from the sack of Constantinople."

Hines jumped up and headed out, leaving me alone with the great man. Plunkitt looked me up and down, cap to buttons. He seemed to like what he saw because he snapped open his humidor and produced two big fat stogies, one of which he handed over to my own good self.

"What are you expecting from all this mischief, in the way of emolument?" he asked, offering me a light.

"A chance to pick up the pieces," I said.

Chapter

Eighteen

So we set out, the whole brain trust, me and Goo Goo, Newburgh Gallagher and Marty Brennan and twenty or so Gophers, plus my lads Art Biedler and Hoppo McArdle and Billy Tammany and Eddie Egan and Chick Hyland, all strolling over to the rail yards west of Tenth just as pretty as you please, like tourists on a sight-seein' expedition, except that I would estimate that the amount of weaponry we was carrying that day was nigh enough to fight a small European conflict or two.

The sun was heading down over the Palisades as we made the yards. Imagine if you will a feast spread out before a starving prisoner. That was the Central Yards to us. I gesticulated in the direction of a handful of railroad cars, hooked up to an engine. "Ain't that a Jew's eye, lads," I said. "Riches beyond compare. Just sittin' there waitin' for us to take it."

Goo Goo looked around suspicious. "Where's the bulls?"

"Shorthanded tonight," I replied. "Go on, Georgie—show 'em."

Little Ranft scooted out from behind me, tossed a glance over his shoulder and then vanished down into the yards. It wasn't easy—to get near the cars you had to climb down halfway to perdition, exposed as a baby's bum, which was why we generally staged our raids in the pitch-dark. But Georgie could move like nobody's business and in a trice there he was, down below. He picked the first lock he saw so sweet it made your mouth water, dashed inside the car, and the next thing we knew there he was, standing back on solid Tenth Avenue ground with a fur coat in his hand.

Goo Goo was impressed. "Nice work, Raft," he said.

"The name's Ranft," said Georgie, trying to sound like a tough guy.

"Too hard to say," says Goo Goo.

"Go to it, lads," says I, gesturing. I didn't have to say nothing. The Gophers was already clambering over the fences and down the drops and heading for the cars with lockpicks and bolt cutters. Goo Goo's eyes were ablaze and even Happy Jack had a genuine smile on his face for once.

Billy and the lads could hardly believe I was dawdling. "Hey, hurry up, there won't be nothin' left for us," etc., they more or less chimed. But I just stood there, waving encouragement to the troops below until every last man jack of 'em had vanished into the booty.

Weren't my lads even more astounded when I led them across the street and right back over to good old 352. Them mugs was wonderin' pretty good by this time, but they was well trained and, even better, loyal as death, and so up the stairs we went on the double, right to the roof, where May was waiting, like I told her to do.

"Hurry up," she said. "It's startin'."

We could hear the sounds of gunfire even before we reached the railing. The muzzle flashes down below looked like lightning bolts in the gloaming, followed quick enough by the *pop pop pop* sounds of the .38s and .45s and the shrill sound of the police whistles and once in a while the thunk of a club on skull. I could hear our lads firing back, but the resultant return fusillade was something to behold, and I made a mental note to try and never be caught against odds like that and if I was, then at least to give as good an account of myself as I could before they finally got me.

In the twilight, the last of the sun still visible behind the Jersey hill, it was hard to see, but see we could, or at least imagine. Maybe it's memory and maybe it's just fantasy, but to this day I have a vivid picture of Happy Jack, the smile finally wiped off his face at last as he falls with a couple of slugs in him; of Newburgh and Brennan dying twin deaths; of the rest of the gang beat up, head-busted and collared in a way that would have made old Monk proud, and if you tell me that I couldn't have seen it from where I was, why then I'll tell you you're a liar, because what's bein' there got to do with it?

The Centrals was waiting in the cars of course, just like I suggested, and I wish I could have been close enough to see the look on Goo Goo's puss when he hammered open a lock and found a gat sticking in his ribs.

It was about this time that the reinforcements arrived, motorcars with sirens, tires screeching, whistles blasting. More cops than I ever want to see come pourin' out of the vehicles and go charging down into the yards, clubbing my mates from hell to breakfast.

The sun dropped out of sight behind Jersey, a big ball of orange flame. "I guess this means you're the big cheese now," May said.

That realization was just then sinking in on the rest. I could see the looks in their eyes, congratulating themselves on being so wise as to have thrown in their lots with me. Tammany had taught me well: the only thing that counted was power, and it didn't matter how you got it, as long as you kept it.

"As a great man says: I seen my opportunities and I took 'em," I said grandly, turning my back on the rail yards and the carnage and the North River and directing my attention east, where it now belonged.

Chapter

Nineteen

So MANY MYTHS have attached themselves to the deaths of Luigi Mollinucci and Willie Henshaw that it's past high time to set the record straight. The same goes for what happened to me at the Arbor Dance Hall and for what happened to Little Patsy at Nash's Cafe. There are times in your life when nothing happens forever, wish otherwise as you might. And then there are times like these, when half of everything that's ever going to happen to you gets decided in a few short seconds, and no goin' back. I guess God only has a certain amount of time for each individual; I only wish I had a little advance warning of the moment I had His complete and undivided attention.

I was over at the Tiger a few days after the Gophers got themselves mashed by the Centrals. There was smiles all 'round the Wigwam as I entered, and in my brain them smiles was for me, on account of what I'd done. By the time I got up to G.W.'s lair, the smiles was for real.

"Mr. Madden," says himself, "let me congratulate on you, for sure isn't Tammany a happy and grateful outfit this fine morning."

I looked around the room and there was Jimmy, naturally, and another big mug I didn't recognize. He was dressed in the same outfit everybody at Tammany wore, only he was sportin' a bow tie—not too swell, but none too shabby either. Normally I don't like conducting my business in front of strangers, but this wasn't my bailiwick, and so I took the compliments like a man.

"'Tis a grand thing when a number of problems can be solved with a single bold stroke," Plunkitt was saying when I started listening again. "There's a new wind blowin' down from Albany these days, and even we of the Wigwam sometimes have to bend along with it unless we want to get blown away. And that wind says the lawless days of the gangs is over. I seen it coming myself, back in the days of Monk and Kelly, but now it's well and truly here, and make no mistake." He cast a beneficent glance around the room.

One of the strangers spoke up. Shows you how dumb I was back then, it was only then that I recognized him as Big Tim Sullivan his own self.

"The gangs is gone because the conditions that bred 'em is going," says Tim. "Tammany's doing its work well. Why be a shtarker when you can just as easily hold elected office? The Irish don't need crime anymore—we got the law on our side."

G.W. took over. "Think of the law like it was a box o' tools," he said. "Some of 'em you use a lot; some of 'em you ain't used in dog's years, although they're right there should you need 'em. Some of 'em, like a hammer, you can use for all sorts of things: to pry open a jar, or smash a window, or tamp down a tack. Well, the law ain't no different. That's why we make laws but hardly ever repeal 'em—you never know when one's gonna come in handy."

"Which brings me to my point," says Big Tim, who really was big, especially when he was standing up, as he was now. "We're after passing a law upstate that makes it a crime to carry a firearm in the State of New York."

"Why would you want to go and do a screwy thing like that?" I asked, polite as I could.

"Because we can," said Big Tim, which after all is the First Law of Politics.

"Because we want the mugs to understand who's rulin' this roost," said Jimmy, and at that moment I knew he was really going places. "Because we want to show the goo-goos that we mean business. Because—"

"Because bangers is okay for some canary bird fresh from the jug," says G.W., "but not for a newly minted Tammany man." He paused so I could take his meaning. "Such as your own good self "

I thought I was going to fall over right then and there, like I was shot.

"Oh sure, we'll still need the services of some hard gees from time to time," says Tim. "An election is a war and the polling place is a battlefield. To my way of thinking, people will always need a bit of persuading to vote often and to vote right each and every time. And we'll be there to help. But we don't need sluggers anymore—we need thinkers."

In my brain I agreed with Big Tim, but in my heart I wasn't so sure, and I certainly wasn't about to forsake the heater that Monk gave me in order to make a man out of me. Which rod was stashed where it always lived, in the waistband of my trousers, snuggled up to me even tighter and more private than Freda, Margaret or Loretta.

Plunkitt wedged his seegar between his teeth and clamped his jaw tight. Then he opened his arms, motioning to me and Jimmy to step inside them, which we did. He hugged us both close, and I had to admit it felt good since I hadn't been embraced by a man since my own dear Da departed, if you don't count Monk's pounding me on the back from time to time, and I guess my friendships with G.W. and Monk mighta been a way to compensate for Da's loss, as them headshrinkers nowadays say, but I don't hold to none of that, which if you ask me is for sissies.

Himself smothered us for a while, then let us out for air. "Tammany needs fine young specimens like the two of you," he said. "Therefore, I want you both to promise me now, on the graves of the Irishmen who fought and died back home, and right here in front of Big Tim Sullivan the workingman's friend, that you'll always work together, never double-cross each other, and that you'll split the take fair and square."

It was an easy promise to make and we both made it.

"Jimmy here will be runnin' for—and winnin'—the leadership of the eleventh district next year, against Jimmy Ahearn, a tough sonofabitch if there ever was one who's beaten him twice, but I have a feeling three's going to be a charm. You know where the eleventh is, Owen?"

I shook my head no. It was the first time Plunkitt had even been familiar with me, and I glowed.

"That would be uptown, Morningside Heights and a piece of Harlem. Sure, our colored brothers are movin' in like Noah's flood, but that don't signify. Jimmy'll represent the darkies same as the whites. As for you—"

I pricked up my ears.

"You'll continue about your business in the twentieth ward, same as always. Except that allowin' as how you're operatin' under the personal protection of meself and the Tiger, there are a few things I'd like you to attend to. To show your good faith and capabilities, about which I have no doubts."

I asked what those few things might be.

"Really only one, when you get right down to it," said G.W. He stubbed out his cigar on his desk and tossed the butt into the spittoon. "I want the Hudson Dusters eliminated from the body politic, and I don't care how you do it. Big Tim's law ain't going to take effect until next year, so the way I see it, you've got six months or so to . . . re-organize the West Side right and proper. Jimmy will see to the finances: salary, expenses and whatnot."

I allowed as how I was happy and honored to do so.

"Just keep your name out of the papers and your fingerprints off the evidence. Keep any unpleasantness to a minimum, cut yourself in on any business dealings generously but not greedily"—he directed his gaze toward Jimmy—"and always remember who your friends are."

I wasn't sure but I thought I'd just been invited to marry what was left of the Gophers to Tammany Hall, a marriage made in Heaven. "Don't you worry about a thing, sir," I said, trying not to sound too eager, but probably failing.

Plunkitt looked at me all avuncular. "One more thing, Owen," he said. "A word about combat, be it political or otherwise."

I was listening hard.

"No matter how tough you are, you can always lose. The question is not how you handle victory. It's what you make of defeat."

We shook hands all around and I left as close to the top of the world as I'd ever been, but with the summit still firm in my sights.

Chapter

Twenty

THINGS WENT FINE ENOUGH at first. Me and the boys took charge of the Kitchen right quick, and soon enough wasn't some folks referring to me as the Duke of the West Side. Without resorting to too much violence, we made it plain to the merchants and voters of the ward that from now on we'd be giving the orders and that if they had trouble whatsoever with any stray or rogue punk, they should come to us. The best part was the fairy story that the terrible Gophers had been destroyed by the Centrals, which meant that we officially didn't exist, which meant there was no public outcry from the goo-goos to clean up the city, which meant I was in the enviable position of eating my cake and having it too.

We also made it clear to the Dusters that they was expected to stay in the Village, and not roam north of 14th Street if they knew what was good for them; penning them in I had figured for the first step. With my chum Tanner Smith in place, I could keep pretty good tabs on the Dusters, who were destroying themselves with the white powder anyhow and therefore weren't much of a threat to anyone except themselves.

I was starting to pile up some real money too, except that I couldn't very well show much of it to Ma. I gave her a lot of malarkey about working for Tammany in a minor organizing capacity, but with real prospects for advancement, and she seemed pleased as she nodded off after a glass of cordial or two. May by this time was working as a domestic, for a family of six kids over on 36th Street, with a sober mother and a crippled father—a sandhog who'd lost both his legs in an accident digging the Ashokan Reservoir in the Catskills—so I didn't feel uneasy about her being in service, although just in case, I had some of the boys keep an eye on things. Marty was Marty, running up a modest rap sheet of petty burglary busts in a sad-sack imitation of my own good self. He did three months in the Tombs and came back not a bit wiser.

Some of my swag I plowed into a proper clubhouse I rented from a horse-shoer named Keating and which I called the Winona Club after a lass in the neighborhood I had taken a brief fancy to in between my visits with Loretta. My youthful fumblings with Freda had long since turned into more accomplished amorous artistry, and I liked to think I knew my way around the more piquant parts of a woman's body the same way I could get from Rector Street to the upper precincts of the Kitchen without giving the route a minute's thought.

The Winona Club sat on the second floor of Keating's building. It had its own private entrance, and in short order we had fixed up another in the rear, so that if trouble came calling, there were a couple of ways out. I outfitted my first club with a big bar and a little Steinway, and there was always plenty of local gals who could be persuaded to come up and keep the gang company, some several of whom I was carrying on with more or less regularly. There was always music, as well as a bottle of whiskey on my table, because in them days I was under the influence of thinking that thinkin' went easier if not better with booze.

Every now and then things could get a bit rowdy, what with the girls squealin' that Georgie or somebody had pinched their bottoms, or a couple of the lads in particularly high spirits whalin' away at each other, which I let them do so long as they didn't break nothing of value.

One night when we was having some particularly boisterous discussions, Keating came bangin' on the door, beefin' about the noise. I guess you could say I'd had a few, because my inclination was to laugh in his face, which I did.

"You'll have to be quiet up here," says he, "or I'll put you out of my house." He looked the very picture of indignation, Keating did, his big blacksmith's arms all pumped up with righteous wrath.

"You'll put *me* out of your house?" I could hear the laughter from the gang in the background. I drew closer to him, knowing that if he was to take a swing at me, he'd be dead on the floor in two shakes of a lamb's tail. "Mister, did you ever hear of Owney Madden?"

His mouth was workin' but sayin' nothing, which indicated to me that his brain was workin' as well. There was a look in his eyes at my name that I'd seen on the face of the sergeant when he beheld the great Monk Eastman.

I backed away a little, letting my coat fall open just a little so that he could get a good look at my arsenal: my Bessie, the knucks and the .38.

"Well, mister—I am Owney Madden!"

I thought he was going to soil himself then and there. "It weren't me that was complaining, mind you," he sputtered. "It was one of them nosy neighbors next door."

I looked over at some of the boys. I didn't have to say nothing.

"Why don't you let me have a word with 'em," he continued, backpedaling. "They's reasonable folks, I'll warrant."

"They'd better be," says I, showing him the door we reserved for strangers and trouble.

Every now and then a bull got it into his thick skull that he ought to trump me in for some imagined malfeasance or other, shinin' his buzzer, as it were, all of which the Tiger quashed faster than you could say Jimmy Hines.

One day while I was in temporary custody, clipping my nails, a bull came up to me. "Newspaper fella outside says he want to talk to you. Says he'd like to know how a big shot like you spends his time."

"I don't talk to no newspaper fellas." Talk about rats.

"Could be good for you, Madden."

"Could be better if you'd let me at your sister, copper."

I thought he was going to slug me for a minute there, but he just laughed, which I hated even more than a slugging. "You mugs are all alike," he said. "Cheap punks with smart mouths and chips on your shoulders."

Well, that got my Irish up. "Gimme a piece of paper," I growled, and he did. Here's what I wrote:

Thursday—Went to a dance in the afternoon. Went to a dance at night and then to a cabaret. Took some girls home. Went to a restaurant and stayed there until seven o'clock Friday morning

Friday—Spent the day with Freda Horner. Looked at some fancy pigeons. Met some friends in a saloon early in the evening and stayed with them until five o'clock in the morning.

Saturday—Slept all day. Went to a dance in the Bronx late in the afternoon and to a dance on Park Avenue at night.

Sunday—Slept until three o'clock. Went to a dance in the afternoon and to another in the same place at night. After that I went to a cabaret and stayed there almost all night.

All of which was true. It was a grand life and as I look back on it now, I didn't realize how good it was. Which of course is true of all of us in our youth.

Everything woulda been swell except that I had to run into Luigi Mollinucci 'round about September of 1911, a few months shy of my twenty-first birthday. You remember him, the fruit stand owner's kid. Well, that was then and this is now: in the interim since I first met Mr. Mike and thus indirectly Mr. Monk, the little wop had growed up and, wouldn't you know it, was after seein' my sister, May, and her not yet eighteen.

What's worse, by my lights, was that he was pals with Fats Moore, the yegg what had mugged my mother way back when. Fats was still in the neighborhood, hangin' around the fringes of some of the gangs, making a small name for himself as a slugger, newsstand-burner and lush-roller. Some of the kids were starting to look up to him as a big man, but to me he was the pure phonus balonus and always would be.

Luigi, on the other hand, had graduated to running his dad's fruit stand. I didn't think much about this one way or another, until it gradually dawned on me that I was seeing more and more fresh fruit in our household, even with nobody dead, which Ma could certainly not afford on Bridey's wages. I knew enough about figures to put two and two together and come up with Mollinucci. With which evidence I confronted May one early autumn evening when a pear suddenly appeared on our table.

"Are they growing pears on 30th Street now?"

She laughed, real innocent, like I was making some kind of a joke. "Ain't it nice?"

"Where'd it come from?"

"Got it from the vendor's."

"Which vendor?"

"Over Ninth way."

"Never liked that fella."

"Well, it was free, if that makes you feel any better."

That made me feel worse. "You know you shouldn't ought to go over Ninth by yourself. Not a good element there."

May laughed again, not knowing how much she was agitating me. "I didn't. He came here."

It was all I could do to keep from jumping out of my chair. "What do you mean, he came here?"

"What I said. He brought this 'round just before you come home. I wasn't here so he give it to Ma, just before she gone out to work."

"I think I'll take a walk," I said, picking up the pear.

"Hey!" said May, but I was already out the door and striding toward Ninth.

Don't get the idea that I was jealous of May's havin' a suitor or anything, when she was old enough. Such things were a natural part of life. But being already experienced in the ways of women, I knew what was on the sonofabitch's mind, and I was going to be damned to Hell for all eternity if I was going to let him put his greasy mitts on my sister.

Which is what I was going to explain to him when, what do you know, I spotted the guinea in question with Fats, toddling down 30th Street toward Eleventh Avenue. They'd both already had a couple and it was about that moment when I wished I'd brought Billy or Chick with me. I trailed them west down the long block, past the rail yards, but as luck would have it, just about at the corner Fats and Luigi stopped and then Fats turned around and looked right at me.

"Hey, lookit if it ain't the banty little rooster from Hell." He leered a little, or at least I thought he did. He was bigger and fatter than when last I'd seen him, neither of which development favored him particularly. "Gettin' any, Madden?"

"Not unless you count your mother, Fats, and I don't, even if everybody else does," I said. My quarrel wasn't with him at this moment, and I didn't want him interposing his fat Irish gob between me and Luigi.

Even Fats was smart enough to spot this for an insult. He stuck out one big mitt and tried to clobber me with it, but I dodged around him to get face-to-face with Luigi. I thrust the pear right in his puss. "You forgot something."

He stood there real cool. "Take it easy, Fats," he said to Moore. "Madden didn't mean that nasty crack about your mother . . ."

I could feel Fats relax a little behind me, but just in case, my left hand was sneaking into my back pocket and coming out with a fine blackjack Loretta had given me for a present.

". . . because everybody knows that Madden don't have to leave home to get his."

From this point on, as far as I'm concerned, whatever happened, happened in self-defense. One of the things you may recall the great Eastman teaching me was how to fight with both hands, and had that ever come in handy on more than one occasion.

I wheeled and caught Fats behind his right ear with the Bessie and he went where he belonged, down at my feet. I think Fats puked as he fell, and so now I was even madder when his meal landed on my shirtwaist. Which incident gave Luigi a chance to scoot, for sure didn't he see the Reaper in the aggrieved person of me coming for him at that very moment.

He barreled across Eleventh, heading for what he thought might be the safety of the North River, but I was too quick for him, and tackled him in a few steps. He came up begging but I came up swinging and I caught him a glancer just to the right of his jaw, which dazed him a bit so that he stumbled back and his heel hit the curb and down he went again.

"I didn't mean nothin', honest I didn't." The same dreary excuse mugs always have when they know you've got 'em dead to rights.

I had to make sure he didn't get up. I couldn't let that kind of talk float through the neighborhood, in and out of the mouths of every layabout, mort and mab and so pulled my Smithie and put a hell of a shanty on his glimmer, to wit: I shot him in the head. Luigi died right there on the spot, on the street, blood oozing out one of his ears, where my bullet had gone in, and a big gaping hole on the other side of his head, where the slug had gone out, and it served him right.

I was still breathin' easy as I looked around. Luckily for me, Eleventh didn't have a lot of people on it, not like Tenth, but there were still a few passersby, drunks mostly, and one or two of the more incautious had actually stopped to watch my dance with Luigi and were standing there gaping at me like fish flopping on a pier.

We looked at each other for a nonce, me with my gat still in my hand, them with their parcels and packages. God only knows what I woulda done next except that Art and Johnny miraculously appeared at my side.

"Beat it, everybody," said Art.

"You didn't see nothin'," added Hoppo. "All of youse."

"Sure they did," I said, still in a daze. "They saw everything. They saw this punk die, which is what'll happen to any mug crosses me on my turf. Which is what'll happen to them if they so much as open their gobs. They saw me: Owney Madden of Tenth Avenue." I was shouting now, full of inseparable rage and pride. "Owney the Killer!"

Police whistles brought me to. I have a dim recollection of Art or Johnny or both of 'em dragging me away quick time, of ducking down into the stairwell of one of our cribs and into the railroad tunnel that ran over to Pennsylvania Station from Death Avenue and finally poking my head aboveground a block or so from 352, the coast clear.

I heard later that the bulls showed up and grilled everybody who'd thought he mighta seen something. I heard later that one or two of 'em might have mentioned my name in a temporary fit of civic rectitude. I heard later that one or two of 'em vanished to Hell or Connaught before they could give any evidence. I heard later that nobody else said a word. I heard later that I'd retrieved the pear as we ran. I heard later that I ate the whole thing.

Chapter

Twenty-One

You MAY HAVE GOT THE NOTION along the way that I was hell with the ladies, which was true. Maybe my head was swelled by all my successes, but I held the notion that pretty much any dame I fancied was mine on my say-so, and you know what? I was pretty much right. Not wishing to crimp my style, I was spending most of my time at the Winona, although I still looked in from time to time at 352, to make sure everything was all right there, but May and Ma were doing fine on their own, and Marty, well, I didn't see much of him, largely because around this time he got sent up the river for three years on an assault charge.

I've never understood why fellas that don't have no talent for it still want to be gangsters; it would be like wanting to be Paderooski without knowing a do from a re from a mi. I knew I was born to the life from before the boat, but the plain fact of the matter was that Marty was never going to amount to much in the gangland department. Neither was Georgie, but him I let hang around because I liked him and because the girls liked him. Even Georgie, though, had found more profitable occupation tea-cozying with the East Side married ladies up at the Plaza Hotel, where he could put his talents as a gigolo to splendid use. There was another guinea he worked that racket with, name of Valentino, of whom you've probably heard. To hear Georgie tell it, the bloomers was rainin' down on them thick and fast, and I believed him.

We were having a beer one night at the Winona after he got off what he called work. There was two kinds of lipstick across his cheek, and his collar was blotchy with sweat and tears and perfume and God only knew what else, plus he smelled like kisses and cigarettes.

"Got an idea," says Georgie.

"Who you kiddin'?" I asked. We was friends, so I could talk to him like that.

"Rudy's idea, actually. Has to do with the picture business."

"You mean them nickelodeons over in Jewtown?" That would be Second Avenue south of 14th.

"They don't call 'em nicks anymore. They're photodramas. Picture shows . . . Anyway, Rudy's heading out West, thinks I should join him."

"Maybe someday."

"You think?"

I looked at Georgie. He was a good-looking kid, no doubt about it. "Can you act?"

"What difference does it make?"

He had me there. "Give it a few years. Let's see if folks take to it in a big way." His face fell a little. "Besides, you're too young for California. Not to mention small. Do a little growin' first, why don't ya?"

"Rudy says all them nickels add up."

"Let's count our nickels here first."

Anyway, there I was one evening, holding court at the Winona. Freda and Margaret were both there, as was most of my boys. Billy and Chick had landed jobs with the Tiger, so they came around only once in a while now, and Eddie had got himself sent to college for a stretch for doin' I forget what, even though he was of course innocent. Which meant that Art and Johnny had more or less become my bodyguards. After that business with Mollinucci, I hardly went anywhere without 'em, except to some young lady's chambers, and even then I sometimes had them standing guard outside, to make sure I wasn't disturbed in my ministrations by anything as inconvenient as a father, brother or husband.

We were going over some business, namely, the amount of money the gang could earn by various malefactions. The income of the Gophers was mainly derived from safecracking, second-storey work, stickups and holdups, shake-downs and collections for Tiger, of which we got a piece.

"Punching?" asked Art, who was the one who could write.

"Couple a bills."

"Blacken both eyes?"

I thought a second. "Two bucks apiece."

"Nose and jaw broke?"

"Call it ten."

"Ear chawed off?"

"Gotta be at least fifteen."

"Slashed cheek?"

"Anywhere from one to ten bucks, depending on whose cheek it is."

"Shot in the leg?"

"Let's say up to twenty-five."

"What about the arm?"

"Same, only start countin' at five."

"How come?"

Johnny smacked Art in the shoulder. "It's harder to hit an arm," he said.

"Maybe for you. Bomb-throwing?"

"Five bucks to fifty bucks." Pineapples were expensive.

"The Big Job?"

I thought about this for a moment. My first Big Job had been done gratis, but that was on account of my temper. This was business.

"A hundred simoleons and not a penny less."

Art and Johnny both whistled. To any chump on the street, a hundred bucks was a fortune—a month's wages—and here they could earn that in a day. I woulda thought it was a fortune too at one time, but not anymore.

We was so wrapped up in all this business that none of us noticed that Loretta Rogers had sat down and was havin' a glass of whiskey a couple of tables over. Normally I woulda been alerted to such a development, my standing order being that I was to be notified whenever one of my babes was on the premises, to avoid unpleasant situations, but I also had declared I was not to be disturbed while discussin' matters financial, which in the minds of the boys clearly superseded order number one.

There was something else that might have had something to do with it. To tell you the truth, I was tirin' a little of Loretta. She was sweet—nicer than Freda by twenty city blocks—and she had a set of lungs on her that a fella would kill to get his hands on, but she was awful light upstairs, and I had found out what every guy discovers sooner or later, which is that you can't stay in bed with 'em all day, much as you think you'd like to.

The first I knew of Loretta's presence was that she was standing next to our table, a glass of rye in her hand and looking none too chipper. The color had gone out of her face, her hair was mussed and unwashed and frankly she didn't smell too good, like she'd been sick not long earlier and I mean English sick, not American.

"What's new, what's blue and how do you do?" I said as jaunty as I could muster.

"Not so good."

I remember the room getting very quiet right about then, something it never did, except it was just my luck.

"Owney," she blurted, "you got me in trouble."

We had a bell system at the Winona, manned by a lookout. One pull meant it was a gang member, two signified somebody from the Tiger, three indicated the visitor was someone we had to do business with, even if we didn't like him, and four meant an inquisitive copper. Repeated clanging meant run like hell.

Before I could say anything, the bell rang. We all stopped counting at five.

Loretta screamed as the bulls' battering rams started pounding down the doors. This was no time for yelling, though, and so, quick as sewer rats, up jumps me and Art and Johnny and we start pushing furniture against the entrance right quick. Mugs started dashin' this way and that, especially down the back staircase to the cellar, where they could disappear into a dozen tunnels beneath the streets.

Our tables and chairs was losin' the battle against the cops' pile driving. "What about the clunker?" asked Art, referring disrespectfully to the piano. I shook my head no, because in my opinion you should never use a fine instrument as a doorstop.

My desire to preserve my Steinway, however, is what lost us the battle, 'cause the rams were tougher than Keating's cheap front door and down the latter came, followed by a host of coppers led by a big sergeant.

Most of the gang had hightailed, leaving just me and a few of the boys to deal with the situation. Before you go thinkin' that was cowardice, though, let me say that it was more like prudence, because a footloose gangster is far to be preferred to one caged in the Tombs. There was nothing for it but to stand and fight.

I yanked my gat out of my waistband. "I'll shoot the gizzard out of any copper what tries to come in!" I shouted, but those Irish pigs were crazy-brave, and they kept on coming until somebody whistled a bullet and that somebody mighta been me.

That was the signal for some several minutes of general fracas firing. Bullets went poking through walls, shattering glass windows and busting up the appointments until we all more or less ran out of ammo about the same time.

As often happens in these kind of wild gunfights, nobody got hurt serious. The sarge mighta got winged a bit, but it was your basic standoff, except we was outnumbered and presently they fell upon us, clubs at the ready. One of the dirty bastards tried to take a swing at Loretta, which naturally had me runnin' to protect her, especially in light of her recent information, which meant I had to turn my back on the bleeding sergeant for a moment and that's when he caught me alongside the head and down I went, face-first into the floorboards, and once again had the ignoble experience of waking up in durance vile.

Chapter

Twenty-Two

THIS TIME THE CHARGE was violating the Sullivan Law, if you please. I was informed of same by none other than my old friend Becker, who had risen to the rank of lieutenant and normally wouldn't be connected with punks like me, except for he'd made an exception.

Becker was standing outside my cell in the Tombs with another fella, a well-dressed little Jewman who didn't say nothin', but I could tell they was chummy. "We've got you now, Madden," says Becker, a cigarette hangin' from his lips. "We know all about Mollinucci and you'll fry for that, sure as hell, witnesses or no witnesses."

I didn't like his tone but there wasn't much I could do about it, on account of I was still spittin' up blood from the beating I took. I coulda sworn my head was busted into a baker's-dozen chunks, and I wondered how it was that I could even move my fingers, so sore were my arms. My right leg wasn't feelin' none too good, and there were bruises across my chest and back. I'd looked better, that's for sure.

"I'm only sorry I can't let you step outside so I can knock you down again," he said. "But I guess all good things come to him what waits." He crushed out his cigarette on the bars and tossed the warm stub at me. "Let's go, Herman. We got business to discuss."

He walked away, chuckling to himself like he was funny or something. The fella Herman, though, hung back just a bit and quick as a flash he too tossed something at me, except it wasn't a fag butt but a card. A business card, with a name on it: "Joseph Shalleck, Esq., attorney-at-law," which I grabbed before it could hit the deck.

When I looked up, Herman was giving me a fisheye. "Be smart, kid," was all he said. Then he scuttled along in Becker's wake, with Becker none the wiser.

I got to spend the night in City College, courtesy of the City of New York, and the next morning found myself in a holding pen at the criminal courts, waiting my turn. Ho-hum. There wasn't a gangster worth a tinker's damn who hadn't been here a million times before, including my own good self. Bein' in the Tombs or the pen was like a class reunion at one of them nancy-boy schools, only tougher, but I wasn't much in the mood for greeting at this point because to tell the truth my schnozz was out of joint on account of I hadn't heard boo yet from the Tiger nor any of its minions.

There I was, waitin' till they called my name, startin' to despair of any good Christian soul's ever turning up to commit a corporal work of mercy when along came another little Jewman, like the first one, only littler. I liked him straight off: he was dressed plenty swell, like he was almost somebody, right down to his spats, and he carried something I'd never seen before, a briefcase. There weren't many briefcases around the Kitchen in them days.

"Joe Shalleck," he said, and I recognized the name. "Herman Rosenthal sent me."

"Herman the friend of that dirty bull Becker?"

"He ain't no friend of Becker's, don't worry about it, in fact you can put your mind to rest on that score, so let's get down to brass tacks here, but like I said don't you worry none 'cause I got it all fixed, arranged, what have you, and all you gotta do is do exactly what I tell you to do is all you gotta do, do you get me?"

Of course he said that in a tenth of the time it takes me to write it down.

"Tammany's left you up the creek, teach you a lesson and whatnot, and if it ain't for your good luck in runnin' into Rosenthal, who happens to be my uncle Hyman, they call him Herman here, Hyman too old country, too Jew if you catch my drift, anyway if it weren't for the luck of the Irish, black Irish I'd say by the looks of ya, well then you'd not only be up the creek you'd be up the fucking river, if you take my meaning, which I'm sure you do."

I looked at him blank, but it was beginning to sink in. This is the way the Tiger learned you a lesson but good and that lesson was, who's boss.

"You are one lucky harp, Madden. Hey, screw!"

The screw in question opened the cell and let us out. We made our way into the courtroom, where Becker was standing with a smirk on his ugly kraut mug, and Shalleck whispered to me: "Uncle Hyman's in gambling, and he pays off to Becker like a Tenderloin whore. Hates the sonofabitch, but what's a yid to do?"

"Is Rosenthal really your uncle?"

"They're all my uncle, if you go back far enough, to Poland I mean, and boy do we ever. Go back to Poland. Not that I would, you understand. England, maybe. You're English, ain't ya? I hear Bob's your uncle there. Kind of a fixture of speech—"

The judge called my name and little Joe shuts up and steps up like David facing Goliath.

"How do you plead?" asks Hizzoner.

"Innocent as hell," says Joe, turning to me. "Take off your shirt and get up on the stand."

That one caught me by surprise. Because in an Irish household nobody sees you without your shirt on, nor obviously your trousers, not even a wife her husband or a hubby his spouse. We undress in the closet, like decent folks.

I balked like one of them pitchers for the Highlanders, which is what the Yankees was called back then, when they was in last place, and who knew a change of name and venue could make all the difference? We all sure did.

Shalleck coughed. Not just a little cough, but a great big loogie one, so that the judge musta thought he'd had a shock and was about to keel over. As he was bent over, with everybody all solicitous-like, he suddenly coughed once more, real loud, and at the same time he give me a shot in the ribs with an elbow I never saw coming, but which message I received loud and clear. I took off my shirt and took the stand.

I had no sooner got up there, and the courtroom was still gettin' over what everybody thought was a shyster's seizure, when there was an even louder collective gasp and who should waltz in at that moment but the Mayor of the City of New York his own grand self. Down the center aisle comes William Jay Gaynor, big as life. I'd never seen a Mayor up close before, but I knew that he was a pal of Charlie Murphy down the Wigwam, or at least that Charlie thought he was.

The thing about Gaynor was he was reform. What, you might ask, is one of them reformers doin' runnin' on the Tammany ticket? But that was the Tiger's genius—if it was reform that the city, or at least the damn newspapers, wanted, then by God Tammany'd give it to them. Which it did in the person of W. J. Gaynor. Tammany-style reform.

Gaynor strode up to the front row and, his bullyboys having cleared a place for him, plunked his hoity behind down and stared at my poor half-naked self about to testify.

"Can you tell the court that you was only playin' cards last night when the coppers busted in and beat you about the head and shoulders, inflicting the grievous wounds that everybody who's got at least one eye in his head and ain't drunk can plainly see?" asked Joe, now completely recovered.

"I sure can."

"And furthermore can you tell the court that this attack was completely and totally unprovoked in any way, shape or form and that furthermore to my previous furthermore you did nothing whatsoever and in no wise to provoke said wanton attack upon your person or the persons of your friends, nearest and dearest and so forth and so on?"

"You betcha."

"Did you at any time discharge a firearm in direct contradistinction and violation of state law number"—here he mumbled something—"better known as the Sullivan Law?"

"Umm—"

"Let me rephrase that. Is it your testimony that you at no time were in possession of the Colt .45 automatic that was found on said Winonan premises, whether discharged or not, and that furthermore and so forth you are fully cognizant and aware of the provisions of the Sullivan Law, having had them explained to you by none other than Big Tim himself in the precincts of the Society of St. Tammany, otherwise known as the Columbian Order or more popular as Tammany Hall?"

"If you say so."

"Yes or no?"

I had to guess, but Joe helped me out with another explosive cough, which made his head bob up and down like something out at Coney.

"Sure."

"No further questions. Mr. Mayor?"

I was still sitting in the dock, shirtless, as Mayor Gaynor stepped forward to address the court. I thought the judge was going to faint dead away, but he propped himself up pretty good after he leaned down and took a stiff one from a flask beneath his robes.

Shalleck spoke directly to the judge. "If it please the court, the Mayor would like to say a few words, maybe even issue a proclamation or general order or two, I dunno, take it away, Yer Honor sir."

I got to admit Gaynor looked like a Mayor, which most of the Tammany Mayors did. But Mayors, I knew, was considered small praties by the Wigwam: its goal was to elect a Governor and maybe even a President.

Instead of saying anything, Gaynor stuck out his hand and one of his dangling flunkies smacked a piece of parchment into his paw. W.J. unfurled it like it was a flag or something and began to read:

"Order Number Seven. I, William J. Gaynor, Mayor of the City of New York, do hereby declare that it is henceforth illegal and unlawful . . ."

All Tammany pols were masters of the pregnant pause, and Billy Gaynor was no different.

". . . unlawful," he repeated solemnly, "for any . . . patrolman . . . to use his nightstick, daystick or billy club . . ."

The courtroom was all ears now, as was I. The only person who didn't seem to be hangin' on every word was Shalleck, who knew it all by heart already.

". . . billy club on any person or personage resident in said City of New York, under any circumstances . . ."

Another gasp and shuffling of feet amongst the spectators. One of them, probably a Printers' Row hack, got up like he was hit by lightning, with half his arse out the door and his ears still in the room, listening for the punch line.

". . . unless that patrolman or officer of the law, in the lawful pursuance of his duties, is prepared to testify in a court of law"—he looked around the room to let everyone know where he was—"that use of said club or implement was in defense of his life."

I could see Gaynor was enjoying himself tremendously. The reporter followed his arse out the door and so missed the next bit:

"God help any patrolman, lieutenant or even captain if a citizen—honest or otherwise"—and I guessed that included me, even without his fisheye—"makes a complaint of an unlawful clubbing."

Gaynor lateraled the parchment to the flunky, who rolled it up. "There's simply no place in a civilized society for such behavior." He looked at the judge, who didn't need to think twice.

"Case dismissed," he said.

May was waiting for me outside the courtroom. She threw her arms around me and kissed me like she had lost me for twenty to life. Shalleck stood off to one side and I was about to introduce him to my sister when there was a tap on my shoulder and who should it be but Jimmy Hines.

"You caught a break today," says he.

"No thanks to you," says I, still a little bitter.

"Yeah, well, politics ain't beanbag, as they say."

I woulda thought Jimmy woulda been happier, but he was all business, and it was about this time I realized that the courtroom was no place for sentiment or weeping and wailing and gnashin' of teeth, as it says in the Bible, but instead was an arena where the law was a football and the various accusers and accuseds were the fellas whose job it was to kick it around until it bore no resemblance to whatever the solons had in mind when they thought it up.

"Cost the Tiger some money," says Jimmy.

"I'll bet."

"You'll bet. You'll pay. We ain't runnin' no charity."

"I get the picture."

"Be sure you do. Otherwise, there's plenty of yeggs who will."

I don't want you to think that Jimmy was angry. On the contrary, he was as even-keeled as ever, a little smile on his face. From a business point of view, this was perhaps the most valuable lesson I ever learned, and haven't I done my damnedest to pass it on to my boys, right down to today.

"No hard feelings, huh?" said Jimmy, punching me in the arm and winking to Joe as he left.

Shalleck watched him disappear as he handed me back my shirt. "Trust him?"

I buttoned up. "Sure. Why not?" I asked.

"Schmuck!" he said, and socked me even harder.

Chapter

Twenty-Three

LORETTA AND I GOT MARRIED a couple of days later. Our daughter followed along in due course. Loretta wanted to call her Dorothy, which being her own unused real name made some sense, although why she didn't use it was beyond me. My superior choice was Margaret Mary Madden, which turned out to be her name, although we sometimes called her Marjorie, in the Irish way of givin' a body one name and then callin' him or her another, just for variety's sake. Loretta fought me on this for a couple of minutes, but I made it up to her in the way boys do and never once did she suspect that just maybe my thoughts of Margaret Everdeane might have had something to do with baby Madden's moniker.

Which brings me to Willie Henshaw.

Willie was a clerk in a dry goods store—Wanamaker's, I think—and somehow in the course of his duties he chanced to encounter and take a fancy to the selfsame Margaret Everdeane, with whom I was more or less regularly indulging my amorous proclivities on an unofficial basis after my nuptials.

For I must confess that Loretta I was well and truly tired of even before she got in the family way, and when I tried to slake my thirst with Freda, I learned she had toddled off and taken up with a Duster who called himself Little Patsy Doyle just to spite me for Loretta, which meant I had no other course but to resume relations with Miss Everdeane. Marriage and childbirth, however, have a way of cramping a man's style, so I was back at the old flat on 32nd Street more than I cared to be, which got me plenty sore, and well, when the cat's away . . . Margaret met Willie, with what consequences for all of us you're about to learn.

I only met Willie once, and that was the day I put a bullet in him on the Ninth Avenue streetcar, coming back down from the Amsterdam Opera House, whence I had trailed both himself and Margaret as he was escorting her to and from a performance. Art was driving and Hoppo was in the front seat of my new Ford T, which wasn't much but was the best they had, and I sat in the back smoking, waiting, thinking, until Art give me the signal and I sighted Willie and Margaret coming out of the theater.

"Beat it," says I, getting out of the car and squishing my fag under my heel.

I don't know what sort of bill of goods Margaret was retailin' to Henshaw, but it was plain as day even though it was the middle of the night that Willie was mighty sweet on her. I knew from experience that it didn't take much to engage Margaret's affections, so I figured I'd better cut Willie off before affections turned to passions and what have you. One of my rules has always been what's mine is mine and God help the man who tries to steal from me.

I got on after them at 60th Street and settled into a seat several rows behind. I even paid the conductor when he came by, which ordinarily I wouldn't have done, except that I didn't want to cause trouble until I wanted to cause trouble.

Margaret lived over 39th Street between Ninth and Tenth, while Willie was a Villager, as I had gleaned from Tanner. I hated the Village because every time I thought about it I thought about this Little Patsy Doyle bum and the fun he was having with my Freda, whom I guess you could say I was still sort of in love with, if I was ever in love with anybody.

The tram hit Margaret's stop, and I waited to see what they were going to do. I was surprised and Willie disappointed when Margaret only gave him a peck on the beak and he just waved good-bye as she hopped off and headed for home. It woulda been so simple for me to jump off right behind her, stroll her home and visit awhile, but the trolley had started moving again and I stayed aboard.

Willie was looking up at the ceiling, oblivious to all around him, as boys in love will be, which was another reason I had decided never to fall in love, at least not the crazy moony kind. He was a nice-looking kid, fresh-faced, but his mind was elsewhere, which is never a place you want your mind to be when you need it.

"Sixteenth Street," said the conductor.

Willie got up and so did I. As the door opened I reached into my waistband and took out my Smithie.

"Hey, Willie," I said.

He turned back to look at me and I could see his eyes widen as he grasped his fate and then I shot him in the belly, his guts splattering the doors and windows and even an old lady snoozing nearby as his body tumbled out the door just as it started to close and the streetcar started to pick up speed again.

Here's the thing about firing a gun in close quarters: nobody can believe it's happening. Which is why so many yeggs get away with it. The noise, the smoke, the shock, the blood—they have a way of anesthetizing the witnesses, so they don't know if it's Tuesday or Killarney by the time the bulls get around to grilling them. In this particular instance, I could have waltzed outta there. But I didn't.

Call it the showman in me. Just as the trolley started to roll, I yanked the emergency cord and sent a couple of nickel-nursers who'd blown their supply of nickels at the corner saloon sprawling into the aisles, wondering what hit 'em. Some say it was Henshaw's body rolling under the wheels that brought the car up short, but don't believe 'em.

As the car slammed to a halt I marched toward the driver's station. I think the poor schnook thought I was going to blast him too, but instead I shoved my piece back into my pants and reached for the trolley bell, which I tolled a couple of healthy clangs for poor dead Willie.

Everybody on the tram was looking right at me. "I'm Owney Madden of Tenth Avenue!" I shouted. "The Duke of the West Side." I glared at everyone on the tram, to make sure they never forgot my face and never remembered my name.

When you jacked a trolley, the doors stood open until the crate got rolling again and so I sauntered out into the night, cucumber-cool. They say the first murder is the hardest and by my lights they're right on the money. This one was a piece of cake.

The hell of it was 'twas Willie what gave Margaret the dose. Which is what she told me when I showed up at her door by way of an alibi. Which is why she hadn't let him come visit her that evening. Which is why I spent the rest of that night enjoying Margaret's company not in her boudoir but in Bellevue, so modern medicine could work its magic.

Chapter

Twenty-Four

As usual, I got up the next day around two in the p.m., having been out most of the night thanks to Willie. Loretta had taken baby Margaret out for a push in her pram, so I had the luxury of lying in bed half-awake for a half an hour or so, with no squalling babies or whining women to bother my reveries.

I dressed, breakfasted on some cold rolls and an apple and then sauntered out into the street. I guess you could say I was feelin' more than a little cocky that day, what with a second scalp on my belt and me feeling like not just the Duke of the West Side but the king of the whole damn town. I was runnin' through my mind just how, or even if, I was going to mention what had happened last night to May, and had pretty much decided that I wasn't going to when these pleasant thoughts were interrupted by the blast of a police whistle and somehow I just knew it was blasting for me.

If it seems like my life was at this period more or less one run-in with the Law after another, you would be right, because it was seeming that way to me as well. Before my ears had registered the sound of the cops' klaxon my feet were already in motion, instinctively. My brain, meanwhile, had turned to thoughts of which of the passengers on board the trolley the previous evening might have ratted me out, and I was already figurin' revenge as I sprinted like hell up Tenth.

The problem was they had me pretty much out in the open and there were plenty of them too. When this many bulls showed up all at once, it made you wonder whether there wasn't something else going on, such as for instance a double cross, but there was no time to fret about that. If I managed to get away clean, there would be plenty of time for settling scores, and if I didn't, well, I would have plenty of leisure time in the Tombs or up the river to chew things over.

I hit the intersection of 34th and Tenth flying. I could have sprinted right and headed east, hoping to lose myself in the crowds that started milling proper once you got past Seventh. Instead, though, I kept on across the road-way and then dashed left, barreling toward Ninth, making for the safety of a place I knew well, namely, Mr. Mike Callahan's bar.

The thing about me in them days was that I was some kind of quick and I knew the beefy bulls were as likely to catch me as they were to jump to New Jersey. So damn me to hell and gone if here don't come more pigs, lurching and blowing hard around the corner from Ninth.

I had to judge fast and I did. I could make it down the service steps of Callahan's before the first of the blue lugs could take a swing at me, and I did that too.

Five or six steps and I hit the door hard.

It crashes open and there I am, in Mike's cellar.

I almost skiddooed on some beer foam down there in the dark, but this was no time to lose my balance because I could hear the shouts from street level and the heavy footfalls of some brave rounder chasing me.

Through the long dark cellar, up the stairs and into the bar.

Mike, wiping some glasses, sees me, sizes me and nods over his right shoulder at the stairs up.

Through the half-glassed door, hoping I wouldn't shatter it because I didn't want to cause Mike no damage, and then a flat rush up and up and up.

Noises behind, heavy breathing, more than one breather, whistles, Jesus, you woulda thought I was a menace or something.

Three floors up, four, then I was through the door and onto the roof.

The big wide city sprawled before me, ripe. I took in the view while I caught a brief breather and then the door clangs and bangs once more and this time it's not one bull or two, but at least three, or maybe half the damn force, and one of 'em cries out my name, but I haven't been exactly filing my nails and before he gets the final "n" out, I'm off again, flying.

The West Side back then was pretty much all of a piece, by which I mean the buildings was more or less the same height. And here's where you could appreciate the difference between New Law and Old because with Old you can just run like hell, dodging the smokestacks and hurdling the dividing walls without having to worry about plunging down one of the air shafts, whereas with the New you did, or you died.

It may occur to you that at this moment I was pretty much scared on account of the bulls clearly had my number and were hell-bent on nabbing me, but the truth is I was never happier than when I was up on the roofs of the city and it was right about this moment that it came to me that it was silly being a Gopher, scuttling about in the dark, when you could be a mighty American Giant Homer, soaring where you liked.

So I ran and ran, the cops' voices growing ever fainter as I put some distance between ourselves. I hopped from one address to another, sailing above the streets, trampling on the rooftops, shouting with joy, and I wished my sister might hear me and share my pride.

I'd managed to make it all the way to the west side of Eighth at 39th when I figured it was safe to come down now. The whistles had long since been silenced, the footfalls quieted; the noise of the city wafted up from below, but there was no danger in it.

I halted and holed up between a chimney and a vent pipe, tucking my legs beneath me like some Buddha. Perched above the town in makeshift rook I must've nodded off, for when I came to, the sun was setting, which meant it was high time I stopped fooling around and went to work.

I rose and scooted down the fire escapes, the usual tableaux unfolding behind the curtains. Here a man in his undershirt was busily polishing shoes. A floor lower, a couple of children played in a room by themselves, their mother fast asleep on the bed, one hand clutching a sack. On three a couple was arguing loudly; the woman had a big red welt across her back but she was giving nearly as good as she got and I found myself rooting for her as I passed by.

On two there was an old woman sitting by herself, staring into space and listening to a phonograph whose needle had finished its job in the matter of sound reproduction and was scratching away at the interior of the record.

I rode the sliding ladder halfway the length of the first floor and dropped to the sidewalk.

I shoulda knowed Becker would be there, waiting for me. He emerged from the shadows like the very divvil himself, the flame of a match signaling his malevolent presence.

I made to flinch and run, but instead of clobbering me Becker just held up his hand. "Smoke, punk?" he asked.

I allowed as how I wouldn't mind, but you can bet I was pretty leery accepting the fag, in case he tried to sucker-punch me. "What's the angle?" I said, inhaling.

"Taking the night air."

"What's the beef?"

Becker took a long drag like he was in no hurry to reply. "Who said anything about a beef?"

We stood there like a couple of pals, puffing away, saying nothing.

Becker threw his fag down and ground out the butt. "Kid named Henshaw got himself killed last night."

"I'm all broke up about it."

"Rumor is you did it."

"Impossible. I was home with my mother."

He reached into his side pocket and I caught a glimpse of some heat under his armpit. My own cannon was in my pants and I wondered if I could get to it before he shot me down.

His hand came out of his pocket. Matches. "The hell of it is, the only witness fell down the stairs this afternoon and broke his neck."

"Guess things are tough all over."

He lit another cigarette. "Heard Hymie steered you to Shalleck."

"I don't remember."

"I'll stop by the Winona tonight to refresh your memory."

"So I can refresh your bank account."

"Guess you're not as dumb as you look."

I had to hand it to Becker, playing both sides of the street like a pool hustler fleecing the house. "So what was all this hugger-mugger about?"

"Exercise. I like to keep my boys fit."

"They still ain't faster than me."

Becker flicked his fag into the gutter. "Pretty tough guy, aren't you, punk?" he said.

"If I have to be."

He buttoned up his coat. "Know what's the difference between us?"

I did, but I didn't say.

"Some folks may hate me when they see me in the street, but more of them like me, because I'm all that's standing between them and mugs like you. Which means I can pretty much expect to be visiting Mrs. Becker in the comfort and safety of our marital bed every evening. Whereas it's precisely the opposite with yourself: some of the yeggs in this shithole of a precinct may like you, but more of them hate you and what's worse they fear you, and there's damn few'd shed a tear if you was to disappear tomorrow. If I was a betting man, I'd wager that my chances of expiring with my boots off are a lot better than yours."

"I'll take that bet," says I.

Becker turned and walked away, confident as all get-out. "I thought you might," he said over his shoulder, and disappeared back into the shadows.

Chapter

Twenty-Five

Businesswise, everything was jake. The swag was rolling in. As long as we kept delivering at the ballot box and stayed out of the newspaper headlines, just about anything the Gophers did was okay by the Tiger. The Winona was renowned far and wide as the best clubhouse on the West Side, with the choicest onions and tomatoes—which is what we called dames back then—the most scrumptious chow and the best music this side of Broadway. I demanded it.

Speaking of which, I was spending more time on the White Way than before, as the theater was exerting an increasing fascination on me, as was the prizefights at the Garden, not to mention the picture shows which were now all the rage; maybe little Georgie had something there. I figured there was dog biscuits to be made in both them rackets if only I could figure out how, and so I decided to start working on that problem right after the elections of 1912.

First thing was we had to get Jimmy Hines elected district leader over Ahearn, and so Joe Shalleck and I threw ourselves into that particular task. Now, here was the problem: Jimmy Hines was a good-looking lad, but he was a by-God-terrible public speaker, as tongue-tied a paddy as ever lived.

Joe and I tried everything we could think of to improve Jimmy's speechifying, but he was still a blacksmith up there on the stump and you woulda thought he was after shoein' horses instead of tryin' to win votes. Even with this handicap, Jimmy had lost to Ahearn by only twenty-seven measly votes the previous election, which to me was an indication not so much of failure of delivery but lack of muscle at the polling place, which I was in a position to deliver and how.

"Okay, so Jimmy, you gotta be more effective is what I'm trying to tell you, more mellifluous. You can't just stand up there waxing platitudinous and whatnot when your audience is down below looking up at your trousers and half the men are wonderin' if you're packing and half the women are wondering how much you're packing, if you get my meaning, which I'm sure you do 'cause even you Irish must have sex once in a while, otherwise how could there be so many of you?"

"What Joe's trying to say—" I began.

"What Joe's trying to say is exactly what Joe *is* saying," said Joe. "You gotta look the part. Why the hell should a bunch of dumb Jews and Irish elect you to anything if you rodomontade like the village smithy or maybe the village idiot? People don't want their pols to look like them, they want them to look like pols, but not too much, you understand, you still gotta have that man-of-the-people crap, makes 'em feel better, makes 'em feel that any one of them could be standing up there on the stump flapping his jaws, except that you look a little too much like any of them, if you catch my drift, and that's what I'm also here to fix, besides and in addition to your speech patterns."

"Plus you lack muscle," I said edgewise.

"Plus you lack muscle, which is what Madden's here to fix. Their sluggers have been better than our shtarkers, but that's gonna change. Heads gotta be busted and I'm talking theirs not ours, right, Owney?"

I nodded.

"I mean fer chrissakes, that's the American way of story and song, do unto others before they can do unto you. So we're gonna do unto. Think of Ahearn's head as one of those anvils you used to pound on." Shalleck's head rotated and looked at me. "What's that big mug's name what runs Ahearn's gang?"

"Spike Sullivan," I supplied.

He spat. "Jesus, don't you micks have any imagination? Spike Sullivan, for crying out loud. Who thought that up, his mother? Anyway, here's what we're going to do—"

"Here's what *I'm* going to do," I took over, because if you didn't remind Joe who was the shyster and who the client once in a while, he could get confused about the relative positions of each. "We're going to tie up Sullivan and his gang forty-eight hours before the votin' begins. Your mistake in the past was going after them after the polls opened. Let me tell you, that's too late. We gotta put him out of commission long before that."

"How're you going to do that?" asks Jimmy. For a Tammany fella he pretty much didn't know his arse from his elbow sometimes.

"Why, have a drink with him of course," I replied as if that was the most obvious thing in the world. "Bury the hatchet on your behalf down at Degnan's saloon. Tell him no hard feelings and so forth, we're all Irishmen here and what the hell's the difference between a Ahearn and a Hines, and business is business, we can work together no matter who wins."

"Then what?" asks Jimmy.

"He'll agree if he's smart."

"Then what?" asks Joe.

"Then the boys are going to come in and beat him to a pulp. The night of the election he'll either be in Hell or attended by the Sisters of Mercy, unconscious. And who votes for a dead man unless we want them to?"

Jimmy's speeches improved. His organization improved. A couple of days before the voting, I met Sullivan for a drink; Spike wound up in hospital minus one ear, with two broken arms and a concussion. On election night Jimmy won by fifteen hundred votes, most of them cast by the living. I gave Johnny and Art a bonus, which was election night off.

Which is what I was intending to celebrate when Loretta spoke up. I'd gone home after it was clear that victory was in the bag, intending to change and then step out on the town with Margaret, who was pretty much cleaned up by this point.

"How come I never see ya?" my wife whined. "We're married, ain't we? All I get from you is the old frozen lamp."

"You oughta know." I went over to baby Margaret's crib and looked down at her. I loved the way she gurgled when I picked her up. She seemed to like me, but I didn't know enough about kids to be sure.

"Well, what choice did I have? You know you can't get a girl in a condition and not act like a man."

"Maybe I shoulda thought a that. Maybe you shoulda too."

Loretta poured herself another drink. Truth to tell, the sauce wasn't agreein' with her. She was starting to get that puffy look dames do what drinks too much, and her beam was most definitely broadening.

"You promised to take me out on the town tonight."

"I changed my mind," I said, jiggling Margaret, which always made her smile. "Besides, I gotta go back uptown, for Jimmy."

She started throwin' things. Loretta always chucked whatever was handy, which is why I kept the breakable furnishings to a minimum. It mighta been an ashtray, I forget. I covered the baby's noggin just in case her aim had improved.

"Oh Jimmy Jimmy Jimmy. You'd think he was a dame the way you spend so much time with him." She stopped flingin' stuff and flashed me a little smile she must have thought was sexy, but wasn't. I put Margaret safely back in her crib, and couldn't wait to get out of there.

"Don't ya love me no more?" she whispered.

Didn't that make me feel like a real heel? I sorta did love her, in a sisterly way, and while I sure preferred the company of my old girlfriends, I still had a little tiny soft spot for Loretta, because after all she was the mother of my girl child.

She put her arms around my neck and pushed her chest close to mine. Baby or no baby, she still had swell headlamps and I was always a sucker for a healthy pair of lungs. The next thing you know we'd done it, the kid none the wiser, and now she was up and getting dressed I could fully appreciate how wide in the beam she had got, and began to feel disgusted with myself and her and us.

Loretta pulled her best dress—and with my money let me tell you it was plenty good—over her head and wriggled into it. She spun around and modeled it for me as I was shaving.

"Where we going?" I asked, because I knew I was stuck. With any luck, I figured we could step out for an hour or so, by which time she'd be stinko and then I could have one of the boys wheel her home and go have some fun.

"The Arbor," she said.

I don't know which is worse: that I wasn't paying attention or that I was. The Arbor was at 52nd Street and Seventh. Used to be called the Eldorado but then one of the waiters, a Tammany man named Dave Hyson, bought it and fixed it up nice with some Tiger boodle. Even way back then there was drinkin' laws, closing times and such, which tended to crimp a lad's style, but they was easy to get around as long as somebody formed a social club. So the Arbor's attraction, in addition to its dance floor, was that it was the Dave Hyson Association, which meant it could stay open to all hours, and it did.

"For sure I ain't goin' to that ballum rancum," says I.

"Aw come on," she wheedled. "Gimme a little cush."

I wasn't crazy about going to a racket like the Arbor, but I figured Hyson knew which end was up and there wouldn't be no trouble. To tell ya the truth, there was one other reason I said yes to Loretta, which was that the Arbor was a hangout of Little Patsy Doyle, who'd taken Freda away from me, and I figured that if I ran into him, it wouldn't be the worst thing that ever happened. Which just goes to prove that even I could figure wrong from time to time.

I rang up May on the telephone and she came over to sit with baby Margaret, and Loretta and I got into the car and drove uptown.

"This is going to be swell," said Loretta.

"If you say so," I said.

She nuzzled my neck with her head and rubbed her bosoms against my arm. They may not have been what they were before the baby, but they were still something.

"Trust me," she said.

Chapter

Twenty-Six

AFTER BECKER LET ME SKATE for waxing Willie, people were plenty scared of me. There was hardly a place on the West Side I'd walk into where some mug or other would start quakin', like I was going to pop him one right then and there. I wasn't just Owney Madden of Tenth Avenue anymore. This was when I realized that a reputation is a mixed blessing: it could bring you respect, sired by fear, and it could bring you attention, whose dam was curiosity.

The thing about the Arbor was it had an entrance on 52nd that led to a long bar on your right and a big dance floor straight ahead. Food was served at tables upstairs, which ringed and overlooked the dance floor on three sides, so you could dine on and fancy a dish at the same time.

Loretta headed straight for the floor to turkey-trot and bunny-hug and grizzly-bear and whatever dances was popular back then; I left the light-fantastic stuff to Georgie. I was hungry, though, all that electioneering and lovemaking having put a hole in my stomach, so I made for goin' upstairs for a bite to eat and something to drink.

There was a hush when the crowd got a load of us. It started at the bar, spread across the dance floor, and pretty soon the whole damn room was quiet as the grave and all eyes were on me, as if they expected me to make a speech or something, but that was Joe Shalleck's department, not mine, and so all that I said was: "Go ahead and have your fun. I ain't going to bump off nobody tonight." Nobody seemed particularly relieved.

I settled into a table above the floor, lookin' down. I was trying to sort out how I felt about the various dames and drabs currently inhabiting my world and my bed, and to tell you the honest truth, I didn't really have a clear idea of what I was going to do. On the one hand, I'd done the right thing by marrying Loretta, because that's what a man does when his little friend gets him and a lady into trouble, but I'd already had plenty of cause to regret the rashness of my honor.

On the other hand, I still plenty fancied Freda, which was pretty remarkable because I'd been knowing her for some several years, and yet she was one of those dames you never quite got tired of. Her figure was a Wonderland ride of never-ending delight, and she had a sweet disposition that's rare in a dame, in my considerable experience.

From time to time I glanced down at the floor, where Loretta was cuttin' a rug with some mugs, but I recognized them and I knew that they recognized me and wouldn't think of gettin' fresh with her.

A pretty waitress kept my glass filled. After about the third drink, I started to chat her up, just for the practice. "What's your name, dearie?"

"Mary. My name's Mary. I'm from Mayo."

"That's what they all say."

She blushed a little. "What's wrong with 'Mary'? It's the name of the Holy Mother of God."

"Holy Mother of St. Patrick!" I exclaimed. "You don't say?"

"She does say," pipes up a voice behind me, and I could hear trouble straightaway.

Mary from Mayo sidled away, her task accomplished, which was to keep me distracted for a minute while the three Dusters who were even now surrounding me had got themselves into position. She flashed me a little look of regret and farewell as she went.

I turned to face the speaker, but he was talking to somebody else behind me. "Hey, Patsy, whadda you t'ink of a mug what calls a lady a liar?"

"I think he needs to be taught some manners, is what."

I knew that voice, so even before I turned and came face-to-face with the ugly gob of Little Patsy Doyle, I knew who it was. Because the hell of it was, Little Patsy was none other than my old friend Fats Moore, even bigger and uglier than before, and with a memory as wide as the river.

"Hello, Madden," says he. Drink had gotten the worse of him, but not as worse as the dust. He had this crazy look in his eyes, like he didn't know whether to shit or go blind and was halfway thinking about both, if you could call that thinking.

"How's tricks, Fats?"

"Name's Doyle now," he said.

"In that case, how's your mother's tricks?"

I thought he was going to punch me, but instead he just laughed that village-idiot laugh of his, which was the signal for his two boys to start in to chortling. The noise of the music below drowned out their yucks and I suppose that if you'da looked up, all's you woulda seen is four yeggs having a fine old time.

A mug with multiple monikers was nothing new in our profession. Multifarious handles came in handy when you were pinched, especially by a copper that didn't recognize ya. Monk himself had a bunch of them, including Edward Delaney, Joseph Morris and Joseph Marvin. I'd been known to throw around a falsehood or two in my times in custody. But to change your handle for real—well, that just shows you what kind of sap Fats was.

"Pretty sassy for a dead man, ain't ya, Madden?" said Fats, and I could feel the unmistakable shove of steel in the small of my back where one of his boys had jammed a hand cannon.

It's a fair question to ask whether I was nervous, and you'd probably expect me to answer yes, but the fact is that in a tight spot like this you really don't have time to be nervous. About all you have time for is to concentrate on each moment and anticipate the next. Long-range planning is not really on the table, as it were.

Accordingly I took a quick inventory of what I had on my person at that moment. Twin .45-caliber Colt automatics, brand-new 1911s like the soldier boys was gettin', one under each armpit in fine leather holsters I'd pinched from a Jewman down Orchard Street way. Brass knuckles in my right pants pocket. Sapper in my left pants pocket. Monk's .38 in my waistband. I could break the nose, split the skull or shoot the eyes of anyone to my right or my left.

Here's what I could reach at that moment without drawing undue attention or, worse, return fire: nothing. Patsy's other mug had jammed some heat into my midsection, while Patsy himself shoved his mug into mine. His breath was starting to smell real bad.

"Hear you're still plenty sore about Freda," he breathed.

"What've I got to be worried about, Fats?" I replied. "You ain't exactly a shirt-collar ad."

That got a little yuck out of the boys, which meant that Fats had to flash them the shut-up sign, which meant I could turn my head for just a moment and shoot a glance down toward the dance floor toward my wife, who was dancing away. I couldn't tell whether I caught her eye or not, but I didn't get a second shot because the guns in my ribs poked me harder.

"I gotta admire your taste in frails, Madden," says Patsy, following my gaze. He waved at her and by God if she didn't wave back, all gay and carefreelike. "Nice of her to let me know you'd be here tonight."

If I could've killed him at that moment, I would have, even though it meant my own life. But I had no weapon at the ready, no freedom of movement. All I could do was stand there and wait, and think. I guess it was a measure of how much I trusted Loretta that I didn't trust her at all.

Something happened right at that moment; the band stopped playing or the band started playing, or somebody got into a shouting argument with somebody else. I dunno. What it was, it was a moment's distraction, the kind that come and go by the dozens on any evening among company. Maybe it was even Mary from Mayo dropping a stack of dishes. I can't remember.

What it was it lasted just long enough for me to grab ahold of the sap and spin around, swinging. I caught the mug behind me right on the button, breaking his nose, but instead of going down, he stood there for half a second, his schnozz gouting, that crazy cocaine look in his eye, and I realized my error, which was you can't hurt a Duster, you have to kill him, and I hadn't. My time was up.

"You don't have the guts," I said to one and all. I was wrong.

It's funny what you remember at a time like this. The first shot was the worst, but the only good thing I can say about it is that if it don't kill ya, it deadens the pain of the others, which it more or less did. I felt the pain, heard women scream, felt myself toppling onto the table, knocking off the plates as the bullets still slammed into me, one after another, eleven in all, tattooing me from breastbone to groin like I was some Coney carny freak, each tattoo coming out blood red.

My head musta hit the table, which is what put me out like I was dead and saved my life, because the next thing I know some medicos was leanin' over me, bringing me around as best they could before loading me on a stretcher. A big bull was there too and even in my condition I managed to recognize him: Happy John Corcoran, the cop who'd busted Monk.

"Who shot you, Owney?" said the giant mick.

Here's an amazing but true fact. Despite the gunplay, there was plenty of folks still in the Arbor and not one of 'em had seen or heard a thing. Including my own good self.

"Nobody. Nobody shot me." My voice sounded strange, like it was being filtered through day-old coffee grounds. I wondered how long it would take me to die. "I done it to myself." Which, when you stop to think about it, was more or less the truth.

They had my nice clothes torn open, staring at my wounds. "Will ya look at that mess?" says one of the sawbones. "No sense takin' this carcass to the hospital—better make it the morgue."

I croaked that I hadn't croaked and I'd be damned if I was going to see the inside of the morgue while I was still breathin', which by the way was getting more and more difficult. "Try that and I'll kill you," I moaned.

That widened the smile on the lips of Happy John. "I don't think you'll be killing anyone for a long time, Killer," he said. I was proud he recognized me.

The last thing I recall was bein' wheeled into the cutting room. My lower belly felt like it had exploded and I could feel the blood soaking through the holes in my shirtfront. "Get busy with the knife, Doc," says I to the first guy in white I saw. "I can feel it real bad."

Then I retched up a lungful of blood and grabbed for my fiery abdomen and instead of touching flesh all I got was a handful of gore.

That's when I passed out. It never occurred to me to pray.

Chapter

Twenty-Seven

I WAS IN FLOWER HOSPITAL three weeks, which beats bein' in the morgue for three days anytime. I only remember the last week or so—I guess I was off my nut half the time, babbling about my mother and dear old Ireland and whatnot, the kinds of things a mug babbles about when he thinks he's had the course. They tell me the sawbones tucked right in, digging six slugs out of my gut, suturin' up arteries and stuff. Five of the bullets was buried too deep and so they decided to leave 'em inside me as a souvenir. They say every last one of the shots just missed tearin' apart a vital organ or two, and that while I was carved up inside like a Christmas goose, almost everything was able to be put back in relatively good working order. They said it was a miracle.

I dunno about miracles; I left that department to Ma. Frankly I didn't believe in 'em. I'd seen too many mugs clipped with a stray shot and die right on the spot, while other bastards you could beat half to death and the next day there they were, big as life. The way I figured it at that moment was that me and Fats, or Little Patsy, or whatever he wanted to call himself, was square. We'd each tried to more or less kill each other—although I took it as a fault on his part that he needed a couple of mugs to help him out—and Providence or Fate or Lady Luck had decreed that so far we was fightin' a draw, which I was determined to rectify, for sure doesn't the Deity, like the Tiger, hate a tie. Kissing your sister, as the man said.

I didn't want for company. Ma and May were there every day, even when I was unconscious, and I have a sneaking feeling that a prelate from St. Mike's might've waved some holy water my way. I was bandaged from my chest to my jewels, and May helped the nurses change the dressings. Even out as cold as a tomato can, I could feel her hand in mine, long into the night.

Art and Johnny were there every hour of every day, standin' guard outside the door. In gangland you always got two shots at your target: once on the street and once in hospital, so it had become the custom to have a couple of triggermen standin' near your bedside full-time. They felt terrible about what had happened, but I told them, once I could talk proper again, that it wasn't their fault, but from now on they should consider themselves on permanent detail, and they did.

My case officer was a sweet little onion of a nurse, a colleen from County Tipperary named Mary Frances Blackwell. I thought that was pretty funny because Blackwell's Island, in the East River, was where the penitentiary was back then, the nuthouse too, but she didn't think it was funny and after a while I didn't either. On the rare occasions when my room wasn't crammed with family members, gang members, bulls or simple well-wishers, Mary Frances was there ministerin' to my every need but one.

Not for want of tryin'. One night in my second week, when my head had more or less rejoined my body, I found Mary Frances lyin' beside me.

"You're going to make it," she said. "I can feel it in my bones."

I tried to contact various parts of my body, with no luck. "I wish I could feel my bones," I said. "Not to mention yours."

She giggled a little the way Irish girls do when a lad's said something naughty. "Fresh."

"Guilty as charged," I breathed. "Throw myself upon the mercy of the court."

"You're lucky this court shows mercy," she said, opening her mouth and pressing her lips against mine. I took a deep drink of her and then settled back, pooped. Her hand was moving over my body, my poor shot-up body, and it pains me to relate to you that said body wasn't respondin' to a woman's touch in the way that it would have just a fortnight or so prior.

Some dames mighta up and left right then and there, but not Mary Frances. She gave me one of those smiles she doled out to patients, and then she gave me one of those special smiles she didn't dole out for every Tom, Dick and Harry. And boy oh boy did it ever feel good, even though I knew there wasn't going to be any payoff. They say that nice girls don't do it, but in my experience the only girls you'd ever want to have anything to do with do it and how.

"How was that?" she said, rising. There was color in her cheeks now, that glow that women get when they're being women.

"What do you want?"

What a thing to say. "Whattya mean, what do I want, ya dumb ape? Nothin', is what."

She rose up on one elbow and pulled her nurse's uniform back in front of her. I had to admit she was plenty fetching. "You paddies are all alike. We're either the BVM or a two-bit whore, Mother Mary or Mary Magdalene. There's gotta be somethin' in between."

"If there is, I ain't met it yet."

This time it didn't matter whether I was an invalid. She smacked me but good right across the gob. "You just did."

She started to rise, but even in my condition I managed to get my arms around her and bring her down for another kiss.

The thing about broads is there's a short time for talkin' and a long time for action, and luckily I was experienced enough to know the difference. That was also the night I learned that package or no package, there was still a passage that ran straight to a woman's heart, and it was up to a clever lad to find it.

Chapter

Twenty-Eight

I woke up the next morning to find not Mary Frances but May Madden at my bedside. She emerged from behind a huge bouquet of flowers that preceded her into the room, as beautiful as ever in the early sun. I kissed her gratefully. Art and Johnny was right behind her, and Chick and Billy as well. That's when I knew I wasn't going to die, because otherwise Chick and Billy and the Tiger wouldn't have bothered with me. The only person missing was Eddie Egan.

"Where's Eddie?" It was amazing how improved I felt.

"Got hisself kilt," said Billy. "Shivved, in the Big House."

"Why?" I was sorry to lose Eddie, especially bein' as how I needed every man jack.

"Crossed a screw," says Chick.

"Shouldn'ta oughta done that," says Billy. "Screw was his friend."

"Screws are never your friend," says Johnny.

"What's the score?" I asked.

"Down a couple," says Chick.

"Duster took a shot at me the other day, eatin' a sandwich at Callahan's," says Art.

"That's neutral turf."

"Better tell Patsy that 'cause he apparently don't know no more."

"Anybody hurt?" A moment of silence. "Who'd they get?" I insisted.

"Mr. Mike," says Art, sheepish.

"How bad?"

"Dead bad."

Before I could say anything, May cut in. "I hope he goes to Hell. I hope his whole goddamn gang goes to Hell."

"Workin' on it," says Johnny.

"That's my sister," says I with admiration. "Names."

"The two mugs was Billy Devaney and Frankie Di Palma." Answers came fast, furious and various.

"Status?"

"Late. Floaters."

"How?"

"Perforated."

"What's the Tiger's stance?"

"Officially neutral."

"What about Jimmy?"

"Wishes you well. Just lookit them flowers."

"Patsy?"

"On the lam."

"Where's the lam?"

"We'll find out. Gotta little bird."

"Who?"

"Freda."

I felt a stirring in what was left of my innards. May gripped my hand tighter.

"Loretta?" I inquired.

"Who knows?"

"Who cares?"

"That bitch."

"Hey," says May. "She's Mrs. Madden to you until my brother says otherwise."

I think they all said they was sorry, which they damn well ought to have been, because after all Loretta was still my wife and they had no cause for disrespect.

All this talk was taking some toll on me, and I sank back into my pillow, thinkin' about basically two things: shooting Little Patsy's fat eyes out of his head, and Mary Frances. I must have closed my orbs a moment. "He's tired," says May. "Anything else you wanna say to him you can say to me."

The meeting would have ended right then and there except for another voice plunging through my darkness. "Mr. Madden."

I looked up to see the angel face of Nurse Blackwell.

"Your wife is here."

I'll never forget the way she said that word. *Wife.* Like it was the dirtiest word in the English language. Attached to the dirtiest whore. I wouldn'ta let her in, except that she had my daughter in her arms.

Chapter

Twenty-Nine

ALL THE BOYS SHUFFLED THEIR FEET, like they was makin' ready to blow. Mighta been my imagination, but I thought Hoppo reached into his jacket. I held up my hand.

"Let her in. Art and Johnny, outside. Chick and Billy, tell the Tiger I'm in no need of plantin' just yet." I glanced at Mary Frances. "Okay."

As Loretta came into the room, May shot up. "I'll come back when she's good and gone," and that's how I knew how things were going to stand for Loretta and me. "First I got some business to take care of."

The room was empty as Loretta sat down beside me, baby Margaret cradled in one arm. "Lemme have her."

Loretta put Margaret in my arms and I have to confess that a great wave of feeling swept over me, a kind of feelin' I wasn't exactly used to, but which I guess the poets call love. Not that kind of love, mind you, real love. Here was this helpless little creature, doing so much for me, and I couldn't do nothing for her. I had a heart full of love and I was about to plunge a knife into it, open it up and pour it all on the floor.

"You gotta believe me." She gave me a hideous smile she probably thought affectionate and sincere. "I didn't know."

I kissed my little girl. She had her mother's cheeks, but she had my cleft in her chin and most of all she had the Madden blue eyes: narrow, with a hook at each end almost like a Chinaman's. Ma's eyes. May's eyes. My eyes.

"He come over and I recognized him. Fats, the kid from the neighborhood. Said he wanted to end all this trouble between the Gophs and the Dusters. That all it took was you and him meetin'. That if I set it up, I'd go down in history or something like that. Anyway," she said, brushing what I thought was going to be a tear out of her eyes, but it was only her hair, "things is gonna be different now, just you wait and see."

"Let me tell you how things is gonna be now," I said. Behind Loretta's fat head I could see Mary Frances, glancing around the doorjamb. I didn't care if she eavesdropped and my eyes must have told her so.

And right behind her, May, standing alone off in the distance, down the hall, talking on the telephone and pretending not to notice.

"This is the way things is gonna be, not just tomorrow but forever and ever amen." I took a hard breath. "I'm going to let you live. Every bit as long as I do."

Even as dumb a twist as Loretta was could hear by the tone of my voice that I meant business. Her big eyes were fixed on me, terrified, and her brain was trying to translate what I'd just said into terms she could understand.

"But I'm not going to ever see you again. The boys'll find you a dump up in Yonkers, as close to New York City as they can. So close you can see the Bronx line. So close you can smell it and taste it and whatever else you want to do to it. But not cross it."

She didn't get it.

"They'll have standing orders that the first time you so much as set a toe in the City of New York, your daughter loses a mother."

Now she got it. Crying, real tears, not croc drops.

"No more dances, no more parties. You'll devote the rest of your life to Margaret, seein' that she's raised proper, Catholic, and not a whore like you. I don't care how much it costs. You'll put her in the best schools, buy her the best clothes, take her to the best places. Just one thing is off-limits to her."

"What is it?"

"This." I managed to sweep one feeble arm. "My world. My life. This is no world and no life for my daughter and it's not for you anymore either. She deserves better. You don't. That's why you both get the same sentence."

"Ain't you ever gonna see us no more?"

My head sank back weakly on the pillow. "Get out."

I knew she'd make a scene and sure enough if she didn't. She threw herself on the bed and kicked up such a fuss that Mary Frances was on her like a shot, heavin' her to her feet. Loretta was still caterwaulin', so M.F. hauled off and belted her a good one across the chops, a smack so loud it startled the little girl, who let out a tiny fuss that I kissed away as hard as I could, knowing it was probably the last time I'd have the chance. "Get her out of here," I said.

Mary Frances grabbed Loretta by the arm and jerked her upright. "I tell ya I didn't know!" Loretta screamed as May walked in.

The look my sister gave me at that moment was something I'll never forget: contempt and fear and respect and love, all rolled into one, and it would take me years to sort them all out.

"We found him," she said. "Holed up in a West 40s whorehouse with some of his boys. Around the corner from Nash's Cafe. They're in there drinking every night."

I was so proud of her I coulda kissed her. "How?"

She gave the wickedest gleam you ever seen a Catholic girl give. "Freda told me. The old lovey-dovey hokum works every time."

I flickered my eyes in Mary Frances's direction and she got the message. Out the door went Loretta. I held on to my daughter for a few moments more as I spoke to May.

"What would I do without you?"

"That's what I been tellin' you for years."

We looked at each other in a new way. May approached my bedside and leaned down toward me.

"Just you and me, huh?" I asked.

"That's the way it's always been," she replied. "You've just been too dumb to figure it out. Maybe you're finally starting to."

I squeezed my daughter tight one last time and handed her over to my sister. "Give her back to her mother."

I was asleep before they left the room. For the first time since I was shot, I had no dreams.

Chapter

Thirty

By THE END OF THE THIRD WEEK I could more or less get to my feet, except when I was on my back with Mary Frances. Biedler and McArdle shadowed my doorway, invisible but omnipresent. The only stranger they let through came near the end of my stay. Tanner Smith, my spy in the Dusters. I trusted Tanner but, just in case, both Art and Johnny were there with me.

"Info's jake. They'll be at Nash's tomorrow night."

"How many guns he got?"

"Five or six. By the time you get there they'll be too baptized to care. And if they do, they won't care for long."

All in all, things were working out just fine. "This is it, boys," I said. "One last move and then—there's no more Gophers, no more Dusters, no more Marginals, no more Parlor Mob or O'Briens. There's just one big West Side gang, and we're goin' to be runnin' it. This ain't gonna be no nickel outfit no more, breakin' into railroad cars and rollin' lushes. We can't just keep stuffin' green under our mattresses and hopin' it'll grow. We gotta get *professional*."

"I'm glad you brought that up," said Tanner. "Meet Frenchy."

He signaled to Art, who signaled to Johnny, and at that moment I thought maybe I'd been double-crossed by my own boys, a feeling that got graver when I saw what was comin' through the door: one of the biggest monkeys I ever seen, six foot six if he was an inch, and plenty of muscle to hold it all up. He was wearing a brown suit with brown shoes and was holding a blue fedora in his massive right paw and I swear to God he was sportin' yellow socks as well. If he was going to join my gang, the first thing he'd have to do is learn how to dress.

"Please ta meet ya, Mr. Madden," said the giant, "I'm George DeMange."

Something about his face looked familiar, the way his forehead pressing down and his jawbone pressing up were fightin' over the little territory between 'em. Then it hit me: he looked a little like Monk, if Monk had been halfway decent-looking and a hell of a lot bigger.

"His middle name is Jean. Everybody calls him Frenchy," said Tanner. "Or Big Frenchy."

"Actually I prefer 'George,' " said the giant.

"He don't look it, but he's a whiz with numbers. Cards too. Can tell ya the odds on just about anything."

I looked him up and down, mostly up. "Prove it. If you take two hundred fifty-four dollars and product it by five, subtract the age of my sainted mother and divide by sixty-four dollars and fifty-five cents and the result is eighteen dollars and ninety-eight cents, then how old's my ma?"

Without hesitation he said, "Forty-five."

"And she don't look a day over it," said Tanner.

"You made a mistake," says Frenchy. "The result is eighteen dollars and ninety-seven point seven five three six seven nine three one eight cents. You shouldn't cheat yourself, whether to the plus or minus. It's bad for business. You do that too often, the odds turn against you."

"Can you keep your mouth shut?" I asked Frenchy.

"I'm good at numbers, not extemporizing."

"Where you from?"

"The Village. Folks from Canada, I think. Maybe France."

"Drinkin' man?"

"No more than social."

"Handy with a gat?"

"Prefer a shotgun. Better odds." He folded his massive paws in his lap. "Frankly I don't much like killin', 'cept when I'm playing poker and even then I just mean symbolical." He shot a sheepish look around the room. "Hope that ain't a problem."

"We got plenty of boys who can handle themselves in a dustup," I told him. "You mind the business and everything'll work out fine."

A look of relief wafted across the big mug's face. "Gee, thanks, Mr. Madden."

"Owney."

That brought back a cloud or two. He shuffled his bulk gracefully. "If you don't mind, Mr. Madden—I'd prefer to keep things a little more formal. Business, you know."

"Then call me Owen. How's that?"

He brightened and nodded and forever after he was "George" to me and I was "Owen" to him. We shook on it and I signaled the boys.

"Art, pick me up here, back entrance, tomorrow night at nine."

"Why don't you come with us now, boss?"

I shook my head. "Somebody I got to say good-bye to first."

They cleared out and I rang the bell for the nurse.

Mary Frances came in, with that look in her eyes that women get when they know you're going to say good-bye without having the guts to actually say it.

"Thought you might need these." She wasn't crying, not even close.

In her arms she carried all my weapons of war, wrapped neatly in a set of hospital towels. Everything I needed to deal with Mr. Doyle was present and accounted for, including a whole extra box of ammo. I coulda kissed her, and I did. "From your sister, May," she said.

"You're a real pal, Mary Frances Blackwell."

She fought back tears hard. "I had a brother once." She wouldn't look at me, but instead snapped open Monk's .38 and started shoveling shells into it, like she'd been doing it all her life, the tears running down her pretty face in earnest now. "Name of Frank Blackwell. Come over on the boat with me, started runnin' with the Parlors. One night he made the mistake of crashing a Duster dive. Something about a girl. They took him out feet first, lacking his head. I identified him in the morgue by the birthmark on his leg."

"What can I do?"

She gave the cylinder a vicious spin, checked all the chambers, snapped it shut and handed it over.

"Kill 'em all," she said.

Chapter

Thirty-One

THE BATTLE OF NASH'S CAFE is legend now, but I'm here to tell you exactly how it was. Rivington and Allen was bigger, and some of the shoot-outs down at Nigger Mike's in the old Monk Eastman days may have had more rounds expended, but I don't think there was a one up to this time that could rival Nash's for expert gunplay. It was like a prizefight, with two of the best shots in the city going toe-to-toe for the first time.

Mary Frances snuck me down a service lift so that the hospital records would alibi me, and I mowed her molly for luck as I got into the backseat and pulled my overcoat over my head. My stitched-up belly hurt like hell, but as I thought about what we were going to do, the pain began to pass, and before we even got to Eighth and 41st Street I was feeling my old self. We glided by the 22nd Precinct station house just to make sure nothin' was up, and it wasn't.

Johnny sat next to me in the back. Art rode up front. I was surprised to see who was drivin': little Georgie Ranft. Him I hadn't seen for a while, not since he started wearing fancy pants and dancing for a living, if you can call it that.

"Hiya, boss," he said. He was even wearing a chauffeur's cap, what an actor that kid was.

"Might be some lead," I said.

"This I gotta see," he replied, and stepped on it.

"Wrong. You stay in the car while we're taking care of business, or else you get out right now and if you won't get out, I'll have Art tap you with a sap and put you to sleep."

Georgie looked both mad and relieved. "Aw, you never let me have any fun."

"Safer that way."

It was half snowing, half raining that night in late November as we pulled up. This was all to the good, because it meant we could pull our collars up and our hats down and nobody would look twice at us. We came through the front door one at a time, first Art, then Johnny, and me bringing up the rear.

I knew going in we were outnumbered, me and Hoppo and Art, but we had two advantages, the first of surprise and the second of marksmanship. True, I was in somewhat weakened condition, but I wasn't exactly planning on hand-to-hand combat, just a few well-placed slugs finding their marks, and then back to the hospital, where nurse Blackwell would vouch for my whereabouts.

I scanned the joint, looking not so much for trouble, which is what we were bringing, but for trouble spots, bottlenecks, unexpected combatants, interfering civilians and the like. There was a clump of mugs down one end of the bar, one of which in particular stood out.

He wasn't much more than a kid, fifteen or sixteen, light on his pins, like a dancer; like I was as a kid, or Georgie was now. Smooth. He was skinny, also like me, but not as good-looking; well dressed, like me, but not as well dressed. Taller than me. I hated him on sight.

I took a place at an unobtrusive lounge table, my hat still low over my left eye, and this time when the waitress came over, I waved her away.

"Waitin'," I barked.

I featured Freda, sitting cross-legged on a barstool, her skirts hiked up high, her blouse cut low, lookin' like far more than your ordinary occasion of mortal sin.

Next twist I saw was Margaret, chattin' up a coupla fellas at the bar, laughin' and tossin' her head back the way she did. Maybe it was just my mood, or maybe it was my recent experiences with Mary Frances, but she didn't look so hot to me anymore. The lads, though, I did have eyes for, since they was the two punks who fed me some lead at the Arbor. I nodded to Art, which meant these two bozos was marked for death.

No Patsy.

The thought flickered across my mind that I was bein' set up again. One day you can trust a bloke and the next day you can't. Alliances shift; power changes hands; greed or lust will all of a sudden get ahold of your best mate and ruin him for life. Trust is the only thing we got in our racket, and once that's gone, well, sir, you are in real trouble. So you spend half your time making friends and the other half worrying about them and sometimes it's hard to tell which is which.

These musings was flittin' through my brain, so that I almost missed Little Patsy's big entrance. He'd been in the loo and was still fastening his trousers as he lurched toward the bar, buttonin' with one hand and gesturing to the barman with his other. I was glad I wasn't going to have to shoot him in the shitehouse. Freda flashed him a lamp, threw her arms around his neck and started in to spooning as he reached for his beer.

I rose and moved through the crowd, keeping my face shielded by my hat as much as possible. Ordinarily a gentleman such as myself would remove his hat in the presence of ladies, but the females in Nash's by and large were no ladies, so, protocol be damned, I kept my hat on and tacked in close to the bar.

". . . all busted up about it," Freda was saying.

Patsy took a big draught. "Don't know what you saw in that runt anyway," by which I took he meant me.

"Me neither," agreed Freda. Dames always make the best double-crossers; comes natural to 'em, you ask me. "Just another punk." She ran her hand up his free arm. "Not like you, Pats."

Fats slid his free hand down in the direction of Freda's arse, which was territory I claimed as my own. "Might as well just stay in the hospital, he'll have a quicker trip to the morgue." Patsy seemed very proud of himself. "I got boys all over the West Side, waitin' for him to show." He slammed his beer mug down on the bar and called for another as I moved in closer.

Out of the corner of my left eye I could see Johnny, and out of the corner of the other Art hove into view. Our strategy was to form a triangle; no one in our line could stand that kind of crossfire, and since the bar was pretty close to the entrance, we aimed to be out the door and into the car before any lurkers could get us in their sights.

I was armed pretty much as I'd been that night at the Arbor, a .45 in each holster and my .38 in my pants for good luck. The reason for this was simple. In a serious gunfight you could lay down an awful lot of firepower with the twin .45s and if one of them jammed, why you always had your handy revolver to finish off anybody still standing.

Most gangsters back then was pretty much as dumb as dirt, but wouldn't you know it, the kid spots me as I approach. One more mug in a hat pushin' toward a bar shouldn't be the cause of no notice, but there you go. He had that sense.

I'm slipping a hand into my coat just as the kid taps Fats on the shoulder and directs his attention my way. Fats, Little Patsy—his eyes met mine and I knew I was made.

Fats shoves Freda hard and she goes flying off the barstool, which is what saved her life.

Her drink goes flying, spilling all over the mug next to her and shattering on the barroom floor.

Pow, it splinters into a thousand pieces sounding like a shot, and every mug in the joint reaches for his heater before the last shards of glass have finished spinning.

My first slug caught Fats in the lung, drilling a hole through his shirtfront and coming right out his back, which also dropped the yegg standing right behind him. Two more shots from the .45 hit him in the throat and the lower jaw.

Even hit this bad he didn't fall right away, but just stood there looking at me, stupid as ever for a blink or two, then hit the deck as dead as McKinley.

This I remembered later, because at that point I was already blasting the two punks who had popped me. I clipped 'em both, one with each hand, knocking them off their barstools into kingdom come glory hallelujah. Hoppo and Art had opened up as well, and all I can say is that I'd trained them good, because Dusters went down like they was shot, which of course they were.

By now there was screaming and general carrying-on among the women-folk. I stood there for a moment over the body of the late Fats, our long score finally settled in my favor. I looked up and saw Freda's eyes all alight and Margaret's echoing her sentiments and I felt a brief tingle through my poor penetrated loins because nothing gets a dame hot and bothered like blood.

A hand on my shoulder brought me around. "Let's beat it," says Art.

On the way out I caught the bartender's eye and give him a look that said forget about the cops till we're gone and forget you ever saw anything, in fact forget your own name for a while, and I thought by return flicker that he got the message.

We were out the door now, Art and Johnny sprinting for the car. Georgie had the wagon all fired up and in gear, and I swear it was buckin' like a prize racehorse. But I'd only taken a few steps when I noticed I was bleeding pretty bad. The Dusters had got off nary a shot, but then again they sort of had, because my stitches had popped and was starting to leak pretty good. I felt gravity having its way with me, and the closer I got to the car the farther away it was, till there was at least a mile of wet pavement for me to cross, and I could hear the sirens already starting up in the distance, which reminded me I ought to turn back and shoot the bartender for disobedience, but Nash's doors were just as far away as Georgie's car, which I wish I could tell you was a Nash, but Nashes didn't come along till a couple a years later.

It was pouring down rain now, and pretty obvious that I wasn't going to make it. Another half-step and then something else popped, and then another something else, and now I was in real agony and I could see the cop cars tearing up Broadway and so I waved for Georgie to scram.

Johnny was half out of the car, half on the running board, reaching toward me, when the first bullet creased my hat; I could hear it splinter the doorjamb behind me.

My first thought was those coppers were some shots, until another slug whizzed past my ear. It woulda hit me pretty much square if I hadn't already been falling, which is what saved my life on this occasion, because the shooter musta figured he'd got me a good one.

I caught myself with my left hand as I hit the sidewalk. The cops were almost upon us now and Art and Johnny were both firing out the windows. "Step on it, George!" I shouted with the last of my strength, but I don't think anyone could hear me.

Falling down behind the car gave me just enough protection to grab a quick breather. I knew the bulls would grab me, sure as shooting, but I wanted to see my antagonist and give him what for before they nabbed me.

Then a shape stepped out of the shadows across the street and I knew right away it was the punk I'd seen in the bar, the one who'd clued Fats in to my presence.

Somewhere along the line I'd dropped both my .45s so I yanked Monk's .38 out of my pants. I came up firing as the cops poured out of their paddies. I could hear the mook grunt in pain as I slammed one into his leg.

I tossed the Smith to Johnny through the open window. "Scram," I cried, and this time they heard me. Little Georgie hit the pedal so hard Art and Johnny almost went flyin'.

Then the cops were on me and that was pretty much that.

I held my hands up to show I wasn't armed. Luckily nobody shot me. I took one last step in their direction, punch-drunk, and went down for the count.

Chapter

Thirty-Two

My FIRST STOP WAS BACK IN HOSPITAL, where the docs sewed me up again, like regular piecework I was gettin' to be, and when I came to from the surgery, one of them stuck around long enough to have a little chat with me. A couple of big bulls stood in the doorway, like a matched pair of iceboxes, which is how I figured I was under arrest.

"Not a helluva lot we can do, I'm afraid," he said. "We tried the first time and we tried this time, but there's no way to get those slugs out of you. Two of them are near your lungs, two buried in the walls of the stomach and the fifth one we can't even see, it's sunk so deep in your gizzard."

"How long I got?"

The sawbones gave me one of those Jewish shrugs, like Shalleck's only not so confident. "Up to you." He fished in his pocket for one of those pieces of paper docs always seem to have handy. "Can you read?"

I didn't see what that had to do with the price of tea in China, but managed a nod. He thought for a moment, then wrote something down: "Dr. Sweet," it read.

"Tell him Dr. Mendoza sent you. He'll take good care of you."

"You didn't say what hospital he's at."

Dr. Mendoza got up to leave just as, wouldn't you know it, Shalleck comes charging in, followed by a couple of mugs in white smocks pushing a couple of carts. "He's not at a hospital," said Mendoza. "He's at the prison. Sing Sing."

Shalleck caught that last bit as he skidded to a stop in front of my sickbed. "I hate that word, so harsh, so unnecessary, so positively penitentural fer cryin' out loud, jeez, Doc, have a heart, why don'tcha, the future this boy's got in front of him."

I didn't like the sound of Joe's last remark.

"What's the disposish?" I croaked.

"Soup for you, steak and dessert for me." Joe snapped his finger at the two men in white and before you knew it they was whipping dishes out of the carts. They weren't doctors, they were waiters. "We got business to discuss."

Joe grabbed a cup of soup and started ladling it to me. "You're in the soup now, an ill wind blowin' nobody no good, least of all you, like I said, really in the soup—mmm, speakin' a soup that's not bad, I had Delmonico's send it over—and while I'm doin' my damnedest, Jesus, Mary and Joseph and all the saints in Heaven, as you goyim say, are you ever in *Scheissdreck*."

He stuck the spoon in my mouth again and I sucked down some bisque. "What's the beef?" I asked.

"Murder One, maybe Two, we're hondeling."

"Dusters?"

Instead of answering, Joe sprang up and started bawlin' at the bulls. "Hey, beat it outside, you bozos, this's privileged conversation, as in you don't get to hear it, eavesdrop it or poach on it in any wise whatsoever, get me?" Like a sheepdog, he herded them outside the door and slammed it shut. "Where was we?"

"Dusters?" I prompted.

"Tragically deceased." Joe tucked into the steak.

"Witnesses?"

"Plenty."

"They'll never yap."

"You might be wrong there."

"Who they got? The bartender? I knew I shoulda—"

"Worse."

"How much worse?"

"Real much worse. Margaret and Freda."

"Which one's singin'?"

"You like duets?"

I could hardly believe this terrible news. "What's in it for them?"

Joe tossed the soup spoon aside and lit up a cigarette. He blew some smoke in my direction and it tasted good.

"How about not having to cuddle up with Old Sparky on a cold winter's night, for starters? As opposed to you, if they make the Big One stick."

"What about the Tiger?"

"Sittin' this one out until they see which way the wind's blowing out of City Hall's ass." He stuck the cigarette in my mouth and let me have half a drag. "You are some little lulu—can't you keep your mug out of the papers? 'T'snot like Tammany didn't give ya fair warning."

He plopped open a copy of the *Graphic*. "Shame of the Streets," squawked the headline. The picture was worse. There was I, lying in the gutter, looking about as close to dead as I ever hoped to see myself. I was glad my mother took the *Sun*.

"Art and Johnny?"

"The girls ratted. Bulls picked 'em both up an hour ago. Art was in bed with his girlfriend; Johnny was drunk in a blind pig. They'll fry if you do."

"Georgie?" I was worried about little George. The boys could take care of themselves, but George was just a pretend tough guy.

"Amscrayed."

"When do we go to court?"

"Soon as you're able."

"We got a strategy?"

"We always got a strategy. Problem is so do the other guys."

"Anybody we can buy?"

He wolfed a piece of cheesecake. It looked good. "Workin' on it."

"Work harder. Somebody must owe us somethin', or be eatin' cherry pie where he oughtn't."

"If he is, we'll find him."

It was right then that I realized somebody was missing. Somebody important. "Where's May?"

Now it was Joe's turn to shrug. "Dunno. Prob'ly with your Ma."

"Find her," I barked, mad. I could feel the stitches pull.

"Take it easy. You wanna bust a gut fer chrissakes, Jesus," said Joe, reaching for his hat.

I felt awful, the shadows coming back over my brain, my chest on fire, my heart cozying up to the lead.

He yanked the door open. "Try to stay out of trouble, will ya?"

In such a state as I was it's hard to say when and if you pass out, nod off or just blink for a moment, but whatever it was I did it and then I smelled her, felt her cool hand on my forehead, sensed her dark curls brushing across my face, restoring some of the life that was leaking from my heart.

Chapter

Thirty-Three

MY TRIAL was in all the papers that month of May 1915. To hear them tell it, I was personally responsible for every bad thing that occurred in the City of New York, as if I'd do anything to hurt the only place that had ever let me call it home. I made a little vow then and there that I'd never speak to a reporter as long as I lived and I'm pleased to say that's one covenant I never had the slightest trouble keeping.

The state, in the unpleasant form of D.A. Perkins, wasn't takin' no chances. Judge Nott's courthouse was ringed with bulls from the Elizabeth Street station house, and they wouldn't let any of my friends or well-wishers into the courtroom except for George DeMange, whom I insisted was my business manager. Big Frenchy, who always did have trouble finding a suit that suited him, looked a little goofy standing there, his wrists and half his forearms shooting through his cuffs, but Shalleck vouched for his bona fides and there he was, bigger than life.

While I'd been on ice at the Tombs, Art caught eighteen and Hoppo won lucky thirteen up the river, and they both took it like a man, with nary a peep. Which was good, because Joe's strategy was to paint me as a kind of victim myself, not only of the Dusters' slugs heretofore but of my own lads' hot-headedness.

You may object that was a mean and low-down sort of thing to do, double-crossing your own as it were, but it was done all the time, and no one thought the worse of you for doing it. For that was the prerogative of the boss, to get his flunkies to dangle for him if they had to, that was part of what they were paid for, and like I said, my boys sucked it down good and hard and silent.

The girls both testified against me, and I'd be lying if I said it didn't get me a little hot under the collar to see them both sittin' there on the stand, crossing and uncrossing their pretty limbs and ankles, batting their peepers at the jury johnnies, mixing a how-do-you-do with a come-hither whenever it suited their purposes, which was more or less all the time, for the sole reason of settling my hash. Such as:

Q: Is it true, in your experience, that the defendant is a no-good, low-down, no-account lowlife?

MARGARET: You said a mouthful, bud.

Q: Do you recognize said lowlife?

MARGARET (pointing at me): That's the selfsame bastard right over there.

And:

Q: Would it be fair to say that this here bum in the dock is the same churl who relieved you of your virginity?

FREDA: And how.

Q: Which was more or less against your will?

FREDA (confused): More or less.

Q: Which is it?

FREDA (thinking): I coulda never tole my mama on account a da shame.

Q: But you loved him?

FREDA: Sure, I guess.

Q: Why are you testifying against him now?

FREDA: On the Saturday before Easter I made up my mind to tell the truth, because I wanted to go to Communion, and I knew I couldn't if I lied on the stand.

Q: And did you?

FREDA (flummoxed): Did I what?

Q: Go to Communion.

FREDA: I forget.

I wrote 'em both off on the spot, which frankly I was glad of in the case of Margaret, but a little wistful in the case of Freda, owing to how far we went back and all. One thing was for sure, which was as a consequence of all this gunplay, I was shedding dames at an alarming rate.

Shalleck didn't much bother with either of the broads, asking only a few perfunctory questions, mostly regarding their indubitably checkered pasts, until the judge had to gavel him and remind all and sundry 'twas me on trial here, not the frails.

Then it was my turn in the box, but in Joe's hands I was merely standing in for the late Little Patsy, and my testimony was mostly to elicit what a great and grand shitheel the little punk had been, right down to the extent of his filling me full of lead on the last occasion of our meeting, which I could tell scored some points with the twelve good and true.

"In other words, and in your humble estimation, would it be fair to say that the late unlamented, excuse me lamented, decedent Mr. Moore aka Doyle was more or less asking for the fate what befell him at Nash's, to put it another way, did the dirty sonofabitch deserve what he got or even more?"

Needless to say, I was ordered not to answer that particular query as the district attorney did his imitation of a Mexican jumping bean and the judge pounded away at his desk like he was pickaxing for gold or something and somewhere in the back of the courtroom the ancient drab that was Moore's ma got loudly weepy.

"Shut up, ya old biddy," I shouted, which got me gaveled good and pronto.

Shalleck waved aside the interruption. "So your testimony is, if I may paraphrase or indeed phrase, what's the difference, that at no time during the recent unfortunate gunplay in the matter of the lamentably late Fats did you have in your possession any kind of firearm, gat, pistol, revolver, sidearm or what have you, nor did you employ, use, utilize or otherwise handle said, or check that, unsaid, heater in the course or noncourse of any such activity in any wise?"

I took my best guess. "Are you kidding?"

"No further questions."

The smirk on Perkins's face told me he didn't believe a word of what I just said, although frankly that made two of us. He was a clever bastard, I have to give him that, needlin' me about the girls, implyin' that maybe I wasn't man enough to handle them the way a man should, which frosted me something fierce.

"They say you're quite the lover boy, Madden," he cracked, and I coulda cracked his skull for it.

"That's for them to say and me to prove," I replied.

He fussed with some papers, the phony. "You seem to have lost your wife somewhere along the way. Hard thing to do." He took off his glasses and glared at me. "Lose one's wife."

"Only if you call Yonkers lost," I said, and that got a laugh.

Perkins got kinda huffy. "I'll have you know I'm from Yonkers," he said.

"I rest my case," said I, which got an even bigger laugh.

That made him plenty sore, so he started in on me but good, draggin' up all sorts of ancient history regarding my various arrests and so forth, paintin' me plug-ugly till I couldn't take it anymore and I got up and started yelling that I was being railroaded, that they might as well just take me outside and shoot me for all the chance I had to get a fair jig.

"Objection on various and sundry grounds, Your Honor," shouted Joe, finally coming to my assistance.

Bang! "Sit down, Mr. Shalleck."

". . . true that your brother Martin Aloysius Madden has also been arrested for the crime of . . ."

That tore it. I jumped out of the witness box and caught Perkins square on the kisser with a roundhouse right. "You can needle me all you want," I bellowed at him, "but you leave my family out of this, you dirty shyster!"

I coulda sworn I heard some applause as they subdued me and started carting me back to the icehouse.

"The state rests," sputtered Perkins, picking himself up off the ground.

Seven hours later they dragged me back into court to hear the verdict: guilty of first-degree manslaughter. Judge Nott asked if I had anything to say before he pronounced sentence, and before I could open my beak Joe was up on his feet, pleadin' like hell, sayin' what a splendid lad I was . . . but let him tell it:

"Your Honor, this here is a very fine boy. Oh, sure, he done some wrong things here and there, but I must perforce remind Your Honor that this here immigrant lad come to our shores nearly an orphan and has he become a public charge or throw himself upon the dole? He has not. He has not, Your Honor. And furthermore, he has prospered in our great City of New York, taken care of his brother and sister and above all his beloved Ma in a manner befitting their prospective station, for being Jewish I don't know much about this, but I'm told on very considerable authority that the Maddens was royalty back in Ireland, until the late lamented English occupation of that sceptered, er emerald, isle—"

The judge spoke up. "That was more than six hundred years ago, Counselor."

"The limeys are still there, ain't they?"

He had Nott there. "You may proceed."

"Owing to all these extenuatin' circumstances, not to mention of course the fact that my client is absolutely innocent of all charges, we ask for mercy."

"Thank you. The court will now pronounce sentence."

Nott shuffled some papers, pretending to ruminate. Joe sat down and whispered to me, "Would you believe this guy don't have a single vice? Ain't human, you ask me . . ."

I got not less than ten and not more than twenty in Sing Sing. Shalleck leaned over and said, "Don't sweat it, we'll lean on the girls, knock some time off, you're out in eight or my name ain't Joe Shalleck."

I could see from the look on my Ma's face that she was taking it hard, but I knew that eight was easy time I could do standing on my head. Her head was down and she was sobbin', but my sister, May, was looking straight ahead, not at me but at the judge, her eyes full of vinegar. I tried to flash her a glance, but she kept looking daggers straight ahead.

"Lawes is okay for a warden and I hear they got a great doc up there, a regular Hippopotamus of a sawbones."

I remembered the card Dr. Mendoza gave me as a bull or two slapped the cuffs on me. The judge in his black robes departed and Joe went sprinting after him, but I neither wondered or cared because my sister, May, was runnin' to me. "Owen!"

"Where ya been?" I breathed, even though they was starting to drag me away.

Ma was right behind her, as black of raiment as the judge, but her sable was widow's weeds, sorrow and heartbreak a decade on, not phony dispassion.

Then May managed to interpose her sweet form between us and the bulls, which wasn't easy. "Lay off, ya big apes. Can't you see he's talking to his mother? You got mothers, ain't ya?"

I wasn't too sure about that, but it seemed to work. "You always told me I was going places, Ma," I said with as much courage as I could muster. I thought my insides were going to explode. "That I was going to be a big man. Well—look at me now." I held up my shackles. "A big man."

My mother's tears were terrible to behold. I suppose if I'da been wiser at that point, I would've realized she wasn't crying for me, but for all of us, the whole family, the living and the dead.

"I won't be after visitin' ya," she sobbed. "I don't t'ink me poor heart could stand it."

I threw my arms around her as best I could. "Don't worry about me, Ma."

"Come on, punk," said one of the screws, "the Big House's waiting for ya." He tapped me on the shoulder hard, and I woulda clocked him if I hadn'ta been holdin' on to my Ma.

"May'll take care of ya," I breathed to her, "and I'll be back before you know I'm gone."

Before me and the screw even made the door Shalleck was there again, waving some kind of magic document in his mitt. "Mr. Madden has been classified as a Class C prisoner—restricted prolonged tractable group."

"Huh?" said the bull.

"That means you should only take it easy." My lawyer thrust the piece of paper under the screw's nose, which made him relax his clutch a little, for which I was thankful. While the guard puzzled out the writing, Shalleck said to me:

"While you're in college, I'll be workin' on the girls getting them to change their stories, and like I say don't worry about it even a little bit because everybody changes their story from time to time, even the four evangelists, you're surprised I read the New Testament, well don't be, it's my job to know what they're sayin', and as for dames, well you knew about dames, they're changeable."

"Hey, Harry, c'mere and take a look at this," the guard called to the bailiff and the two of them studied the order like it was in Egyptian or something.

"So that's why what's happenin' to ya ain't so bad because there's no dames up at the Big House, just mooks, and since you're not one of them fairies actually pines for a stretch up the old river, hell, you got nothing to worry about. Keep your nose clean and Lawes'll take care of you and before you know it you'll be runnin' every racket in the joint."

I must have grimaced in pain from my wounds. May clutched my arm.

"Look at it another way," said Joe. "It's like medical leave or something, like you was shot up in a war and now you're recooperatin' at the state's expense. The meals'll all be catered and that Doc Sweet is some kind of wizard with a scalpel, Jesus he'd have to be, what with all the shot-up mugs he sees."

The uniformed clowns had finally finished reading the order. "Seems okay to me, but it's outta my bailiwick," said the screw. He gave a yank on the cuffs. "Get moving."

Big George was still standing in the spectators' area but I could hear his voice boom: "It'll all be here when you get back, Owen. And more."

I nodded at May, who was comforting my mother. "Make sure she is too."

As they finally pulled me away, I could have sworn I saw Mary Frances standing at the back of the courtroom, a silent sentinel blessing my passage to the other side.

The next time I saw the sidewalk the year was 1923.

PART TWO

Chapter

Thirty-Four

J OE CAME TO SEE ME nearly every week. "You're doin' great, huh, how's the health, don't worry about a thing we're workin' on it, and lemme tell ya the Tiger is pleased and proud as punch at the classy way you're doin' this time, Owney, just you keep on doin' it and everything's going to be okay—okay?"

"Okay," I'd say, and then little Joe would go waltzing off, back to Manhattan in one of my cars, at my expense.

As Shalleck predicted, Lawes liked me, made me a trusty even. I pretty much had the run of the joint and believe it or not, it didn't cost me a penny. I'd never met somebody so straight before and at first I assumed Joe or Frenchy was cheapskating me, but no, Lawes couldn't be bought and that was that. He let me have my pigeons in peace, grow flowers and whatnot. For the head screw, he wasn't so bad.

One day early on in my incarceration I got the shock of my life when the Warden and I were taking the air together in the yard when I saw somebody that looked awful familiar. My face must have betrayed my emotions, or maybe I even said something, which I didn't often do around Lawes unless he asked me a question.

"What's the matter, Madden? You look like you've just seen a ghost."

"A specter for sure, Warden," I responded politely. For wasn't I looking right at none other than my old nemesis Becker, the copper. He didn't look so grand now, chained to a gang.

The Warden let out the merest puff of a laugh. "How the mighty are fallen, eh, Owen? The great police lieutenant Charles Becker, brought low by a common gambler named Rosenthal. Don't you read the papers?"

"I musta been havin' some troubles of my own just then. What happened?"

Warden Lawes looked at me like he was a little surprised I didn't know. "Mr. Rosenthal penned an ill-advised article in the pages of the *World* detailing the, er, interest of certain members of the force in his affairs—"

"You mean shakedowns?"

Lawes didn't seem to mind my rudeness. "—the upshot of which two days later he, Rosenthal, met a most violent demise."

"Becker popped him?"

"So the jury decided. He and some others."

"Well, did he?" I thought of poor sad Hyman, and how he gave me a break when nobody else was likely to, and I felt sorry for him.

Lawes gave me a wise look. "It's not my job to settle such questions, boy," he said. "Wiser men than I have already done so. I simply carry out their decisions."

"Whether or not they're right."

Lawes gave me a little smile, as if we were both, at that moment, on the same side. "We all have our jobs, son."

I looked back Becker's way. He'd lost a lot of his hoity-toity hauteur; he was just another mug at the moment. A couple of screws stood near him, watching his back.

I jerked my head in their direction. "What's with them?"

That got a broader smile from the Warden. "Insurance," he said. "Becker wouldn't last ten minutes in the yard or the workhouse without someone's sticking a shiv between his ribs. It's my job to keep him alive."

"How long?"

"Until he sits down with Old Sparky."

I could hardly believe my ears. The thought of a police lieutenant going to the chair flabbergasted me. The chair was for mugs, not cops. That was a real eye-opener, let me tell you.

"Who else took the rap?" I was curious.

"Gyp the Blood, Dago Frank, Lefty Louie and Whitey Lewis. They all walked the last mile, just before you got here."

I let out a low whistle. Gyp the Blood! Becker was running one of the toughest little gangs in New York.

I looked at Becker and saw a dead man. "When?"

"He goes to the chair tomorrow, by order of Governor Charles S. Whitman—the same man who, as district attorney, convicted him. A fearful symmetry, eh?"

I didn't know much about symmetries. "Ain't that some tough luck."

Lawes surveyed his yard, his empire. "This institution is full of object lessons for the wise lad who will heed them."

That night I bribed a screw to let me visit my old friend Charlie with some of my leftovers from the meals Delmonico's was sending up the river. It was very late, well past midnight, but I knew that a fella on death row don't get much sleep the night before he meets his Maker, and sure enough, Becker was sitting bolt upright on his cot.

I was packing some cigarettes. "Smoke, punk?" I whispered. No sense rousing unbought screws.

He didn't even bother to look up as the guard opened his cell door. "What's the angle?" he said.

"No angle," says I. "No beef either."

Now he looks up. What a difference a uniform makes. "Looks like they caught up to both of us."

"Know what's the difference between us? I'm out in ten, maybe less . . ."

"And I'm out in one," he finishes.

I took the smoldering fag out of my mouth and offered it to him. He wasn't responsive, so I stuck it in his mouth, man-to-man.

"Never figured you for the big hike." Nobody ever does. "How come?"

Becker puffed for a while, sucking his last breaths through the weed. "No choice. Once you're in . . ."

I let it drift a sec. "Long time ago a wise man said something to me."

"So what?" He was almost finished with his cigarette.

"So it's wisdom. He said, 'Some folks may hate me when they see me in the street, but more of them like me, because I'm all that's standing between them and mugs like you.' "

"Smart fella."

"If I was a betting man, I'd wager that my chances of expiring with my boots off are a lot better than yours."

"I used to be a betting man."

"So did Rosenthal."

I clocked him right on the point of his jaw, plenty hard, knocking what was left of the cigarette out of his mouth and sending a trickle of blood down his jaw. Becker, though, never moved, never flinched, but took my payback like a man. "Have a nice ride, Charlie," I said, motioning to the screw.

"See you in Hell, Madden," he said. "There's always room there for one more."

The next day I wheeled myself in behind the guy that threw the switch, and so it was that I got to watch Becker fry. I half thought he'd go yellow, kicking and screamin' and beggin' and pleading and calling for his mother like most of the other so-called tough guys, but he didn't. He shook off the hood, and as they strapped him in and put the magic beanie on his head, he just sat there, staring into space, trying to catch Fate's eye and maybe a break too, and in that instant I looked at Becker I beheld Monk Eastman.

The first jolt didn't kill him, and I heard through the vine later that they underpowered the juice a little, just for laughs, on account of everybody hates a crooked cop, especially one who gets caught. So they overcompensated on the second jolt, which nearly took off the top of his head. His hair on fire, Becker bucked and jerked, his eyeballs bulging, the veins on his forearms popping, until his tongue turned black and a trickle of piss ran down his pants leg, and that was the end of him.

Most of the witnesses averted their gaze at that point, but me I'd seen men die before and so it wasn't a big deal, except for his eyes, his dead eyes, dead before the second wave crashed over him, dead before he'd even sat down, dead like Monk's, dead.

I'd been so focused on Becker that I hadn't bothered to eyeball the witnesses, who I'd made for screws and reporters. I shoulda known that little Joe would be there. He was sitting near the back of the witness chamber, for once emotionless, and I had the sense I was peeping in on him in a private moment, but I couldn't help it. Joe kept his hat on the whole time, even when the prison surgeon checked Becker's pulse and listened to his heart. The doc carried a clipboard in one hand and when he'd finished giving the late Charlie the once-over, he made a few notations and handed it to the warden.

"Sentence carried out on this day, July 7, 1915, by order of Governor Whitman," said Lawes. "Charles Becker, rest in peace."

It wasn't Becker whose rest I was worried about, though. I chanted as much in hebe as I'd glommed from Monk for poor Rosenthal, who was good to me when he didn't have to be, and then sneaked back to my cell.

Chapter

Thirty-Five

Such was my last view of Becker and my first view of the great Dr. Sweet, who I got to know pretty good and pretty often. Them damned Duster slugs was makin' my stomach ache something fierce and after enduring a lot of jokes about my bellyachin', I got an appointment with the sawbones. First thing I did was mention Dr. Mendoza, which turned him kindly on the spot. He put me up on the table and started feeling around.

"Is it worth it?" he asked while he was pokin' me. Dr. Sweet spoke in a low monotone, as if everything was more or less the same to him, which it more or less was.

"Is what worth it?"

"This," he said, and pressed down hard. I thought my head was going to fly off and hit the ceiling, the pain was so intense. "And this." More torture.

After a while he let me up. "Yours isn't the worst case I've seen, not even this month," he said.

"Case a what?"

"Lead poisoning."

"Gee, I feel better already."

Dr. Sweet stepped back to get a good look at me. I wasn't much of a sight. I'd lost at least ten pounds, more like a full stone, what with all my adventures recently, and my strength was shot. I wasn't cuttin' much of a figure, gangsterwise.

"Had a prisoner in here the other day, a lifer," said the doc. "Thought he was a hunchback. Had been treated all his life as if he were a hunchback. I got his shirt off and had a look. He wasn't a hunchback. He had a huge cyst that had never been treated, never even properly examined, and it had grown and grown until it was bigger than your head. I removed it and you know where that man is today?"

I said no.

"Playing center field for Sing Sing baseball team."

I whistled.

He was writing as he was talking now. "Missing ears, missing noses—last year I reconstructed practically an entire face for one poor unfortunate."

"What was his name? Maybe I knew 'im." But the doc wasn't listening.

"It's not the bullets they left in you which are causing your distress," he said, handing me the slip of paper, which he had folded over on itself. "It's the ones they took out. How many did you say? Six?"

"So I'm told."

Dr. Sweet shook his head in deprecation. "Surgery has come a long way in just a few short years, and we're continuing to make advances at a rapid pace. Your wounds are ulcerating."

"What's that mean?"

"Suppurating. Becoming necrotic."

"Say again?"

"They'll kill you if we don't fix them—soon." He pointed at the piece of paper in my hand. "Take that to the Warden. It's a request for a pass, for medical emergency." He handed me back my prison stripes. "I want you in surgery tomorrow morning, seven A.M. sharp."

Well, Dr. Sweet was every bit the artist with a scalpel as I'd heard, and after he got finished with me I was better if not perfect, and from that moment on I knew I'd never go to another doc but him as long as I could.

One of my regular visitors after I got out of recovery was Georgie Ranft, and was I ever glad to see him. Each week or so, Georgie would fill me in on the gossip, who was deceased, who just shot up, who was banging who, that kind of stuff. He got handsomer every day, Georgie did, and he still hadn't given up the idea of being a gangster, but now his main notion was to become one of them Hollywood actors in the picture shows. His buddy Valentino had done it and Georgie figured so could he. Why the hell not? Didn't seem to take any brains.

"Only one problem," he said one day.

"What's that?"

"What if they find out about, you know, us?"

"How they gonna do that? Your name never came up at the trial."

"Yeah, well . . ." Georgie seemed fretful that his Hollywood career was over before it even had started.

"Tell 'em it's just rumor. Innuendo. Insinuation—and that kinda stuff don't have no place in the United States of America."

Georgie didn't seem too sure. "What if they keep asking?"

"Tell 'em it was research."

Well, if that wasn't the old open sesame. From then on, Sing Sing was one big stage to Georgie, and as we wandered around, he'd be after asking me what's this and what's that till I wanted to slug him. I took him all over the prison, to the laundry room, the library, the exercise yard, the hospital—he pretty much saw the whole shooting match, took it all in too.

Another mug I was pleased to see was my own brother. Marty had been after makin' it in a variety of occupations, including dancer, hod carrier, ditch digger, stableboy, handyman and a bunch of others, but had come a cropper at each and every one of 'em, thanks to his love of horseflesh, dogflesh and girlflesh, each one of which is expensive.

Marty had been doin' some other stuff too, namely time. In the past four years he'd been nicked for burglary on a couple of occasions, breaking and entering, and violating the Sullivan Law, which malfeasances won him a stretch in stir.

"What the hell's the matter with you?" I yelled at him. "You know somebody's gotta take care of Ma and May."

He looked sheepish and stupid. "Sorry, Owney. It won't happen again."

"You're damn right it won't." If there weren't screws around, I woulda smacked him. But he'd brought me some cigarettes—the real kind, not the prison kind—and a pie that Ma'd baked, so I was feeling kindly.

"You gotta help me, Owney," he said, and he said it so pathetic that I couldn't say no to him. A man's got to take care of his family, as everybody knows, and since my family was now in Yonkers and might as well have been on the moon, I had to revert to my original group of relatives, which was okay by me. "I mean, look at you—"

"Yeah—look at me," says I. "Doin' a stretch for manslaughter, like a cheap hood."

"But you ain't no hood—nor a cheap one neither. This thing here, this is just a howdyacallit, a passing fancy. You'll be righter than rain when you get back on the outside, you can count on that."

"You're the one who's counting on it, I'll bet, ya bum."

Marty looked real sad, and I realized I didn't have to insult him anymore, that he was going to be a friend in addition to being a brother.

"Sure I'm counting on it. And why not? We's brothers, ain't we?"

"Always have been, always will be," I said. "When I'm out, I'll need ya. Just like, right now, I need to count on ya. Think ya can manage that?"

I swear to our dear departed Da there were tears in his eyes. "Lay a bet on it," he said.

"I will—but you won't. I want ya to lay off the ponies and the mutts and the twists, hear me? Sure, go ahead and have a good time, but don't blow nothin'. George—Frenchy—will give ya what he calls a stipend."

"What's that?"

"Bread. Moolah. Dough. Hang on to it. All I ask in return is—"

"Yeah?"

"Nothing. You're my brother." I reached across the table and we shook on it. One of the guards thought we might be passing something between us and started over to take a look.

"Whaddya lookin' at, ape?" I snarled. I pointed to my trusty stripes. "You see these? The Warden himself gave 'em to me, and let me tell you, brother, I earned 'em. So back off, you smackoff."

I had one last question for Marty. "How's the girls?"

He lowered his eyes. "Ma's doin' fine. Still workin'—"

That got me mad. "She knows she don't have to do that. Ain't Frenchy takin' care of her and May?"

"Yeah, but—"

"But what? Either they're gettin' the dough or they ain't."

"Oh they're getting it all right. It's just that—"

"Just that what?" My impatience was about ready to bust loose, and the guard was getting ants in his pants again.

"Just that May, well . . . she ain't always around."

I jumped up. "Whaddya talkin' about, she ain't always around? What's she doin'?"

That was enough for the guard. "Okay, Madden, trusty or no trusty, that's it for the day."

But I wasn't finished yet. "Where is she?"

Marty jumped back. The other collegians, their mouthpieces, their frails, their mothers, their brothers, the screws—everybody stopped yapping for a minute to see what was the matter.

Marty took a couple of quick steps back, stumbled over his chair and sat down hard. I guess the guards must've thought I'd clocked him or something, because they started in to runnin'. I put up my fists, ready to give as good as I got, almost.

My brother managed to get to his feet before the first club fell across my shoulders. "An accident!" he cried, and that slowed them down some. All but one screw, who must have been deaf or something.

His club was high over his head as I caught him right in the old solar plexus and most of his lunch went flyin' as a direct result. I ducked as it decorated the tabletop, spattering Marty with green peas and some chicken. I caught his chin with my knee as he hit the deck.

Then the rest of the press-gang was on me. I held up my hands to show I'd acted in self-defense and the clobberin' I got was relatively minor as a result.

My heels were dragging as I shouted to my brother. "Find out where she is," were my last words to him, "if it kills her."

Chapter

Thirty-Six

You may have been surprised to learn that Sing Sing had a nine. It had an eleven too and a basketball team. There were races run on a more or less regular basis as well. Inside those quarried stone walls, we had ourselves some right regular sporting events, the better to make us sound in mind and body, as well as soul.

Shot up as I was, I was exempt from the strenuous life. The warden and I understood each other, and so I was left in peace to tend to a little garden he let me use, to raise a bird or two and spend my evening in the prison library, readin' up on this and that. I'd never had much truck with formal learning, but after cracking a hardcover spine or two I got the hang of it, and pretty soon I was devouring those volumes like popcorn at the Bijou. The books had mostly been donated by well-meaning ladies, which meant that a lot of the tomes was concerned with manners and morals as their class defined 'em. But once you pushed past the etiquette and the religious tracts, there was plenty of useful stuff and I read it all.

I read one book about General Custer, who'd gone and got himself killed by the Red Indians in Montana. Since I'd been in an ambush myself, I felt a twinge for the numerous poor paddies who'd joined the Seventh, only to find themselves on a lonesome hill, water gone, horses dead, arrows and redskins everywhere, traveling all that way from Ireland just to die for nothing in the middle of nowhere. I learned that their favorite song was "Garryowen," which means "Owen's Garden" in Irish, and so I called my little prison plot Garryowen, a place where I could sit in the sun and watch the athletic goings-on around me.

Baseball I liked but didn't quite understand; I'm told you have to be born to it. American football seemed to me a pansy imitation of British rugby and if there was one thing I didn't have no time for, it was pansies. Basketball, throwing a big fat medicine ball through a peach bucket, didn't make no sense, and as for running around in circles, well, I had enough of that in my regular life without wanting to make sport of it.

What I did like, though, was boxing.

Now, you may object that 'twas boxing that killed my old man and put the dent in Monk from which he never recovered. All of which was true. But it was also boxing that got me, Marty and May over this side of the ocean, for which we was more than grateful.

There was no finer place outside Madison Square Garden to see the manly arts than the Big House. First, you had plenty of mugs what liked to fight. Second, you had plenty of guards to make sure the rules was followed. Third, you had plenty of spectators, each to cheer, whistle and holler for their man. Prison was made to order for boxing, and it's a wonder that they don't hold legit prizefights there on a regular basis, for what better place to see two stout lads pounding away at each other, with no penalty to be paid?

Luckily, Warden Lawes was of the same mind as yours truly, the happy result of which was that weekly boxing matches were a part of the entertainment program during my time up the river. I made a point of attending as many of them as I could, duties and health permitting. Nor was I averse to the laying of one or two side bets, just to keep my hand in on doings various and illegal, in preparation for my return to civilization.

On one particular occasion, which I have cause to remember well, a big Negro named Washington was mixing it up with an Italian of particularly swarthy complexion, much to the savage delight of the assembly.

"Knock the nigger for six!" shouted one white man, who I recognized at once as a fellow English subject.

"Put him down, Giordano!" cried an olive-skinned dago, rooting for his own.

Me, I had the darky at 8 to 5, and pretty confident of the odds I was. I watched him with half an eye, putting the gloves to the guinea's face on a consistent basis, until the Italian's nose had listed to one side of his face and one of his brown eyes was no longer observing the world in quite the same way as heretofore.

I was mentally contemplating my tote board when a tug at my sleeve brought me 'round. "Mr. Owney?"

It was little Hiram, the Tammany shoeshine boy. Except that he wasn't no boy anymore. I was glad to see him, but I was sorry to see him.

"What'd they nick you for?" I said, my gaze still fixed on the bout.

"Kill the nigger!" shouted one of the inmates.

Hiram paid him no never mind, as the coloreds say. Neither did Giordano, who took another one on the chin from Washington that buckled his knees.

"White boy ain't got no talent," observed Hiram calmly.

Washington followed up with a combination to the wop's breadbasket. Down went Giordano. I backed away to avoid the spray of blood. "None whatsoever," I agreed.

"I ain't nicked," said Hiram. I noticed then he was sporting street clothes. "I just visitin'."

Giordano was pretty much down and out by now, so I sat back and waited for my wagers to come rolling in. Hiram and I shook hands, and I didn't give a tinker's damn whether some of the punks woulda liked a white man shakin' with a colored, because after all I had more in common with him than with them.

Hiram's gaze was still fixed on the makeshift ring in the prison yard. "That's my uncle," he said, nodding in the direction of the victorious Washington.

I held out my hand as another loser slapped a pack of cigarettes into it. "What's the trouble?"

"Murder One."

"That's trouble."

"Chair."

"He sure can fight, though."

"That was the trouble. Killed him a man with his bare hands."

I watched as they carted Giordano out of the ring feet first. "I bet." Another couple of packets were slapped my way. "Such things happen." I didn't have to remind myself. "Seen it myself, once or twice."

I counted my winnings in a flash. "How's the champ?" I asked.

"You mean Mr. Jack?" asked Hiram. "He fine . . ."

"Heard about the Willard fight in Havana . . . tough break." The screws were breaking down the ring, and two of them were already escortin' Washington back to his cell. That was what he got for his talent—some fresh air. I saw him cast a rueful glance our way as he trundled back to confinement.

Hiram shook his head. "I seen the whole thing, 'cause I was in Mr. Jack's corner, helpin' out."

I couldn't wait to hear about it. Everybody was talking about the Johnson–Jess Willard fight. "Is it true what they say? That he threw the fight?"

I thought Hiram was going to smack me. "If Mr. Jack was goin' ta throw dat fight, why he go twenty-six rounds in dat heat?"

"How did Willard put him down?"

Hiram sighed. "Mr. Jack went out 'cause he was tired and it was so hot down there in Cuba, Mr. Owney. So damn hot."

"Did he quit? I can't believe a man'd quit."

Hiram spat hard, like he was shining some fancy dogs. "Hell no he don't quit. He just walked away is all."

"On his back?"

"You goes how you goes."

The screws were clearing the yard. "Tell me," I said.

"In the twenty-fifth Mr. Jack tole his white wife to leave the fight, and she done got up and left. You shoulda heard the crowd, Mr. Owney, the things they was yellin' at her, callin' her a nigger's whore and suchlike, when all she done was love a man for bein' a man, no matter the color of his johnson."

"I wish somebody'd love me like that."

"They was yellin' at him too. 'Kill the Black Bear! Put the damn nigger down!' Oh, Mr. Jack had his fans too, but mostly it was white folks there and you know how they felt about Mr. Jack and his white girls."

"He told his wife to leave?"

"I guess he didn't want her to see what was comin', 'cause in his heart he musta *knowed*."

"What he was going to do." I could see it.

"Then he went out there for the twenty-sixth and damn if that white man didn't look huge—huger than Mr. Jack ever was, and Willard he chase Mr. Jack around the ring till he get him in a corner and he start in to whalin' away on Mr. Jack, hittin' him with everything he got, and Mr. Jack try to defend hisself, but he's just too old and tired now, and then Willard hits him with a right cross that's got two hundred forty-five pounds loaded behind it and it catches Mr. Jack flush on the button and down he go."

"Hard?"

Hiram was still in Havana. "Down he go and as he hits the canvas he throws up his arms in front of his face and don't you just know it, that's when the flashbulbs go off, a million of 'em if there was one, and that's the picture everybody see the next day, of the black man lyin' on the deck, with his hands over his face like he was afraid or somethin', except that we knew Mr. Jack weren't afraid of nothin', jes' shadin' his eyes from the sun is all, and the white man standin' over him crowin'." Hiram finally took a breather. "You know what he say when he come out the ring?"

I shook my head.

"'Alone,' he said. 'At last, they will leave me alone.'"

We were pretty much by ourselves in the yard now. A couple of the screws clumped off in the distance, watching us. I was grateful to Lawes for the slack. "What's he gonna do now?" I asked.

Hiram picked up a kit lying at his side. "I dunno. Fight a few exhibitions. Make some money. 'The Great Black Hope.' Mostly, though, he openin' up another club, like the one he had in Chicago back there a while ago."

"What kind of club?"

"Music, dancin', a place for folks to disport theyselfs."

"Sounds like a good business."

"Folks need some fun in they lifes."

"Tell me about it."

We walked together into the main hall. Instead of leaving by the front gate, though, Hiram started to peel off in the direction of the Warden's office.

"Where you going?" I shouted.

"To see the Man," he replied. Then I noticed that his kit was his shoeshine works. Jack Johnson or no Jack Johnson, Hiram was back to earning a living.

"What about Jack?"

I think Hiram took the question as more of a remonstrance about Johnson's straitened circumstances, but in truth I was only after asking about his well-being.

"Even champs got to work," said Hiram with a shrug. He gave me an address uptown, Lenox Avenue. "Come see us when you out."

"Count on it," I said—an easy promise, for I always did love a fighting man.

Chapter

Thirty-Seven

MAY FINALLY SHOWED UP several months into my confinement, and I must say she looked great. I had forgotten how beautiful she was, and even in the short time I'd been gone she'd grown up even more. I suppose it was the burden of taking care of Marty and Ma that had matured her, but not aged her.

I was more than a little agitated, after what Marty had said, but she come bustlin' into the chatter room so sweet and pretty that I didn't have the heart to call her on the carpet. Marty was just as protective of her as I was, now that he was after bein' a real brother again, and we were both long since men of the world. Sure hadn't I often been out and unaccounted for myself, even if I was a fella; but this was modern times now, and girls was people too, or so they said.

I'd instructed Frenchy to give her whatever she needed and he must have taken both of us at our word. She was sporting a fancy new dress, very modish, one that bared her graceful arms and dipped down a little in the front to show a modest bosom. Her eyes were the same clear blue, and her skin was still west-of-Ireland pale.

"What kept ya?" were my first words to her. I suppose I coulda chose them better, but that's what I said.

The screws were keeping their distance but were still giving me the weather eye after my late outburst. One or two of them, I noticed, was giving May the once- or twice-over, which got my Irish up, but there wasn't nothing I could do about it, so long as they maintained their distance.

Then she gave me a smile that melted whatever hardness had formed on my heart, and in that smile was all the explanation she needed to give. "Ma,

Marty . . . you know, Owen . . ." She gathered her thoughts a moment. "I can't stand seeing you like this."

I gave her a tough, bitter little laugh, to show it didn't bother me none. "Part of the cost of doing business, sis," I said.

"Speaking of which," she said, relieved. May started fillin' me in on what was happening back in town in that same matter-of-fact way she'd had since we were kids, no emotion, no sentiment, just the bald-faced chips fallin' where they may. It wasn't the first time I wished my sister had been born a guy, so she and me could have been proper partners.

May's news wasn't particularly good. Since I got canned, and with Art and Johnny up the river too and Chick and Billy workin' a more respectable side of the street, and Eddie dead, the gang was pretty much leaderless. The cops managed to pick a lot of the boys off, one by one, and Tanner Smith, who was left alone to try salvage things on the muscle end, couldn't quite get the job done. It didn't surprise me none when May told me he was dead.

"How?"

"Shot."

"Where?"

"In the back."

"Where?"

"The new Marginal Club."

"Where?"

"Eighth Avenue, where else?"

"Who done it?"

"Nobody."

"What for?"

"Who knows?"

"How'd it happen?"

"He was sitting with his back to the door . . ."

"I told him a million times never do that."

"Mug sashayed in, clipped him, waltzed out."

That was pretty much it for the Gophers, as I saw things. With me on ice, Tanner dead, it was down to Big Frenchy to hold things together while I figured a way out of here.

She must have read my mind. "Just you and me now, huh? In this thing together. The way we always wanted it."

Things was moving too fast for my taste. "I told you I don't want you mixed up in the rackets."

May never got mad, she just got cold, and I could feel the chill across the table. "There ain't no more rackets. Isn't that what you were just thinkin'? The gang is done, finished. All that's left is us."

"Lower your voice."

"You and me."

"There'll be other gangs," says I.

"But you won't let me be in them either."

"You don't have to get sore."

"Well, I am sore. Plenty sore. Sore about the way you've been treatin' me."

Now, that got me sore. "I've treated you swell, your whole life. Ain't I took care of you when Ma couldn't? Didn't I buy you nice things as soon as I could? Don't I love you? What more do you want from me, May?"

If I coulda reached across and touched her right then and there I would have, and hugged her and told her I was her own dear brother, put on earth to take care of her. I wouldn'ta cared if the screws had laughed, or talked about it like it was sissy or something. It was part of my promise to Da when he lay dying not to let him down, ever.

But I couldn't, and I didn't. "Get Shalleck up here pronto."

Her face fell. "Sure. Whatever you say."

"Sorry, sis," I said. "C'mere, give us a kiss."

I forgot that kissing wasn't allowed, not even between a brother and his sister or a son and his mater, so I leaned forward and May leaned forward and I could smell her perfume now, our hands nearly touching.

And then I caught the looming presence of the guard over my shoulder, heading us off. We both pulled back. "Don't make it so long next time, okay?" I asked her. I didn't want to have to beg.

"Count on it," she said.

Every man in the joint watched her leave. "Nice little number you got there, Madden," said the screw.

I socked him right on the button, for which I did a short stretch in the hole. It was worth it.

The thing about the hole and about time itself in stir is that it don't go the same for us on the inside as it does for the folks on the outside. It goes both faster and slower, and here's why.

On the outside people go about their daily business, rising in the morning, working a full day or more, returning in the evening to scan the papers and have dinner with the family. Or so I'm told, anyway. Each moves along at a prescribed pace, not differing much one from the next, and so it is that you go from youth to married to the grave without hardly noticing what's happening to you until it's too late.

True, on the inside, things are plenty regimented, but it's a different kind of regimented. There's a lot of petty rules about rising and shining, lights out and whatnot (and how is that different from the outside?), but because your world is so closed, the effect is even more pronounced, which means that once you get into the rhythm, the days whiz right on by. Which is why when I hear a fella's been sentenced to such and such much time, I have to laugh, because unless it's life, that kind of time you really can do standing on your head. Because you're just a clown in the circus, and the circus is the only game in town.

Therefore, after the first few months the time went sailing by, which is why it's hard for me to now recollect exactly what happened when. I knew a war had broken out back in Europe, and there was talk we'd soon be in it. I even heard a crazy rumor from one of the Jewish punks fresh up the river that my old friend Monk Eastman had enlisted in the Army. I could hardly imagine anything barmier, but he swore it was true.

Anyway, the next thing I remember is this:

"Dame here to see ya, Madden," said a screw.

I rose up off my bunk. Doc Sweet had been keeping a pretty careful eye on me and my Duster souvenirs, which were still giving me some considerable discomfort.

I was looking mightily forward to seeing my sister again and so it was that I made my way over to the visitors' room and caught sight of a dark-haired girl I expected to see, except that it wasn't the dark-haired girl I expected to see, but another, and that other was none other than Mary Frances Blackwell, my own dear nurse.

She was in uniform, Mary Frances was, and she greeted me like I was her long-lost brother, only closer. I wanted to kiss her right then and there; instead I sat down.

"Hiya, kid," I said. "How's tricks?"

She just laughed in my face. "Still the tough guy, eh?" she said. "Look at you—ventilated, incarcerated . . . least you're not incinerated."

I got the joke. "Not yet, baby."

"Thought you might like to say hello to an old friend."

I gave her a good up-and-down. "Who you callin' old?"

She blushed. "How's about *dear* friend, then?"

"Deal."

We chatted a bit, catching up on old times. I didn't really care what she was talking about, I just liked talking to her. Rather, I liked watching her talk. Watching that pretty mouth I knew so well as it made its way around the words. Forming vowels and consonants and whole syllables like God creating the world. I could have watched her talk all day.

She'd quit Flower Hospital recently, I finally realized she was saying.

"Got a better offer."

"One of the big city hospitals, no doubt. I always had you pegged for big counselor things."

"Actually, no—it's out of town."

I wasn't happy to hear that, since I was looking forward to seeing M.F. again once my counselor sprung me from the joint.

"Gee, that's too bad," I said. "Hope it ain't far."

"Not too far—thirty, forty miles from town."

"Where is it?"

She flashed me a blinder. "Right here, stupid." It took me a second to figure out what she was talking about. "I'm Dr. Sweet's new nurse."

My time was about to get a lot easier. "You don't say."

"Try me."

I didn't mind much going in for treatment after that, which I did quite a lot. Mary Frances and I were able to spend some very pleasant hours together, especially when the doc got me made an infirmary trusty.

One evening Mary Frances and I were lying together on one of the cots. The chop shop was closed, and unless anybody got caught in a mangle or met with an unfortunate accident, we was home free.

She brought it up first. "Do you love me?"

"What kind of a question is that to ask a married man?" I remembered her reaction to Loretta in hospital.

"Did you ever love her?" she asked.

"What do you think?"

"Then why—"

"Oldest reason there is."

I poured us both a stiff drink of some sacramental wine I'd filched from the Catholic chapel. "Here's to love," I toasted.

"Hey, you don't have to make fun," she protested.

"I ain't makin' fun," I said, kissing her. "I'm making love."

Here was the best news. Them Gophers had more or less done me a favor in that while my johnson was back functioning more or less as before, it was shooting blanks forever after.

We got that over with in half an hour or so, and during the next several years Mary Frances never brought up the subject of love again. That was one of the things I liked about her.

So it went. May came to see me pretty often, sometimes with Frenchy, sometimes with Georgie, sometimes alone. There was never another harsh word between us, and I thought to myself how good she looked, how happy, how her cheeks were full of color and life and how her eyes sparkled.

"And that's the lay of the land," said Frenchy, giving me a report. We spoke in code. Frenchy would tell me about his travels hither and yon and from that I could glean the direction of our businesses, which unfortunately had started heading pretty much south as far as growth was concerned. Pilfering the railroads was not as lucrative as before, and while we were still makin' money supplying the various saloons, blind pigs and tigers, that racket was leveling off. Frenchy was doin' a helluva job preserving capital, squirreling it away in banks and drops all over town.

"You didn't tell him the best part," coached May.

They put their heads together and had a quick conversation that clearly made Frenchy uncomfortable. The thought flashed through my mind that maybe there was something between them, that maybe the big fella had betrayed my trust with her, and then I cursed myself for my suspicion and felt like a regular heel.

"One more thing," said George, trying to figure out how to put it.

I hate suspense. "Hurry up, I ain't got all day." A lie.

"They just passed a law that says no more booze," said May. "No more manufacture or sale, effective first of the year." That would be 1920.

"We're outta business," says Frenchy.

There had to be a loophole. There always was. "Drinkin' okay?" I asked.

"Totally legal," replied May.

It came to me in a flash. "Then what's the problem?" I asked. One look at May and I knew that she knew that she and I knew which way was up.

"Get ready," I told Frenchy.

"For what?" the big lug asked.

"For more than you ever dreamed possible," said May.

We spent the next couple of years planning, and while some of the other gangs got the jump on us, by the time I was ready to hit the streets, we were ready to go—bigger and better than any of 'em.

"Not less than ten" meant, in the parlance of New York State, somewhat short of ten, as far as years was concerned. Good as his word, Joe leaned on the girls, who modified their stories in exchange for certain emoluments. Joe leaned on the Tiger and in particular on Jimmy Hines, who, in exchange for certain emoluments, leaned on the Mayor, who, in exchange for certain emoluments, leaned on the Governor, who . . .

The appeals court knocked eighteen months off my minimum, which meant that, combined with time off for good behavior because Warden Lawes had taken such a shine to me, I was out in eight, on parole. Governor Alfred Emanuel Smith, a favorite of the grand sachem Charles Murphy his own good self, personally signed the order.

Those were the days when the Irish took care of their own.

Chapter

Thirty-Eight

THERE WAS A FLEET OF CARS waiting for me when I strolled out the gates, wearing the same clothes I had on my back when I went in, which weren't exactly fashionable now that it was 1923. Buick six-cylinders, a couple of Franklins and a Hupmobile they might have been, but they was all tricked out alike, with shiny chrome trim and a string of lights across the roof like they was some kind of tribe or something.

There was a human welcoming committee as well: Joe and Chick and Billy and the two Georges great and small, Marty and of course May, glorious May, in a sundress and a fetching little cloche bonnet and didn't she look swell.

Mary Frances saw me off at the gates. She was older now, which I couldn't exactly hold against her, me being at this time thirty-one years of age, but the wrinkles around her eyes most distinctly gave me a sense of time having passed, especially in the harsh sunlight of the outside, my own time ticked off on a pretty girl's face.

"Am I gonna see you again?"

"Depends."

"On what?"

"How long we both live."

I thought she was gonna slap me. "What kind of thing is that to say?"

"Realistic."

"Tell me you love me."

I looked around. "With all these mugs watchin'?"

Her face fell a little, but she was a brave gal, I had to give her that. "I get the idea."

I started to head out the gates.

"One more thing," she said, and it was the way she said it that arrested me. "Thank you."

"For what?" I said.

"For doin' what I asked ya."

If there's one thing I like, it's gratitude. "Thanks, pal," I said, and left the Big House behind me.

May threw her arms around me and kissed me, and Marty shook my hand, right after Joe and Frenchy, and then we all piled in the automobiles. I drew the Hupmobile, which was decorated with funny crisscross thingies I later learned were called swastikas, an old American Indian sign for good luck, or peace, or some such sentimental nonsense.

"Where to, boss?" said the driver, who turned out to be Georgie Ranft. He looked sharp.

"Am I glad to see you," I said, and boy did I mean it.

Shalleck sat in the front with Georgie, May in the back with me and a fella I didn't recognize, who'd been sitting there all along.

"Who's the mug?" I asked. The mug introduced himself. "Larry Fay," he said. "These are my taxicabs."

I'd never ridden in a taxicab before. "Pretty swell," I said, admiring the leather upholstery and the curtains the passengers in the back seat could draw for privacy.

"Watch this," said Georgie. He hit the horn, and I'll be damned if it didn't play "I Wish I Could Shimmy Like My Sister Kate."

"That's somethin'," I admired.

"That's nothing," says Fay, and gives a high sign out the window, triggering a symphony of melody like he was Toscanini or somebody. "Somebody Stole My Gal." "Toot Toot Tootsie." "Way Down Yonder in New Orleans." We were a right regular chorus line.

"We change the tunes every couple of months or so," said Fay. "Keeps the customers happy."

I was impressed with all this musical culture, but even more did I want to see the last of the Big House. "Step on it," I said to Georgie, who floored it. The force of the acceleration threw me back into the seat, but May just laughed and held my hand as off we went.

"Some bucket a rust, huh?" she said.

As we tore along the Westchester roads, Shalleck handed me a bottle of something wet and almost cold. I took a swig and nearly puked. I fumbled for the window and managed to spit the shite out. Everybody laughed.

"Needle beer," says Shalleck. "Pretty awful, huh?"

I was still wiping my mouth off but managed to mumble, "I thought beer was supposed to be illegal."

"It is," said Fay.

"This sure as hell ought to be," says I.

"Comes from a brewery in the Bronx owned by a guy—" says Georgie.

"—who calls himself Dutch Schultz," finishes Fay.

The name was familiar. "Used to run the old Frog Hollow gang," I recalled.

"Not that Dutch Schultz," said Fay. "He's been dead for years."

That made sense. "I remember Monk talking about him. How is Monk, anyway?"

A brief silence.

"Fought like a tiger," said Fay.

"You shoulda seen the medals he brought back," said Joe.

"Got his rights back," said Fay. "From Governor Smith himself."

"He's dead," said May.

Another silence.

"How?"

"Bought it from a Prohibition agent," said Shalleck. "Couple a years ago. Found him lyin' on the sidewalk near the Wigwam at 14th and Fourth. Buried with full military honors. It was in all the papers."

"That's what he got for goin' straight," said Fay, who I liked already.

It took me a while to get the whole story, but what happened was this: After he got out of jail, Monk really did join the Army and fought with O'Ryan's Roughnecks in the Great War. He was a hell of a soldier of course, killing jerries left, right and center, the upshot of which was that when he got back stateside, Governor Smith restored him to full citizenship. The lure of the chisel was too strong, though, and after the Noble Experiment got launched, Monk started running booze in tandem with one of the agents, a mook named Jerry Bohan, who put five bullets in him.

The idea of Monk Eastman dead took some getting used to. Especially at the hands of a copper. Especially on the steps of Tammany Hall. "How much time's this Bohan doin'?" I asked Joe.

"Minimal."

"Find him."

"Already have," supplied May. "He's hanging out in a dive on the Lower East Side."

I flung the beer flask out the window, having made my first rehabilitated appointment. "Who's the new Dutchman?"

"Kraut kike from Yorkville named Flegenheimer, moved up to da Bronx when he's a kid, gives the rest of us a bad time and a bad name, yids like him," said Shalleck. "Just gettin' started in the rackets, but he's throwin' some pretty good muscle around already. Never guess who's workin' for him."

"I'll bite."

Georgie turned around. "That little mook what took a pop at you that night outside Nash's."

I could feel May stiffen from the memory. "Missed me. I got him in the leg, I think, I dunno, it was dark." He'd be my second appointment.

"Harp name of Jack Diamond," said Fay. "They call him Legs."

"I call him dead."

"Easier said than done," said Shalleck. "Kid knows how to move. Light on the pins, easy on the eyes, smooth as a silk shirt. Quite the ladies' man, I hear. Ain't that right, Miss Madden?"

"How would she know, Joe?" I snarled.

"Hey, holy cow fer chrissakes, I didn't mean nothin' by it, it's just that your sister is a lady, in case you haven't noticed lately . . ."

"Let's don't talk about it, all right?" said May, and how could we say no to a lady. "We're supposed to be celebratin' today—ain't that right, Larry?"

"You betcha," says Fay. "Pull over, George."

We were in a deserted stretch of Westchester nowhere, north of Yonkers somewhere along the Hudson. Georgie played "My Sister Kate" again and the cars pulled over, one after another, off the road and down to the water.

When we got to the shore, Fay jumped out and May jumped with him. "Close your eyes, Owen," she said, and I wouldn'ta done it for nobody but her.

"Hold it . . ." I could hear the boots of the cars openin', stuff rustling around.

"Hold it . . ." I hate surprises.

"Hold it . . . Okay—open 'em up!"

There was the most perfect picnic you ever saw, laid out for a lord. And at every place, a bottle of champagne.

May and Fay was already poppin' the corks. The bubbly was flowin' like the great river itself and two seconds or so later my glass was filled to over-flowin' and toasts was being proposed all around.

"To success!" said Georgie, who was marked for it.

"To freedom!" said Shalleck, whose people lacked it.

"To the future!" said Fay, who wouldn't have much of it.

"To us!" said May.

The champers tasted like real frog, not like the treacle we sold at the Winona. I asked Fay where he got it.

"France," he said. "Didn't have to cross no ocean to get it neither."

I didn't know much about geography, but I knew there was an ocean between here and Europe, having crossed it once. "France ain't part of America."

"That's where you're wrong, smart guy," said Fay, laughing at my ignorance. "Look at a map sometime. There's an island up Canada way, called St. Pierre."

"So?" I hated it when people made fun of my ignorance.

"So it's a part of France the way, say, New Jersey's a part of America."

"He's right, Owen," said Big Frenchy, who knew about such things, or should have. "Listen to Mr. Fay."

Larry told his story. About how he was a taxi driver in New York and one day this drunk says to him, "Montreal," and Larry says, "Hey, mister, that's pretty far, ain't it?" but the mug don't care and forks over a wad and Larry drives him to Montreal and dumps him and never sees him again, but it don't matter, because the whole point of the story is that Larry's in Montreal now, where he sees booze goin' begging. So he takes the opportunity to fill up the boot with whiskey and drives it back to New York, where it sells for a buck on the dime, and before you can say Seagram's 7, Larry is makin' money hand over fist, expanding his taxi fleet, buying a small armada of speedboats to scoot up and down the coast, working with a Boston paddy named Kennedy, a New York mick named Big Bill Dwyer and a wop named Costello to land the booze on the Cape, or in Jersey somewhere, and everybody's bakin' up some serious dough, and the long and the short of it is that he wants to cut me in.

"Costello ain't no guinea name," I objected. "That's Irish through and through."

"You never heard of a name change? Used to be Seriglia, Castiglia, something like that. Everybody wants to be Irish these days."

" 'The Irish was born to rule.' A great man said that to me once." I turned to Fay. "What's in it for you?"

He didn't hesitate. "Protection."

"From who?"

"Punks like this Dutchman. Like Legs."

"Mugs is everywhere, Owen," said Big Frenchy.

"Which is Larry's point," says May. It seemed to me she and he were a little too cozy, but this was no time to think about that. Especially when she said: "Meet our new partner."

Somebody had refilled my champagne glass. "What can I do for you? My gang's shot."

I thought May was going to sock me.

"Not for long," said Fay. "Besides, you know what I see when I look at you?" I hoped I was looking my best. "Jimmy Hines. Tammany. The whole damn Democratic Party. Maybe even the whole damn country."

Fay raised his glass. "Here's to the Eighteenth Amendment and the Volstead Act. Long may they flourish. Long may we prosper."

I drank to that. My head was swimming, not from the booze but from the possibilities. A couple of hours ago, I was just another yobbo, leaving the can with two cents in his pocket and wanting a shoeshine. All of a sudden I was partners in a front company that was making plenty of legitimate green and with a back end that was sky's-the-limit.

"What's in it for me?"

"Money, dames, you name it."

I looked over at May. "Don't need no dames."

"Everybody can always use dough."

"How're we fixed?" I asked Frenchy.

He dug around in one of his cavernous pockets and pulled a fistful of little ledger books. He opened each one and toted up the numbers in his head. "After allowin' for interest and not countin' whatever our investments done today, and near as I can figure, we got about—"

"It don't matter what you got," interrupted Fay. "It's what we're *gonna* get."

"How much?" This to Frenchy.

Frenchy blushed a bit. "Okay, we got exactly one million two hundred thousand five hundred and seventy-two dollars and forty-eight cents." The big lug blushed a little. "Until tomorrow, when I recalculate the interest."

I looked at him like he was off his noodle. "What are you, hockey?" I said. "Where'd that come from?"

Frenchy took a little notebook he kept in one huge pocket and consulted it. "Protection. Newspaper slugging. Fencing of swag from New York Central Railroad. Blind pigs and tigers." He glanced up. "We turned the Winona into a pig, low overhead, high profit. Opened a bunch more."

Back to the ledger. "Poll watching and other services to Tammany Hall. Plus I've been playin' the market." He gave a massive shrug. "Liked the odds."

Fay was looking at me. "We got a deal?"

I was looking at my sister. "To us," I said, raising a glass to Monk and Plunkitt, to Francis and Mary, to Jesus, Mary and Joseph and all the saints, past, present and to come.

Chapter

Thirty-Nine

PROHIBITION HAD PUT A KIT and caboodle of legit businesses out of business, so there were plenty of formerly going concerns available for ten cents on the dollar. One of them turned out to be on Tenth Avenue, not far from my own dear 352. It was called the Phoenix Cereal Company, formerly the Clausen and Flanagan brewery, which had tried to sell near beer, but nobody wanted to drink it. They wanted the real stuff. And since this Dutchman character uptown wasn't giving it to them, I figure it was up to me to do it. I had Frenchy buy the place for cash.

For what Fay and I'd realized was that, far from putting the likes of us out of business, Prohibition was just about the biggest and best gift anyone could have wished for. I learned from Hines later that Tammany had fought it tooth and claw, only to be overwhelmed by a motley crew of goo-goos, midwestern Protestants and frigid women.

Still, part of me suspected the hidden paw of the Tiger behind it all. Just because you outlaw drink don't mean that people is going to stop drinking. Far from it. Absence makes the heart grow fonder, as the poet said, but not abstinence; and the absence of John Barleycorn was going to be plenty felt. When a man's worked up a thirst, then someone is going to have to slake it, and one of those someones was going to be me.

Which is why I suspected complicity down the Wigwam. However long the Experiment lasted, fortunes were going to be made by men bold and brave enough to see their opportunities and take 'em. And once the country got good and sick enough of Prohibition and them what brought it, why then there would surely be Democratic administrations in Washington as far as the eye could see. You could count on it.

Folks today got Prohibition all wrong. They think it was about bootleg whiskey and bathtub gin, and in part it was, but in small part. Mostly it was about beer, because beer is what America drank. The Irish drank it, sure, but so did the Italians and the Germans, and I'd even known a few Jews to imbibe on occasion. The workingman enjoyed his brew after a long day, and so did the ladies, even though not many of them would admit it, owing to their sensitivity on matters relating to the passing of gas, not to mention their figures. Even little kids drank beer; it was like water, only better and healthier, 'cause at least it was brewed, whereas the water, most of it came right out of the rivers and streams and collect ponds, and God only knew what lived or was dumped in that water. You ask me, water's killed more folks than beer ever did, but try telling that to a goo-goo.

Now, the amazing thing about Prohibition was that, after the first couple of years, many of your big towns, being sensible places not given to religious or sexual hysteria, gave up entirely trying to enforce the law, and left it up to the feds to do the dirty work. Old Frog and Toe was one such municipality, especially what with the Tiger bein' on the side of the workingman and all, and we quickly found there weren't going to be no trouble from John Law if we kept our heads down and our noses clean.

Which got me and Larry to thinking. Why not combine our various interests and start thinking big? I mean, really big. Sure Larry was making a fortune using his taxis to run booze, and I was making some dough offering muscle and political clout. But why not go further? No one ever went broke giving the American public what it wanted, and what it wanted right now, more than anything, was a drink.

Here's the thing about the liquor business: When times is good, as they was then, when people are workin' hard and makin' money, then folks want to drink, unwind with a little hot toddy or glass of cordial after a long day. And when times is hard, men out of work, business bad, aren't they even more in need of a drink then, to kill the pain, still the doubt and offer that fleeting glimpse of happiness that can only be found in a bottle?

This was the genius of what we were doing: the more biscuits we made, the more taxis we could buy, and the more taxis we bought, the more booze we could run all over town. Cops, even feds, didn't stop taxicabs very often, and even if they did, they had to know where to look for the shipment. We didn't just stick it in the boot anymore; no, we had our fancy cars specially outfitted with drop-down compartments in the backseat that could only be opened by the driver. A passenger could pull the privacy curtains, knock on the glass and have himself a party—a party that would vanish the minute the Law hove into view. But why drink in a taxi when you could drink in a club?

Besides, the taxi business was a tough racket. There were competing companies, and I do mean competing, just like the shtarkers and sluggers in the newspaper wars. To own the corner of Lexington and 42nd or the area around Pennsylvania Station was to mint money on all the rubes that was pourin' into the city, not knowin' up from down and scared of the els and streetcars and subways, none of which they had back in their hick towns. All you had to do to win their trade was play a little rough.

Frenchy and I managed to pull together some boys from the old days and some boys from the new days. We never had the kind of numbers Monk did in his salad days, or even the Gophers did at their apogee, but the great thing about New York was there was always a new group of lads maybe wantin' in brains but plentifully endowed with muscle, desirous of taking a shortcut up the arse of a city that wouldn't let 'em onto Park Avenue unless they fought their way there.

All we needed was product. The Phoenix still had its official Treasury Department permit to manufacture near beer, but nobody wanted to drink that tiger sweat when they could get the real stuff. The first bottle of Madden's No. 1 beer rolled down the chute about a year after I got out of college. The man I hired as my brewmaster was none other than the son of old Wagner, our former landlord, who'd taken his old man's place at Bernheimer and Schwartz until the goo-goos closed it down.

In light of my unfortunate experience at the Arbor I myself had forsaken the Creature—not for any moral reasons, but because it had proved inimical to my survival—so when Reinhard Wagner handed the bottle to me, I hiked it to Larry Fay, who took a swig and pronounced it fit for human consumption.

One of the Phoenix's advantages was that it took up pretty much the whole city block, which meant a big stretch of road front on Tenth—one-twentieth of a mile, to be exact—two side streets, plus lots of loading docks in the rear. To make matters even more convenient, it was only a hop and a skip from the Central rail yards, the happy scene of so many youthful adventures, which meant that shipping upstate would be no problem, provided the right amount of moolah was schmered around.

All I asked of my boys was that they played straight and they shot straight. I couldn't forbid drinking, but I didn't encourage it neither, unless they got in dutch and needed a little courage to back themselves up. A couple of beers was always good for putting the fight into a lad, in my experience, which meant I didn't entirely begrudge them drinking whatever fell off the trucks once in a while.

Within a couple of months we had nearly a million half-barrels rolling down the service ramps, netting us a tidy profit of seven million bucks a year. All it took was water and yeast and hops and someone who knew what he was doing, all of which we had in abundance. The hard sauce was tougher, which is why we got it from Canada or, better yet, hijacked it from one of the rival gangs that was springin' up all over New York, and with whom we had started trading shots and I don't mean highballs.

This is where my old Gopher training came in handy. One time we knocked over a private home up in the Berkshires somewhere near Stockbridge that was stocked to the ceiling with quality hootch. We managed to jack most of it into our vehicles. Only problem was the cops stopped one of our trucks somewhere around Bedford, just my luck the one I was ridin' in, and there I was, a parolee aboard a hijacked booze truck. They wanted to bust me right there, but I managed to convince the cop with a case of wine and a couple of bottles of malt that I'd been out hitchhiking, and how was I to know it was a booze truck?

So all that poteen needed a place where it could flow free and unimpeded and that's how Larry and I came to open our very first club, the El Fey.

The thing was that folks, our kind of folks, needed a place to unwind late at night, a place you had to dress up to go to, a classy dump where a fella could meet a dame and not have to worry overmuch about the preliminaries if you were both in the mood. A place where you could have a decent meal and wash it down with some spirits, where you could hear a band and enjoy a floor show of girls who forgot to wear their overclothes that night.

Back in my Gopher days you had your blind tigers and blind pigs, but they was no proper place to take a filly to, filled with hoods and mugs of all descriptions, places where there was plenty of gunfire from punks who didn't know how to shoot straight, drunk or sober. The Winona Club had been my first attempt at what the papers were now calling speakeasies, but I didn't have the resources to do it right. Now I did.

The other thing needed was girls, and there was nobody better at finding them than a Swedish fella I'd met on my wanderings about town named Nils T-for-Thor Granlund, who was from Lapland, of all places. You know I'm telling you the truth because you can't make this stuff up. Granny had the best eye for dames I ever saw; he'd worked as a picker for both Ziegfeld and Earl Carroll, and if your taste ran to dolls barely older than fifteen who looked good naked sitting in a giant champagne glass, then Granny was your man. Nice work if you could get it, and Granny got it.

Which is how I met Texas Guinan. She'd been knocking around New York, nightclub work here and there, and we got mighty chummy, if you know what I mean, but it turns out she had even more of a yen for fifteen-year-old broads in champagne glasses than the customers did, and so the two of them was a match made in somewhere, 'cause Granny put the pulchritude onstage and Texas, brassy Texas, got the suckers sucking down the booze until the girls were even prettier than they were in real life, and we were all even richer.

I don't want you to get the idea that the El Fey or any of our other clubs later were in any wise knocking shops. I strictly forbade it, and Granny was such an old prude that he wouldn't even let his girls sit at the tables with their mothers, brothers or boyfriends, and as for dating any of the mooks that came in, forget it. I'm not saying that Larry didn't help himself to the talent from time to time, and whenever Georgie come 'round, well the squealin' was enough to bust your eardrums, but by and large things was pretty respectable—respectable enough not to get closed down very often, but disrespectable enough to give a mug the feeling that he had a shot.

I did let the girls guy the law a bit. They even had a song they liked to sing, which Texas herself led 'em in:

> The judge says, "Tex, do you sell booze?"
> I said, "Please don't be silly.
> I swear to you my cellar's filled
> With chocolate and vanilly."

Most of all, what struck me was how easy this all was. Sure there was some rough stuff from time to time, whether it was clientele getting outta hand in the clubs, speaks that didn't want our booze and every now and then a necessary killin' or two. But God bless America: here our very own government had up and handed to enterprising young lads like me riches beyond the fancies of avarice, and no end to it in sight.

I took a chunk of change and leased a couple of apartments in a swell new dump at 440 West 34th Street, closer to Tenth than to Ninth, down the road from St. Michael's parish church, and just a short stroll from the Phoenix. I put Ma and May in one flat; the other, the penthouse, I kept for myself. It was a swell place, and I had it fixed up to a T. On the roof, I built a fancy new pigeon coop, plus a trophy room because let me tell you my birds was winnin' prizes every competition I put 'em in. I knew my Da would have been proud of me.

The Phoenix was hard to miss, an enormous pile at the corner of 26th and Tenth. It looked like a brewery, it smelled like a brewery and it was a brewery, as everybody in the Kitchen knew. More important, everybody in the Kitchen knew it was *my* brewery which meant that nobody in the Kitchen knew it was my brewery. And after all them years of battlin' the roundsmen, I began to look upon them as friends, almost, for with the proper donations to the Benevolent Fund, they could be made to go suddenly blind whenever they were in the neighborhood. This is how you had patrolmen, lieutenants and police captains able to retire to their estates in the Catskills or the Adirondacks or the Jersey Shore without costing the taxpayers a cent over their annual salary, and what could be wrong with that?

The thing about a bribed cop is, absent the presence of a meddling bunch of goo-goos, a businessman could mostly expect that cop to stay bribed. It was a sad fact of life in New York that pretty much every thirty or forty years there was a commission impaneled to investigate so-called corruption, which it more or less did, depending on who got to 'em, and then another voluminous report would be issued with much cluck-clucking and hand-wringing and the like. That report itself would soon be gatherin' dust in some city archive, the newspaper would have moved on to some other shame of the city and business could be transacted in peace for another generation or so. The last one had been the report of the Lexow Committee back in 1894–95, which had taken the Wigwam down a peg for a while, but then life went on. It always did.

In any case, our cops stayed bribed, especially if they knew what was good for them, and so any enforcing of the Volstead Act was pretty much up to the federals. I hired as many off-duty and former coppers as I could to be my guards, with the happy result that if there was a raid coming on, we would be notified plenty in advance.

Of course every Eden has its serpent, and in our case it was the Department of the Treasury. Federal agents were harder to bribe than city cops, not because they were more honest, but because they were fewer and farther between. They didn't have relatives or business interests in New York, not the way a copper did, and sooner or later they'd go back to Washington anyway, so it didn't make much sense to offer 'em a bribe, nor for them to take one. Therefore, not only did we need a reliable set of informers down Centre Street who would warn us about any activity from Washington way, we also had a series of alarms and signals that made the Winona Club's look like baby talk.

One afternoon I was sitting in my office at the Phoenix, which was near the front of the building, overlooking Tenth. After my fox-trot with Patsy at the Arbor I fixed things so that I always had plenty of outs should I get in a tight spot, and in this instance I'd rigged it up so's I could scoot down the stairs and out through a disused Central Railroad tunnel and be struttin' on Broadway before the feds could pin their badges on.

I had the place done up in what they were soon calling Art Deco style, everything black and white except my big wooden desk, and everything— and I do mean everything—sleek and stylish, much like my own good self. Some joker'd cracked open King Tut's tomb a coupla years before, and so Egyptian jazz was everywhere, but I liked it anyway.

I was sitting alone when the buzzer under my desk sounded and I hit the intercom.

"Officer wishes to speak with you," said Frenchy's disembodied voice.

"Ask him if wants to buy a carton of cereal."

"Says he knows you."

"All the cops know me."

There was a brief pause and then Frenchy came back on the wire. "Says he knows you from the old days. Says he's a friend. Says he don't want no trouble. Says—"

"Shut up and send him in."

I took a .45 out of my top desk drawer and slipped it in my suit coat pocket. I liked cops as much as the next guy, but there was no sense in taking chances.

A rap at the door announced his arrival: two short, one long.

"It's open."

The door swung wide and the first thing I saw was Frenchy's bulk, occupyin' most of the doorway.

The second thing I saw was my old friend Branagan.

Time hadn't been particularly kind to him, but then time is never particularly kind to anybody. Time just goes about its business, heedless of human entreaty, artifice or subterfuge, and then kills us dead whenever it gets the urge. The City of New York, on the other hand, was treatin' him swell— Branagan was sporting captain's insignia.

"I thought you was done with patrollin'," I said by way of greeting. "Cashiered, as it were."

"Things change," says he.

"It's okay, George," I told Frenchy, who withdrew.

Branagan plopped himself in the chair opposite. His hair had turned gray, and he'd lost, rather than gained, weight, but he'd turned in his roundsman's tunic for an officer's raiment.

"Nice uniform. No hard feelings?"

"Thought we could do some business," says he.

"You never did stand on ceremony."

"Why bother when there's dough to be made?"

He had a point there. "How much?" I didn't like Branagan, but I did admire a man who got right down to business and didn't let bygones get in the way of the present.

"Depends on what the information's worth to you."

I offered him a drink, which he accepted. "Why you doin' me favors?"

"Times change."

"Meaning I got money now."

"And I still got the Law."

"Makes us even, then."

"Are you gonna listen or are you gonna yap?"

Over the course of the next half hour or so, Branagan laid out past, present and future. What had happened to him in the aftermath of Monk's apparition. Suspended. Travelin' a bit out West—he got as far as the Great Salt Lake and the country of the saints. Homesickness. Letters here and there. Reinstatement—the Tiger taking care of its own. Risin' through the ranks in precincts near and Brooklyn while I'm on ice. And here we are, nearly twenty years on, face-to-face once more.

"Another drink?"

"Well—I am on duty," said Branagan, reaching across the desk for the glass, "so maybe just this one more."

"Drop by the El Fey tomorrow and the rest of 'em'll be on the house."

"Count on it."

I lit up a cigarette. The first hit of smoke always seared the hell out of my lungs, but the pain wasn't bad once you got used to it. "What do I get in return for my hospitality?"

Branagan glanced around the room like Commissioner Enright himself was lurking in the shadows. "You're gonna get hit."

"When?"

"Tonight."

"Mooks?"

"Feds."

"Why?"

"Make an example of you."

This was not good news. Ordinarily there'd be no problem. But a big ship-ment of beer was being loaded onto my Pierce-Arrows and it needed to get where it was going.

"Make 'em disappear."

"They got authority."

"Look at this." I pointed out the window. Up and down Tenth, the entire block between 25th and 26th was jammed with idling trucks, each waiting to snake around to the loading dock and take on its supply. "I got authority. You got authority."

Branagan was trying hard to follow.

"Where them feds gonna park?" I asked him, and answered. "No place legal, that's where. You know how they hate to flash a badge until the last sec-ond? They're gonna drive right up and double-park and come charging in here like they own the joint. But you ain't gonna let 'em."

I could see the glimmer in his eyes. But not only did I see understanding about this evening's drill, I saw a dope havin' a glimmer at the future, and lik-ing what he saw. That was where we were going to beg to differ. "Capeesh?"

No one could capeesh like an Irishman. I watched the whole thing. As soon as the first of the feds' crummy Fords pulled up and sure enough double-parked, they were harassed on the spot by traffic patrol. Since they didn't want to blow their cover, they pulled away, to look for a legal spot, but I'd made sure the boys had taken every available spot for blocks in every direction, so about fifteen minutes later back they come, and this time they double-parked and the hell with the cops.

No sooner were they out of their cars, though, when another group of patrolmen descended on them, demanding identification, which the feds of course refused to provide. The cops threatened 'em with arrest for vagrancy. Voices were raised, then fists. Meanwhile, a couple of wreckers arrived and started towin' the feds' cars. One by one they went galumphing down the street, bouncing like bar drunks, with the feds in their suits standing on the street scratching their bums in wonder at the cheek of it all.

Eventually they managed to impound some of my empty trucks—for about five minutes—until Shalleck hustled into court and pointed out to a sympathetic jurist that the feds didn't have a leg to stand on, that just because they mighta smelled beer brewin' doesn't mean there necessarily was beer brewing, and even if it was, it could have been near beer, which after all was not only legal but kosher, or maybe not kosher but still legal, and anyway who cared because of the separation of church and state, or even shul and state, and of course the judge, a fine man name of Aaron Levy, agreed, and I got my trucks back, Joe got his fee, Branagan got a month of free drinks and the feds got egg on their face.

Which didn't keep them from trying again of course. Pretty much the same thing happened every time they came back, so that after a while they completely stopped speaking to the New York City Police Department, which so angered our splendid mayor, Jimmy Walker, that he told them they weren't welcome in the great City of New York if that's the kind of attitude they had, and we all thought and hoped a war would break out between the cops and the feds, but it never quite did and more's the pity. I had to give them credit for stick-to-itiveness, but as the poet said, it's the hobgoblin of small minds.

Made them plenty mad, though. I guess I was riding too high to fully appreciate it at the time, but when the feds get mad at you, they stay mad for a long, long time.

As for myself, I had one bit of unfinished business with the feds—namely, a mug by the name of Jerry Bohan, the man who shot Monk Eastman—so at the end of all the rigmarole on Tenth Avenue I slipped over to the Lower East Side, asked a few questions, moseyed downtown a bit, tucked around a corner or two and in short order found Bohan sitting on a barstool in a sad-sack joint called the Blue Bird, run by a fella name of Brosnahan, who I just happened to be after knowin'.

Chapter

Forty

THE IRONY OF THE FACT that I was walking through the doors of what had once upon a time been the New Irving was probably not lost on me, although I didn't stop to think about it. Monk's old place, the scene of much honest mayhem in the good old days, and here I was, big as life, for this day only, the great man himself, reincarnated. And if it was Easter Sunday to boot, well, that was simply poetic justice.

Bohan wasn't much to look at, but then assassins are usually not a patch on the great men they dispatch. It went without saying that everybody in the joint knew who I was except for Bohan himself, which was to be expected, because a federal in my experience was about the dumbest form of life there was, except for a Republican.

"Whaddya know, whaddya say?" says I, sitting down at the stool next to him.

"What's it to you?" He was at least three drinks ahead of me, and already belligerent.

"A beer," I said to the barkeep. "Madden's No. 1."

"Swill," said Bohan.

"Name your poison," says I, taking a draught. Even though I didn't drink anymore, it was mighty good. "What's yours, friend?"

"What's it to you?" he snarled.

I picked up the bottle and looked at the label. There was my name, big as life, emblazoned across the bottle's belly, right in front of an artist's rendering of the Phoenix Brewery its own good self, all red brick and smokestacks, old Tenth Avenue come to life.

"You know what the papers said about Monk when he came back from France, Jerry?" He gave me a rheumy look. "'Monk Eastman Wins New Soul.'"

I cracked the empty bottle over his head as hard as I could, which was saying something. That was the signal for the bartender to drop onto the floor and forget he'd ever seen my face, and for what few patrons who were in this fine establishment of a Sunday to start to scatter, and for Jerry it was the signal to reach up and grab his bleeding scalp, which meant that, defenseless, he was a sucker for receiving the broken half of the bottle right in his face. It caught him across the bridge of the nose, which meant that both shards gouged into his eyes, blinding him on the spot.

A more pathetic sight than a blind man, his eyes streaming with blood, Oedipus calling for his mommy, there isn't, but in my heart there was no mercy at all, just the vision of Monk lying there, whether bloodied in the Bronx barn or on the pavement outside the Wigwam it didn't matter, my Monk, my father.

Bohan had fallen off his stool and was kneeling on the floor, mumblin' and mutterin' to beat the band.

"You know what this is, don't you, boy?" I said to him as calmly as I could, removing one of my pistols from my waistband.

I never saw such blood. "Oh God Jesus Mary and Joseph and all the saints please sir have mercy . . ."

I conked him but good with the butt of a .45, which drove him down face first into the floor. "Answer my question."

I'll give Jerry Bohan this. He managed to push his torso up, elevating his puss to my knee-level, all the while whining for mercy and asking questions of eternity it was not my place to answer.

Normally it is against my rules to beat a man when he is down, but in the matter, I decided to make an exception. I swung the automatic, catching him on the jaw, which knocked out a few of his teeth, not that he was going to need them where he was going.

"Answer me."

It always makes it easier on me when a man who knows he's about to die gives up and makes it easier on himself. Luigi had fought me, Willie had never seen it coming and Fats had had it coming. Jerry raised his head one last time, praying through blubbery red-flecked lips, and I might have felt sorry for him, except that I didn't.

"Tell me," he pleaded, because I guess in the end we all want to know why we're getting it, why here, why now, why.

"Redemption." I shot him once through each bloody eye and left him there on the floor, the New Irving floor that had absorbed so much blood it was almost human. Now Jerry's blood was mingling with Monk's and the score was even.

I tossed a couple of bills on the bar as I departed. "Drinks on the house," I said. "Make 'em doubles."

Chapter

Forty-One

THE EL FEY WAS OKAY and so were the other clubs, like the Livingstone on East 58th where the pink lemonade went for a buck and a half, which was a profit to me of about $1.48. Along with the Club Abbey, the Silver Slipper at Broadway and 48th Street was Texas's favorite, and it made her a star. "Hello, sucker," she'd say, and no truer words were ever spoken. What I liked about Texas was that she got it. "Never lose the purple mantle of illusion," she'd tell her girls. Good advice.

I ran all my joints on the up-and-up. One night Winchell told me that a new scribbler on the block, kid name of Whitney Bolton, had told him some society dame was claimin' she got shortchanged by one of my waiters. I rang up Bolton and told him to come over to my office in the Longacre Building in Times Square—used to be Longacre Square until the newspaper got fancy pants. The waiter was waiting for him when he got there, the overcharge of $21.90 in his paws, which he handed over to Bolton on the spot. Then I fired him.

"What's your beat, Bolton?" I asked the newspaperman after the waiter was gone.

"Gangland, Mr. Madden," says he.

I dropped by his newspaper a couple of nights later. He was sitting at a messy desk, pounding an Underwood, what a way to make a living. City rooms are noisy as hell, but this one fell silent as I moseyed along, and I made sure everybody got a good look at me, especially Bolton's editors, as I stopped in front of his desk.

"Close your jaw," I said. "That's better."

I could see the fright in his eyes. "What—?"

"Relax." I looked around and saw the editors standing in their office doorways. "We'll just shoot the breeze a couple of minutes and then I'll be gone."

"Why—?"

"You're covering gangland, aren't you? Well, this shows 'em you know what you're talking about."

As I left I could hear typewriters being pounded once more. I found out later that Bolton's editors were so impressed he got a ten-buck-a-week raise the very next day. And I never had no trouble from him, ever.

Still, I wanted something special, a real classy joint that folks would come to for miles around. Something out of the ordinary, with topflight chow, the best performers, the prettiest girls. I found it uptown, smack in the middle of the Dutchman's precincts, which was pretty much the true beginning of our friendship, and the trouble between us, which is often more or less the same thing.

How it happened was Hiram.

Hiram was no kid anymore and neither was I, and since our reunion at Sing Sing I'd taken a friendly interest in his career, especially because I was plenty interested in the fight game. Seems that Hiram had graduated from shine to rubdown boy to trainer, and had himself a stable of colored boxers that he trained in a gym up on 125th Street, which by this point was pretty much completely brown.

As part of our investing strategy, George and I had bought pieces of several fighters. Now, I may be a white man, but I never let a little thing like color interfere with the sweet science or its financial rewards. When Hiram told me about a boxer named Harry Wills, a tough Negro they called the Black Panther who Dempsey was ducking, I decided to take a spin up darktown way to have a look at him.

I found Hiram in the gym, seegar in his mouth, admiring his boy. "Ain't he pretty? Lookit the way he move. Beautiful. Damn!"

I could see why Dempsey was ducking Wills. He was coiled and quick, a right regular black panther indeed, with sinewy muscles and flashing fists. "He's too quick for Jack, that's for sure," I said.

"Colored boys is always too quick for white fighters," said Hiram, not even bothering to glance over to look at me. With the evidence in the ring, I could hardly disagree. "Look at the jab. He bust up Dempsey's nose in round one, that's for sure." Hiram spit out of the side of his mouth. "Harry'd clean his clock."

"Hell, *I* could bust Dempsey's nose. He's through, washed-up."

Hiram featured me sideways, keeping an eye on his pugilist. "Tex Rickard tells me Dempsey's gonna fight Tunney."

"Irish got to stick together."

"They never give colored no chance."

I watched as Wills got off a couple of fancy combinations. "Right you are. Furthermore, Tunney's going to beat Dempsey. And then he's gonna be champ."

Hiram spat harder, a big brown ball of phlegm that missed the spittoon and splattered on the hardwood floor.

"It's the way of the world, Hiram," I said. "It's our time. Someday it'll be yours. Just be ready for it, 'cause they're only gonna give you one shot."

Hiram brought a small hammer down on the time bell. "Okay, Harry, come down here and meet Mr. Owney."

The glistening Negro slid through the ropes and a cornerman took off his sparring gloves. My hand disappeared into his and we shook. "You got what it takes, kid."

"Thank you, sir," said Wills.

"You got some nice moves there."

"Thank you, sir," said Wills.

"Good luck to you."

"Thank you, sir," said Wills, and shuffled off to the training room.

"Too bad he ain't gonna get his shot."

I wasn't telling Hiram anything he didn't already know. "White boys don't want to fight colored, not heavyweights. Ever since Mr. Jack, they want the champ to be white."

We walked together out of the gym. There was a horde of humanity in there, but I was the only white man. "How's Johnson? See much of him?"

Hiram brightened a bit as we trotted down the stairs. "He runnin' a supper club now, the Deluxe, up where the old Douglas Casino used to be."

"Lenox, right?"

Hiram nodded. "At 142nd. Northeast corner. It ain't open yet, but he prob'ly there. Don't got much else to do these days."

I got an idea. "Feel like a walk?"

Hiram did, and half an hour later we were climbing the stairs up to the Club Deluxe. It was on the second floor of a nondescript two-story building, with a theater on the ground floor. The theater wasn't very successful—the Renaissance Casino on 133rd was eating its lunch—but the Deluxe was still in operation. Barely. Even before I got to the top of the stairs, I could see that

Johnson was going to need some help. It wasn't that it was shabby, exactly, just tired and run-down and deflated, like an old boxer after he's been knocked down for the last time. Jack had had plenty of knockdowns in his life, not in the ring, but from the law. That was something we both had in common.

I don't know what I expected, but the last way I expected to meet Jack Johnson was jamming with a combo around an upright piano. Sax, cornet, drums, if I remember right. And bass of course. I'd forgotten that he was a bull fiddle player—cellist too—and let me tell you that bull fiddle looked more like a viola in his big hands. I think he coulda picked it up and played it like one, if he'da wanted to.

I didn't want to disturb them, and so Hiram and I stood in the back, in the shadows, listening. The tune was "Bye Bye Blackbird," and I never heard it played better. When it came time for the bass solo, Johnson plucked that bull dry, made it sing and cry and whisper. The other players just stepped back and listened, the drummer laying down a trap beat, just enough to support Jack wherever he wanted to go.

Believe it or nor, it was at that moment, watching that big African toss that fiddle around, with the other players smiling and snapping their fingers, and the piano player tossing back a fresh cold one while he had the chance, and one of the waitresses, mid-twenties, lithe, startin' in to shimmy, that I got the idea that, if I do say so myself, changed the course of popular music.

The music stopped and I started to applaud, two lone white paws clapping on 142nd Street. Black faces turned toward me as I stepped out of the shadows, and for a moment there I thought there might be trouble, or at least some hard feelings, but Hiram was right beside me and the minute Jack spotted him he broke into a big grin and gave everybody the high sign and the next thing I know I'm shaking hands with the champ.

"Mr. Jack, this Mr. Owney. I tole you about him years ago. Now he a big man."

The fighter they called the Galveston Giant looked at me and I knew that he knew that I knew that he could squash me like a roach if he wanted to, which luckily he did not.

"I am pleased and delighted to have the honor of making your acquaintance, sir," said Johnson in a soft East Texas accent. That's the way he talked, real fancy, all class, and I liked him straightaway.

At the time I met him, Jack Johnson was forty-eight, a good fourteen years older than my own good self. That may sound middle-aged to you, but believe me back then it was old going on elderly, especially for a boxer. Pushing fifty, even a regular workingman was already yearning for retirement. A fighter had one foot in the grave, if he was lucky.

Jack snapped his fingers and the shimmying colored gal brought us some beers. One sip was all it took to tell me he was serving the Dutchman's dreck, which was going to have to change.

As she set the beers down, I couldn't help but notice how pretty she was, how light her skin, and for a minute there I thought she might be white, since I knew that Jack liked white girls plenty, but she was what dark folks call high yaller. Up to this point I had never thought one way or the other about colored girls, having met damn few of 'em, but as I say my mind was workin' overtime now.

"Now, what can I do for you, mister?" asked Johnson.

Instead of gawking at the dame, I should have been thinking about what I was going to say. If I had, I probably would've thought to say something about Johnson's fight career, how he made hamburger out of Jim Jeffries and the other Great White Hopes, right up to Jess Willard; or his problems with the Mann Act, or his travels around Europe, but no, the first words out of my mouth were:

"How much you want for it?"

Normally I would never blurt business right off the bat, like a Levantine, but I was shook up in the presence of greatness.

Johnson counterpunched right away. "What is it about my establishment that indicates to you that I am in either want or need of partnership or sale?"

I felt like a real jerk, especially with Hiram's left shoe bouncing off my shin. "Nothing whatsoever, Mr. Johnson," I said. "I just thought maybe we could do some business together."

The giant smiled. Jack was running to fat, like all old fighters do, his belly spreading, his tits drooping, but the muscles in his arms still bulged through his T-shirt. "Mr. Watkins tells me you're in the liquor trade." He reached for his beer and downed it. "This concoction is decidedly inferior."

I could second that motion. "Maybe that's why you're having trouble drawing people. You ought to try mine, Madden's No. 1. Best brew in town. Ain't that right, Hiram?"

Hiram didn't have to say nothing. "I am inclined to agree, upon information and belief." Johnson stroked his clean-shaven chin, the one that had taken so many punches over the years. "I could mayhaps take on a fiduciary partner or two, in order to improve and refine the surroundings, the libations and the comestibles."

Now he was talking.

"Got it all figured out already. We'll form a corporation. My associate, Mr. George DeMange, will be the secretary. In exchange for a cash payment of"—I watched his face carefully—"two hundred thousand dollars, you'll be employed in an executive capacity, to lend your name and prestige to the joint. Welcome anytime, everything on the house, you get the picture . . ."

Jack nodded. "And in return?"

"We get one hundred percent. Straight buyout, with you as the front man for as long as you wish."

Johnson trained his big brown eyes on Hiram. I couldn't tell if he was blaming him for bringing me up here or thanking him. "You're asking me to throw my last fight, Mr. Madden," he said.

There was an awkward moment. The musicians were still at their perch, silent. The waitress had stopped pretending to serve and was standing stock-still. Hiram, well, Hiram had pretty much stopped breathing. Show time.

"How hard did Willard hit you? With the last punch." That was either the right thing or the wrong thing to say, and I would soon find out, either the easy way or the hard way.

Reflexively Johnson made a fist and then opened it again. His eyes were elsewhere. "Combination," he said softly. "It was a combination. He came out for the twenty-sixth, and he knew he had me and I knew he had me. I just plumb had nothing left. He struck me with a left jab in the face, then a right to the stomach. Then another left to the heart."

"What did you feel?"

He looked at me like I'd never been in a fight, and I never had, not in that kind. "Pain," he said. "Nothing but pain. Everything else is silence."

I sat there in the Harlem club, picturing that awful scene in Cuba.

"I dropped my guard, the way one does when one has taken two shots in the midsection, and that's when he caught me flush on the jaw, and the next thing I knew I was on my back in the broiling Havana heat, trying to shield my eyes from the sun and finally hearing something I hadn't heard before up to that point. Something my beating heart had drowned out heretofore."

"What was that?" I had to lean forward to hear his reply.

"White people."

He drank the last dregs of his beer. "In that moment it occurred to me that I had finally given them, after all my years in the ring, what they came to see. A white heavyweight champion."

He threw the bottle against the wall. It didn't stand a chance. "You're right. This beverage is completely unacceptable. When might I expect the down payment on our transaction?"

"Mr. DeMange will be here tomorrow morning at eight o'clock sharp with payment in full."

"Do I need or want to know where this money came from, Mr. Madden?"

"Not at all, Mr. Johnson," said I.

He let out a big sigh, and then he stuck out a bigger hand. We shook, and no matter what happens to me in the rest of my life, I can always tell people I shook the hand of Jack Johnson, heavyweight champion of the world.

First thing I did was change the name to the Cotton Club. You might have heard of it.

Chapter

Forty-Two

THE COTTON CLUB was what brought me and Dutch together, and kept us working together right up until nearly our last night together. It's funny that we should both have departed the great city of the Manhattoes on the same day, but I don't suppose that's any less believable than the fact that John Adams and Thomas Jefferson died on the same day. They didn't like each other any better than Dutch and I did, but they admired each other, and sometimes it takes two great, if flawed, men working together to bring Americans the kind of country they want and deserve.

We fixed up the joint spectacular, and they're still talking about it today. Feature a jungle with a stage, a dance floor and places for four or five hundred customers and you'll have the idea. They didn't call the Cotton Club the Aristocrat of Harlem for nothin'.

At first, most of our musicians came from Chicago. The reason was simple. Unlike our girls, colored players was mostly a bad lot, and a fight that started downtown at the Club Abbey could easily continue ninety blocks north. I didn't want no trouble—couldn't afford any, being on parole and all—and so I called up the Big Fella, Al Capone, in Chi-town and had his boys send me musicians that mostly didn't know each other. For it's sad but true that your average colored likes to fight as much as your average Irishman, which is why I guess when the paddies first come here, the white folks had a hard time distinguishin' us from the darkies. Take a look at any of the political cartoons of the period, if you don't believe me: there they are, the mick and the coon, two apes sittin' side by side and scaring the bejesus out of the proper folk.

I didn't know Capone then, not personally. I knew he'd come out of Brooklyn and had run with the last of the Five Pointers, so in a sense he was one of Paul Kelly's boys, but New York had changed, and already Monk and Paul were lifetimes ago. There was no point in holding imaginary grudges when there was business to be done.

We welcomed everybody as long as they had the price of admission, which was steep, with a couple of exceptions. The doormen, who were colored, were under strict orders not to admit Negroes, whether on their own or in mixed groups. Once in a while I bent rule number one to let in some coloreds known to me personally, such as Hiram, whom I'd hired as my valet and man Friday for thirty-five dollars a week, and of course I kept my bargain and Jack Johnson was always welcome—hell, you can't ask for a better front man than a former heavyweight champ—and so I guess you can say we invented the whole idea of the pug-turned-Vegas-greeter right there on Lenox Avenue.

Another rule concerned women: no unescorted dames after six P.M. in any of my clubs. It wasn't just that I wanted to keep the easy-virtue element out; it was to spare my married clientele the embarrassment of being sought out by the wife and being caught with the girlfriend. Or vice versa.

I had one other special rule, which was more or less the reverse of the previous: my sister, May, was only to be admitted by herself, as long as I was in the house. No dates, no groups, only solo. Of course my mother was never to be admitted, under any circumstances. Marty could do as he pleased.

Inside and out, a no-fighting policy was strictly enforced, the result of which the Cotton Club was the safest place in darktown, bar none. We wanted only the classiest people in our joint, and any overt razorwork, slicing or gunplay scared the high-class element away.

We sold Madden's No. I—showcased it, in fact. For those wishing to indulge in the finer bubbly, we offered champagne at thirty bucks the bottle and a fifth of whiskey for eighteen. The chow was good and pricey, and as for the girls . . .

The girls were young as legally allowed and maybe not even, and so fair that half of them could have passed for white and probably did. One or two later married high-society boys, whose blue-nosed families were none the wiser. I'd asked Granlund to help me out, and while colored gals was a little out of his line, he came up with some real winners. We put 'em in the skimpiest outfits we could get away with—good legs was a must—and choreographed them to a fare-thee-well. No show ever went up on that stage without I gave it the high sign.

Only trouble was my keen ear soon realized that we needed a better band to accompany our revues. The Cotton Club Syncopators was just okay, and when its leader, Andy Preer, passed away of natural causes, I thought it was a tough break for Andy but a good break for me, because now I had an excuse to find something really terrific, especially with a new season coming up.

Fella named Jimmy McHugh was one of our music johnnies, and he said he'd heard a swell group, eleven pieces, called Duke Ellington and his Washingtonians. Problem was Ellington was gigging at Gibson's Standard down Philly, and so I'd called a mug I knew, Boo Boo Hoff, and asked him to have a collegial word with Clarence Robinson, the proprietor, about my chances of employing Mr. Ellington and his band. On the night I'm recounting I was waiting for Boo Boo to bring back Robinson's response.

At the Cotton Club everybody who was anybody, and everybody who wanted to be somebody, showed his face. Jimmy Walker was a regular, toodling in most nights after midnight; no wonder the press called him "the Night Mayor of New York." I always kept his table stocked with champagne. Tammany lads came often, including my old pals Chick and Billy, now men of property and position; we used to joke with Billy that his last name had to be worth a job someday, and now here he was, a district leader named Tammany. Police captains came with their wives, police lieutenants came with their mistresses, detectives came with their girlfriends and patrolmen came with their whores. It was swell.

Writers and journalists ate it up and why not? That moocher Winchell came by to collect scoops, hobbin' with the nobs and pretendin' like hell he hadn't been born just a few blocks away. Damon Runyon was just the opposite. He told everybody he'd been born in Manhattan, which was true, except he forgot to mention it was Kansas.

We got so big that we was killin' the Harlem competition—Small's, the Exclusive, a bunch of others. And that's why Dutch Schultz paid me a visit that night.

Although we hadn't met facewise up to this point, Dutch and I had an agreement that Manhattan north of 110th Street and all of the Bronx was his liquor territory, while I took the rest of the island plus Brooklyn. Nobody lived in Queens in them days and Staten Island wasn't worth fighting over. The deal had been negotiated by Frenchy for me and for Dutch by the punk named Legs Diamond, but Legs had struck out on his own and I was wondering how long that deal could hold.

You may be wondering why I hadn't revenged myself on Jack Diamond for taking that shot at me back at the Arbor, but that was bygones as far as I was concerned. He was just doin' his job. You can't go through this life tryin' to settle each and every score, just the ones that counted, and I figured as long as Legs hadn't done nothing more to me, a live-and-let-live policy would obtain.

This, by the way, is another thing folks today get wrong about the gangs back then. Jews employed Irish, Irish employed Jews, everybody employed Italians, even the Italians, who also employed Irish and Jews. That was the way it was back in the days of Monk and Paul Kelly, and that was the way it was during Prohibition. That's how we all learned to work together, and who's to say the country isn't better off for it? It wasn't going to happen on Wall Street, that's for sure.

May and I were sitting at my usual table in the back with Frenchy, who was playing solitaire. I was enjoyin' the show and looking out over the sea of furs and jewels and she was just being beautiful. Once in a while at first, some mug would mistake her for my girlfriend, but he got straightened out real quick if he knew what was good for him.

Frenchy dealt a tableau, turned over a card or two, then folded.

"Why don't you play the hand out?" I asked.

He looked at me like I was stupid. "No point to it," he said. "I can tell how it's going to go."

"Then why bother, if you can figure it out after a couple of cards?"

"It's fun is why," he replied, dealing himself a fresh layout. "Look who's here."

"Mr. Madden," said a natty fellow in specs. "How are you this evening, fine sir?"

Runyon sat down with us, schnorring as usual, and talking up his latest project, which was stories he was writing about gangland and all the "colorful characters" therein. "Like you, Duke," he said.

I told him if he ever so much as thought about putting me in one of his stories, I would cut his heart out and mail it to his mother back in Kansas.

"All life is nine to five against," he said.

"Not if you're already alive," said Frenchy, calculating his cards. "Then it's even money."

"You got me all wrong," Runyon stuttered. He'd had a few, so he wasn't as wary as he otherwise might have been. I'd already had to explain the facts of life to Winchell, that he could plug my bands, my booze, my babes in his newspaper columns but on no account was he ever to mention me by name nohow nowhere. Walter thought of himself as a tough guy, but that was a figment of his imagination, like most of the stuff in his columns, and he did exactly as he was told. I couldn't have asked for a better press agent than Winchell, which is why, unlike some mugs, I never had to hire one.

Runyon, on the other hand, was a more formidable chap. He was bright and brave, he'd walk into any kind of situation—brawls, shoot-outs, what have you—and stay just as dapper as when he left his house in the morning. Too bad he was such a drunk.

"I'm not using real names, I'm using aliases."

Now, that was thinking like a hood. "Such as?"

"Such as the one I'm thinking about for you, for example."

Frenchy looked up from his cards and shot Runyon a look, just so I didn't have to. I knew that his shotgun, fully loaded, lay under the table by his feet, just in case. George DeMange believed in insurance.

"Just look at you: neatly groomed, impeccably attired, elegantly turned out in every wise and all respects. Who else could you be but—Dave the Dude?"

I wasn't sure if I liked that, and told him so.

"Aw, give a fella a break, why don't you? Wait till you get a load of the story. It'll kill you. You know that old crippled dame you always give a quarter for luck to, the one down on Times Square?"

"Apple Annie?"

"You mean Miss Osborne," interjected my sister. "I hear she used to really be somebody. A great beauty too."

"That's what drink'll do to you," I said. "Just look at George here—he used to be mistaken for Georgie Ranft all the time."

The big lug looked up from his patience game, I think it was Canfield. "Lay off," he said. May laughed and kissed him on the cheek.

"Not Apple Annie—her name's Madame la Gimp."

"La what?"

"Mother of a Spanish princess-in-law, or something like that. I haven't worked it all out yet."

"Let me know when you do." I signaled for the waiter to refill his glass. "Who else?"

"Gee, thanks," he said, swallowing it whole. "How about this one: Regret."

I looked at George, who'd won three in a row at Canfield. How he did it without cheating the talon I'll never know. "What kind of a moniker is that?" he asked, switching Napoleon at St. Helena, which I preferred to call Forty Thieves.

Runyon was about to answer and then I seen his eyes get a faraway and over-the-rainbow look in 'em.

"Why don't you ask him yourself?" he said, jumping to his feet and making his own regrets.

The band struck up some new number—I think it was "The Best Things in Life Are Free"—but my mind wasn't on the music, or even on Damon anymore. Instead it was on three gorillas in tuxes and a dame dressed to kill waltzing across my dance floor and makin' a beeline for my very own table. It was 1927, and my life was about to change again.

Chapter

Forty-Three

THEY WERE A FUNNY-LOOKING LOT. The guy in the lead wore his monkey suit like he was born in it; it fit him so well that only my practiced eye could pick out the heater under his left armpit and inside his left ankle.

The second mook couldn't have been more different. He was short and round and bald; he looked like a beach ball that had been invited to Cinderella's ball, except that he didn't have nothing to wear and so pulled the first rag he could find out of the closet.

Bringing up the rear was a little fella, about my size. Like me, he was trim and well built, but unlike me, he was manifestly a slob. I could see the stains on his bow tie from halfway across the room and I would have laid you dollars to donuts that his socks didn't match. No matter what duds you draped over him, this guy would always come up lookin' like he'd slept in them, not to mention dined in them.

The great Dutch Schultz, in all his fleshly glory.

The two mugs with him, I knew from reputation, were his triggerman, the sleek Bo Weinberg, and his portly abacus, Otto Berman, who some folks called Abbadabba and Runyon called Regret, on account of his sad brown eyes. He reminded me a little of Rosenthal, Joe's doomed dead uncle.

The dame took me one whole second to spot. Mary Frances Blackwell, done up to the nines, yet in this environment still as anonymous as all get-out . . . In my clubs every broad was beautiful.

"Hello, Dutch," I said. "Been looking forward to this powwow for a while." The trio started to sit down, but I held up my hand. "Pat 'em down, George, all except the dame." For a big man, Frenchy was plenty fast: before

Schultz could utter a word, George's big mitts had run up and down his legs and armpits. "Shirtwaist .45 is all. Nothin' too dangerous."

Dutch was all smiles, no hard feelings, he'd do the same to me in one of his clubs.

"Otto don't carry," said Bo—whose Christian name, pardon my French, was Abe—flashing open his jacket to show what he was packing, twin .45s. Bo was very good, all class, and I found myself wishing he worked for me. "For ten thousand smackers a week he's brains, not brawn."

"Sit down, boys. You too, miss."

Waiters came running without being called. Berman and Weinberg both eyeballed May and took off their hats. My topper was already off, but I rose half out of my seat as Mary Frances sat down, and got a quick look into her eyes. Recognition, definitely. Reproach, possibly. Regret, absolutely.

I woulda said something and maybe she would have too, except it was Dutch, naturally, who opened his beak first. "What the fuck's with you Irishers anyway, for crying out loud?"

Silence all around for the nonce. Bo and Berman were used to their boss's famous crudity, but I knew for a fact that my sister wasn't and neither I hoped was Mary Frances.

"Watch your mouth, Dutch, we're all friends here."

"And tryin' to stay that way," said Abbadabba, leaning over with a stage whisper.

"I'm not Irish," said Frenchy.

"Which leaves me you must be talkin' about and I was born in England," says I.

That's how angry Dutch was, so mad he didn't notice May right off, the way most blokes did. "Yeah, well, I was born in the city but everybody thinks I'm from the Bronx, so that don't prove—holy cow, introduce me to the tomato, why don't ya?"

Dutch looked at May. I looked at Mary Frances. Bo looked at the colored girls on the dance floor. Frenchy looked at his tableau. Otto looked at his chewed nails. May looked into space. The band played "My Heart Stood Still."

I caught the whole show. She was a brave girl, my sister, not afraid of hard guys. Dutch may have been a bum, but dolls went for him. Then again, dolls go for pretty much everything in pants, so maybe that doesn't prove anything. I spied his glance Maywards and didn't like it much. "I thought you liked blondes. It was in all the papers."

Mary Frances flinched a little. She was going bottle-blond, but she wasn't quite there yet.

Dutch couldn't take his eyes off my sister. "Yeah, well, you can't eat at Childs every night, can you?"

"Except she ain't no tomato."

"Nor an onion either," says May, offering her hand. "I'm May Madden."

At this point we had ourselves a right regular comedy, because I wasn't sure whether Mary Frances could distinguish between my wife and my sister, and neither could the Dutchman.

He looked at me with a little confusion on his hound-dog puss. "I thought your wife was . . . you know . . . upstate."

"His sister," said May. "You heard of sisters?"

The Dutchman pushed himself back in his chair and finally took off his hat. "Hoboe and Poboe, two peas in a pod," he said. "You Englishmen, you are a type."

"May, why don't you and Mary Frances go powder your noses for a while?" I said.

"You know her?" asked May and Dutch, both more or less at the same time.

"I know all the girls named Mary," I told my sister, kissing her as innocently as I could.

"I don't have to powder my nose," said May.

"Then go fix your hair."

"Her hair's fine," said Dutch. He gave Bo a shot in the ribs, to redirect his attention. "Ain't her hair fine?"

"Fine," said Bo, wandering back to the colored girls.

"I think our mother's calling you," I said.

More glances, too numerous to mention. At last, May and Mary Frances rose. "We'll be back later, boys," said May. "Try not to talk about us while we're gone."

"Count on it, sister," said Dutch, leaning back in his chair and stretching out his short legs.

May took Dutch's hand for a moment—what a diplomat my sister was—and then moved off with Mary Frances.

"Sister or no sister, that is some tomato," said Dutch.

"She's not for you, Dutch," I said.

Something in my tone must have caught even his tin ear. "Who're you saving her for, Madden?" he sneered.

"She's not for anybody." Even though it was plenty warm in the club, and getting warmer by the minute, I could feel myself growing very cold.

"This is a sensitive subject, Mr. Schultz," said Frenchy.

"Must be a Catholic thing, huh, Bo?" said Schultz to Weinberg. "Jeez, these Catholics—no wonder nobody likes 'em."

"Arthur," said Otto Berman, "we're here to discuss business, not sex or religion."

"Those are the fun things," said Dutch.

"I promised my father a long time ago I'd take care of her, and a deathbed promise is more than a promise—it's an oath," I said.

"And you think keeping her virginal is protecting her?"

"Owen thinks what he thinks, and I think that what he thinks, whatever he thinks, is right," said Frenchy.

Dutch finally decided to lay off, which was the healthy course of action. "You don't have to get sore about it."

"You wanted to see me?" I asked Dutch.

He finally got down to brass tacks. "I mean, I'm up here in coontown, minding my own business, getting the whole place under control, keepin' the chimney sweeps happy with the policy rackets, and all of a sudden you'd think it was St. Fucking Patrick's Day." He wasn't mad, but he wasn't exactly brimming with bonhomie neither.

"What seems to be the problem?"

"This Diamond guy is giving me fits, and now this fuckin' Coll, Jesus, I do these micks a favor, give 'em a break, and this is how they repay me, jackin' my trucks, sticking up my bagmen. Gloryoski, where's the goddamn honor?"

That wasn't a question I was prepared to answer but luckily I didn't have to because at that moment two things happened. First, the girls came back from wherever girls come back from, and second, a wave of applause rippled through the crowd.

I rose in honor of the ladies and looked to see what's the ruckus all about.

Now, there are ripples and there are ripples. There's a ripple when a doll walks through a room. A lapping little wave when a doll who's also a dame sashays through a room. There's a splish-splash when a mug who's nobody strolls through a room. And a wave when a mug who's somebody cock-walks through a room.

And there's the tidal wave that crashes through a joint when a dame who's not quite a doll but everybody thinks she is, and a mook who's not quite a mug but everybody thinks he is, ramble down the alleyway, all eyes upon 'em, and well-deserved too.

The stud looks like two million bucks as he canters in, if his kraut-wop folks could only see him now, and on his arm he's got a babe that every bozo in the joint not only recognizes but has humped in his dreams.

Of course I'm talking about Georgie Ranft, my old pal, and the dame du jour, the one and only Miss Mae West. Come to pay their respects to the Duke.

"Hello, Owney," says Georgie, pretending he almost knows me.

There's something about a broad who's already so famous, so famous for being sexy, that freezes every other woman in the place. I couldn't swear in a court of law that Mae West was the most gorgeous piece of girl I ever laid my peepers or paws upon, but she sure made you think she was.

"Mae West, Owney Madden."

Mae and I eyeballed each other for a moment. "So you're the famous Owney Madden."

I was already up on my feet, reaching to shake, but instead she caressed one hand across my face, like I was a little kid. "So sweet . . ."

May and Mary Frances watched me like I was a movie star or something. "Yeah?" I said.

Mae's hand paused in the vicinity of my nose, then slapped me hard. "And so vicious."

That stung, but so what? "Loved you in *Sex*."

"Everybody does." Another slap. "Say somethin' original."

I took it and I liked it. "You ever need a backer . . ."

She stopped slapping and started laughing. "I'm okay on my back. It's the front I'm looking for help with." She swung her porch around plenty so we all could get a good look. "Ain't we all, girls?"

"Would you like a drink, Miss West?" asked Frenchy, coming to my rescue.

So here was the situation: Me, I was flanked by my sister, May, my former girlfriend Mary Frances and my friends Georgie and George. Dutch was partnered by Otto and Bo, with his eyes roaming from Mae's *poitrine* to May's to Mary's, in descending order. And each and every one of us males at that moment with a loaded roscoe.

"What took you so long?" said Mae.

I noticed that Mayor Walker, Beau James himself, was leading the applause, just beamin' at her, which was pretty funny considering that he was the guy who indirectly put her on ice at Blackwell's Island for a stretch, but that's politics and strange bedfellows for you. I made a motion that meant: send another bucket of champagne over to the Mayor.

Which got my focus back 'round to Mary Frances, who, half-blond, looked better to me than ever, even though Dutch had his hand halfway up her skirt.

The thing about me is I'm not jealous of dames once I've finished with 'em. But I wasn't sure in my own mind whether I was finished with Mary Frances or just getting started, so I wasn't crazy neither about Dutch's familiarity with her nor about his evident prurience as far as my own dear sister was concerned.

Mae gives Beau James the fisheye and gives me the look—you know, that look of hers. "I hear we got somethin' in common, sweetie," she says with a smile. "We both done time." You couldn't beat Mae's timing.

Jimmy Walker, only the little worse for wear, stands up. The dame not his wife with him discreetly kept her seat. One of our waiters refilled Hizzoner's empty glass before he knew it was empty. New York had Mayors in them days.

"A toast," he toasted, nodding in our direction, "to the first lady of New York." He might have been referring to Mrs. Walker, but he wasn't. "Whose pulchritudinousness, whose fecundity, whose sheer—"

"Spit it out, Jimmy," chimed some drunk.

"—benefidence," sputtered Walker, "has made our fair city happier, our happy city fairer and, dare I say"—he took a gulp—"holier."

"Than thou," completed the lush.

Walker turned toward the heckler. "Than you," he topped. "Schmuck."

The crowd roared. The waiter filled his glass once more as I signaled to the orchestra to play a quick fanfare.

Mae looked around the room. "All I gotta say is," says she, "if this is the way the Mayor of New York treats his ex-convicts . . ."

All ears and eyes on Mae.

"—it's a wonder he ain't got more of 'em!"

Jimmy Walker laughed out loud, and it was a while later that Mae told me privately she'd adapted that line from Oscar Wilde, but I think we were in bed at the time and I didn't much care one way or the other.

Sleek little Georgie piped up. "Well, we gotta be going . . . makin' the rounds, you know."

Truth to tell, I was glad to see Georgie go. He was one fella I could never compete with when it came to dolls, and the looks he was dartin' at Mary Frances and my sister were making me uncomfortable.

"George," I said to Big Frenchy, "make sure Miss West's next show has our full financial backing." I turned to Mae. "What's it going to be?"

She thought half a second. "A little number I call *Diamond Lil,*" she said.

"Put me down for one hundred percent."

A little smile crossed those notorious lips. "In exchange for . . . ?"

"Fifty percent of the box and six pairs of ducats a night."

"I guess I can share." She touched Georgie on the arm. "Come on, big boy, let me show you a good time."

All the men stood, even Dutch. "So long, mugs—be seein' ya in the funny papers."

Georgie raised an eyebrow and then he sailed away, trailing along in the magnificent wake of Miss Mae West. I signaled once more to the band, and they struck up "June Night" or some favorite as we sat back down to business.

"Jeez, what a fat ugly broad."

"Arthur," started up Berman, but Bo cut him off.

"There's gonna come a time when they won't make women like that anymore," he said. "I just hope I don't live to see it."

"Anything can be arranged, Bo," said Dutch, who hated being contradicted.

I looked over at May, to see if maybe she and Mary Frances had to go visit the loo again, but this time she just ignored the hint, and I didn't feel like making a federal case out of it, so I let her sit there and pretend not to listen.

"Let's see if we can help each other out here, like friends and neighbors." I hailed another waiter, who brought over several bottles of Madden's No. 1.

Dutch looked at his without drinking it. "This is one of the things giving me *tsuris*," he said.

"You call this *tsuris*, I call it business. It's not my fault if my beer's better than yours. I thought you wanted to talk about Jack Diamond."

"Legs," said Dutch, "is out of control."

"Didn't you used to work with Jack?" I asked.

"Way back when," said the Dutchman. "But now Joey Noe and me got a good thing going in the Bronx, and I don't need Legs no more. In fact, what I need is for him to disappear. Permanently."

"I don't like Diamond any more'n you do," I said. "His clubs are down in the 50s, like the Hotsy-Totsy. My old turf. He's more of a pain to me than he is to you."

I turned to George. "We doing business with Legs these days?"

Frenchy yanked one of the ledger books out of his pocket and consulted it. "You could call it that. He still owes us for the last few beer shipments. Guess he's too busy chasing skirts to take care of his books."

"That's just it!" said Dutch loudly, and I could see a couple of police captains glance our way, to see if I needed any help. "The fuckin' guy is chasin' so many skirts minus stockings that he don't have time to tend to business, so he's gotta steal from honest businessmen like you and me. Only guy I know gets as much trim as Legs is Bo here, but I can count on Bo to give me an honest day's work for an honest day's pay. Ain't that right, Bo?"

"That's right, Dutch," said Bo, brushing an imaginary speck from his lapel.

Dutch was so agitated he finally took a sip of my beer. "Not bad," he said, wiping his lip with his sleeve. "How many times do you have to shoot a guy before he falls over and stays down?"

"Only once if you're doing it right."

"Easy for you to say."

"Damn right it is. People have been saying the same thing about me since 1912, and I'm still here."

"Something tells me Legs ain't going to be so lucky."

I was getting the picture loud and clear. "Are you askin' me or are you tellin' me?"

"Think of this as a courtesy call," said Otto Berman diplomatically. "Mr. Schultz has come here to inform you of some of his business plans, because—"

"Because of, you know," blurted Dutch.

I had no idea what he was talking about.

"Mr. Madden doesn't know, Mr. Schultz," said George.

"Arthur, I think it best if we—" said Otto.

This was starting to get me sore. "What is it that I don't know?"

Even with all the music and the noise and the clinking of glasses and the dancing colored girls, the Cotton Club seemed a very quiet place to me all of a sudden.

Then Mary Frances spoke up. It was the first time she'd opened her beak all evening. "You don't know what Legs has been saying about you. And your sister."

Well, now I was plenty sore. "What kinds of things?"

Mary Frances tossed back her curls. "Rumors. Boasting. The usual mug stuff about guys and dolls."

If Legs was there, I would have shot him on the spot. "Did he say anything about my sister?"

Otto wiped some sweat off his brow. Frenchy put a hand on my shoulder. "You know how mooks are, Owen. All talk, no action."

"So you're gonna have Bo pop Legs," I said, trying to calm down. "I'm sorry for this, May."

She looked kinda pale. "Don't worry about it."

"Eventually," said Dutch. "He's hidin' out upstate somewhere, but we'll find him, and when we do, Bo and Abe and Lulu'll be there and that will be the end of Legs Diamond. Tough break about whatever broad he's banging. I hear the new one is quite the dish. Kiki something. If she was a blonde . . ."

"What about the other half of your problem? Coll? I thought he worked for you."

Dutch, as usual, was ready with an answer. "He did, but he just popped one of my boys, Barelli, over nothin'. Killed his sister too, just 'cause she was there. Guy's a fuckin' madman." Dutch got an idea; I could see it in his eyes. "Say, why don't you put him down? He's one of yours."

"A Kildare lad, through and through. Folks live in the Kitchen." I shook my head. "He's just a boy, Dutch—can't be more than seventeen, eighteen."

"That's a man in my book."

"I'll think about it."

My eye caught a signal from the doorman, whose name was Bert. As you know from riding trains and dealing with Pullman porters, all colored boys are named George, but we already had so many Georges around that I decided that all the black boys who worked for me would be called Bert, after Bert Williams, the great entertainer, and none of them seemed to mind.

Bert and me had a whole series of hand signs that woulda done Urban Shocker and his catcher, Pat Collins, proud. This particular one—a tug of his doorman's cap, followed by a brush on both lapels—meant there was an urgent message for me, that the messenger was going to deliver it in person and that the messenger was jake.

To my surprise the messenger was none other than Boo Boo Hoff, who'd come straight up from Penn Station. I'd always told my boys I like good news over the phone and bad news delivered in person, and here came Boo Boo, so I could guess what Clarence Robinson's answer was, and now it was up to me to formulate a reply.

"What's the word, Boo Boo?" I asked as he approached our table. He featured the gang and stopped, taking off his hat like a good boy.

"Could I have a word with you in private, Mr. Madden?" he asked.

"Sit down and have a beer instead, you've come a long way," I invited.

"Gee, thanks." He couldn'ta been more nervous if he was face-to-face with his Maker.

A waiter rushed over. "A beer for Mr. Hoff, and would you mind going up on the roof and getting me a piece of cardboard what's lining one of my pigeon cages at the moment?"

The Cotton Club waiters knew better than to ask questions, and so in two shakes of a lamb's tail Boo Boo had his beer and I had my cardboard, which was fairly dripping with pigeon shite.

"Gimme a pen, George. One that writes."

Frenchy took out a splendid Cross in the shape of a baseball bat I'd given him as a present in honor of Ruth's hitting sixty home runs that summer. I turned away from the group, rubbed away some of the ordure and started in to writing.

"What the hell you doin'?" asked Dutch, but I wasn't finished.

"Makin' a medical suggestion. There."

I turned back to the group and showed them what I'd scrawled on the liner:

"BE BIG OR BE DEAD."

I handed it to Boo Boo. "Take this back to Robinson and tell him I expect Ellington's band to be at Pennsylvania Station by two tomorrow afternoon, checked in to a colored hotel by three o'clock and up here playing at the club by seven."

Boo Boo jumped to his feet and made ready to grab the sign.

"Finish your beer first," I said.

Chapter

Forty-Four

I'VE MENTIONED THAT OUR BUSINESS INTERESTS were flourishing, and so they were. Everybody was makin' money, honest or otherwise, and more important, everybody was spending it. Stock pickers couldn't rake it in fast enough, coppers couldn't put their hands out quick enough and bartenders couldn't set 'em up smart enough. It was like a giant wheel of money that just kept spinning and while the smart eggs knew it had to stop someday, the suckers just kept plunkin' down their dimes, hoping to take one last ride.

Looking back, I guess you could say that 1929 was more or less my high-water mark, just like the rest of the country. The clubs Larry and I ran were going gangbusters. Thanks to Winchell and Runyon, Texas Guinan's name was in all the papers and mine wasn't.

The brewery was operating at full capacity. Me and a dapper little Hebrew named Joe Gould were investing in various fighters, including the heavyweights, so I got to go to plenty of fights at the Garden and profit from them too. I lived at the top of 440 West 34th Street and raised generation after generation of Columbidae. My sister and my mother lived in a big flat on the floor below, and I was paying for a place for my brother, Marty, at 452 West 96th, telephone RIverside 9–4313, where he was nightly entertaining a nice young lady named Kitty.

Mary Frances and I saw each other on the nights she wasn't with Dutch. I could tell the state of their affair from the color of her hair, and on this evening it was darker rather than lighter.

"You ever gonna get married?" she asked. We were lying on my bed, with the view east into the city. Even flat on my back, I could see down 34th all the way to the Waldorf on Fifth, north a little to 405 Lexington Avenue, where the new Chrysler Building was going up, and let me tell you it was some sight, even without its topper.

Ignorant of school learning as I was, I nevertheless had a great appreciation for fine architecture, and Mary Frances was one of those rare dames who was more beautiful without her clothes on than she was with them on, not needing the purple mantle most women rely upon to make their way in the world. She was still slender, small-breasted and narrow-waisted, her diadem set off against the changing color of her topside.

"I am married," I reminded her.

MFB rolled over to reach for the cigarette case I'd given her. It was pure silver, embossed with her initials. The covers fell away from her and I got a good long look at her shape, smooth and round the way God intended such things to be, and at that moment, if I was going to love a woman, I guess I'd have to say I loved her.

"Match me," she said. I did. "Love me?"

"What kind of a question's that?" I replied, shaking out the match before it burned my fingers.

She took a deep drag and handed the fag over. "The kind girls like me ask."

"Why?"

"Because it's the only one left."

I blew the smoke out of my lungs. It hurt. "Divorce is against my religion."

She kissed me, hard. "So's this."

"Gotta pick your poison."

I hate when girls cry.

"Would you, could you . . . ever?"

Mary Frances pushed the covers back and exposed my body from chin to toenails. I hated the way I looked, shot up and scar-tracked, but she knew each and every wound, had practically been present at their creation, and she kissed and caressed each one like it was an old friend. "You almost died that night."

"Didn't want to."

"Me you neither."

She rolled over, opened her arms and made her legs receptive. "I want to."

"Me you too."

We did it again, with the abandon of lovers without consequences. At times like this, what the Dusters done to me seemed like a small price to pay for my pleasure, until my pleasure was over, and then I remembered that it was just about the highest price a man could pay and still call himself a man.

I guess there must have been something stimulating about our conversation, because I gave a particularly good account of myself, and finally we both fell back exhausted, our duty done, to suffer the little death that comes to all lovers.

"I see the way you look at her," she said. I was half-asleep. I took a wild guess.

"Who? Mae?"

She seemed surprised I'd got it in one. "And that's okay?"

"Why wouldn't it be? We're both free, white and twenty-one."

"Yeah, but—"

I threw my arms around her, ready for round three. "But nothing."

"I never woulda thought—"

"Don't think, then," I said, smothering her tender mouth and drawing her breath into mine.

Chapter

Forty-Five

Back to business. By now, even the feds had pretty much given up enforcing Prohibition, and Hoover trumped up a typical goo-goo commission, this one named after some clown called Wickersham, to prove that what they thought had been such a swell notion just ten years earlier that they went and amended the Constitution was now a rotten idea and what they needed to do was of course amend the Constitution again. This, I thought, was the true genius of goo-goos and reformers everywhere: that they never had to admit Reform was a mistake, and if it was, then all it took was more Reform to set it right.

I had the cops eating out of my hand, all except my old pal Branagan, who was starting to bite that hand what fed him, mostly in the form of small shakedowns from time to time. The problem with me and Branagan was that we each had too much on the other. He, my priors; me, his desires. Branagan had lost none of his taste for lasses, and here was the amazing part: that while he'd aged, the girls he went for hadn't, which meant that it took some of the town's more exotic establishments to keep both his big head and his little head happy.

So one fine day he demanded more than his usual, and I refused, and the result of which was that the cops padlocked the Cotton Club for a few months and fined me, but that was okay because it meant two things. One, that as far as I was concerned Branagan and I were quitclaim and two, I could fire the manager and hire two fellas who knew guns and broads and how to keep 'em apart: Harry Block, to run the place, and Herman Stark, to produce the shows. Herman was the smart guy who came up with the idea for the "Cotton Club Parades," as well as the fella who told Harry to hire a little sheeny songwriter from Buffalo, which I did and here's how.

One morning I had Hiram drive me up to the club to take care of some business. Hiram was my man now, and a better wheelman I never found. People looked at me strange when I called him my friend, because no proper white man was friends with the colored back then, but being Irish I was no proper white man in the first place and anyway Hiram and I went way back, and we had a lot more in common than we did with most others, plus we actually liked each other.

Funny how small a dump is with no one in it, at night, when it was packed to the rafters with swells, you could swear the whole City of New York was cheek-to-cheek, but at eleven A.M. it seemed forlorn and a little tacky. Power of illusion, and never underestimate it, whether in business or dolls.

Anyway, there was a swarthy kid sitting at one of the rehearsal pianos, fiddling around, and I figured he was one of the boys in the band, although I didn't recognize him.

"Who's that?" I said to Harry Block.

"Says he's a songwriter." Harry always had a seegar in his mouth, couldn't live without one, and so he didn't like to say much.

"Colored boy?"

"Jewish."

"Name of?"

"Arluck."

I ambled over, but Arluck was so lost in his tinklin' of the ivories that he didn't hear me coming. I listened as I approached; the tune was melancholy. I myself am partial to up-tempo numbers, but like most Irish I liked a sad song every now and then, especially when sung by a dish. He jumped as I clapped a hand on his shoulder.

"You shouldn't oughta let mugs sneak up on you like that, kid," I said. "Ain't healthy." I looked at his notepaper. "Whaddya call it?"

He stayed cool. " 'Ill Wind,' " he said. "I call it 'Ill Wind.' "

"Let's hope none of it blows our way." I leaned on the piano as we conversed. "You always write such sad songs?"

"Sometimes I do, if that's the way I feel. Colored folks call it the blues."

"Sing a little of it." He did. "Nice voice."

"My father is a cantor in Buffalo, New York. He taught me to sing."

"So why ain't ya singin' there?"

"I'd rather be here."

I liked this gonoph, full of moxie. "You know who I am?"

"I can guess."

"Make you nervous?"

"I haven't done anything wrong."

Good answer. "You don't mind working with colored?"

That got him a little riled, the way I hoped it would. "Mind? Mind! That's why I came here—to New York City. To Harlem. To work with the best. The fellows in the band say I'm the blackest white man they ever met."

"I bet they mean that as a compliment too," I said.

"You bet they do, Mr. Madden."

"Call me Owney."

"No, I won't. I'll call you Mr. Madden until the day comes when I'm more famous than you are, and you call me Mr. Arluck."

I shook my head. "That day ain't never comin'."

"Why not?"

I changed the subject. "What's with the blues?"

Hyman settled down. "Not everybody's lucky. Some folks have it tough. They can't make the rent, their girlfriend's left them—"

"Ellington's got a number, 'Mood Indigo.' Something like that?"

"Something like that."

"I don't like it as well as I like 'The Mooche.'"

"Tough to choose, with Ellington."

"Between the devil and the deep blue sea, huh?"

"Something like that. The blues are how they, black folks, express themselves. They're how I express myself."

I looked him over. He was wearing an okay suit and trying to grow a little mustache. "You don't look like you're so bad off. After all, you're working for me." I thought he would faint. "Fifty bucks a week. So start earnin' it."

"Okay!"

He launched into another number he'd written, a snappy bit that had me tapping my toes. "It's called 'Get Happy,'" he said, pounding away. He was one of those guys who could play and talk at the same time. I never understood how they did that.

A girl, barely sixteen, was standing off in a corner, shy as all get out, listenin' raptly. I motioned her over.

I had a rule about underage kids, having been one myself once. The whole notion of underage workers was just another screwy reform idea in the first place, but even gangsters had to observe it, at least in the breach, so the deal was we could hire as many of them as we could get away with, but any mug who so much as gave them a dirty look was out the door in a flash.

"What's your name, honey?" I asked.

"Lena," she said.

"Workin'?"

"Chorus line."

I took a good look at her. The chorus girls wore nothing but a string of bananas, a couple of strategically placed leaves and a smile. On stage, she looked like a small bronzed goddess. To me, now, she looked like a star.

"Can you sing solo?"

"Yes, sir, Mr. Madden," she said.

I pointed at Arluck. "Can you sing his swill?"

She nodded. "We've been practicing."

"Then hit it."

I listened a few bars, that's all it took. I reached in my pocket, took out a roll and peeled off a set of bills for each of 'em. "Here," I said, handing Arluck and Lena a couple hundred simoleons apiece. "Buy yourselves a yacht."

"But I get seasick," said Hyman.

"Then buy yourself an egg cream," I said. Egg creams were new back then and you didn't even have to be Jewish to like them.

"What's it really for?" asked Lena, smart girl.

"The future," I said. "And, kid"—I'm looking at Arluck now—"lose the name. All the best people do." A couple of weeks later he was callin' himself Harold Arlen, a big improvement if you ask me.

But she was Lena Horne and that's the way she stayed.

Chapter

Forty-Six

Arluck wasn't the only one singing the blues. Dutch Schultz was too, because a few of his mugs got themselves killed, including his partner, Joey Noe. I think if Joey hada lived, things mighta turned out different, although maybe not, because Joey was smart, although obviously not smart enough. But he didn't live—Legs killed 'im, ambushed him, and so the trap that Dutch thought he was setting for Legs turned out to bite him on the bum, and boy did the Dutchman ever hate that.

Life in gangland was startin' to turn violent, which was always bad for business. The problem with most of the gangsters was that, unlike me, they didn't have no memory of the bad old days of the shoot-outs under the els—hell, the els was on their way out themselves—or the big fight between Monk and Paul Kelly, or the Arbor and Nash's.

That's when I realized that I was nearly thirty-eight years old. Thirty-eight was already old for anybody, but for someone in my line of work it was ancient. I attributed my longevity to a number of things, including smarts and savvy, but truth to tell, the eight years I spent up the river didn't hurt, neither. Bein' on ice isn't the worst thing that can happen to you, especially when the ice was as relatively pleasant as mine was, and hitting the sidewalk smack-dab in the midst of Prohibition was the luck of the Irish, if you ask me.

To give you an idea of the kinds of things I was involved in, I'm going to share something with you no one has ever seen, and that's my private note-book. George kept the books, several sets of them: one for us, one for prospective investors and one for the tax man. There was one other book that not even George saw, and that was my book. It was just a little harmless-looking date book, small enough to keep in a man's breast pocket, which is where I kept mine.

In it, I maintained a running tally of our cash on hand, adding and subtracting as necessary until the product got too big to hide, and then I sent it somewhere nice and safe. You'd be amazed at how quickly numbers can add up, so just in case you think I'm bragging, here are a few choice entries from 1929:

George and Owen, $5,000. That was our cut of the various operations. We always made sure that, no matter what happened, we got paid and we split it square. That's why there was never no trouble between us. Everybody should have a friend like George. George lived pretty frugally, but he had a beautiful girlfriend named Jane. I mean she was some dame, a dame and a half, and he swathed her shape in ermines and furs, and I mean mink and beaver and rabbit and fox, until pretty soon she started referring to herself as Mrs. Fox, and that's how George got his alias, Mr. Fox.

Back, Jack Diamond, $500. Maybe I was a soft touch and maybe I was a born diplomat, but one of the ways I kept the peace for so long was to always lend a mook a nickel or a dime if he needed it. I never let a guy get too deep into me, nor I into him, because serious indebtedness leads first to gratitude, then to resentment and finally to murder. But I did believe in keeping guys on a string, in order to ensure civility. No mug worth a mother's tears would welsh on a little debt, nor would he kill for one. If Dutch wanted Jack dead, that was his problem—well, so did I, but not after I was good and through with him, which meant through making a buck off him.

Loan Harry Block, $5,000. Harry was my manager at the Cotton Club and I wanted him to be happy. He was making me too much money for him to be otherwise, and if he liked dames and ponies, well, didn't everyone? His boss was Herman Stark, who also oversaw the Abbey, which was in the Hotel Harding, and later on the Stork, where that Okie Sherman Billingsley was our front man.

Rent, Silver Slipper, $506, and cheap at the price. The Slipper was a money machine; after the theaters let out, folks would come pouring in for a glass of champagne and a show of near-naked girls. Cover charge was two bucks, three on Saturday, the food and drinks were good and expensive and the floor show . . . Granny found the girls and wrote the revues, whose highlight was always an "Oriental Slave Ballet," which mostly consisted of getting the girls into as little clothing as the law allowed. Bunny Hill, Virginia Magee, Myrtle Allen, Ripples Covert. Best of all was Beryl Halley, all class even when she was practically starkers. Which was the way I liked her.

Loan George McManus, $10,000. You may have read about Hump McManus, a good friend. He was in the poker game at the Park Central with Nigger Nate Raymond and Titanic Thompson the night Arnold Rothstein welshed on $320,000. A few weeks later—the night Hoover beat Al Smith, in fact—Arnold laid down half a million bucks on the Republican, then never collected on account of he went and got himself shot in Hump's rooms at the Park Central and died over at the Polyclinic Hospital. Hump and Nigger Nate both beat the rap, and I was there to help them out. No sense any more trouble. Besides, I didn't want anyone to think I had something to do with it. I liked Arnold. I really did.

Israel Levy, $10,000. A business partner and good friend who helped me operate the Hydrox Laundry on Hooper Street in Williamsburg, Brooklyn. The tax man said I needed a job to explain my income so I bought one.

For Laundry, $72,000. It was amazing how handy laundries were when it came to laundering money.

Loan Van Higgins, $2,000. Vannie was a "lobster fisherman" from Brooklyn. I never saw no lobsters in Brooklyn, and I suspect Vannie didn't neither. He'd worked for both Legs and Dutch in the rum-running enterprises and was now laboring for me. He and I were taking aeroplane flying lessons together. I never really got the hang of flying, but Vannie was pretty good.

Downtown, $8,915. What the Tiger owed me that week for services rendered.

Father Cashin, $500. I believed in taking care of the padre, even if I hardly ever went to Mass.

Loan, Frank Costello, $10,000, about whom more later. We were getting mighty chummy, even though he was a wop with an Irish name.

Flowers, $100. I sent a lot of flowers.

Hiram and Maid, $2,000. Never spent money better in my life.

Joe Shalleck, $5,000. Lawyers were expensive, but they were worth it, until they weren't.

Owen Yonkers, $200. Rent on Loretta's place. Margaret was seventeen years old that year. I wondered what she looked like, whether she looked like me, and what her mother told her.

Duesenberg Car, $7,000. A Model J Murphy, J-211 to be exact, a bargain (the dealer was a friend, plus he owed me), and you can just eat your heart out. They didn't come any better than a Doozy, especially in our line of work, and this one was a real dilly. Two hundred and sixty-five horses squeezed into eight cylinders, two overhead camshafts; that little darlin' could do 89 miles per hour in second gear, and once I hit a top speed of 116 on the open road. Complete with speedometer, ammeter, tachometer, brake-pressure gauge, altimeter and barometer, plus a stopwatch that worked right down to the split second. You could have her fitted out however you liked, with gold fixtures, leather interiors, vanity case, passenger instruments, radios, bars. Some of them were even upholstered in silk. And quiet? You could sneak up on a mug so softly that he'd be dead before he heard the motor. I loved that baby. Still miss her.

Sent Away to Europe, $124,000. I also parked money in Florida, mostly in the racetracks.

Loan Jim Braddock, $500. One of my fighters, along with Primo Camera and Maxie Rosenbloom. The first two became heavyweight champs of the world. Slapsey Maxie was a light-heavy who couldn't punch his way out of a paper bag, but beat Slattery for the title in 1930. They both always needed money. All fighters always need money. Everybody needs money.

Cops, $200. I rest my case.

Trenton, $10,000. We owned Jersey then. Still do.

But the thing that made 1929 such a truly swell year was this: that's the year I finally realized my dream of all us immigrant boys—harp, hebe and dago—stopping battling for a while and getting together. The place was Atlantic City and there we changed this country forever. You may not read about it in the history books, so that's why I'm tellin' you now.

Forty-Seven

ALTHOUGH BUSINESS WAS SURE ENOUGH good for me, it wasn't much good for my family life. I mean, without Loretta and Margaret, the only family I had was my Ma and Marty and May, but things had got so busy that I frankly was neglecting my duties. I guess I made the mistake that most men make, that of thinking that just because you're working hard for your womenfolk, they don't need something else as well.

I was deep in conversation with Stark and Harry Block one early summer afternoon about the upcoming meeting of the Seven Group down on the Jersey Shore. This was a gang of gangsters comprised of Frank Costello and Lucky Luciano from Manhattan; Joey Adonis, who thought he looked like a Greek god, representing Brooklyn; Longy Zwillman, who was my man in Jersey; Waxey Gordon and Nig Rosen from Philly; Lansky and Siegel; Johnny Torrio, the old Five Pointer who had trained Capone in Chicago; and Nucky Johnson, who was a hood who happened to get himself elected Mayor of Atlantic City, which is why the meeting was going to be held on his turf.

"I dunno, Owney," said Stark. "What if it's a setup?"

"They're all friends, Herman."

"You don't have any friends. Nobody does, in our business."

"What about you?"

"I'm different. I can't do what you do. They can."

"And do," added Harry Block.

"It ain't just gonna be them," I said. "We're inviting the Dutchman—"

"That crazy sonofabitch," grunted Stark.

"Capone, Greasy Thumb Guzik and their pal Moe Annenberg are comin' in from Chi-town—"

"Annenberg the newspaper shtarker?" asked Harry.

"He ain't sluggin' no more. Moe's a big shot now. Cooking up a race-wire scheme that I want in on. Plus Abie Bernstein and his Purple Gang from Detroit, Moe Dalitz from Cleveland—"

"Great, more Jews," said Harry Block. Harry was of the opinion that there were enough Jews in the rackets already, without there being more.

I looked over at him. His seegar was working overtime. "When are you going straight, Harry? Be sure to tell me in advance so I can get a new manager."

"Too late for me, but one of my kids is going to City College."

"You call that goin' straight?" asked Herman.

I continued my litany. "Danny Walsh from Providence, John Lazia fronting for the Pendergast operation in K.C."

Herman whistled. "Quite a group. What about Maranzano and Masseria?"

Now, there was the big question. The M&M boys were currently battling each other for supremacy of the old Italian Black Hand. They thought it was a big deal, but as far as I was concerned that was yesterday's news.

I liked Joe the Boss, I did business with him. To my mind, he was far smarter than that preening popinjay Maranzano, who thought he was some kind of Sicilian don, and who disparaged Costello because Frank was from Calabria instead of Sicily. That's the kind of chump Salvatore Maranzano was, goofy for Sicilians when he should have had an eye for talent from any-where. It was an expensive mistake to make for a guy whose dream was to be *capo di tutti capi,* boss of all the bosses in woptalk.

"Ain't coming. Too old-fashioned." I settled back into my chair. "I remem-ber the days when the politicians used to pull us around by our ears. Burn this newsstand, slug this ape, keep these fellas away from the polls, make sure this guy votes early and often. Now we call the tune and they jig to it. Look around. Nobody gets elected in Kansas City without Tom Pendergast's say-so, Capone has Big Bill Thompson in his waistcoat pocket and Tammany's got its claws so far into Al Smith and his boy Frank Roosevelt that it ain't funny."

"I don't trust that cripple," said Stark. "Look what he's done for Al, and us, since he got elected governor last year—nothin'."

"Aw, he's okay. In fact," I said proudly, "I've written to him, asking for a complete pardon for my manslaughter rap. Clean jacket, that's what I'm lookin' for, and I have every reason to believe I'm going to get it."

"Never happen," said Herman. "Bet you a hundred bucks."

We shook hands on it, and I steered the subject back to Atlantic City. "Nucky's hosting, puttin' everybody up at the best hotel—the Breakers."

"I thought that dump was restricted," said Harry. "No Jews, no Catholics." He looked across the table. "None of us could get in there, that's for sure."

"Nucky's got it all fixed," I said, looking at my watch. "George and I'll leave next week and when we come back—well, things is going to be different, all over the country."

"I'll believe it when I see it," said Harry, lighting another seegar from the glowing stub of the old one.

The Duke and his orchestra were sounding great, we had a swell lineup of talent and our girls was prettier than ever. The Dutchman was having some serious trouble with the colored policy makers he was tryin' to displace—I'm talking about Brunder, Pompez, Joe Ison and their muscleman, Bumpy Johnson—not to mention that hex queen Stephanie St. Clair, who some said put a spell on Dutch, but to me lead poisoning is lead poisoning and voodoo has nothing to do with it. I didn't want any of our coloreds getting involved, because I knew most of 'em played the policy rackets—colored people always did—and I also knew sure as shooting that Dutch and Abbadabba were cheating them blind, and when word like that gets out, that is a surefire way to start trouble.

One day I'd caught Hiram with a bunch of policy slips in his hand. "Where you goin' with those?" I asked.

"Droppin' 'em off for my mama."

"Shouldn't ought to play policy, you know that."

"I know that, Mr. Owney."

"Then what the hell you let your mama play for?"

"She jes' likes to is all."

"Well, don't let me see you throwing away my money on stuff like that."

"Okay, Mr. Owney."

I don't know whether Hiram paid me any mind, but one thing I did know was that you couldn't win at policy, which was also called the numbers racket. Poor Negroes picked a three-digit number from 100 to 999 and put a penny or a nickel on its nose. If you hit, the payoff was 500 to 1. So that was a gyp right there. The winning number was supposed to be the last three digits of the handle at one racetrack or another, which was published in the newspapers the next day. Otto Berman figured out a way to pay off only on penny-ante stuff, and cheat big winners, by checking all the policy slips and then getting a bet down by wire and changing the tote at the last minute. The suckers never knew what they was missin'.

Anyway, I didn't want this policy war between Dutch and the colored boys getting any wider. Ever since Little Patsy, I'd tried to keep my irish in check whenever possible, but when Bert the doorman give me a sign, and then Harry all of a sudden stopped talking, and I saw Legs Diamond and his brother Eddie in my club, well, I thought about firing Bert on the spot, except I figured he was scared of Legs, and you'd be too, in his place. Legs had been pointedly not invited to our little beach party, and the last thing I needed was to have him spotted in here.

I was up and out of my seat in a flash, just as Legs and Eddie sat down at a table. One of the waiters saw me coming and vamoosed pronto, which left Legs waving his hands in the air, and I was just hoping and praying he'd start to shout or something, because then I could throw him right out on his arse, but he kept his gob shut just long enough for me to get there and for him to see me.

"No Irish need apply," I said as unfriendly as possible. I still hadn't forgotten that shot he took at me when he was just a punk, even though I was one slug to the good as far as he was concerned.

Legs just about laughed in my face. "You know my brother, Eddie."

"He can't apply either. Only colored in the band, on the stage and in uniform. Plus we don't hire geeks, spastics or cripples."

Legs looked around the room at all the beautiful girls getting ready for the evening's acts. "Thought I might find our mutual nonfriend the Flegenheiming Dutchman in here instead." I swear he was about to put his feet up on one of my tables, then thought the better of it. I wished Frenchy and his shotgun were both here.

"Why don'tcha try one a his joints?"

Legs gave me that nasty little smile of his. "Yours are better."

"If it's Dutch you're looking for, take it elsewhere, Jack," I said. "I don't allow trouble at the Cotton Club. Besides, ain't you got enough lead in you already? You're the only guy I know's been shot more than me."

"Just a little friendly chat," said Eddie.

"You don't know how to have a friendly chat, Eddie," I said. "The only thing you know how to do is exchange gunfire, which I'm not particularly in the mood to do with you right now. Maybe later."

A waiter hovered. "These gentlemen are leaving soon," I barked and turned back to Legs.

"How the hell could you shoot Red Cassidy and his pals right in the Hotsy-Totsy? Your own club? And then rub out your own bartender and waiter so they couldn't testify? No wonder nobody trusts you—Jesus, he's spitting up blood." Eddie had TB, as everybody knew, and everybody knew it was going to kill him unless everybody else did first.

Eddie's coughing spell was terrible. Blood was coming out of his mouth and dribbling down his chin. Legs threw his arm around his brother to help him through the spell, and I guess the only nice thing I can say about Jack Diamond was that he was a family man, like myself.

At last Eddie managed to get himself under control. "He's okay," said Legs, "just needs a little fresh air is all. We're going up to our place in the Catskills tomorrow."

"I'll have one of the boys drive you. Every cop from here to Albany'll be on the lookout for your cars."

Legs looked at me crossways. "We'll make it." Then he glanced up and over my left shoulder.

"I think maybe you boys ought to beat it," said big George, and was I ever glad to see him, looming over skinny little Legs. He was wearing his great-coat, which meant his shotgun was cuddled up alongside his right leg.

"Why we gettin' the air?" snarled Legs. "Ain't I buying my beer and booze from you now?" That part was true. The fight between him and the Dutch-man meant I was now his major supplier, and I appreciated his business.

I turned to George. "Keep an eye on Eddie. Legs, let's you and me go upstairs, where it's nice and private."

Legs and I walked to the back of the house and then up my private stair-case, which led out onto the roof. I always had two men stationed there, to prevent anybody from sneaking up on me. They grabbed Legs as he came through the door.

"What's the big idea?" There was no fear in Legs Diamond's eyes, I had to give him that.

"Relax. If I wanted to kill you, you'd already be dead." The boys had come up with two pistols, a blackjack and a throwing knife. "They're just going to relieve you of your artillery for a while."

It was a clear, cool evening up on the roof. The lights of the city glowed bright to the south, fading away as Manhattan stretched north. To the east, the Bronx twinkled, and for some reason in that instant I thought about Monk and his battle with Kelly way back, and hadn't the Bronx changed since then. Everything had changed, but everything was still the same and I was trying like hell to hang on to it.

I made my way over to my pigeons, with Legs following, and took out a bird. It was a Giant Runt, sort of like Legs himself, or maybe Dutch. Diamond and Schultz may have hated each other, but they were birds of a feather just the same. I tossed him up in the air, and off he flew, circling the roof and then heading south, disappearing into the night.

"He's on his way down to the Lower East Side," I told Legs. "The old Five Points. I keep some coops down there, visit the birds from time to time, get a whiff of the old days. You don't remember the old days, Legs."

"I worked for Little Augie Orgen, didn't I?"

"Fat lot of good it did him too. I guess you couldn't help it Lepke and Shapiro shot him so hard his hat flew off his head."

"They shot me too."

I was still looking out over the roof, to the south. "That's just my point. You're slowin' down. You been hit too many times."

"Bullet ain't been cast with my name on it."

"I used to think that. Then I got eleven of 'em, special delivery."

"Didn't kill ya, did they?"

I thought about what Dr. Sweet had told me, about the pains I still felt. "Not yet."

I turned back to Jack, who looked bored. "Listen to me closely, Jack, because I'm only going to say this once and I'll deny that I ever said it if anybody asks. This thing between Schultz and you is going to end badly, for both of you and for all of us. Do you know why? Because Lepke and Gurrah Shapiro and the Bug and Meyer Mob are tougher and hungrier than we are—"

"Buncha Jews, running with the guineas—"

"—and in this business it's the hungry and wise who eat the foolish and well fed. You got your rackets upstate—hell, you practically own Albany—so my advice to you is get back up there and leave the rackets down here to people who can handle 'em. I don't plan to stay forever, but I sure as hell do plan to get out alive."

Legs bristled. "Think I'm going to let a few sheenies push me around?"

"It's not just the Jews, Jack. They ain't long for the rackets themselves. You've seen their kids, smart kids, who work hard and are goin' places. How long do you think they'll want to stay in the rackets, killing and being killed, when they take their law degrees from City College and relieve mugs like us of our cash, right up to the minute they strap us to Old Sparky and fry us?"

Legs snorted. "You scared, Madden?"

That offended me. I didn't have to prove my courage to this punk. I kept my temper as I replied: 'No, I'm not scared. I'm smart. Smarter than you, leastways . . .'"

"Sounds to me like it's you who should be thinking about retirement."

I took a deep breath and gave him one last chance. "Long time ago I worked for Monk Eastman. 'Prince of the Gangsters,' the newspapers called him. Toughest guy I ever met, who'd put you in the hospital soon as look at ya. Like a father to me . . ."

"Ancient history."

"Shut up and listen, you dumb harp. Monk and his gang fought that wop Paul Kelly and his Five Pointers to a draw. There were tough Jews in those days, and there still are tough Jews. Benny Siegel is as tough as they come, and little Lansky is even tougher, you wouldn't know it to look at him. But they're on the wrong side of history. The Italians are coming—"

"You talking about Maranzano and Masseria? Them Mustache Petes? They're too busy killing each other off to give us grief."

"Eventually they'll succeed. There'll be a power vacuum on the East Side. And who's going to take their place? Not an Irishman or a Jew. No, it'll be someone like Frank Costello or Joey Adonis or even Masseria's boy Lucky. Guys like us, we gotta decide whether we're going to go graceful or go bloody."

Legs ground his cigarette into the roof. "I was right—you are yellow."

"Have it your way, smart guy."

"Tell that punk Schultz I want to see him."

"Watch out for Dutch. He's meaner and crazier than you are."

"Ever hear of the luck of the Irish?"

That almost made me laugh. "Sure I have," I said. "We got plenty of luck. Only problem is it's all bad. Good or bad, in the end it's all bad. A real Irishman knows that. A stupid one forgets it."

"Forget it," said Legs, looking at his watch. "I gotta go get my girl. She can't sneak out until her mother goes to bed."

I chuckled. "Ma thinks she's still a virgin, I bet."

He chuckled harder. "Not just Mom."

So there you have it. I tried to warn him, but some harps are dumber than others, and Jack Diamond was sure one of 'em. So was I, because I didn't figure it out until a few days later, after I got back from Atlantic City, when I went to visit my Mother.

Chapter

Forty-Eight

THE FAMOUS ATLANTIC CITY conference got off to a comic opera start. Nucky Johnson may have been the Mayor, but the desk clerk at the Breakers had all the clout the day we checked in.

I was in the lobby talking with Frenchy when I saw Capone and Jake Guzik coming through the door. Al wasn't all that tall but he was plenty big, and besides, how could anyone miss the scar? Frank Galluccio gave it to him free gratis when the Big Fella made a smart remark to Galluccio's sister at Frankie Yale's Harvard Club. We had gallantry in them days. Of course the Big Fella ended up hiring Galluccio and murdering Yale, born Uale—that's the way the cookie crumbles.

The Thumb was nattering on about something in that thick Chicago-Russian-Jewish accent of his. How Capone, who didn't speak so good himself, understood him I'll never figure out. I featured the food stains on the Thumb's tie, and I knew there'd be trouble as soon as they came toe-to-toe with Osgood, a little chicken in a bow tie who was manning the reception desk and even now giving them the old fisheye as they approached.

"Mr. Brown from Chicago," smiled Big Al. "And my associate, Mr. Smith."

Osgood—it didn't matter whether that was his first, last or middle name, he had to be Osgood—pretended to look through his reservation book, but I saw him slip his hand under the desk where I assumed the buzzer was, to summon help.

"Get Nucky. Fast," says I.

No matter if Frenchy could've run like Bronko Nagurski, he wouldn'ta been fast enough, because at this moment along comes Luciano and Little Man Lansky, who greet the Big Fella like long-lost friends, and the clerk just shakes his head and then whispers something in the ear of the manager, who's showed up by now, and the two of them make a big fuss of flipping through the reservation book and finally the manager looks up just as Capone turns his attention to him, and I'm wondering if the manager has his life insurance paid up good and proper, how many next of kin he might leave behind, etc., and then I see the manager shake his head, sorrowful, and he says:

"I'm terribly sorry Mr., er, Brown, but—"

"Who the—who're you?" asks Al.

"I'm Mr. Billinghurst, the manager," says he. "Unfortunately we have absolutely no record of any reservation in that name."

"Must be some kinda mistake on your part," says Capone. "Fix it, before I—" Greasy Thumb jabs him in the side with his elbow, because we're not supposed to put the finger on Nucky, for appearance purposes.

"You're certainly right about that," agrees the manager, working hard to save his life and not even knowing it. "Brown is a, er, common name and . . . let me see . . . Brown, Brown . . ."

"Before I get unhappy," says Al.

The manager gives him a big phony Protestant smile. "We wouldn't want that now, would we, Mr. Brown?" says Billinghurst, drawing out the diphthong. The best part of this farce is that Billinghurst is probably the only man in America who doesn't recognize Al Capone. The St. Valentine's Day Massacre had been just a couple of months earlier. Everybody in the land had seen the photos of the seven stiffs lyin' in puddles of blood against that garage wall on Clark Street, and everybody and his sister Sadie made Capone for the brains behind the rubout, and still this mug doesn't get the picture. Well, they say ignorance is bliss.

The manager shakes his head like his dog just died. "I'm terribly sorry for the inconvenience, but I'm afraid we'll have to make other arrangements for you, at a hotel more . . . suitable."

You don't think of Capone at a loss, but here he was. Lansky says:

"Somethin' wrong?" Luciano says:

"This mug givin' ya a hard time?" while Guzik says:

"C'mon, Al, let's take a walk," and just then who but Johnson comes struttin' in like he owns the dump, which he unfortunately don't. Johnson was a big fella, bigger than the Big Fella himself, which was a good thing for him considering what was about to occur.

". . . I'm fairly certain that the Ritz or the Ambassador will have accommodations that will be to your liking," Billinghurst is saying. Johnson is sidling up, real smooth, like he's going to take care of everything, but Capone steps in front of him and blocks his path. I see Al's scar is gleaming white, which it did when he got mad, which was pretty often.

"What the fuck are you tryin' to pull here, Nucky?" says Capone, loud enough to freeze blood.

"Calm down, Mr. Brown," says Johnson, still trying to pretend everything's jake.

"Relax, Al," says Jake, hoping that everything's gonna turn out ducky.

"I ain't gonna calm down, you miserable piece a shit," says Al to Nucky.

"Settle down, Big Fella," says Luciano, trying to intervene.

"We're businessmen, with business to transact," reminds Lansky, trailing behind.

I guess Nucky didn't like Al's choice of words. "Who are you calling a piece of shit, you fucking gorilla?" he replies, and then I thought the two of 'em was going to go at it, right there, and let me tell you, hand-to-hand, no weapons, I think Johnson might've taken him. "This is my town and I ain't gonna let no guinea goombah from Chicago push me around."

"Jesus, I ought to put Nucky in the ring with Carnera," I said to George, who was once again by my side.

"You'll need a good undercard," said Frenchy calmly. "Take him out in one punch."

So you got all these big guys and all these little guys screamin' and yellin' and the manager is shouting something about calling the cops and Johnson is shouting something about being the Mayor, he owns the fucking cops, and now the manager finally figures out who the hell he's dealing with and what little color he had in his face drains all the way down to his shoes, whereas Osgood is nowhere to be seen, no dope he, and all the guests are heading for the exits as fast as they can and meanwhile more gangsters are showing up, including the Purple Gang Jews who let me tell you do not look anything like Osgood or Mr. Billinghurst and then here comes the Dutchman and I figure that's all we need, it's just a matter of time before somebody breaks out his heater and then we really got trouble.

'Twas Lansky what broke it up. The little yiddeleh somehow manages to interpose himself between Johnson and Capone and like a sheepdog starts shooin' 'em both toward the front door, where the limousines are still idling. He steers Capone into one just as the cop cars pull up, sirens going full blast, and there's that fool Billinghurst, who's got more guts than brains, pointing, and Johnson waving at the cops to stand down. Meyer gets the back door of the limo open and Nucky gives Al a shove into the backseat and slams the door. "The Ritz," he says, and the car roars off.

That was the first day.

I heard that when they got to the Ritz, Capone was still ape, even after they got him up to his room, rippin' the pictures off the walls and generally carrying on. I think that's when it struck me that maybe he was going a little squirrelly on us, which turned out to be true. Dose of syph he got from one of the teenage whores he'd made into a mistress back in Cicero. Some said it was the tax-evasion case that drove him over the edge, turned him into the Wop with the Mop on the Rock, but you ask me it was her. Beauty-and-the-beast type of thing.

Speaking of which, once everybody was settled in, I sent for Mary Frances. Dutch had turned his attention to some other woman not his wife, and what the hell the kid really loved me, or said she did, so I brought her down on the train and who should show up with her but Georgie Ranft and one of my pugilists, Maxie Rosenbloom. They all spent most of the time on the beach, very sharp in their new bathing costumes, and Georgie turned so many pretty heads that I really didn't have to worry overmuch about his getting his paws on my frail. I introduced Mary Frances around the gang, and so she met Meyer and Frank Costello and of course Charlie Lucky.

The next day, once everybody was set up at their rightful hotels, and the damage at the Ritz had been repaired, we met stag at one of Johnson's dumps near the Boardwalk. It was a big banquet room in the President Hotel, the kind you seen in the movies about us, with a head table and a bunch of hoods including myself sitting at the wings. By agreement, Lansky and Johnny T. were the hosts. Torrio even led us Catholics in a prayer before we started. Then Lansky got up, took a sip of water and spoke.

"Gentlemen," he said, "we stand today on the precipice of a new order in America. The world is ours, if only we got it in us to take it."

"Not to mention keep it," said the Dutchman, who was already drinking.

Lansky ignored him. Even though they were all brother Hebrews, there was no love lost between Dutch and the rest of the Jews. Dutch was a pretzel, the kind whose folks came from Germany, while Lansky and the rest had come out of villages in Poland and places even worse. I never heard Dutch say a nice word about any of 'em, called 'em kikes and whatnot, which was a mistake, as things turned out.

"Lemme tell you a little story," continues Lansky. "Happened back on the Lower East Side when Benny and I were kids."

"Where is Benny?" shouted someone, maybe Joey Adonis, maybe Lepke, I dunno.

"Prob'ly banging some broad," said somebody else, maybe King Solomon from Boston, mighta been Nig Rosen, I forget.

Lansky held up his hand for quiet. "He's traveling. The point is Benny was entertaining a young lady in some old warehouse—"

"What a romantic," says Chuck Polizzi, Dalitz's partner in Cleveland.

"—when in walks Charlie Lucky, back when he was still Salvatore, fresh off the boat. You all know what a gentleman Charlie is. Well, he sees Benny on top of this broad and he mistakes her squeals of delight for cries for help, so he grabs a two-by-four and starts remonstrating with Benny about his head and shoulders."

"Beat some sense into the Bug, maybe," says my old pal Boo Boo Hoff, which gets Meyer's attention.

"Out of him is more like it," says Abie Bernstein. "Jeez, that guy—"

"You know Benny don't like nicknames, Boo Boo," says the Little Man. "Anyway, Charlie is whacking Benny pretty good, and the dame really does start yelling now, so in I rush and see Charlie whaling on Benny." I noticed Luciano smiling at the memory.

"I'm on top of Charlie in a flash. I don't care if Charlie starts beating on me too, as long as he lays off my friend Benny. Charlie turns to me and is about to conk me a good one. Then he gets a good look at me and starts laughing at the little runt who wants to fight him."

"I was laughing so hard I never seen the punch from Benny coming," says Lucky.

"Benny popped him a good one and they both went down," says Meyer. "When they got up, we all decided to shake on it, be friends, and we have been, from that moment on."

"What happened to the broad?" asks Vince Mangano.

"Who cares what happened to the broad?" says Lansky. "She was just a broad. The point is, even back then, we realized that we had to work together if we were going to get anywhere. What was the point of Charlie Lucky shaking down Jewish kids for protection when we could all join up and really make things happen? And you know who watched over all of us, gave us counsel, wise advice? This fine man on my left, Johnny Torrio. Take a bow, Johnny."

Johnny stood up and everybody broke into wild applause. He was a mild, dapper sort of fellow, the kind of guy you'd expect to find running a shop somewhere, or maybe selling you a life assurance policy. Everybody liked Johnny, even his former protégé Capone, who had tried to kill him in Chicago but just ended up retiring him back to Brooklyn, best thing that ever happened to him, really. Johnny bowed and then indicated Capone, who'd motioned to be heard. "Go ahead, Al," said Meyer.

Capone rose and scratched his nose for a minute. "You all know how much I like baseball," he began.

That got everybody's attention. Just a month or so earlier, Capone had personally beat to death two of his best triggermen, Giovanni Scalise and Alberto Anselmi, and another mug named Hop Toad Giunta—some say with a baseball bat, others with an Indian war club. Anselmi and Scalise were the torpedoes who popped the great Dion O'Banion right there in his North Side flower shop. That had pretty much decided the war between the Irish and the Italians in Chicago, and the St. Valentine's Day Massacre was the icing on the cake. They say in Chicago that Scalise and Anselmi were the best, even better than Machine Gun McGurn and Golf Bag Hunt, of the North Side mob.

"In fact, as a youth in Brooklyn, I played a little myself. Still got a pretty good swing." Nervous laughter, big smile. "Or so they tell me. You should hear them cheer me at Cubs games." He took a beat, then boomed: "And booin' that bum Hoover!" The mugs loved that, let me tell you.

Now—and this is the part you won't believe—Capone reaches under his chair and I swear I don't know how it got there but he comes up with a Louisville Slugger, the real McCoy, moves to the front of the room and takes a couple of practice swipes. I could see the smiles frozen on Lansky's and Torrio's faces like old Happy Jack's puss. I also saw a couple of the honored guests reach inside their monkey-suit jackets and then remember that all heaters had been checked at the door, for insurance purposes.

Even though most of us weren't American citizens, and I include myself in that group, since I was still holding a British passport, we were patriotic. Behind the dais there was a big American flag, all forty-eight stars on it, plus framed pictures of the Jersey Governor, whoever he was, and President Hoover.

"First I heard of this meetin'," said Capone, "I didn't like it one bit. Thought it might be a con job, a setup." Whoosh went the bat. "Or, worse, a hit."

Pow! Capone got good wood on the Jersey Governor, knocking the picture from its holder and sending it flyin'. "Now," says Capone, barely breaking a sweat, "I know it's a hit. In fact . . ."

"Mr. Brown" wandered back over to the head table. I think I remember seeing Johnny T. flinch a little, but Lansky he never budged, never even blinked. I guess he figured if he was going to get it, he was going to get it and he might as well check out with his dignity intact, if not his head.

"In fact," Capone said with that big scarfaced grin, "it's a home run!"

I never saw anybody swing a bat harder, and that included the Bambino.

Capone hit the portrait of Hoover so hard it flew into a million shards of shite, which is what all politicians deserve, in my opinion.

Al dropped the bat and I swear you never saw such a look of relief on the mugs of grown men. He held out both empty hands to his audience, like an opera singer soaking up applause, and boy oh boy did everybody cheer, like their lives depended on it.

I was surprised when the next mug to rise was none other than Big Frenchy, who besides Nucky was just about the only fella in the joint bigger than the Big Fella. George wasn't as crazy as Al, but his size commanded respect, if his elocution didn't.

"Um . . . ," he began looking over at me. "Say, Owen, have you got your watch with you?"

I had no idea what he was trying to say, but I held up my wrist to show I was wearing it. It was a fine little piece that had fallen off a truck a couple of years back, and it kept good time too.

"Mind if I take a look at it?"

I looked around the room, but everybody seemed to be in on the racket excepting for me. Maybe I don't have much of a sense of humor, but the last time I looked around a room at unsmiling gangster faces, I got it but good.

I slipped the timepiece off my wrist and handed it to the man next to me, Boo Boo Hoff, who passed it along to Mangano and so on up to the dais and Frenchy.

"Nice," said George, dropping it on the floor and crushing it under his weight.

There wasn't a sound in the room then.

"Aw, gee, Owen, I'm sorry about breaking your watch," said Frenchy.

He crammed one huge mitt into his pocket, fished something out and held it up for all to see.

It was a real beaut, a Swiss baby with a solid gold wristband. Even at a distance I could see my name spelled out with diamonds across the band.

"Here's another one for you." I could feel the color coming back into my face. "From me and the boys, for makin' all this possible. You're a real pal."

I rose as steady as I could, the watch making its way down the ranks toward me. I pushed it over my wrist and thrust my left arm into the air.

I had never had so much applause in my life.

We broke up into smaller groups then, carving up the territory of the United States of America for ourselves. One thing we all agreed on was that neither Maranzano nor Masseria was going to have any part in our plan, nor was Legs Diamond. Charlie Lucky passed the death sentence on all three of them, even though at that time he was technically still working for Joe the Boss. I liked Joe; he didn't have much class—he rivaled the Thumb in the amount of chow he could slop on his shirtfront—but he was an okay grease-ball in my book. Still, if Charlie Lucky said he had to go, then he had to go.

General Motors or U.S. Steel couldn'ta done a better job than we did in splitting up territories. All the big East Coast bosses got theirs, Boston, Philly, Jersey. New York was big enough for everybody, and so Charlie and Meyer took the East Side, Lepke took Brooklyn, I took the West Side, the Dutch-man got uptown and the Bronx and we all took pieces of Staten Island. Dalitz had Cleveland and a chunk of the Midwest, while the Big Fella retained Chicago, with the proviso that he finish off Joey Aiello the way he did the Terrible Gennas—Mike the Devil, Bloody Angelo, Tony the Gentleman and the rest of them—which he did the next year. California was declared an open state.

There was one other caveat for Big Al: thanks to the Massacre, the heat was on, even though he was disportin' himself at his estate on Palm Island at the time. Everybody felt—okay, Lansky felt—that Capone would be doing us all a favor if he gave himself up on something piddling like a gun charge and do a year at the Eastern States Federal Penitentiary in Philly, to which he agreed. It was a good example for all of us, and especially for me.

So the conference, which began so badly, ended up pretty well. We had established the Combination, or the Syndicate, or the Outfit, or the Com-mission, whatever you want to call it. At the final banquet Al and Nucky even embraced each other, like they was brothers, and then everybody went home.

Speaking of brothers, did you know one of Capone's brothers was a law-man? We didn't either, but since he never bothered any of us, it didn't matter. Just shows to go you, though, that sometimes you can't even trust a member of your own family.

Chapter

Forty-Nine

I GOT HOME AROUND NOON and the first thing I did was go visit the old lady. All them mugs had got me to thinkin' about the finer things in life, of which women were most definitely included. And after disportin' myself with Mary Frances, I was feeling the need for a less profane form of female contact.

"Hiya, Ma," I said, blithe as all get-out. I threw my hat on the table and headed straight for one of the easy chairs. A picture of my Father stood on a table beside it. "Hiya, Pop," I said to the old photograph.

The view out the window was spectacular. She and my sister could see all the way across town, all the way to the East River. "Long way from Ireland, huh, Ma?"

Atlantic City had got me all jaunty this particular afternoon, but Ma more than counterbalanced me. Usually she was quiet, the more so as she got older, but this afternoon she was mousier than usual. Folks from the west of Ireland usually don't have a lot to say under the most garrulous of circumstances and these weren't them.

"Maybe not so far as you might think."

I had no idea what she meant by that, but in my long experience with Ma, either she'd explain herself or she wouldn't and there wasn't much I could do about it except wait.

I swept my arm toward the picture window. "You're telling me you'd have all this if you'da stayed back home?" I felt like making an exception to my abstinence and pouring myself a celebratory drink—whiskey and soda were always on the sideboard, in crystal decanters, at my behest—but I refrained. She didn't.

One thing I had to give Ma was that she could always hold her liquor. Years of practice, I guess. "Maybe not all this," she said, and I started to nod. It's always nice for a boy to finally put one over on his Ma. But she wasn't finished.

"Maybe not this fancy furniture. Maybe not this big flat and this fine view, although what the use of that is I'm sure I can't tell ya. Maybe not this money you give me either, cash money it is too. But there's plenty of things I would have back in Ireland."

I walked facefirst into it like a common palooka into a roundhouse right. "For instance?"

She sat down, hard, in the other chair, and I could see she was beginning to look and feel her age. "I'd still have an eldest son already defeated by life, who consorted wit' bad companions, couldn't hold a job and barely keep himself out of jail."

She had me there, but she was just warming to her subject.

"I'd still have an unmarried daughter, searchin' for a man who could stay sober past noon and who wouldn't beat her when he finally came home, smellin' of liquor and lipstick."

Another shot to the chin. "High time to work on that." I still found it hard to think of my sister as a woman.

She gave me a quick, darting look that sent a shiver through my heart. "Maybe it's after high time you did."

I stood toe-to-toe with her and got ready to take her knockout punch. "What else would you still have?"

She took a deep, exhausted breath. "I'd still have a rebel son who thought he was smarter than everybody else and maybe he was, until one day he found out the hard way he wasn't. A son who'd shamed me by his actions, who disgraced the family name. And I'd still be sittin' home, no matter how humble, waiting for the day they brought him home to me, wrapped in a sheet, suitable for buryin'."

I tried to put up my dukes, but I was already out on my feet.

"There is one other thing I'd still have."

"What?"

"I'd still have my husband."

Down I went, face first onto the slippery canvas. Which is where I was when the door opened and my sister came into the room.

"Hiya, sis," I mustered.

She didn't seem glad to see me; in fact, she was surprised, like I'd caught her at something she shouldn't oughta do. I would have figured something was amiss right then and there, except that something else was even more amiss.

May was still wearing evening clothes, party clothes, her cheeks were red and flushed, her breathing heavy, and there was a big welt across her bare shoulders.

Every fight I ever saw, even the ones I fixed, a man only had but one single opponent, and when he went down, there was a ref to step in quick and prevent further clobbering, but this bout was different.

May and I just looked at each other for a moment, and if two minutes ago I'd realized that I'd never really known my Ma, then you can imagine my mystification when May double-teamed me and threw the kayo.

"I'm going ta bed now," she said, trying to sweep by me, or step right over me.

I was on her in a flash, grabbing her by her naked shoulders and shaking her, trying to shake some sense into her, some sobriety, some fear maybe, I didn't know what. "Where the hell have you been?" I shouted.

"Owen . . . ," said my mother.

"Shut up, Ma! Where you been?"

May pulled away from me and did something she'd never done before. I was ready for a slap, but instead she just laughed in my face.

"Wouldn't you like to know, Mr. Big Brother? Mr. Big Shot! Tough guy who can push little girls around and make them dance. Well, I got news for you, buster—"

"May," I said, trying to calm her down. "Come on. We're a team—remember?"

That just got her even more agitated. "Some team. You never let me do anything. You never let me go anywhere. Well, I'm not a child anymore, I'm a grown woman. Look at me."

"Come on," I said, trying to calm her. "You're still my kid sis—"

She ripped open her dress and right through her slip, enough to expose both her breasts. I turned away, but she grabbed me by the ear.

"Look at me. Look at me! This is what men want to see. This is what you don't want them to see. This is what I'd like them to see. Because I'd like to live—not die a shriveled-up old maid."

I reached for her, trying to cover her up. "May, you're—"

She pulled away. "So go ahead and look. Because this is what *you* want to see too."

I couldn't listen to talk like that, not from my own sister. I reached for her.

"Don't touch me. If I'm going to be touched, it's going to be by a real man. A real tough guy, who loves me and appreciates me for my brains as well as my body."

Now I got it. "Who is he?" I said, my blood turning to ice water. I walked very purposefully over to the phone. "Give me his name and I'll have a couple of the boys take care of him right now." I gave the operator the name of the Cotton Club and asked her to place the call.

May ripped the phone out of my hands. "I'll never tell you. Never. You know why? Because he's married. Married, just like you, with all your mistresses and girlfriends and lovers. Married to a woman he doesn't love, because he loves me. And I love him."

May stood there, her bosom heaving. I would have gone to her and comforted her, except that first I had to take care of this thing with my sister, the sister I had loved since the day she was born, the girl I had protected on the ship and raised on the streets, the girl in whom I had confided all my hopes and plans. May.

"You give me his name, and this is all over in an hour," I said very softly. But she just stood there, looking at me with a look of utter hatred on her face, and I could hardly believe I was staring at my baby sister.

Our mother came up behind her and draped an Irish shawl around her shoulders, restoring May's modesty. "I'll never tell you," she spat. Then she rushed to her room and tried to slam the door.

I yanked her out of the doorway and smacked her around pretty good. I had to hit her a bunch of times before she spit out the name. I hated to bloody my sister's face, of all people, but what choice did I have? You'd have done the same thing.

Finally I heard her whisper, "It's Jack. Jack Diamond."

I dropped her onto the floor and spoke to my Mother. "Keep her in there. Don't let her out and I don't care how she wheedles. You need food, I'll send it over. She needs a doctor, one'll be here in five minutes he knows what's good for him."

I grabbed my hat. "Everything's gonna be all right, Ma," I promised. "Just like old times."

Chapter

Fifty

THE FIRST BULLETS chinked my armored Duesenberg just past Columbus Circle. The shooters picked up my trail as I was coming up Eighth, and slipped in behind me real smooth with the merging traffic. I wasn't looking for them, but I noticed them soon enough: soon as we cleared the circle, the tommies opened up. This is what I got for being mad and being alone.

Lead kicked up my steel-reinforced boot and ticked off the back window's bulletproof glass, but bulletproof or no bulletproof, I knew that I was in trouble. It was still almost a hundred blocks to the safety of the Cotton Club, where Frenchy was. We tore up Central Park West, scattering schoolchildren and young mothers as we went.

My Doozy could really run, but even a racing car can only run so fast on Central Park West, so I cut into the park, hoping to open up a lead. The tail car, a big Packard, was almost as fast, and kept up pretty good, blasting away as it came.

I couldn't believe this was happening, right after Atlantic City. I was trying to drive and figure out who would be dumb enough to try to hit me in broad daylight. I didn't think any of the boys with which I'd just broke bread would welsh so quickly, not even the Dutchman at his craziest, which meant that it must be somebody who wasn't there, and that pretty much narrowed it down as far as I was concerned, if I lived that long.

I got one of my pistols out of my shoulder holsters, but there was no sense firing until I had a target. The twists and turns of the park drive meant I wasn't able to put much distance between me and them, and so I decided the only way I was gonna shake 'em was to kill 'em.

We were up high, nearing 110th. My first thought had been to lose them in the park, shoot right out back onto Eighth and outrun them from there, but this plan was getting me nowhere fast, so when I hit the roundabout, I took a hard right on 110th and then a left on Lenox, rolling down the passenger's side window as I sped along. The thing about Lenox is it's a nice broad boulevard, with plenty of room to maneuver, which I proceeded to do.

We crossed 116th going about eighty miles per hour and just when they thought I was going to floor it, I hit the brakes hard.

That Duesenberg didn't even squeal as she slowed. Instead it was like the Doozy had stopped cold and the Packard all of a sudden caught up. I could see the surprised look on the driver's side as we suddenly came starboard to port and I didn't even have time to think if I recognized him when I shot out his left eye. I have a dim recollection of the bullet crashing out the back of his skull and splatting the window opposite, which distracted the triggerman beside him just enough that, when the dead man slumped over the wheel, I was able to take him out too.

Two shots, two kills; I said a silent prayer for Monk Eastman as the Packard started to swerve out of control. The backseat tommy johnnies got off a few desperate last rounds, then one of them dropped his cannon and leaned over the front seat, scrambling to regain control of the car. I fired at him and must've got him in the left shoulder because he flipped over on his side and then the Packard spun out completely, clipped a parked Chevrolet, flipped over twice, careered over the sidewalk and exploded into a storefront, mighta been one of those storefront Jesus joints the Negroes like so much.

Given that there was only two mooks who wasn't invited to our little beach party, and both of them paddies who sunburned easy, I had pretty much narrowed it down culpritwise. Then I thought over the whole roster of my colleagues and pretty much opened it up again. That was one of the problems with this business: when your enemies are your friends and your friends are your enemies, it's hard to know which you'd rather have.

The papers the next day said "Four Killed in Harlem Auto Accident," by which they meant the four white men in the Packard. There was no description of any of the damage, because newspapers didn't much care about coloreds one way or the other, and that was about it, because I phoned Winchell and got him to squash any further coverage if he knew what was good for him.

I'll tell you, though, the thing that really put a damper on my day was when I got to the Cotton Club and there was Herman Stark telling me that Vincent Coll had grabbed Big Frenchy and wanted $35,000 for him alive and nothing at all for him dead, and what was I going to do about it?

Chapter

Fifty-One

"WHAT HAPPENED?"

"Went out to get a sandwich. Vincent grabbed 'im."

"When and where?"

"Seventh Avenue, outside the Argonaut."

"We sure it's Coll?"

"Rang about an hour ago."

"Where's he got George?"

"Westchester somewhere."

"Still alive?"

"Best of our knowledge."

"Did you talk to him?"

"Briefly."

"What'd he say?"

"Pay 'im."

I had to think about this for a minute. It wasn't the money, exactly, although $35,000 was a lot of dough. And I liked George, couldn't do business without him. It's just that I didn't like the precedent, as the shysters say. You start paying ransom for a mug, next thing you know, some ape is grabbing the whole zoo. You gotta draw the line somewhere, and the question I was facing was whether that line was on my side of Frenchy, or Vincent Coll's.

I pulled a thumb in the direction of my car. "Get those dents out pronto," I said.

I never liked Coll, Irish or no Irish. I knew his folks, and they were decent enough, but there was something wrong with Vincent from the start. He was still a kid, and looked like a cross between a choirboy and a movie star.

Famine Irish, catnip to the dames. But he was missing a screw or two. I'd known plenty of stone killers in my time—hell, the tabs said I was one myself—but Coll was different. Just like Jack and Eddie Diamond, Vincent and his brother Peter were both no good. The last thing I needed was two crazy micks, make that four, loose cannons all, and so I decided to call Dutch.

The rules was like whacked like, but I never liked them rules. What with my clubs and various other business enterprises and all, I was trying to keep the muscle to a minimum. Oh, I wasn't against killin' a harp when he needed killin', as Little Patsy Doyle proved, but there was something unseemly about the entire enterprise, something untoward, and for this hit I preferred to contract out.

I finally rousted the Dutchman out of bed with one of his babes. I don't know what it is about a mug with a gun to a dame, but even the nicest girls drop their knickers pronto when they meet a real hard guy, and Dutch had as much success as any of us in that department, even though he had no manners of any kind and never did learn how to treat a lady.

"Who is it?" the nameless dame said, and I could just tell over the wire she was blonde too.

"None of your business," I said. "Gimme Dutch."

I could hear various noises and while I waited I thought about May, and May and Jack, and then started to get really mad. I was steamin' by the time the Dutchman came on the line.

"What is it?"

"That gobshite Coll."

"What else is new—hey, lay off, will ya?" I could hear broad noises in the background and then the sound of a hard smack. "What's the situation?"

"Grabbed Frenchy. He's shakin' me down,"

"Whattsamatta, ya don't love me no more?" That was the twist. Another slap and she shut up.

"Where are you? Slipper, Fey, Livingstone or Cotton?"

"Cotton."

"Be there in a half." Since you could practically spit into the Bronx from Lenox and 142nd, I knew he would be.

I went up on the roof to visit my pigeons, have a smoke and think things over. The new Yankee Stadium was only a few blocks away, just across the Harlem River; I could practically hear the crowd noises. In my mind I watched the Bambino swing the bat, which made me think of the Big Fella and the way he swung the bat—talk about your Murderers Row—and then there was the Dutchman, running a comb through his greasy hair.

"This fuckin' paddy, this sonofabitch piece a shit Irisher, how many times I gotta tell ya, he's gotta go. I don't care what you say, he's gotta go and he will go, if I have to do it myself "

He looked at me like I was objecting or something.

"The sonofabitchin' bastard has been hijacking my beer trucks and generally fucking me up and down the Hudson River for the last six months." Dutch plunked himself down next to me and the birds. "Jesus, between him and Diamond, I don't know who to hate more." He turned to me: "You're a smart guy, Owney—who should I hate more?"

"Your call, Dutch. It's all the same to me. All's I know is one or both of 'em took a shot at me today, and I'm plenty sore about it."

I offered him a cigarette and we talked things over but good, not just the hit, but the beer business, about politics, about Roosevelt's chances to make the leap from Albany to Washington. We talked about Dewey, an up-and-coming lawyer agitating for an appointment to the D.A.'s office. Dewey was a Republican, which meant he was a reformer, which meant he was a goo-goo, which meant he could be trouble. That's the kind of relationship we had; most people didn't like Dutch Schultz, but you could talk straight with him, and as long as you were both armed, there was never any trouble.

In the end we decided that both Legs and Coll had to go. There were lots of things we were all willing to put up with, including a rubout or two, but hijacking booze and kidnapping aides were out of the question.

"They being micks and all, seems only right you should put 'em down," said Dutch.

"Ixnay. I got a grudge against Vincent. That don't look good to the cops or the newspapers."

"What's in it for me?"

"Thirty thousand dollars. Double that for both of 'em."

A thought occurred to Schultz, which didn't happen very often unless it involved a heater. "Jeez, what if Coll tries to grab one of us while we're lookin' for him? That crazy sonofabitchin' bastard—"

"Maybe you got a point there." It wasn't that I was yellow, but you never knew what the Mad Mick might be up to. Untethered, he was nuts. It behooved us, as my Mother said, to be careful, to play this smart.

"Maybe I'll go down to Polly Adler's and stay there for a while." Ugly little Polly Adler ran the classiest whorehouse in town, conveniently located on West 54th Street, practically next door to Dutch's own Chateau Madrid and just down the street from Legs's Hotsy-Totsy Club.

It's a good thing Big Frenchy's gone these many years now, because I never did have the heart to tell him that Dutch and I discussed his fate dispassionately, the way businessmen ought to discuss things.

"What if you just pay?" Dutch asked.

"Maybe I will, but I want my money back."

He gave me a look. "You goin' soft?"

"Goin' smart." I finished my fag, right down to the butt, even though my lungs hurt like holy hell. "Got enough holes in me to last a lifetime."

"You gonna pay both of us?"

"One thing you gotta learn, Dutch," I said. "Patience. I'm a long-term investor. Plus I know you won't let me down."

I sent a couple of my lesser boys, who were expendable and didn't know it, up to Westchester with a suitcase two days later. They came back with George, not much the worse for wear. His clothes were a little mussed, like he slept in them, but otherwise he looked all right to me.

"What took you so long?" he asked, miffed.

"Business," I replied. We'd waited the extra day to see if Coll was serious about the kidnapping racket, as opposed to simple murder. Because if he wasn't, if he gave us back a corpse in exchange for our dough, then we wouldn't bother with him if he nabbed somebody the next time, assuming he was still alive to do so.

"Am I worth it?" I could see he was a little sore.

"That's up to you," I joshed.

Except to say yes or no, George didn't speak to me for forty-eight hours.

Chapter

Fifty-Two

M<small>AY GOT MARRIED</small> in 1931 at St. Mike's to a fella named Jack, but it wasn't Jack Diamond. There was a Democrat district worker officer, name of John F. Marrin, Jack, who done a few things for me. I liked Jack. I liked him for a number of reasons. He was young, strong, healthy, didn't drink much, was good to his family. I liked his sister, Alice, a quiet religious sort of girl. Most of all, I liked the fact that he wasn't going nowhere, that he was content to be who he was, and wasn't going to get mixed up in what Costello was calling Our Thing, especially if he knew what was good for him.

I gave my sister the choice of marrying this Jack, Marrin not Diamond, or spending the rest of her life locked in her room. You may laugh at that today, but back then we really did things like that, and everybody had a crazy cousin or uncle living in the attic, who only came down at mealtimes, and sometimes not even then, and if they did that often enough, one day one of the kids would tiptoe up the stairs to see if Uncle Dan was all right and there he would be, dead, and so you'd have to plant 'im, and that would be that.

May thought about it for a while, not that there was much to think about, and then she give me her answer and it was, how about that, yes. When I told Jack, it was like he won the Irish Sweepstakes, he couldn't believe his luck. "Take care of her, treat her good. You hit her, you're a dead man. I'll give you one of the apartments at 440. I'll make sure you have a good job, plenty of money, people to watch over you. Only one thing."

"What's that, Mr. Madden?" He was polite too.

"You don't brag about our relationship. You don't mention to nobody you're my brother-in-law. You keep your wife out of my clubs, out of my business and out of my life unless I send for her. Clear?"

He nodded.

"I picked you because you're a good man, Jack. Because I trust you. Think you can handle it?"

Another nod.

"Do you think you can handle her?"

"I'll sure try, Mr. Madden."

"Good lad." I handed him two packages, one large and one small. "Open the big one first."

He tore the brown paper off an elongated box, reached inside and extracted one of Frenchy's prize shotguns.

"Watch it, it's loaded," I cautioned. "For home use only. I don't expect you to ever have to get involved in any rough stuff, but if trouble comes looking for me and finds you or your family instead, this will help you settle it. Now open the other one."

Inside was the biggest diamond ring he'd ever seen. "That's your engagement ring. Give it to her tonight. Don't tell her where it come from. She'll know anyway."

I saw the picture in the paper a few days later. She was wearing a beautiful diaphanous dress with a plunging neckline and a ruffle at the bottom, her long arms bare and elegant. There were three rows of pearls around her neck, a double strand and a single. Her hair was marcelled in high style, but just a couple of curls were peeking out from beneath a broad-brimmed hat of the very latest fashion. Her left hand, with its carefully polished nails, rested lightly on her hip, displaying a diamond-studded watch, which I'd given her, and on her ring finger, Jack's rock. "Miss Madden Engaged to Mr. Marrin," the story said.

What struck me most, however, was her face. Her mouth was crimped in the Madden smile, a small crooked tight-lipped slash that the three of us shared with our mother, and which on her signaled a private emotion so deeply buried no one could ever excavate it. Her blue eyes were angled ever so slightly to the left, as the photographer had probably commanded, but they were still looking right at you, unblinking, frank and wise. They were looking right at me, and always would be.

Marty gave the bride away. Big Frenchy was the best man. Ma and Alice Marrin were the bridesmaids. There were no guests. May cried. I didn't, because I wasn't there.

Chapter

Fifty-Three

ON BEHALF OF FRANK COSTELLO, Meyer Lansky and the rest of the ruling council, I was traveling all over the country. To Chicago, to visit with Al until he got busted by the feds and shipped off to the Rock, and to work with Moses Annenberg on our race-wire racket. To Cleveland and Detroit, keeping an eye on our supply lines. To Florida of course, especially as I was now the major silent investor in several fine racetracks down there. I even got to New Orleans once in a while, to see if we could bring those fellas onto the reservation. But the New Orleans mob was always recalcitrant, and so we mostly left them alone until Meyer could figure out a way to approach them without getting killed.

I guess somewhere in the back of my mind I knew this life couldn't last, and maybe it was time to start thinking about life after Manhattan, just in case. There were two places I really enjoyed going, and they were Los Angeles and Hot Springs, Arkansas, which everybody called Bubbles on account of the natural hot springs found there—forty-seven of them in all, each one percolating along at 143 degrees.

Los Angeles you know all about from the movies and whatnot. What you probably don't know is how much we—and I'm primarily referring to the Big Fella and myself—influenced the picture shows. To this day there's some journalist or producer johnny coming down here to Bubbles to see if I'd sit for an interview or sign away the rights to a life whose rights I signed away to a higher power than Hollywood long go. One of my boys, who drove a cab in his spare time, brought a writer right to my front door on West Grand and told me all about how the guy was a swell fella, I'd love talking to him, etc. and so forth, but one thing I never do is change my own rules no matter what, and those rules said no reporters ever, and if it was good enough for Runyon and Winchell, it was good enough for this mug, and so I told my boy, "You ever bring another reporter to this house I will cut your heart out." He believed me, and that was the end of that.

Producers, though, were another story. For that, I have George Ranft to blame.

You remember Georgie, my old pat from our salad days in the Kitchen. Not cut out for the gang life, but a keen observer of it. As it turned out, our racing businesses were growing mightily, and so I went out to the Coast to see about some investments in Santa Anita and I took Texas and Georgie with me, because they both wanted to be in pictures, and the pictures would want them to be in 'em if they knew what was good for them.

First time I got to Hollywood, I understood right off why the gangs'd never had much luck here: the real gangsters was running the studios. I don't mean those mugs was real gangsters, though they talked tough enough, like their Hebrew brethren back East, but in a real fight I knew they would fold up like a cheap squeeze-box, not like Monk or the Dutchman. Still, they had a similar way about 'em as we did, being used to getting their way and so forth, plus the directors and the actors not to mention the actresses really liked to drink, and the long and the short of it is we all got along swell, and with no one did I get along sweller than Howard Hawks.

Hawks had been at the Silver Slipper more than once, and was quite fond of Texas, so with his help we got her into a couple of pictures, including *Queen of the Night Clubs,* which I think came out around '29, don't hold me to it, Georgie would know. Talkies was all the rage, and nobody could talk like Texas, but whatever she had in the clubs she forgot to bring to the screen—maybe you had to be there—so Hawks was looking to do something else, and one night at the Brown Derby in Beverly Hills he brought up the subject.

"Say, Madden, what would you think about doing a picture about your life story?"

"Sure, Howard," I said, slicing off a piece of choice flank steak, "except that then I'd have to cut out your heart."

Hawks laughed but Georgie said: "He ain't kidding."

"What about the Big Fella?" I followed up. "You know how much he loves publicity. Wasn't he just on the cover of *Time* magazine?"

"You bet, boss," said Georgie.

"You think?" asked Hawks.

"I know. Al loves the limelight."

"What if we make the picture and he doesn't like it?" Hawks looked kind of nervous, who wouldn't?

"Worried about your health?"

"Don't worry," said Georgie, patting Hawks's arm. "They only kill each other."

"Except when we don't."

I saw Hawks staring at Georgie, his face, his shape. Only a bona fide director could stare at another guy that way and get away with it. "What about you, George? Think you'd like to be in pictures?"

I thought Georgie was going to kiss him right there in the Derby. That was another thing a mug in Hollywood could do and not get punched in the chops. If there was anything George Ranft had wanted all his life, it was to be somebody, a big shot, a mug that didn't risk getting whacked by other mugs, except playing let's pretend. A movie star.

"Me?"

Hawks let out his breath. "We'd have to change the name of course . . ."

"You ain't gonna give me no homo name, are ya?" asked Georgie. "Besides, what's wrong with my handle?"

"Yeah," I chimed.

Hawks breathed in. "Too kraut, too hard to say. No offense."

"You got a better idea?" I asked him.

He thought for a moment. "How 'bout we just drop the 'n'? How's 'George Raft' sound?" He looked at both of us. "Got a nice masculine ring to it."

We both thought it sounded just peachy keen, and that's how George Raft was born. Goo Goo Knox was right all along.

A hack named Rowland Brown warmed him up, casting him as a gangster, how about that, in *Quick Millions,* followed by *Hush Money* and *Palmy Days.* I saw them all. George couldn't act much—his tough-guy image was mostly derived from imitating me—but he looked swell, and the dames liked him a whole bunch. The studio was flooded with letters from teenage girls in Omaha.

So I wasn't surprised when I heard Hawks had cast George as the second banana in his new picture, *Scarface,* with Muni Weisenfreund, a Jewish Rialto thespian who'd changed his name to Paul Muni, good idea. The plot was pure Al Capone, the character of Guino Rinaldo was pure me, if I was a wop.

Except for the ending, I liked *Scarface* and so did the Big Fella, who got a private screening from Hawks and gave the director a souvenir tommy gun in return. But let me tell you, I coulda sworn I was looking at myself up there on the screen. Georgie had imitated just about everything about me: the way I wore my fedora, the way I dressed, the way I moved. About the only thing I didn't do was toss a nickel incessantly, the way his character did, but I guess that's what they call artistic license, or maybe it's just acting.

Once George was established out there, it was just a matter of time before we talked Mae into bringing her act West. Ever since *Sex,* I'd been backing Mae's shows on Broadway; after each performance, I'd send one of my boys, usually Georgie, over to the theater to take half the b.o. in cash. That's how *Diamond Lil* got produced at the Royale on 45th Street, and when Hollywood came calling, they bought it too and called it *She Done Him Wrong.*

Anyway, George suggested to somebody that they bring the great Mae West to Hollywood, which they did, sticking her in one of his pictures called *Night After Night.* Raft played a gangster, Mae played herself. I saw the movie and called Georgie in Hollywood. "You thought you were the gonoph," I joshed him. "She stole everything but the scenery." After that she and Georgie were both big stars, and I was proud of them.

The only problem with Los Angeles, which I otherwise liked, was that between the cops and the moguls there wasn't much room or opportunity for real gangsters. The LAPD had a policy that any convicted or suspected gang member from the East who showed his face anywhere in the vicinity of Sunset Boulevard would be arrested for vagrancy and put on the next train for Timbuktu. Needless to say, this was cramping all our styles, but especially mine, since I had interests in the picture business as well as the racing game, and it was mighty inconvenient for me to keep shuttling back and forth between the coasts. One day I spoke to Meyer about it.

"We're workin' on it."

"Who's 'we'?"

"Benny and me. We got a plan." Meyer always had a plan. The only question was whether those plans included you, and how.

"So can you give me a little help?"

"Not at the present time."

Which meant you should only drop dead. One thing I didn't like about Meyer was that he was interested only in business, which come to think of it was the one thing I liked about Meyer. There was no room for sentiment with Lansky, not when it came to the coining of coin, and if he had a partiality toward his fellow Hebrews and the wops he worked with, well, that was understandable.

I'd come to Meyer because, as things were turning out, he was more or less the guy who called the shots. Everybody respected him. He was a little fella, littler than most of us, who tended to be little guys in the first place, but he didn't have no record of killing, so nobody was really afraid of him. You always felt with Lansky you could take him out anytime you wanted to, shoot him, beat him to death with your shoe, what have you, which is why nobody ever did. People were scared of crazy Benny, and you basically didn't want to cross Charlie Lucky, especially not after he whacked his own boss—I mean Joe the Boss—at a lunch at Coney Island. Which is how the Castellammarese War was settled, because somebody had to settle things between the Mustache Petes, and it might as well be someone of the Italian persuasion, which it was.

It seems that Charlie and Joe were one afternoon dining, if you can call it that, because Joe could really shovel pasta down his gob, when Charlie got up to go to the can and along comes a bunch of gunners including Benny Siegel, Joey Adonis, Vito Genovese and a vicious punk named Albert Anastasia— you talk about your '27 Yankees, your Murderers Row, even though this was '31—and that was it for Joe the Boss. That other Mustache Pete, Maranzano, got his a little later, and after that Charlie Lucky was King of the Wops, no questions asked.

Here's the funny bit. Maranzano had hired none other than Vincent Coll to take out Charlie Lucky, and Coll, running late, was coming to see the capo outside his office near Grand Central when the Mad Mick spots four sheeny gunmen heading for the same location, so off he waltzes twenty-five grand to the good without having to do a damn thing. If Vincent had only been on time, he might have saved me a lot of trouble, but I guess you can't change history, only tell it the way it really happened.

Yeah—L.A. One night I'm in my hotel—the Mark Twain I think it was— and comes a cop a-knocking on the door, and I do what I wouldn't do in New York, which is grab a heater, because them L.A. cops was bad, totally unscrupulous when it came to the use of firearms without provocation. Most of their income they derived from shaking down hookers and dope fiends, real low-life stuff. Honest graft they wanted no part of, so you couldn't buy 'em, and even if you could, you couldn't trust 'em to stay bought, which is just about the lowest thing you can say about a man, in my book. This is what happens where there ain't nothing like Tammany or the Democratic Party to take care of the workingman.

"You Owney Madden?" says the flatfoot, who thought he looked like an actor. In my experience all L.A. cops think they look like movie stars, and are just hoping to God they'll find some fella they don't have to sleep with to agree with them so's they can get on with their real careers.

"That's Mr. Madden to you, Officer," I said politely. There was no point in arguing with L.A. cops, I always found.

"Wise guy, huh? How'd you like a trip up to see Mulholland Falls?"

"How'd you like to speak to my lawyer, Officer . . . say, what's your name?"

"Fogelman."

"Might want to work on that."

"Grab your things. We're going downtown."

"Lemme make a phone call."

"Who you calling? Mae West?"

I dialed the Ravenswood in Hancock Park. "Gimme Miss West," I told the operator.

Well, wasn't that the magic word. I could have said "the President of the United States" and the cop wouldn't have been impressed, but Mae West was different. Mae West was a movie star.

"Go on . . ."

"Talk to her yourself, you don't believe me."

She sounded a little out of breath, but otherwise she sounded exactly like Mae West. "Hiya, dearie," says herself.

"Fella here wants to speak with you. Name of Fogelman."

"Is he adorable?"

"Man in uniform."

"Trouble, huh?"

"You said it. Know anybody?"

"The D.A.'s a personal friend of mine. Mr. Fitts."

"Say hi to—" I turned to the cop.

"Come on, smart guy." He grabbed the receiver and slammed it back in its cradle.

We took a ride downtown and by the time we got there Officer Fogelman had been relieved of his duties and assigned to a desk job down on Jefferson somewhere in the colored section. A couple of the detectives drove me back to my hotel, peppering me with questions about Mae and George Raft and all the big shots I knew.

Mae and I had lunch the next day. Seems that just by pure chance Buron Fitts's wife was back East visiting her family that night, and so Mae went over to the D.A.'s house for a glass of cordial and one thing led to another and my name came up and in the time it took us to get downtown Mr. Fitts had already made the phone call consigning poor Fogelman to purdah. That Mae really had a way with words.

Chapter

Fifty-Four

THAT WAS PRETTY MUCH IT for me in the City of the Angels—Mrs. Fitts was only going to be conveniently out of town once, at least to hear Mr. Fitts tell it—so after that episode I turned my attentions south, to Hot Springs, the crookedest little town no one has ever heard of.

Hot Springs had been an open city since as long as anyone could remember, right back to the Civil War. It was a tiny little burg, squeezed in between two hills, North Mountain and West Mountain, which I suppose you could view as the Arkansas equivalent of the North River and the East River of my youth, and it had a splendid row of bathhouses—the Superior, the Maurice, the Quapaw—lining the main drag, where people from all over would come to take the waters.

The town liked to boast that the waters were good for a variety of ailments, whether you bathed in them or drank them, but the main ailment they were supposed to cure was venereal disease, which is what had made Bubbles so popular with the folks up North. A gentleman who'd caught a dose from a drab could leave, say, Pittsburgh on a business trip, scoot down to the Ouachita Range and while away a pleasant couple of weeks or so, especially since Hot Springs had a thriving sporting house district. So you could get cured of one dose of the clap then turn right around and pick up another, all in the same locale.

It was Lansky's idea to go South. Meyer was looking for a spot between our business interests in Florida, which consisted mostly of racing and gambling, and the big cities of the East. A place off the beaten track, but not entirely uncivilized. We looked around, at Nashville, Charlotte, Savannah, but couldn't find nothing suitable. Until one day we were talking about baseball.

Maybe we were thinking back to Big Al's performance at Atlantic City, I dunno, but anyway the topic of baseball came up and of course the Yankees, and I remember that the Yanks used to stop off in Hot Springs on their way north from spring training. It was the kind of town built for Babe Ruth, with food, drink and whores, and no inconvenient lawmen to make trouble for people like Colonel Ruppert, the Yanks' owner. The town also had a thriving gambling industry, which was mostly conducted in back rooms in the stores across the street from Bath House Row, and with all that moonshine being distilled in the Ouachitas, there was booze aplenty.

"I been there a couple of times," I told Costello one afternoon. Of the three East Siders, I liked Frank the best, he had the most class. The Little Man was smart and Charlie Lucky was cunning, but Frank was the kind of guy you could be seen with in public. Nobody didn't like Frank, and Frank didn't like nobody. "There's an Irishman mayor, McLaughlin. We can do business with him. Might be a good play."

"Right in New Orleans's backyard too," mused Costello. He was a big guy even back then, beefy, looked like a well-fed diplomat or something, dressed in $350 suits. Judges loved him and he loved them, especially when they were on his pad, which most of them were. Frank had moved up to Harlem as a kid, which was another thing I liked about him. We were the same age too, older than the other mugs. Plus you had to love a guy whose first beef was robbing his own landlady and then beating the rap. "Sam Carolla, his boy Carlos Marcello—they ain't gefilte fish."

I had another reason for wanting to go to Hot Springs. The Dutchman, who had an eye for such things, had told me about a cute little frail working the gift shop of the Arlington Hotel, Capone's old hangout when he was taking the water. The Arlington was a big fancy pile, commanding the turn of Central Avenue as it threaded its way between the hills, and I could see why the Big Fella liked it. From a fourth-floor suite—Al always stayed in room 442—gunners could command the avenue coming and going, so Mr. Brown could sleep easy when he was in town.

My first stop in Hot Springs was to see Mayor Leo P. McLaughlin—"the Jimmy Walker of the Ozarks," the press called him. He was a type I knew well, a kind of cut-rate Big Tim Sullivan, not as nutso and not as dangerous. He rode around town in a horse-drawn carriage with a pair of horses he called Scotch and Soda and generally was the picture of self-important paddy-whackery. The two of us got along well enough, although he could probably tell I was fixing to move the Combination into his territory, and I could tell that he could tell, and to tell you the truth, I didn't care. I told him I'd be back with a more refined business plan, and we shook hands.

My next stop was the gift shop, to see the little filly. She was as cute as a bug in her pert cloche, with a neat figure and a nice pair of ankles.

"What's your name, sweetheart?"

That was not the kind of question a gentleman asked a southern lady, but I was from up North.

"Miss Demby, sir."

"You got a first name—you know, a Christian name?"

She blushed a little. Maybe she reminded me a little of Freda Horner, maybe she didn't. "Agnes."

"You don't say."

"I do say."

"Always liked that name."

"How come?"

"My mother's middle name. 'The little lamb.' "

"Huh?"

"You know, like Agnes Day, the lamb of God."

She gave me the fisheye. "Is that some of that Catholic stuff? Papa says to keep clear away from that Catholic stuff. It ain't Christian."

"How'd you like a soda, Miss Agnes?"

She blushed again, which meant she'd had plenty of practice. She was obviously used to strange men sweet-talking her. She came out from behind the counter, so I could feature her gams through her dress. It was almost always hot in the South. Diaphanous. Nice.

"I'm working."

"All day?"

"I get off at five."

"Soda shop's still open then, I'll bet."

She gave me the eye. I was taller than she was, which was a plus. "I guess so."

"So we got a deal?"

"I don't know your name."

"Madden."

Now she frowned, and I wondered if my reputation had preceded me. "That Irish?"

"I'm from England, as a matter of fact."

I could see the relief. "For a minute there you had me worried. Papa says—"

"Papa?"

"The Postmaster."

"Pick you up at five."

She was dumb, but not much dumber than most geese. "Papa says I have to be home by seven. Eleven at the latest."

We had a swell time. Agnes showed me around Hot Springs, up and down Central Avenue along Bath House Row, then north, heading out of town. I was driving my Doozy. She was plenty impressed, which was the way it should be with a dame.

"We call this Park Avenue."

"We got one of those back in New York. Maybe you heard of it?"

Ixnay. "Is it as nice as this?"

I looked at the houses, big frame dwellings for prosperous hillbillies.

"Nah," I said. "Not a patch."

I got a good gander at the whole town, better than Dutch had. I have to say it wasn't bad at all.

Because I believe in planning ahead, I wrote her as often as I could. Mostly mushy stuff. "To my Agnes, whom I know to be the swellest fella in the whole world and believe me I met nearly most of the men and women worth meeting in this little world. Agnes, you're the most marvelous girl I have ever met and I adore you and I idolize you with all the love in my . . ." You get the idea. The things we do for safety, if not love.

We were engaged six months later. For the ring I gave her a rock bigger than the Ritz. She'd never heard of that either, but then, she was a Republican.

Chapter

Fifty-Five

DUTCH FINALLY EARNED HIS FEE with regards to Legs Diamond in a Dove Street flophouse in Albany. Even though I'd been keeping pretty close tabs on the family Marrin, I was relieved to hear the girl with him when he died was the dame named Kiki Roberts, a real dish with a mouth on her even fouler than Dutch's, which is saying something.

Bo Weinberg made sure he didn't miss the Clay Pigeon. Somebody—Abe Landau, I'll bet—held Legs down on the double bed while Bo pumped three shots into his head. It wasn't too tough, since Jack was dead drunk at the time, and then he was just dead. Among his personal effects, the cops found some religious medals and a rosary. It was December 17, 1931, the night before my real fortieth birthday. Me, I was in Hot Springs, visiting Agnes, because . . .

I had plenty of trouble at home. Roosevelt, the Governor of New York, had turned me down flat for the pardon which, looking back, was our first indication that he wasn't going to be the compliant Tammany man we'd been promised. Al Smith, his rabbi, had already turned against him, because Roosevelt was making no bones about wanting to run for President in 1932, when everybody knew the nomination by rights belonged to Smith unless he didn't want it, which he very much did.

I hadn't had too high hopes for the election of 1928. Being a British subject, not to mention a convict, I couldn't vote legally, for one thing, although that had never stopped me before. For another, I figured there was no way a country full of thin-lipped, milk-drinking midwestern Republican Protestants was going to elect a Democratic Irishman from the Lower East Side and sure enough Hoover clobbered him. But Al figured he had a real shot this time, because something had changed and that something was what everybody was callin' the Depression.

Money comes and money goes, we all know that, but this Depression really caught the country in the outhouse with its pants down around its ankles and the flies buzzing something fierce. One day everything was jake, nowhere to go but up, and the next folks were running around like it was the end of the world, and down wasn't low enough. We figured it wouldn't affect the nightclub business much, and at first it didn't. But then it did. Because if you read your history books, you'll see that Depression and Repeal pretty much went together like a Packard and a Thompson machine gun, if only you were smart enough to see it.

My more immediate concern was the Mad Mick, who'd gone to ground somewhere after the Frenchy nab, but was still causing trouble. He was plenty sore when his brother Peter, who was almost as crazy as he was, had bought it from Bo Weinberg, and had put a number of Dutch's torpedoes in the ground in revenge. This was making Dutch look bad, especially with my money burning a hole in his pocket. Costello and the others put the finger on him to solve the problem. Then Vincent did us both a favor.

About six months before Bo put Legs to sleep, Coll had tried to take out one of the Dutchman's business associates in East Harlem, fella named Joey Rao. Rao ran Italian Harlem from his stronghold up in the East 100s, enforcing Dutch's policy racket and making sure no other mugs muscled in. Fleecing superstitious Negroes, who'd bet their mother's birthday as long as they could figure out how to express it in three digits, was child's play, and that was such easy money that the Dutchman was facing renewed competition from the blacks themselves, Bumpy Johnson and Stephanie the voodoo queen foremost among them. I didn't have a dog in that fight, but I needed stability on my Harlem flank, because if the colored took over completely—and the white women refused to go up there, except when they didn't—we all had trouble. People were starting to make noises about not wanting to go uptown, what with the bad element and all—why some black people were so violent was beyond me—and Frenchy and I had once or twice discussed whether we should relocate the club down to the 50s, where many of the others were, but I decided that would be an insult to Mr. Jack Johnson.

Rao had orders to shoot Vincent on sight, which I guess Vincent musta heard about because he decided to preempt Joey. On a hot July day Coll and a carful of his boys came roaring around the corner of East 107th, where Joey and a buddy were walking, and blasted everything that moved.

Joey was no fool, and when he heard the screech of accelerating tires, he knew it was Death coming looking for him, so he and his pal jumped into a stairwell as the hail of lead began. Buncha kids weren't so lucky. Coll peppered 'em with .45s, putting five in hospital. One of them, Michael Vengalli, had his stomach blown away. He didn't make it.

Well, the papers went wild. "Mad Dog Coll," they dubbed Vincent, and everybody in the city was out for his blood. It was a real dumb play, death-warrant dumb. The Outfit put a price on Vincent's head, which, when you stop to analyze it, was really a price on our heads, me and Dutch, because it was our territory, which added a certain urgency to our search for Vincent.

That snoop Winchell somehow got a load something was up, and runs an item that a planeload of gunners was flyin' in from Chicago to rub out Coll. Naturally, everybody wants to know where Winchell got this information, not to mention what's he doing broadcasting it, and since he hangs around my clubs, I had to go to bat for him, because as much as I dislike reporters, I figured rubbing out the most famous Broadway columnist in the world was not a good move. Winchell was a cheap schnorrer, but he wasn't no Jake Lingle, the double-crossing reporter Capone had whacked a couple years earlier, which meant that he could be bribed, cajoled or terrorized, depending.

I don't know whether Coll'd been drinking or just readin' the papers, but the next day—it was February 9, 1932—my private phone at the Cotton Club rang, and Fate decreed that I would be there to pick it up.

"Yeah?"

"It's Vincent Coll."

"I'm talking to a dead man."

He guffawed a little in that stupid way of his. I could hear a dame in the background, giggling as well, and I decided they were both stinko.

Above my desk was the "Be Big or Be Dead" sign. I liked it so much I'd had it framed, pigeon shite and all.

"So I read in the papers. Remind me to pop that nosy punk Winchell. How do they let him write this stuff anyway?"

"They say it's a free country."

I could hear his breathing as he thought about what he was going to say next. "How much d'you think you're worth?"

"To you or to my Mother?"

"Don't get smart with me, Madden. Your day is done. You and Dutch, you're finished. You don't have the guts anymore."

"I said that once to a mug, Vincent. You know what happened?" Dead silence on the other end of the wire. "He and his boys put eleven slugs in me. So I guess, looking back, he did have the guts after all."

"I gotta go."

"I thought you wanted to talk business."

There was some muttering at the other end of the line; him and Lottie Kreisberger, the fat chorus girl he married for no apparent reason, were talking.

"Call you back in ten minutes. Be ready with a price."

Coll rang off, I buzzed Frenchy and I was on the blower to Dutch in the Bronx seconds later.

"I found him."

"Where?"

"Don't know quite yet. He's going to phone me in ten minutes. Make that nine minutes."

"So what good's that do me?"

"Don't be daft. Frenchy will have the call traced. I'll keep Coll on the horn. Where's Bo and the lads?"

"One of the clubs, midtown somewhere, I dunno. Hard to keep track of Bo these days."

"Find him. Maybe we'll get lucky."

"Or maybe Lucky will get us." That was the Dutchman's notion of humor.

"Stand by, Dutch," I said, ringing off.

Frenchy and I sat for a moment in silence. It was a nice office, all done up in wood and leather. I liked it plenty.

"Ever think about gettin' out of this, Owen? The rackets, I mean. Leave it all behind, go somewhere healthier . . . you know, sweeten the odds?"

I was playing with a silver cigarette lighter Mary Frances had given me years ago for my birthday. I hadn't seen her for a while. "Too late for anything else now."

"You sure?"

The phone rang. I signaled to Frenchy to get our friends at the phone company on it PDQ.

"Yeah?"

"What's the answer?"

I knew I had to keep him talking. "Still totin' things up."

"What's takin' ya?" I could hear noises in the background, voices, traffic, so I figured he was in a public place.

"Look, Vincent," I said, stalling. "Your folks are from Kildare. Mine're from Galway and Clare. Do you think they ever imagined how their sons would turn out?"

"Who cares about Ireland when we're talking about money?" He was pronouncing his words very carefully, trying to give the impression he was in control.

I looked over and saw George nodding on the other line and writing down some numbers. Then he rang off and gave me the high sign.

"My father died trying to get out of Ireland. Okay, England."

George stuck the piece of paper under my nose: "London Chemist's, W. 23rd Street." I pantomimed for him to call Dutch, but he was already on the case.

"I've come up with a number."

"Give it to me."

"Keep your pants on." Frenchy flashed me another high sign and I knew we had him, if I could just keep him yakking. "Here's how I figured it out."

"Hurry the fuck up, I haven't got forever."

He was sure right about that. "Do you want the dough or don't you?"

"Yeah."

"So listen. I figure if Frenchy was worth thirty-five grand, then I gotta be worth more, right?"

"That's what I was thinkin'."

"And then I thought, what's one of our favorite tools of the trade?"

"Gimme a hint."

"I'm talking ordnance here."

"Huh?"

"Weapons. Bullets, you know—"

"You mean .45s, like the kind tommy guns shoot?"

"Now you're using the old noodle, Vincent. Forty-five is my number. Yours too."

In the background I could hear the sound of the shop door opening and some rapid footfalls. I pressed my ear against the receiver as hard as I could.

"Hey, what is this?" I wasn't sure whether Vincent was addressing his last words to me or to them, not that it mattered.

"Good-bye, Vincent," I said, but the shooting had already started.

They lit up Vincent but good, Bo Weinberg and a couple of his playmates did. At the autopsy the coroner counted fifteen steel slugs in various parts of what was left of the Mad Dog, not to mention the countless others that had gone clean through him while he was trapped in that call box.

Seven shots through the right arm, four in the left, to make sure he wouldn't be able to return fire. A couple in the forehead, one of which wound up drilling its way through his body and into his heart. And of course one in the brain. Except for its glass front, which was shot to hell, the phone booth emerged surprisingly intact. That is the mark of the professional, which Bo Weinberg most certainly was.

A cop named Sherlock—this is God's honest truth—happened to be passing by and chased the gunmen on foot, then commandeered a cab and ran with them up to about 50th, where they disappeared. I sent the flatfoot a bottle of my best champagne anonymously, in tribute to his moxie.

The other end of the line was still alive, although the man on it wasn't. I broke the wire at my end, and that was that.

"What a tough break for the Mick," I said.

"He musta done something wrong."

"Let's celebrate."

Frenchy already had the champers open. "Don't mind if I do," he said, not bothering about a glass. It was the only time I ever saw him take a drink.

Chapter

Fifty-Six

Two days after Vincent bought it, I was entertaining Frank Costello at one of my clubs. I saw Winchell off in a corner, having a drink with some dame, and he looked up to see Frank sitting down with me. After what I'd done for him, Winchell knew better than to shoot off his mouth, but I gave him a quick shake of my head and he returned a brief nod, which translated into English meant you don't see nothin' and you bet I don't.

Frank was hard to miss, with a nose that looked like it belonged on someone else's face, and the first time you looked at him you made him for a mug, which he of course was. But Frank spoke very well, in more or less complete sentences, which was unusual for a wop, and his voice had a kind of authority to it that was lacking in Charlie Lucky and Meyer. Frank was a born diplomat, able to shuttle back and forth among the various dukes and barons of New York and the other cities, mediating conflicts, parceling out new territories and new business, and generally keeping his eye on the ball, which was that the whole world was ours, if we didn't blow it. Of all the fellas I met in my working life, not counting the ones that worked for me, I think I liked Frank the best, and I still see him down here in Bubbles, more than anyone else from the old days.

"We're all thrilled the way things have worked out," Frank was saying.

"Bo Weinberg is a very good worker."

"Leaves a job site in tip-top condition," agreed Frank, knocking back one of my beers. "You could use a guy like that."

Now, that was a sore spot. My guys were not exactly geraniums, but there's a difference between a torpedo and a Michelangelo, and with Johnny and Art gone I was short on artists. After he got out of jail, Hoppo moved out west for his health; Art worked for me for a while, but it wasn't the same.

There was one new kid I liked, thought he had a lot of potential, fella named Charlie Workman, a Lepke protégé who was so crazy-brave his friends called him Charles the Bug. The thing I liked best about the Bug was that he could shoot with both hands, just like the way Monk taught me, and pretty much not miss anything.

"We all could," finished Frank, wiping his lip daintily with his napkin. Frank had class.

"I don't think Dutch would take too kindly to any recruiting efforts."

Frank gave me one of those wise-counselor looks. "It may not be up to him."

"What's that supposed to mean?"

"Listen, Owney," said Frank, dropping his voice and shoving that big hound-dog face of his close to mine. "I like you a lot. You know that. Hell, everybody likes you. But there's pressure on its way and we gotta do something about it, or somebody's gonna feel the heat and we ain't gonna be the ones, if you catch my drift."

I caught his drift, a can of corn if there ever was one. The upcoming presidential campaign was shaping up as a dogfight between the two Democrats, Al Smith and Frank Roosevelt. Once friends, they had become bitter enemies—what a surprise in politics. Roosevelt had promised his old boss that he'd stay out of it but then of course changed his mind. Especially since in the aftermath of the stock market crash and the Depression, Monk's pigeon, Hilda, coulda beat Hoover. Which just proves that even among the so-called better class of people, back-stabbing and double-crossing were the norm and not the exception.

"Who're we boosting?" I asked.

"Tough call," replied Frank. "Al's always been a friend to Tammany and so has Roosevelt. But Al can't win—the country still ain't ready for a Catholic President, especially not some mug from the Lower East Side. Frank Roosevelt, on the other hand, he's got class. Plus he's stupid."

That was hard to believe. "Stupider than the Big Fella?"

"About the same. Anyway, we think we have a better shot with him."

That sounded good to me, although I was still peeved at Roosevelt for turning down my pardon, which I took as both a stupid and an unfriendly thing to do.

"Roosevelt's got a problem, though," said Costello, and he didn't sound happy.

"Besides dumb, what?"

"It ain't what, it's who. It's us."

That made sense. If Roosevelt was going to run for President, he'd have to put some distance between himself and the less savory aspects of New York politics. We were long since used to our friends pretending not to recognize us in public, but what we weren't used to was those same friends being actively hostile.

"Frank's called Olvany, Curry, Hines and the rest up to Albany and given them the word. He's got to look tough on corruption. Judge Seabury's expanding his inquiry into a full-fledged commission, and the word is no one's safe. Not even Jimmy Walker."

That seemed ridiculous to me. "Roosevelt wouldn't dare take on Beau James. He's the most popular mug in town. Without New York City there ain't no New York State, and without New York State there ain't no nomination and without—"

"Maybe," said Costello. "And maybe it don't matter. The point is Frank needs to hang a few scalps on his belt."

"So did Geronimo."

"Which brings me to my second piece of bad news. After Roosevelt's elected President, the new Governor, Lehman's, going to appoint Dewey special prosecutor and bust up the rackets. First guy he's going after is the Dutchman."

"But Dewey's a Republican," I objected.

"Unlike us, pols always figure it's better to have the other side do your dirty work for you."

I saw their angle and didn't like it. Now I was trying to figure out our angle. "So why are we thinking of supporting Roosevelt?"

"So we can control whose scalp gets took and whose don't."

I thought it over for a minute. That was putting too much trust in politicians, in my book. I'd rather trust a Hudson Duster. "What if he's a rat?"

"What if we ain't got a choice?"

I was still thinking about what Frank had said when I got home. It was times like this that I wished May was around, that she hadn't gone off and done that dumb thing she did, that she was free to leave her husband's home and come spend the night with me, the way she did when we were a team.

I was sitting in my chair, lost in thought, when the telephone rang. I'm Irish enough to believe in spirits, fate, etc., and I'll tell you the truth, I thought it was May, calling to say she was sorry, that it had all been a terrible mistake, that I'd been right all along, but when I picked up the receiver, the person on the other end of the line was not my sister but my lawyer.

"You sitting down? You really oughta be sitting down on account of the news, not very nice news I'm afraid, but the only news I got, sitting down, as I was saying, on account a the news I got to give you, so are you sitting down, I mean is your rear end in the chair, because brother it'd better be."

"It was until you called. It's up now."

"Okay, forget the sitting-down part, here's the news: the Treasury Department is about to indict you for tax evasion, just like they did Capone and Waxey Gordon and here comes the Dutchman too, the way I hear it and my ears are just fine, thank you very much."

"How much do they say I owe?"

"Seventy-three thousand five hundred and fifty-three dollars and no cents."

"Pay it."

"Too late. Even if we pay, they still want a pound of tush. But that's not the worst of it."

"What could be worse?"

"Oh much. I just heard the parole board has issued warrants for Gustave Guillaume, Jeremiah Sullivan and Terry Reilly and other employees of the Hydrox Laundry."

Guillaume, a tough gunner we called Little Frenchy, on account of he was littler than Big Frenchy, and Sullivan were both paroled murderers; Reilly was a burglar. All of them were on the payroll.

"So?"

"So what's the matter with you, they've already talked to Izzy Levy."

"Good. He'll cover for me." One of the conditions of my parole had been that I get a job, and so on paper I was working for the Hydrox Laundry in Brooklyn. The fact was I owned it. The fact was that Israel Levy was working for me. And the fact was that he was a relative of Judge Aaron Levy.

"That's just it, he blew it. When they shook him down about you, he told 'em he never heard of you, didn't know you from Adam, you get the picture, deny, deny, deny. Thought he was doin' you a favor and here we are, sad day in this great land of ours when you try to do a mug a favor and it backfires."

"What do you mean backfires?" I asked.

"We sure as hell don't want them pokin' around the laundry, now do we, so we got to play along, which I did, more or less on my own toot, which means unfortunately your parole's been revoked and the long and the short of it is that you'll be arrested in the morning. For tax evasion, like I said."

I guess it says something that the first person I called, as soon as I hung up on Joe, was my sister. And if I rousted her out of bed with her husband, that was only fair.

Chapter

Fifty-Seven

"MARRIN RESIDENCE." A man's voice. Sleepy, not tired.

"Lemme speak to my sister."

There was a pause, a hesitation. "She ain't here right now, Mr. Madden."

"What do you mean she ain't there right now? Where the hell is she?"

"Out. She said she was going out."

"You let your wife go out this time of night and you don't do nothing about it? What kind of a man are you?"

I could feel his embarrassment over the wire. "You know May, Owney," said Jack, getting familiar with me. "She's got a mind of her own—"

"You were supposed to fix that," I reminded him. "That's what I pay you the ten grand a month for, remember?"

"I know, but . . ."

"Find her and have her call me."

"Well . . . I'll try, but—"

"Don't try, Jack. Just do it."

I slammed the receiver back in its cradle. I was still sitting there, trying to decide what to do next, when my doorbell rang. I was mighty popular this evening.

I slipped my .38 into my dressing gown pocket and walked slowly to the door. Off to one side I put my ear to it but didn't hear anything. Then I peeked through the peephole, and that's when I saw it was her.

I flung open the door so fast it almost come off its hinges. And then she was in my arms, hugging me the way she used to, before all this happened.

We held each other for a long time, and I realized how much I'd missed her. All because I was mad.

"Take off your coat and stay awhile," I finally managed to say.

She gave me one of her May looks. "He's a good man, Jack."

"That's why I picked him."

"I'm only sorry I lied to you."

"What do you mean?"

She sat down and I poured us both a drink. Even though I didn't drink no more, sometimes I had to.

"What I said about Jack."

Now I was confused. She could always read my mind.

"About Jack Diamond. Sure, he was pestering me there for a while. But I never had anything to do with him."

I can't tell you how relieved I was to hear that. The thought of my baby sister sullied by that bum was almost more than I could bear. Even if he didn't deserve to die, he did, just because of what he made me go through.

"I was just trying to make you mad."

"You sure succeeded."

"I know. I'm sorry. That's why I'm here. To say I'm sorry. To the only man I ever felt I had to say it to."

I looked at her, and at that moment I knew that it was her I loved, it was her that I'd always loved, and that it was her I'd ever love. Not in a dirty way, mind you, but in a pure Christian sort of way, a selfless sort of way, the way our Da had wanted us to love each other, the way I'd promised him I'd love her and here I was, doing just that.

My troubles with the tax man and the parole board didn't seem quite so bad or so important now. I'd beat 'em, especially now that I had her back.

"I'm going to be arrested in the morning," I told her. She looked so beautiful at that moment, the fur coat I'd bought her tossed over her nightgown, the pearls on her neck, the rock on her finger. My rock.

"What are you talking about?"

"Just heard from Shalleck. Joe'll have me out in twenty-four hours."

"What if he doesn't? Repeal's coming. These mugs don't need us no more."

"He will."

"Yeah, but what if he doesn't?"

I smiled at her, and the years fell away and it was like the old times all over again, just the two of us, up on the roof, holding hands, planning, dreaming . . .

"I got it all figured out. Besides, it might not be the worst thing that could happen."

"I read about Vincent Coll."

The image of the Mick, ventilated as all get-out, flashed before our eyes.

There's a look I'd seen often in dead men's eyes. I'd seen it in Luigi's and Willie's and even Little Patsy's. It is not a look of anger or reproach, or any of them things you civilians might think, because after all you've never been there, and so you've only got your imaginations and the picture shows to guide you. But the real look that dead men get in their eyes just before they're dead, the look that the cops spot in two shakes of a lamb's tail, is this:

Surprise.

"I wouldn't cry for him, I was you. He had it coming, if anybody ever did."

"We all have it coming." She fumbled for a cigarette in her pocket and then realized she didn't have any street clothes on. "Ain't that what you always say?"

I fished a fag out of my pocket and handed her my silver lighter.

"What are you going to do?" she asked.

"What are *we* going to do, you mean?" She'd been right all along. The look on her face, I can still see it to this day, sitting right here in my study at the big house in Bubbles. "I've been such a chump, May. I never saw the play."

She leaned forward, her eyes gleaming, her lips wet. That was the look I loved. "What play?" she breathed.

"The play of you and me together. Nobody knows me better than you. Not Frenchy, not Dutch, nobody. You're like the other half of me. All this time I was pushing you away, when I should have been drawing you close. Because when you get right down to it, who can you trust? Nobody, except your blood."

I thought she was going to laugh from joy. "What do you want me to do?"

I phoned her husband and told him to relax and go back to sleep, that she was here with me. We talked late into the night, until we stopped talking.

Chapter

Fifty-Eight

THE NEXT MORNING—it was February 13, 1932—I came out the front door of my apartment to find a big mick dick named Thomas Horan standing there, waiting for me.

"Owen Vincent Madden?" he said. May was freshening up in the biffy.

"Who wants to know?"

"You're under arrest for violation of parole and are hereby taken into custody pending a hearing on a writ of habeas corpus two days hence." He must've practiced his little speech in front of the mirror, because he didn't look like he was smart enough to make it up on his own, even if you spotted him a sentence or two. "Will you come peacefully?"

"You think I'm going to walk all the way to the Tombs?" I asked him, holding out my hands for the cuffs. I knew the drill.

"Follow me, please."

We rode down the lift in silence. I nodded to the doormen as we exited.

The flashbulbs started popping the minute we hit the street. There musta been a dozen photographers there, plus who knows how many reporters, all crowding around to get a good look at the famous desperado, myself, caught up in the long arms of the Law. Normally I hated photographs, but they had me dead to rights, so I figured I might as well give 'em a show. You've probably seen the pictures. They were in all the papers.

I looked swell. I was wearing a dark three-piece double-breasted suit with a pocket square, light green tie, my best pearl-gray fedora and a scarf. Horan was dressed like a detective. He resembled an icebox somebody had outfitted in a suit.

A crowd trailed us onto 34th Street. Faceless, for the most part, but one kid caught my eye, a kid from the neighborhood, a kid just like me in them dear departed days when I was a kid, Jewish by the looks of him, in suit and cloth cap, a look of adoration on his face, and pride, and fear, just the way it should be. I thought of me way back when, and of Monk and all those who had come before us, and maybe all those who would come after us too.

We got into Horan's car, me and Horan in the backseat. The driver hit the pedal and we were off, heading downtown.

"Sorry about this," says the bull.

"You're just doin' your job."

Horan was about my age, maybe a little bit older. He sure looked older, but then he didn't live as well as I did. "I remember you from the old days in the Kitchen."

I looked him over. "What gang did you run with?" Got it in one.

"Parlor Mob."

I smiled in recollection. "We smacked you boys around pretty good. What for'd you go straight?" Horan was silent. Talk about Regret . . . "Bet your mother made you. Mine tried that with me, didn't work, God bless her."

"You know, I admired you back then, the way you ran things."

The squad car bounced hard over some old paving stones. "And now here you are, arresting me."

"Funny how these things work out."

"I'm hysterical."

"Well, if you need anything, you know, while you're in the can, just let me know."

"Make sure my meals are catered. I hate that college slop." We shook hands and Horan was as good as his word, which was rare in an Irishman, no matter which side of the pond we was on.

Shalleck was waiting for me as I checked in. Joe was dressed almost as sharp as me, but even flashier, which was a difference between us. "We got a hearing in two days, habeas, the usual jazz."

"So I heard. What's the score?"

"I won't kid ya, we're behind."

"What's the inning?"

"Still early, third or fourth, I dunno, I gotta make a few phones calls, call in some chits, but Jesus it's hard now, there's heat on everywhere, what the hell is going on, I can't even find Hines."

"Why don't you ask Judge Seabury?" Right on schedule, another goo-goo commission had come along.

"I hear they're even after Jimmy Walker now."

"You heard right."

"Well, ain't that a kick in the pants, going after the Night Mayor, after all he done for everybody, for the city, for the state, hell for the U.S. of A., him writing that hit song and all, what was it called, 'Will You Love Me in November—' "

"December—"

"Whatever, 'as You Do in May.' Brings a tear to my eye every time I hear it."

"You always were sentimental, Joe."

"Maybe so, but in this business there ain't no room for sentiment, sentiment's for suckers, and we got our work cut out for us now, I mean, we lose this and you're back in stir for another twelve years, fer Chrissakes, and all because of a few lines in the statutes, go figure."

"That's what I pay you for, so things like that won't happen. Statutes or no statutes."

The food arrived at that moment, a nice cutlet with all the trimmings from "21," a midtown speak I did business with.

"And it's money well spent too, it really is. How many times you been arrested?"

"Remind me."

"I'll be your guest. I've been doin' a little research, on account a we gotta make our case for your being a solid upstandin' citizen, and here's what I found out, what I found out was that, datin' back to way back when, you been arrested a grand total of . . . hell, I lost count, but it's more than eighty."

"Not counting juvvy, how many convictions?"

"One."

"I rest my case. Who's the judge?"

"Levy. Do you think I'm stupid?"

"What'd it cost me?"

"Not as much as you'd think."

Aaron J. Levy was the Democratic majority leader, the guy who got Governor Sulzer impeached, the judge who'd freed my lorries from the feds, Israel's boon kin. He'd been on my payroll for years.

"He's a state supreme court judge now, how about that, it pays to make friends, as I always say. So listen I got some ideas how we're going to handle this, it might get expensive, but hey it's only money, right?"

"It's only my money, you mean."

"Whatever."

Joe Shalleck was a wizard in that courtroom. He wasn't afraid of nobody, certainly not Cahill and Brancato, the prosecutors, who were trying to get the writ of habeas dismissed so they could take me directly to the can.

Cahill starts things off by talking about my clothes. "Look at this man," he orders Levy. "See how he is dressed. This kind of arrogance is typical of his kind, and he should be made to fear and respect the law. The question before this court is simple: are the law enforcement agencies running this country, or are men like Owney Madden?"

Well, I knew the answer to that question, and so did everybody in the courtroom, but most important so did Judge Levy, and his was the only opinion that counted.

Up pops Joe, who points out that I was convicted long before the present parole rules were put into effect and that therefore this was prima facie evidence of ex post facto something or other, and I couldn't follow the whole show, but Levy did. He sat up there on the bench, fat and gray-haired in his black robes, and from time to time he would nod and smile at Joe, which only encouraged my little shyster to even higher flights of eloquence.

Near the end of his peroration, Joe whipped out a folded piece of paper from his breast pocket and made a big production of unfolding it, putting on his reading glasses and reading it aloud. "I have here in my hand a telegram from my client, Mr. Madden, to the parole board," he began.

I couldn't recall sending such a telegram, but what did I know.

"In it, he asks only one thing, and I quote: 'a chance to work, to be let alone and to be a law-abiding citizen.' Are we going to deny him, a poor immigrant boy, that chance?"

"This court is recessed for lunch," said Judge Levy, who was always hungry at propitious times.

"How we doing?" I whispered. The courtroom was packed with spectators, onlookers, kibitzers, gawkers, all nattering upon the departure of Hizzoner. There was cops in uniform and cops out of uniform, plus the usual assortment of reporter johnnies, scribblin' like mad. What distinguished them from bookies I couldn't tell you.

"I like our chances," replied Joe, studying a racing form.

The *Times* reported that I was nervous and ill at ease as we waited for the Judge's ruling, but that is just plain hogwash or wishful thinking. As soon as the Judge came back I knew it was in the bag.

He wiped a couple of Reuben crumbs off his lips. "After reviewing the evidence, the court declines to dismiss the writs," he said. "Bail is ordered at ten thousand dollars, pending the court's evaluation of the written briefs." And that was that. Now we had time to cut a proper deal. Make that deals. Because right there, at that moment, in that courtroom, I saw a way out for all of us.

As the gavel slammed down, I caught May's eye and I swear to God she knew exactly what I was thinking. She was always one step ahead of me, was my sister, May. That was just one of the things I loved about her.

Fifty-Nine

ALTHOUGH A TOUGH BREAK for Lucky Lindy, and even worse for his kid, the Lindbergh baby kidnapping was a terrific split for me. Right off the bat, people figured little Charlie was grabbed for dough and that maybe the Outfit was behind it—specifically the Purples from Detroit. I knew the Fleishers and the Bernsteins wouldn't be mixed up in something as dumb as grabbing the kid of the most famous man in America, and so we put out the word to the Colonel that we would be happy, as patriotic Americans, to help him find who nabbed the baby. Given that the Jersey cops couldn't find their arse with both hands, it was an offer he gladly accepted.

It was one of life's little ironies that I found myself working the case alongside Elmer Irey from the Treasury Department. Irey was the selfsame mug threatening me with a tax-evasion rap, and now here we were, with me funneling him whatever information we could find out about the kid. I even sent Joe out to meet the press, to assure the public that all the important gang leaders were doing our bit to find out who'd commit such a heinous crime. Even the Big Fella, doin' his time on the Rock, volunteered to help out, but the feds turned him down cold.

I took the Doozy down to Hopewell a coupla three times, to meet with Schwarzkopf, the chief investigator. I also took up residence for a few days with the great man his own good self and here's why. Once word got out that the underworld was actively involved in seeking-information-leading-to, well, let me tell you every poseur on the planet started showing up, pretending to be one of the boys. "Do you know Owney Madden?" the Colonel would inquire of each and every mug what come through his door. "Yes, sir, why of course I do," they'd to a man reply, upon which I'd emerge from the

next room and most of 'em would piss their pants on the spot and the rest
would just plain make a run for it.

At one point the Colonel was so desperate that he met with a nut job
named Mary Magdalene, one of those phony psychics who always come out
of the woodwork in times of trouble, offering to divine the whereabouts of
the missing beloved. I had a word with her on Lindy's behalf, and she didn't
bother him no more. Nor, coincidentally, did the Treasury Department bother
me anymore, after Lindbergh had a discreet word or two with them.

As you know, they eventually found the kid stiff, coincidentally nailed a
kraut carpenter for the big job and fried him after a fair trial. I have no idea if
he done it or not, but it didn't really matter. The important thing was we all of
us looked like the good guys for a change, which we of course were.

Even more coincidentally, Levy found for us again in the matter of the
parole violation. That rat Roosevelt showed his true colors just about this
time. I never saw anybody follow the papers the way this crook did, calculating every last move, and when he saw that I was up before Judge Levy, what
did he do but release the pardon plea I'd wrote him earlier, in which I said I
was gainfully employed by the Hydrox Laundry. That was all Cahill and
Brancato needed, and they flew it over to the judge saying it was evidence of
my deceitful nature or some such nonsense, because after all hadn't I denied
that very thing at some or other court appearance in the dim distant past, let
the record show.

Nevertheless, good old Levy ruled in my favor and said it was up to the
parole board to show that I'd never been discharged from parole, rather than
me having to prove that I was. "If Madden committed all the misdeeds of
which he is accused, he should have been apprehended long ago."

"Couldn't have said it better myself," said Joe as we discussed our next
move. "In fact, that's exactly what I did say."

"Judge Levy knows eloquence when he hears it."

"I'll say he does, we're planning to vacation together, our families, his and
mine, maybe the Cape, maybe the Island, maybe the Coast, I dunno. But I'll
tell you who doesn't know eloquence and that's Roosevelt."

"He really wants that nomination."

"Too bad he's gonna get it."

"He ain't gonna be good for us or our thing. Not like Al Smith. And you
know why? Because he ain't a businessman, that's why. He don't do business
and he don't know how to do business. Never trust a rich mug."

"Yeah, but he's gonna get it. Mark my words. Because he wants it more
than the other guys. More than Smith, more than Mike Curley, more than

Huey Long, even more than Seabury, that dirty sonofabitch." Between Seabury and Roosevelt, it was hard to choose which one was worse. "Simple as that."

Frank Costello said more or less the same thing when he called a meeting a few days later, up in Charlie Lucky's suite at the Waldorf, the one he rented under the name of "Mr. Ross." That would be the new Waldorf over on Park, which opened in 1931, the Empire State Building having replaced it on 34th Street.

Charlie had more names than any of us, which was saying something. Born Salvatore Lucania in Sicily, in New York he swanned around under the name of Charles Lane, which is the way he registered himself at Barbizon Plaza, or Charles Ross, once he'd moved over to the Waldorf. Sometimes you'd pick up the phone and it was Charlie calling and he'd just say, "This is 312," which wasn't his room number but his way of referring to himself by his initials, 3 for the letter "C" and 12 for the letter "L." He mostly did that when he thought the wire might be bugged. Out of town, though, he was Charles Lucania, Charles Luciano, Charlie Lucky or just plain Lucky.

He and Meyer were both there, as was Jimmy Hines. "Bunch of us are goin' to Chicago for the convention, make sure things run smooth," said Frank. He looked over at Hines. "Me and Jimmy are even roomin' together at the Drake. Nice place, the Drake."

"Nice place, Chicago," said Hines.

"Who we rooting for?" I asked.

"Whoever gives us the best deal," said Costello.

"Whoever we can trust more," said Meyer.

"Whoever's the least dangerous," said Charlie Lucky.

"I hear it's Roosevelt," said Frank.

Jimmy Hines rubbed his hands together, the way he did whenever he smelled money. "Of course it's going to be Roosevelt," he said. Roosevelt had plenty of dough-re-mi.

I still didn't like it. "You're a Tammany man through and through, Jimmy boy," I objected. "No one's been a better friend to the Tiger than the Happy Warrior." That was what the newspapers called Smith, and he seemed to like it. "Hell, he's the mug what give me my parole—"

Hines cut me off. "I don't think either of us is exactly a poor paddy anymore, Owney. I love Al, I really do. He's a great and good fellow. Only one thing wrong with him—"

"—he can't win," said Costello.

"And Roosevelt can," said Hines. "There's been a Republican in the White

House for the past twelve years. Things is dryin' up up here; we need the patronage that Washington can provide. Them goo-goos have had their shot at the trough for the past score. Now it's our turn."

"So you're backin' Roosevelt," I said.

Jimmy didn't have to say nothin'.

"I'm stickin' with Smith," said Luciano. "I don't trust that sonofabitch FDR."

Costello started flapping his big hands. "None of us does, Charlie. The guy's a weasel. But we'd rather have him inside the tent pissing out than outside the tent pissin' in. Meaning that if he owes us and he wins, he can flap his fuckin' jaw all he wants, just so long's the gravy keeps comin' down the tracks."

Charlie looked dubious, which matched my sentiments to a T-bone steak au jus. "Frank," I said, "no offense, but you're a chump. Look what this mug is doing. He'd put his own mother in the can if he thought it would help him. He's got a bag for a wife, he's boffin' every broad he can get his crippled mitts on, he's got Jimmy Walker on the run, Smith hates his guts and worst of all, he's making us look bad."

"That's one of the things we want to talk to you about," said Frank.

I looked around the room and realized I was alone with Lucky Luciano and Meyer Lansky, with no gunners or the Dutchman to back me up. I figured nothing would happen, what with Jimmy sitting there and all, but for just a moment I was after flashing back to the Arbor and I tell you my stomach started to ache again, real bad, and Sing Sing all of a sudden started to look good to me.

It started looking better when Meyer said, "You can go now, Jimmy. See you in Chicago." Lansky waited for Jimmy to shake hands with all of us, collect his hat and find the exit. Hines flashed me a rueful smile as he left, one of those what-can-I-do-I-only-work-here smiles. Then he closed the door and was gone.

"This Dutchman-Dewey thing is gonna be a problem, Owney," said Meyer very softly, the way he said everything. "We got enough problems as it is, without Arthur flyin' off the handle. We figured that since you guys is friends—"

"You might want to have a word with him," chimed in Lucky.

"A friendly word," added Costello.

"Because, frankly, what we're hearing is that Dutch's been making threats. Against Dewey," said Meyer. "To Berman, the boys, that broad he's bangin', whoever'll listen."

The old line about being my brother's keeper suddenly floated into my head, and I wished I knew how the rest of it went, whether you were supposed to be or not supposed to be. "What do you expect me to do about it?"

"Calm him down."

"Be persuasive."

"Reason wit' him."

"You got ways," said Meyer.

"And when we get back from Chicago," said Costello, "we'll all sit down, friends again, and deal with whatever we gotta deal with." He spoke in a flat monotone, especially the "friends" bit, and I knew he wasn't kidding.

"I can manage that," I said, getting up to leave.

"Not so fast," said Charlie Lucky. "We got one other problem."

"What's that?" I asked.

"You," said my friend Frank Costello.

Chapter

Sixty

WE WERE SITTING THERE, the four of us, very close together, speaking in low voices. For some reason it occurred to me just then how many years of my life I'd been sitting in that same small room, talking in that same low voice, and sometimes the people sitting with me were alive and sometimes they were going to be dead, but just hadn't gotten the news yet. I wondered, at our table, who was who.

I thought back to Luigi Mollinucci and to Willie Henshaw, and what they must have seen in my eyes just before I pulled the trigger. I thought about Little Patsy, practically wetting himself when he realized his number was up, and hoped when my time came I wouldn't embarrass myself like he did. I thought of the bodies I'd seen in blind tigers, when a couple of gangsters got to quarreling and one would suddenly pull out a gat and put a bullet through the side of the other fella's head; the way the victim's head, a bullet in one ear and out the other side of his brain, would pitch back, like he'd suddenly passed out; how there would be a little trickle of blood at the entrance and a big missing piece of skull bone at the exit; how sometimes the window opposite would get blown out, or how the bullet would punch a hole in the plaster; and everyone else would still be drinking or smoking cigarettes or playin' cards, and pretend not to notice because after all it was none of their business, because it was only business.

Was I worried? Yes. Was I sorry? No. At that moment, contrary to what you might think, I wasn't thinking about Heaven or Hell. I was only thinking about how to get out of there alive, if it came to that. Because, aside from Monk's .38, I'd left all my hardware at home. Because I was among friends.

". . . we think you should take a vacation," Lansky was saying when I came back to earth. "For your own personal health and safety . . ."

"At our expense," said Charlie Lucky. His right eyelid, the one that got busted up so bad when he went for that ride, was drooping even lower than usual, and he looked even sweatier than normal.

". . . during these times of troubles," finished Meyer.

"You caught a break with Levy, but I don't know how long he can shield you from the parole board," said Costello. "Even bought-and-paid-for robes gotta be honest sometime, otherwise the public will lose all faith in the system. And we can't have that."

"Because we *are* the system," observed Meyer.

"And we'd like to keep it that way," said Frank.

"If Roosevelt gets the nomination, we can all look for big-time heat for a while," said Lansky. "Okay, we can take it. We always have. And if he does get in, then he knows that we know that he knows he owes us, so maybe we got a little leverage here and there."

"And maybe we don't," said Luciano.

"There's something else we gotta face if it's Franklin," said Meyer. "Smith too, for that matter. Soon as he's in, the first thing he does is sign Repeal. Then where are we? I think we are all agreed that the past twelve years have been the years of milk and honey. But once booze's legal again, we gotta find something else."

"Such as?" said Frank, who'd be the front man in anything we did.

"Lepke and Shapiro are running the labor rackets, and we feel this is a major growth area," said Lansky. "The garment district is under their complete control, the longshoremen, the Teamsters . . . we are making inroads everywhere. Remember, if every workingman kicks us back a piece in gratitude for the contract we've gotten him, and if every employer comes across with a nice donation as the price of labor peace, then we are sitting pretty. So that's an area we've got to look at."

"Dutch is already doing that, with his restaurant workers' association," I pointed out.

"Your basic protection racket," said Lansky. "Strictly small beer. Like the policy rackets."

"What else?" I asked.

Charlie says: "There's always broads."

We all knew how much Charlie liked dames, how he'd go through fleets of 'em at a time. I guess it was only natural that he got into the drab racket, which he did with gusto.

"I mean, who is hurt by broads? The johns? Every guy needs a little strange once in a while. I sure as hell do—"

"Like every night," observes Frank.

Charlie let that drift. "The dames? What else are some of these frails gonna do? Their father raped 'em, their old lady beats 'em, maybe some of 'em are, you know, queer for each other, they don't got no talent for show business and they ain't blown the right producer in the picture business, so what's left but their backs? No foul, I say."

Me, I always thought running hookers was beneath a man's dignity but I kept my mouth shut on that. I was feeling more relaxed now, more a part of the group. I had plenty of ideas about what we could do, and was happy to share them.

And I would have too if at that moment Lucky's private doorbell hadn't buzzed.

"Speaking of which," said Lucky. His scar glowed white when he was aroused.

"This is no time for pussy, Charlie," said Meyer, who never had time for such things.

"Wait till you see *this* pussy," said Luciano, throwing open the door.

And there stood Mary Frances Blackwell.

The terrible thing about love is that you never really recognize it until it's too late, or else you can never admit it in the first place, not that there's much difference.

And the beautiful thing is you don't care.

"Sorry, Charlie, I—" She looked at me, and she didn't look at me.

Nobody looked at her except me and Charlie

"Not now, sweetheart," said Charlie. I said nothing.

"I'll call you later," said Charlie. I said nothing.

"Jeez . . . ," said Mary Frances. I said nothing. She sure looked swell.

I guess that's another thing. Dames, once they get under your skin, never change. Age ages 'em, sure, but when you're in the mood, the years just melt away, vanish, and then there she is, just the way you first saw her, in the first flush, in the first rush, in the first bloom.

"Beat it, baby," said Charlie, and she did.

I just never realized before how much she looked like May, until she closed the suite door behind her without another word. I said nothing.

"What a dumb broad, bargin' in on us like that. Gonna have to dump her."

"Looks like she's still got some good years left," said Frank, sucking on a cigar.

"And then there's narcotics," said Luciano, getting back to business.

"We disagree on this one," said Costello.

"We agree to disagree," said Lansky.

Charlie was pretty animated now. "Owney, you think the Dutchman's policy racket makes money? How much you think it makes?"

I knew, but in light of what just happened, I didn't much care. "Twenty million dollars a year." Frenchy had told me.

"What if I told ya you could make ten times that, easy?"

"I'd believe you, Charlie. You're a square gee."

That pleased him. "Them niggers is so dumb they bet on policy and think it's insurance. But dope is somethin' they're gonna love even more than policy. They got a weakness for it, I dunno why, just like the Indians and firewater. Can't resist that shit. Makes 'em feel real good. Makes 'em forget they ain't going nowhere 'cept jail and an early grave. Which, given their lives, is probably preferable. All we gotta do is make it available, nice and cheap, then jack up the price once we got 'em hooked. Like takin' candy from a fuckin' baby."

"I don't like it," said Frank. "Too much heat."

Luciano looked at him goofy. "Are you nuts? Maybe at first, but that's the part that's ridin' on our hip. That's our *investment*. Once the money starts flowin', there's no turnin' it off. And say we kick back twenty percent to the Law? So fuckin' what? They stay out of our way, and we're on easy street like we never dreamed about."

"I still don't like it," said Frank.

"And I don't like Roosevelt," said Lucky. "So we agree to disagree."

"And then there's gambling," said Meyer, stepping in. "Maybe even bigger than dope. Certainly less controversial and dangerous. Billions and billions of sucker dollars a year, for minimal outlay—slot machines, card tables, protection money. All you need is a friendly state government whose elected officials happen to be poor hillbillies and would rather be rich hillbillies, plus a police force of blind, deaf and dumb cops, and you're in business." He looked right at me. "This is where you come in . . ."

Lansky opened an atlas of the United States and pointed to a couple of places. First place he pointed to was Nevada. "Benny is working for us here."

"I thought he was in L.A.," said Costello. "I heard Benny and Owney's buddy Raft have become great pals. I heard Benny wants to be a movie star."

"Bupkes," said Lansky. "This is where the real dough is." We could see he was pointing to Las Vegas, a little town in the southern part of the state.

"Within driving distance of Los Angeles, and the state government appears to be exceptionally friendly to people like us. Plus this is virgin territory, gang-wise. Benny feels, and I agree with him, that this could be a very, very fruitful area for us."

"They don't got too many laws in Nevada," said Costello. "I like that in a place."

"The other territory we're looking at it," continued Meyer, "is here." He plunked a tiny finger somewhere east of Texas, right on top of the State of . . .

"Arkansas. We all been there. Rednecks and hillbillies, mostly. Guys that screw their sisters when their mothers and daughters ain't available. But it's got some of the same advantages as Nevada." Lansky withdrew his finger and started ticking off his points. "First, it doesn't matter as a place, so nobody will care what we do there. Second, the state government is already a criminal enterprise, so all we gotta do is show 'em how to do it right. Third, there's already gambling going on in Hot Springs, so why shouldn't we grab ahold of it." Meyer looked at me. "You remember, we talked about this."

"And I already been there," I said. I'd been trying to improve my language, but hanging around with these guys, it was tough.

"Right, that's what I thought. That's what we all thought. That's what got us to thinkin'. Ain't there some dame down there caught your eye?"

I nodded.

"Good," he said. "That settles it."

I wasn't sure what had been settled but I knew I was getting out of there alive. "You want me to go there and deal with McLaughlin."

"We want you to go down there and shove him over. If he plays along, pat him on the head. If he kicks, get rid of him."

"What about my interests here? The clubs?"

Frank reached over and patted me on the shoulder. "Frenchy and I'll take care of those for you."

"In exchange for . . . ?"

"For a piece of what you make down there."

"You don't expect me to stay there forever . . ."

"Hell no. Jesus, that would be a fate worse than fucking death, you ask me," said Charlie. "Just till we see which way this wind's going to blow over."

"In the meantime we all gotta make arrangements," said Frank. "That's why you need to cool off the Dutchman and put yourself on ice for a while."

"Why isn't Dutch here, Frank?" I asked. "You guys trying to cut him out or something?"

There was an awkward silence around the table. Meyer looked at the floor, Frank looked over my head and Luciano looked even oilier than usual.

"Let's put it this way, Owney," said Meyer softly. "Dutch ain't no team player."

"He don't get along with the group," said Charlie.

"And he sure as hell don't play nice," said Frank. That was clear enough for me, so I decided to keep my mouth shut as Costello looked around the room. "That about it?"

Lansky and Luciano nodded. "That's about it," said Frank.

I got up to leave and this time nobody stopped me. "Have a nice time down in Bubbles," said Costello. "I hear the golf is great down there."

"Come down and visit some time, Frank," I said. "You too, Meyer, Charlie. Bring your sticks."

"We should all live so long," Meyer was muttering as I departed.

On my way down to Bubbles I saw the news that Roosevelt had beaten Smith for the nomination. I felt sorry for Al, who was a good egg, but that's the way the ball bounces.

I heard all about it from Charlie Lucky. Longy Zwillman brought the deal to the Roosevelt camp, Lansky to the Smith forces: the nomination in exchange for calling off the Seabury dogs. There were plenty of delegates for whom the Outfit had done favors, run booze, got girlfriends abortions, and it was time to call in the chits.

I never got it straight whether Roosevelt's men actually agreed to the deal or whether they faked Longy out of his socks, but somebody gave somebody a sign or signal and the next thing you know, FDR was up there on the podium, making his acceptance speech, tryin' to pretend he still had pins under him, and every newsie going right along with the scam.

"I talked to Smith right after, told him how sorry I was," Charlie phoned me later. I was in my suite at the Arlington Hotel. Agnes was in bed with me.

"What did Al say?"

There was a short pause on the other end of the line. "He said, 'Charlie, you have just made the biggest mistake of your life. Frank Roosevelt's word isn't worth the mouth it comes out of. I ought to know. He will fuck you sideways. He will kill you.' "

"Jesus, Mary and Joseph and all the saints," says I, hanging up.

"What's the matter, sweetheart?" Agnes asked me as I turned back to her. I rose and looked out the window, down onto Central Avenue, looking at a little building across the way called the Southern Club and Grill, which sat right next to an apartment building that looked like good old 440 West 34th, shrunk in the Hydrox Laundry.

"Nothing," I said.

"You know I don't cotton to that popish talk."

"Then don't pay me no never mind," I said, trying to speak her language.

When I got back to New York a week later, I found out that the parole board, at the urging of Democratic presidential candidate Governor Franklin D. Roosevelt, had revoked my parole and ordered me back to Sing Sing the next morning.

Chapter

Sixty-One

I wasn't going to go without saying good-bye to my Mother. This entailed being driven down to 34th Street while lying flat on the floor in the back of a car in the dead of night. I got out near the rail yards and dove into one of our old Gopher tunnels, scooted through the usual shite, trotted under 34th Street toward Pennsylvania Station, detoured off to the right, came up the back stairs of 440 and let myself in to my mother's place.

I featured the bulls staked out for me in the front, and I had to laugh that they would think I'd be so dumb as to fox-trot in my own front door, when there were a million other ways into any dump in the nabe, but how would they know that, they were new Irish, fancy-pants, no pigs in the parlor, lace-curtain with hot water and toilets, and some of 'em even with electric fans to keep 'em cool instead of honestly sweating the way we used to.

I let myself in the front door, waking my mother. "Go back to bed, Ma," I barked, and she did. My lines was tapped, that I knew. The first call I made was to Joe Shalleck telling him to stall, and the second call was to my sister, May, a few floors below, but her husband, Jack, said she was asleep, and the third thing I did was call Agnes in Hot Springs and tell her I might have trouble making our dinner date next week, but then again I might not.

"What's the trouble, Owen dear?" she said. Agnes had a kind of sweet disposition that's hard to find in a woman, but then we were still courting. They're all lovey-dovey and sweet-talky while you're courting them, but after the ring, forget it, buddy, you're on your own.

One little detail I had left out of my relationship with Agnes, which got more serious every time I visited, was the fact that I was still legally married. I'm not sure it would have mattered very much—the crazy kid was head over heels for me—and in fact my bein' a Catholic was much worse in her eyes, not to mention her old man the Postmaster's, than being married. There weren't a hell of a lot of Catholics in Bubbles, not to mention Irish, but there were at least two Catholic churches, and the rest of 'em was all heathen Christian of one sort or another.

I have to admit, I never felt very comfortable around Christians, you know, those kind of Christians. Although I couldn't prove it, sometimes I suspected that they hated us Catholics more than they hated the Jews, which didn't seem to make much sense since we both more or less believed in Jesus Christ His Own Good Self, although they were more than a little wobbly about the BVM, which is the Blessed Virgin Mary to you. In fact, I think they even hated us more than they hated the coloreds, especially down South, where the coloreds were at least useful, up to more or less the present day.

Loretta—you remember her—was still alive and living up in Yonkers. I'd sorta lost track of time, but I figured my little girl was almost twenty by now, and there was hardly a month or a year that went by that I didn't wonder what had happened to her. I knew she was still kicking because she kept cashing the checks I sent her, and I had a coupla photos of her at her First Communion and her Confirmation. Still, I realized that Loretta and I were going to have to have a chat sooner or later, especially if I wanted to marry Agnes, which I was seriously considering owing to the present political situation.

For the truth was I had a tough play to make and I was only going to get one shot at it. It reminded me a bit of the situation way back when I had to wreck the Gophers in order to save them, and it was funny that the same bloke should find himself in the same situation twice, but I guess that's what keeps the Man Upstairs amused and interested in our little fates.

The outlines of this play were still forming in my mind as I made my fourth phone call, to Vannie Higgins, the flying lobster fisherman on my payroll. He and I both had taken aeroplane lessons from a retired Army flyboy, Major Thomas G. Lanphier, who just so happened to have been a friend of Charles Lindbergh. In fact, I'd bought a plane from Lanphier, which I was hangaring out on the Island. "Feel like a trip, Vannie?"

"Owney?" I'd obviously rousted him.

"Meet me at Roosevelt Field in an hour, and you can forget about the money you owe me."

"Gee, Owney—have you seen the papers? They're lookin' for ya everywhere."

"What the hell do you think I'm callin' about?" I snarled.

"Ya don't have to get sore about it," said Vannie.

"An hour," I said, and hung up.

I figured me and Vannie could make Hot Springs in four or five hours, and from there I could plan my next move. I hadn't thought Roosevelt would move so fast, but a guy with the world in his hip pocket and the White House in his sights is liable to do anything, which reminded me of my fifth phone call, which was by rights to the Dutchman.

This was my luck that night: Dutch was in bed with a broad, answering the phone out of breath.

"What?"

"It's me."

A girl's giggle, faint and vaguely familiar, and then: "Whattaya want at this hour?"

"We got trouble."

"You're tellin'—hey, cut that out—me?"

"Roosevelt's a rat."

"Knock it off. I'm talkin' to—"

"You've gotta warn everybody. Meyer, Charlie, Frank."

I heard Dutch hiccup. "Fuck 'em. What've they ever done for me?"

"Have it your way. But you might want to think about relocating."

More noises, sex noises. "I'll take it under advisement, Counselor," said Dutch.

"I'm going out of town for a while."

"Have a nice trip," he said as he rang off.

The hell with him. I tried.

Hiram took me out to Garden City in a plain old Chevy, which we figured nobody would be looking for. The cops were so used to seeing me toolin' around in my Doozy, or at the very least a Packard, that a Chevy with a Negro at the wheel and a white man in the backseat, like he was drunk and headin' home to Long Island after a night out on the town, wouldn't look too hinky.

"You want I should wait, Mr. Owney?" asked Hiram, anxious. My first instinct was to say no, but things were different now, things were changing on a daily basis, make that hourly, and so I told him to pull the car into the bushes and watch, just in case.

I stood out there in the dark, feeling like a fool. Worse, feeling like an animal—hunted, and in my own town, the only town I'd ever known and ever cared to know. The one I'd traveled so far to get to, and now this—some cigarette-smoking cripple who'd married his own cousin like some hillbilly boy from Arkansas was driving me out of New York. That's when it struck me that among the Christians, there wasn't hardly any difference between the toffs and the toilers, between the high life and the low life. When you got right down to it, they all married their cousins, one way or another.

The more I thought about the situation, the angrier I got. I began to feel like one of my mug fighters, like Carnera, who'd been told to take a dive—or worse, a coward who was running from a fight. I'd been battling cops all my life, and since when had I run from 'em? Since never is when, and this was no time to start.

This was my state of mind when Vannie finally pulled up. Hiram flashed the lights at me a couple of times, so I knew he was coming, and I was ready for him, a brand-new play in mind.

"You serious about the dough?"

"Why else would I have invited you here?"

"The pleasure of my company?"

We walked together to the hangar where they kept my plane, which was called an Ireland, something I liked. It's hard to believe now, but back then you could more or less come and go as you pleased, and so the night watchman didn't see nothing amiss about two fellas taking their flying machine out for a spin. I made sure the flatfoot saw both of us, chatted a bit, small talk, and then Vannie had the craft ready and I said so long, bet you never thought you'd ever meet Owney Madden, eh, and at that the guard's jaw dropped and I reminded him to keep his mouth shut until we were long gone if he knew what was good for him.

I threw a kit in the crate and stepped in as Vannie fired her up. "Where we going?" he said as the props began to spin.

"Arkansas. You heard of it?"

"Ain't that kinda far away? I told my—"

"Yeah, you told your mother you'd be home for breakfast. But you won't be."

"But—"

"But nothing. You'll do as you're told or you'll be sorry."

"But I got business—"

"We'll take care of it."

"But—"

"Can't you say anything but 'but'? Let me put it this way: if I see your face in New York in the next couple of weeks, you're a dead man."

That seemed to get his attention. "Okay, you don't have to get sore about it," he said. "I was just—"

"Going to shut up. So shut up and listen."

I gave Vannie his instructions, which was to get himself to Hot Springs and make like we'd both gone. Agnes would "put me up" at her father's house on West Grand and she'd store my things there, to prove I'd checked in. I'd had the foresight to grab a newspaper on the drive out, so there was even a copy of that day's *Mirror* for good measure. As for Vannie, he was to stay down there and make himself as scarce as possible for as long as possible, at my expense of course.

The plane was starting to move as I slipped out and hit the ground. I saw Vannie take off, bank, nearly clip a stand of trees, gain altitude and disappear, and hoped like hell he took my threat seriously. I couldn't afford any more double crosses, but if he tried to hand me one, I was in a position to do something about it. Unlike with Roosevelt.

Good old Hiram was waiting for me by the time I trudged back to where the car was hidden.

"Have a nice trip, Mr. Owney?" he said.

"Ask me in four or five days, Hiram," I replied. "Until then, I'm on holiday."

"Where to now? Where you ain't gonna be, I mean."

"How's the Bronx sound?"

"Good as anyplace else not to be," said Hiram, starting up the engine.

Chapter

Sixty-Two

FOUR OR FIVE DAYS was about how much I figured I had before the cops caught up with me, and about the time I needed to put my plan into action.

Here's the way I had it figured: First, Roosevelt was going to beat Hoover standing on his head unless the country saw him as too New York, too Tammany, which it wasn't going to do. Second, he'd have to show he was tough on crime, by which he mostly meant bootleggers like me—a cheap ploy that didn't cost him nothin', seein' as how Repeal was right around the corner. Third, the Outfit was going to be under a lot of pressure, and I knew us well enough to know that we didn't handle pressure very well. There were too many hoods like Charlie Lucky and his gunners, too many crackpots like the Dutchman who got mad and got even pretty much in one motion, and not enough brains like Lansky or diplomats like Costello. Temper had always been our weak spot, going back as far as Monk and his club. Our instincts were to slug first and worry about the cops later, and I include myself in that roster as well.

Fourth, with the heat on, Charlie and the boys would try to grab for everything they could right now. Dutch may have been nuts on the subject of Dewey, but he was onto something. Dewey was a humorless little prig with a mustache who wasn't above shaking down campaign contributors himself, as I heard and believed it. What we were witnessing was nothing less than a reversion to the old days, when the pols ran us instead of us running them. Only this time, they were adopting some of our tactics against us: cutting deals and then welshing, shaking us down for protection, muscling in our rackets. I guess it's easy to be a ruthless sonofabitch when you don't have to worry about the Law, when you are the Law, but if you ask me, it's dishonorable too. Honor is one thing and trust is another, but when both of them break down, you got chaos, which is what I could see coming like the old Death Avenue express.

Thoughts of persons such as Mayor Walker and Jimmy Hines floated through my mind. The Seabury johnnies were after the Mayor full-time now. Beau James! The mug who, when he was Al Smith's right-hand man in the state Senate, had legalized prizefighting and allowed the Yankees, Giants and Dodgers to play baseball on Sunday! And saved the nickel subway fare when he was Mayor, takin' his argument all the way to the United States Supreme Court! What had all them other bums in fancy suits done for the people compared to Jimmy? And what had he ever done to them? But Jimmy'd been too deep in the rackets for too long for them to spare his hide. Between the gangsters and the politicians there was going to be a bloodbath for sure, and whether the bodies were blown apart by bullets or the newspapers was a distinction without a difference.

So here was my agenda: save as much of my businesses as I could, try to keep as much of the peace as possible and get the hell somewhere safe to enjoy my old age. I'd already been as close to death as I ever wanted to be, and had no intention of repeating the experience anytime soon.

It seemed to me Dutch was the key. He had the shooters and the territory. If the two of us worked together and stayed together, we could keep Charlie Lucky and his troops at bay, long enough for us to salvage whatever the crooks in the federal and state governments were going to let us keep.

I sat in the backseat, low, and when we got to Queens, I hit the floor and stayed there until Hiram told me we were in the Bronx, 543 Brook Avenue to be exact, where the Dutchman and Joey Noe had started in the rackets and Dutch still kept a private pad for sentiment's sake. Brook Avenue was a street rendered innocuous by its proximity to Webster Avenue to the west and the railroad tracks to the east in darkest Morrisania.

I told Hiram to wait a block or so away and as my car glided up and idled for a moment I jumped out and hit the buzzer for Dutch's place. After just a couple of punches the door buzzed me in and there I was face-to-face with Abe Landau and Lulu Rosenkrantz. Abe was bald and looked like a college professor; Lulu was balding and looked like a mug. But they was both tough eggs, as good in a fight as anybody I ever saw. Which is why when I hear folks talking, especially down here in Bubbles, about what pansies the sheenies are, I just wish they could have known Dutch, Bo, Abe and Lulu, could have seen them in action like I did.

We were all old friends, but they seemed very surprised to see me when I told them I had to see Dutch in a big hurry.

"He ain't in," said Abe.

"He's busy," said Lulu.

Since they spoke simultaneously, I knew right away something was up. "I don't care if he ain't in or he's busy, this is real important, can't wait, and since when did either of you yeggs know me to give ya malarkey when it wasn't completely called for?"

Abe and Lulu looked at each other and I could see in their eyes they had to admit I was right.

"Yeah, but—" said Abe

"—even if he was in—" said Lulu.

"—and he wasn't busy—"

"—it probably wouldn't be a good idea," finished Lulu.

Now my suspicions were raised pretty high. "I know he's got a dame up there, if that's what's bothering you," I said. "I don't care. I seen plenty of dames, in and out of their knickers."

"But you haven't seen this one," blurted Lulu.

"At least we don't think you have," modified Abe. "Not in a long time anyway."

"Think I care about some old girlfriend?" Abe and Lulu looked at their scuffed shoes. Everybody knew my reputation for looking askance at mugs what tried to make time with my girls. "Forget it," I said. "I'm a new man."

They still seemed pretty dubious. Lulu even started to move in front of me, blocking my way up the stairs. And then Abe did something that caught me completely by surprise: he patted me down and found the .38 that Monk had given me so long ago. Talk about sentiment.

"Kinda old, ain't it?" said Abe.

"I can't believe you done that to me, Abie," I said.

"It's for your safety."

"It's for everybody's safety," said Lulu.

"Okay," said I, "but I want that back. When I come down, you give it to me."

Abe and Lulu were still lookin' dubious as they buzzed Dutch.

"Boys, I give you the solemn word of an Irishman on the head of his mother and his sister that I will not hold you personally responsible for anything that occurs upstairs, and that furthermore I will keep my Irish temper and emotions in check come what may. Deal?"

Abe and Lulu musta been getting tired of looking at each other, because Lulu stepped aside to let me pass.

"Who's he up there with?" I joked. "Mae West?"

As I climbed the two flights of stairs to Dutch's hideaway I was going over in my mind the business proposition I was going to present to him. How we'd combine our beer operations, our nightclubs, to take 'em legit once Repeal hit. How we'd introduce slot machines and card tables into the back rooms of all our clubs for special members. How we'd do our best to keep running the numbers but to keep the dope away from the coloreds, because being Irish I'd had plenty of opportunity to see what the Creature could do to a family, and I didn't want to find out about coke or horse or whatever they call it.

I had it all figured out, see. I had even figured the next step, which was to let Roosevelt have his fun, and to give myself up to the parole board, with suitable fiduciary assurances that I wouldn't have to do much time. To take Frank's advice and put myself on ice for a while, until the storm from Washington and Albany blew over, and then to be there, the last mug standing, to pick up the pieces and to go on with business as usual, as usual.

All these thoughts were in my head and plenty more I've forgotten about, and frankly it's a miracle that I can remember any of them because at that moment I rapped sharply on the door and I could hear laughter from inside and then all of a sudden a pretty girl not wearing much of any clothes opened the door and at that instant I knew why Abie and Lulu had taken my heater away from me because there I was face-to-face with my sister, May.

Chapter

Sixty-Three

I GUESS IT WAS ONLY A SECOND or two that we stood there looking at each other, a couple of strangers united by a mother and a father and separated by a threshold, but it sure seemed a lot longer. I have a vague, dim memory of glimpsing Dutch lying on the bed, a bottle of cheap beer in his hand, wearin' only his shorts and his socks, held up by a couple of garter belts. There's nothing makes a man look more foolish than to be caught in his stars and garters, but there was Dutch and there was I and which of us was the bigger fool at that moment?

"Zat you, Bo?" said Dutch. They say Jews don't drink, but whoever says that has already had a few shots too many, in my opinion.

Neither May nor I could muster words at this moment.

"Bo?" shouted Dutch.

"No," I managed to croak, "it ain't Bo."

"Where the hell is that sonofabitch?" screamed Dutch. "I'll cut his balls off, that motherfuckinsonofabitchinbastard."

I stepped into the room, managing to avoid looking at May. "You shouldn't oughta talk like that when there's a lady present, Dutch," I said.

Dutch managed to point both eyes in the same direction. "The gallant brother, come to rescue the fair virgin!"

I decided to ignore that. "At least, she used to be a lady—"

Dutch was struggling to his feet, sloshing the bottle of beer. "You know what they say about Catholic girls?" he wobbled.

He drew nearer. May remained frozen.

"They might not fuck you on the first date . . ."

"Until you made a whore out of her," I spat.

". . . but they sure will blow you."

The force of *my* blow put the Dutchman on his arse. May grabbed my arm. "Don't," she said in that little voice, and even with all that alcohol in her, she still had something of a head left on her shoulders. Unfortunately she hadn't been thinking with that part of her body much then. "They'll hear you."

Dutch was still sitting in a puddle of beer, looking bewildered. "Madden?" he said. "I thought we was friends."

"We used to be," I muttered.

"That's a hell of a way to treat a friend," he said, rubbing his jaw.

"Put some clothes on," I told my sister.

"How d'ya like my girlfriend?" he burped.

"I used to like her a lot," I said as I fumbled for May's things. Her dress was thrown into a heap in the corner, her stockings were draped over the edge of the bed. As I reached for them, Dutch shot out a hand and grabbed me.

"What d'ya think you're doin'?" he managed.

I slugged him again, hard. I wasn't worried a bit about Abie and Lulu because they knew, they knew the rules, they knew it was my sister, they'd tried to save me from my own folly. After all I was supposed to be out of town and here I was, big as life. They were right guys, even if they were working for this dirty' bastard.

My punch knocked the beer bottle out of Dutch's hand and I picked it up. I was about to hit him over the head with it when this time it was May who grabbed me. "No."

"Go home to your husband."

"No."

"Go home to your mother, then."

"No."

"Then just go home, for Christ's sake."

"No."

I was uncomfortable in that room, facing off against my naked sister, defenseless and beautiful and my own flesh and blood.

"Go home to your brother, then. The one who always took care of you when nobody else could."

I don't think either of us was ever closer to killing each other at that moment. She didn't even bother to cover herself up. Instead she let me have it. I woulda rather've had it again from Little Patsy and his mugs ten times over.

"I would," she said, "but I don't have that brother no more. He's gone, disappeared. The brother I knew was a real man who thought big and dreamed big, and wanted me to be part of those thoughts and dreams. We were gonna be a team, him and me, partners, the way he became partners with Monk and Dutch and all the rest. But he just never could start seein' me as a partner and kept on seein' me as just a girl." She paused. "Like now."

I stepped back, ready for anything. Ready to slug Dutch again, or kill him, or hold her, sweet May, in my arms once more. "How long's this been goin' on?" I asked, throwing her dress at her.

"Long enough."

I had to ask. "What about . . . that other stuff? The stuff you told me wasn't true?"

"What was I supposed to tell you?" she said.

"Let's go."

"You go. I'm staying."

"Don't you love Jack?"

"Don't you love me?"

Dutch had somehow managed to get to his feet. I'll say this about him, he was tough, he could take a punch. I wish some of my fighters had his jaw, and his heart. "I think you better go now, Madden," he said.

"I think you're right, Dutch," I said.

I stepped back out into the hallway. There was no sound from below; Abe and Lulu had too much class to come between a couple of guys arguing over a dame, the oldest argument in the book, and with always the same result somewhere down the line.

"What are you gonna do?" she asked me as she started to close the door.

"I'm going to take a vacation," I said. "A long vacation."

"I wish I could go with you. I wish I had come with you."

"I wish you'd come with me all along. Now it's too late."

She got that look in her eye then, that wise look she'd had since she was a kid. "Owen, are you in trouble again?" She'd been saying that to me since the old days on Tenth Avenue.

"I'm just after catchin' a few birds, May. And maybe lettin' a few fly away."

"I always wanted to fly."

I leaned forward and kissed her lightly on her cheek. "Good-bye, May."

Then she shut the door and was gone. The next time I saw her, we were back on 34th Street, just like we was kids again, only not. I was too dumb to get her play, and she was too smart to keep on playing. Frenchy wasn't the only one who could figure odds.

Chapter

Sixty-Four

I SPENT A COUPLE OF DAYS hiding out here and there, reading the newspaper accounts of my manhunt. The plane gambit had worked well enough. The night watchman had sung his song and there was a lookout for me in Canada and Mexico, whence the cops figured I'd flown. Others speculated that I'd gone to Reno to get a divorce from Loretta, the news of how I was sweet on Agnes down in Bubbles having made its authorized way into Winchell. Finally, Agnes gave an interview to the local rag to the effect of how I was down there and we were very much in love, that sort of malarkey.

All this talk about love got me to thinking and maybe a little randily at that, the result of which I made a phone call to Lucky about that dame and he told me he'd canned her some time ago, she was workin' a crib downtown, and if I wanted her, it wouldn't cost me nothin', we bein' friends and all.

"I can make my own deals, Charlie," I said. "Just gimme the address." Which he did: 23rd Street. The Cornish Arms. The same flophouse where Mad Dog had holed up with little Lottie, just before he ran into Bo Weinberg and his Thompson.

She answered on the first knock, breathless, expectant, needy, broke.

"Hello, lover boy—Jesus . . ."

"Hello, Mary Frances Blackwell," says I.

I went to put my arms around her, but she pushed me away. Not out of disgust or lack of desire. Fear.

"You don't love me no more?"

"I got the clap."

That flashed me back to Margaret Everdeane right quick. "So what? I seen plenty of clap. They got a cure. They got a cure for everything nowadays."

"Not for this clap they don't. It's the big one. Syph."

"How bad?"

She started to say something, opened her mouth in fact; the words wouldn't come but the tears did, plenty of 'em. "Tertiary."

I slept with her that night, just slept. We held each other like children, through all the hours of darkness, the hours of magic, when men and women meet each other as equals, as primals, bodies and souls.

"How long you got?" The light was glancing through the dirty windows, northern light, weak light, New York City light.

She sat up and shrugged, her nightie falling off her left shoulder, exposing her breast, that still beautiful breast no matter what was going on inside her, in the mysterious woman place that no man, however exploratory, however adventurous, can ever understand.

"Maybe a year. Maybe not."

"What can I do?" I assumed the answer was nothing, but it seemed to me the gallant question to ask, the only question to ask.

"Same as always," she said. Then she threw her arms around me and hugged me so tight I thought I was going to expire right then and there, because my breathing wasn't so good, you savvy, what with everything and all, the bullets and the bullet wounds, the healed and the unhealed. She mashed her mouth onto mine, sucking my tongue and my breath, tasting and infusing at the same instant, her last gift to me, her last bequest, her last request.

"Kill 'em all."

Some combo. A syphilitic whore and a sterile gangster, locked in an embrace, genitals that wouldn't generate, generations that would go ungenerated, forever and ever.

"Amen," I said. I pulled on my clothes and left.

The short version is she didn't make it a year. The long version is she never wanted for anything, as long as she lived. I owed her that much, and more. She's up in the Bronx today, with several of my friends, peaceful now.

Everybody was getting pretty worked up about the search for Public Enemy No. 2—that would be me, a testimonial to my ability to stay out of the headlines—and the wrapping up of my business affairs was coming along pretty well when all of a sudden Vannie Higgins shows up back in New York and starts shooting off his mouth.

Charlie Workman brought me the news. "Says he took you for ten grand. Says you never went to Arkansas. Says he don't even know where Arkansas is. Says he flew around in circles for a while, then landed at Teterboro and went to see his girlfriend. That's what he says."

This made me very unhappy. This made me out to be a liar, and worse, made Agnes out to be a liar. "Where is he now, Charlie?"

Charlie was a big guy and sometimes we think big guys is slow, and he was slow enough when he talked, but pretty quick on the trigger when he had to be, which is what I liked about him. "You won't believe this piece a shit," he said, and normally I don't cotton to that kind of language but I was getting pretty mad at Vannie myself. "He and three pals knocked over the Hydrox Laundry, got away with thirty-five hundred bucks and a couple a heaters."

"That all they get?"

"They also grabbed a ring and wristwatch from Edith Schwartz." Edith was the bookkeeper, whose job it was to keep the books as separate as possible.

"Hurt her?"

"More than they had to."

"What's Frenchy doin' about it?"

"Hunting."

"Any luck?"

"I already found him. Red Hook."

The more I saw of this kid, the better I liked him. He leaned forward, hoping to hear the magic words from my lips. I was sorry I had to disappoint him, but this was personal.

"This one I'm taking for myself. You can watch, see how it's done." The Bug flashed me a hurt look, and I knew right then that he was a stand-up guy, a gee who'd do time rather than rat on a fella. "I'm going back to college in a couple of days anyway. Stake him out, set him up and we'll roll."

"Gee, thanks, boss." He was genuinely grateful.

"Maybe you'll do me a favor someday."

We bagged Vannie a couple of days later in Brooklyn, where he was swaggering around, making the mistake of bragging about how he was holding parts of me in the palm of his hand. Hiram was at the wheel and the Bug was beside me as we slid up to Vannie somewhere near the Gowanus Canal.

"Feel like a trip, Vannie?" I said.

I'll say this about Vannie Higgins: he may have been a weasel, but he took it like a man. Even half-drunk, he got into the car without a fuss, sandwiched himself between the Bug and me and didn't open his gob.

We drove out to Garden City pretty much in silence. "Meet Charlie the Bug." Vannie nodded. "Unlike Benny, he don't mind the name Bug. Takes it as a compliment to his guts, in fact. Ain't that right, Bug?"

"That's right."

"That's the truth, Vannie, but don't you worry about Bug. He just feels like a trip too. Never been out on the Island before. Ain't that right, Bug?"

"That's right."

"They say travel's broadening. Ain't that right, Vannie?"

Vannie tried to say something but he couldn't.

"Mrs. Schwartz would like her ring back and her wristwatch. Imagine that, Bug, a buncha mugs in the middle of a cheap stickup heisting a lady's rocks. Don't seem right. Does it seem right to you, Vannie?"

Vannie shook his head.

"Plus of course I want all my money back. Vacations are expensive these days and, well, dough don't grow on trees."

Vannie swallowed hard and turned his pockets inside out.

"I guess we're going to have to make restitution some other way, eh, Vannie? It's like you go out of town and then your best friend starts making time with your girl. No self-respecting guy can have that."

We got to Garden City, near Roosevelt Field. I told Hiram to stay with the car and I told Bug to come with us.

As we strolled into the woods Vannie finally said something. "You ain't really going to do this, are you, Owney?"

I liked Vannie. I really did. "A year ago, two, the answer woulda been no. But things is different now and I gotta make examples and clean up loose ends. It's just bad timing is all."

"What do you mean bad timing?"

"I don't need any more pigeons in my life, especially stool pigeons."

He opened his mouth in protest and that's when I got Da's knife in him, right up through the roof of his mouth. He tried to struggle, but the wind was already out of his sails, and I cradled him in my arms as I jabbed the blade through his palate and, with a smack from the heel of my hand, up through the nasal cavity and into his brain. He died like one of my birds, bloody but peaceful, with only a twitch or two of his legs in protest.

That's what I call merciful.

The Bug and I wrapped his body in a sheet, popped it in the trunk and dumped it in Park Slope, on 8th Street, not far from the hospital, which wasn't going to do him any good at this point, and Green-Wood Cemetery, which was.

Chapter

Sixty-Five

I TURNED MYSELF IN at the front gates of Sing Sing two days later, July 6, 1932. I made an entrance that Raft would have been proud of. I was wearing a three-piece double-breasted green and blue suit with dark oxfords and white spats and a two-thousand-dollar Panama hat with a silk band. I had a reputation to uphold.

Big Frenchy and little Joe Shalleck were with me as we pulled up. "Don't worry about a thing, it'll be all took care of before you can shake a monkey's uncle at it," said Joe.

"What's it gonna cost me?" I asked, handing Frenchy Monk's .38 for safekeeping as he blasted the klaxon to let the screws know we was here.

"Six figures—maybe, I hate to say it, may God close His ears, seven."

"Whatever it takes."

"Peace of mind, you can't beat it with a stickball bat," said Joe.

I shook hands with both of them. "So long, boss," said Frenchy.

"See you in a year, George. A year," I repeated, speaking to George but looking at my lawyer. "If I ain't out in a year, get our money back."

The car roared away, leaving me standing there in front of the Big House. A couple of the screws had poked their heads out to see what the fuss was.

"It's Owney Madden," I shouted.

"Yeah, and I'm the Queen of Sheba," said one wiseacre, a dope named Crocker.

"Open up, ya screw, or I'll rap ya in the snoot."

I saw the other guard staring at me. "It *is* Owney Madden," he said.

"Get outta here."

"No, really. That's Owney Madden. I recognize him."

They were about to start debating my identity in earnest when I shouted: "Get the Warden before I get angry."

I couldn't believe that I had to stand there in the broiling July heat while I waited for these two nitwits to get Warden Lawes, but after about ten minutes, with me wilting, along came Clement Ferling, Lawes's secretary.

"Hello, Mr. Ferling, I'm coming," I shouted.

Naturally Ferling recognized me and got those gates open right quick, and a few minutes later there was the Warden, God bless his soul, greeting me like a long-lost pal and booking me right then and there.

"Where have you been, Madden?" said the Warden. "They've been looking all over for you."

"Jesus, Warden Lawes, am I hungry. Do you think you could possibly send a couple of the boys down to '21' to fetch dinner?"

Lawes snapped his fingers and Ferling went running off to place the order.

"In New York, where else?" I said with a smile, a smile that was returned by the Warden. For a head screw, he was all good, really cared about me who woulda cut his throat without thinking twice about it had circumstances warranted, and maybe that makes him a saint or maybe that makes him a chump, I dunno.

"Why didn't you turn yourself in to the parole board in the city?"

"Didn't want the publicity," I replied.

I had to give up my swell threads for gray prison garb of course, but Dr. Sweet was there too, to give me an examination as soon as I got settled in my cell. The Warden took good care of me right off the bat, excusing me from work detail, letting me raise flowers in the garden, all my usual haunts.

Charlie or Meyer might have got to me had they really tried, but I was more powerful at Sing Sing than they were, and it was about then that I figured out that having a cop next door to you might not be such a bad play as long as the cop was on your side. Since I stayed away from the work details, the laundry and the exercise yard, I was pretty secure.

I was also pretty sick. Those damn Duster bullets was acting up again, and Dr. Sweet had to put me under the knife once more. Before I went out, I asked him whether maybe this time we could get rid of the five slugs still walkin' around with me, but he reminded me they weren't the problem, it was the other six, the missing ones, ghost bullets whose wounds hadn't healed properly. Just before they give me the laughing gas I told him to give it one more shot, so to speak, and he replied he'd do his damnedest, which he did, but it didn't matter in the end, for when I woke up, they were still there, my little Arbor souvenirs.

Here's why I was so sanguine about going back to prison. The state may have been giving me what for, thanks to Roosevelt, but we still had a friend or two on the parole board. At my hearing some of the goo-goos raised the usual fuss about Al Smith's commutation, about whether I did or did not work at the Hydrox Laundry, the old rigmarole about whether I was or was not released from parole board custody, even that jolly little incident with the feds and my beer trucks, all supposedly to prove that I was still in the rackets even after they let me out of stir. I skipped the hearing on account of my health.

"You know what that schmuck Cahill said?" Joe asked me on his first visit.

"I can guess."

"You don't have to guess, I'll tell you. Here's what that schmuck Cahill said, something like 'His hands'—that's your hands, not my hands—'may be red with the blood of his fellowmen, but there's nothing in the record now before us to show it.' You know what I said?"

"I can't guess."

"I popped right up and said, 'I couldn'ta said it better myself,' and then I sat down again."

"How'd it go over?"

"Not too good. They ruled against you."

"Did we take care of it?"

Joe gave me a quick nod, then coughed loud and opened his briefcase to flash me something. One of the screws saw him and started to sidle over. "Beat it, ya mug!" I said, and he stepped back like a good boy.

I could see the name of the parole board members who was on our side, and I could also see the amount of money they and their sons and heirs were going to wind up with if they played it straight. There were a bunch of Irishmen on the board—Fagan, Moore, Canavan—and we figured one or more of 'em was hankering for an estate upstate somewhere. All it took was one million dollars in cash.

"How can we be sure it's on the level?" I asked.

"Simple," said Joe. "It's part up front and part on delivery."

"Not to mention cement overshoes and a dip in the drink if anybody welshes."

"I didn't say that."

"I did."

"I didn't hear that."

"That's what I like about you, Joe," I said as he got ready to leave. "You're blind and deaf—but not dumb." I think he took it as a compliment, but I'm not sure. It was always hard to tell with Joe if he even knew what a compliment was.

So there I was, sitting pretty. From time to time Warden Lawes would call me into his office for a catered dinner, and he'd fill me in on the continuing mayhem in town. One day in early October we sat down for a little heart-to-heart, just like in the old days.

"You're smart, Madden. I always said you were smart."

"Thanks, Warden."

"You're not like those other men."

"Who would they be?"

"Men like Lucky Luciano and Dutch Schultz. Gangsters." The Warden offered me one of his fine seegars, but I told him I'd stick to my cigarettes, even though Dr. Sweet was after me to stop smoking, on account of my lungs and bronchitis and emphysema and other diseases I can't spell, and mostly because, in his opinion, cigarette smoke and holes in one's lungs didn't mix, but I'd been smoking since I was a kid and wasn't about to stop now, although I hated the coughing. "Mark my words, they'll end up like all the other hoodlums—dead in some gutter somewhere."

I'd been in that very gutter, rose from it in fact, but kept my mouth shut.

"But not you, Madden. You've got a head on you—a fine head that ought to be turned toward honest, profitable pursuits."

"The laundry business sure is lousy, I'll give you that."

"You know what I mean." That was what I always liked about Lawes. He knew the score but had to pretend he didn't.

"You could be right about that," I admitted.

"We'll need some flowers for the prison chapel altar next week."

"Happy to oblige."

"Good lad," he said. I got up to go.

"There's one more thing," he said, and I sat down again. He got a grave look on his face as he rummaged through some papers on his desk and came up with a telegram. Although I'm certain he'd already read it, he read it silently to himself, looked up at me, started to say something, then didn't, and then he handed it to me. It was from my brother, Martin, and all it said was:

"OWEN, MAY PASSED AWAY LAST NIGHT."

My tongue wouldn't work, but all the questions were on my face.

"Last night. She found the shotgun that you gave . . ."

I'm told it took four men, including Warden Lawes, to hold me down and still enough for Dr. Sweet to get the needle in me.

Chapter

Sixty-Six

I ARRIVED BEFORE THE MASS, while she was still lying in the John Simons Funeral Parlor at 428 West 34th, between our apartment building and the church. I'd passed it every Sunday morning on my way to Mass, and now here I was in it.

Warden Lawes was kind enough to let me out for the day, as long as I was back to Ossining by nightfall. I told the guard they had to send with me to go have himself a drink or two on me at the bar across the street.

My Mother was kneeling in front of the coffin, mouthing the rosary so only the dead could hear it. I told Ma I wanted to be alone with my sister one more time before we put her in the ground, and she understood. Marty helped her into the next room and I closed the door.

The lid was down, because it had to be. There was no way even the most skillful mortician would have been able to put her back together, although I paid them well enough to try. So I'd bought her a gorgeous mahogany casket with gold fixtures, cost a couple of grand, because I wanted her to have the best, as usual.

"Didn't quite work out the way we hoped, did it?" I began.

"Not the way I hoped. It was supposed to be you and me—"

"And it was—"

"Except there was never quite enough room for me."

Don't be surprised that May was talking back. We Irish know you can talk to the dead, especially the recently dearly departed, and they'll talk right back, even if you're the only one who can hear them. We have some of our best conversations that way. When one person's alive and the other one's dead, that's the only time we can say some of the things we've always wanted to say, but couldn't in this world and that won't matter in the next. I used to wonder what they meant by Limbo and now I finally knew. May and I, we were both in Limbo, just on opposite sides of the waiting room is all.

"I was trying to take care of you."

"You sure took care of me, all right. I hated you sometimes. Didn't you ever feel it?"

"If I did, I didn't believe it."

"How I wished I could be like you. Do what you did, all that you did. I wished I had your moxie, your willingness to hurt people to get your own way. How I envied you your freedom."

"It came with a price."

"So did my imprisonment. Now I'm in the smallest cell of them all."

One of the funeral home workers, an old man, poked his head in, interrupting us. "What do you want?" I groused.

"Thought I heard voices," the old coot said.

"You thought wrong, so go pour yourself another drink and have another think, in that order. Get me?"

"Yes, sir, Mr. Madden," he said. He closed the door and vanished.

"Sorry," I said. "Where were we?"

"Do you ever dream? I used to. Maybe I'm dreaming now. Maybe you are too."

"What do you dream about?"

"Sometimes I dream about Ireland, about when Da and Ma were kids, before they met, before we existed."

"I dream about being way up high, higher than the roof at 352, higher than the penthouse at 440."

"Then what?"

"Jumping."

"But not falling."

"Soaring."

"Like your birds."

"Better. Higher."

"Sometimes I wished you were dead. You know what else I wished?"

"I don't want you to say it."

"That sometimes I wished I was dead?"

"You got your wish."

"And you never quite got yours."

I tried to lift open the lid of the coffin, one of those Dutch door lids, but it was screwed down tight, like somebody was afraid she'd get out.

"What are you trying to do?" she said.

"Kiss you good-bye."

"Too late for that now. Don't worry, it doesn't hurt anymore."

There was a cautious knock at the door, which I recognized as Marty's. "Be right there."

"Guess we gotta break this up, huh?" said Sis.

"Why didn't we have this talk sooner?"

"We couldn't. We were going places, remember?"

"I'm going to miss you."

"At least you'll be with me for my big moment."

The next thing I knew, my brother was putting his hand on my shoulder and telling me it was time.

We kept the funeral small, only immediate family, and so the mourners at St. Mike's included myself, Marty and Ma, Jack and Alice Marrin, Frenchy. Raft was in California, Diamond was dead and Dutch . . . The organist played "The Last Rose of Summer."

I kept my hand on the coffin the whole service, holding her hand through the wood, right up to the altar, letting her know by my touch that I hadn't left her, that I'd never leave her. I rode in the hearse with her and stayed by her side until they lowered her into the ground and started shoveling dirt on her.

I had three bullets in my .38, so right there Frenchy cracked open the cylinder and took one out for me. I threw it into the grave with a prayer and a blessing for what we never had. The other two I kept for myself, until the time was right.

Chapter

Sixty-Seven

Most of the next year I spent in prison. Out on the sidewalk things were happening, mostly not good things. Talk about being on ice: the end of the Castellammarese War was playing itself out, Dutch and Charlie Lucky got to shooting each other, Jimmy Walker resigned and sailed to Europe, Roosevelt got elected, trouble everywhere you looked. Worst of all, Prohibition was on the way out, given the bum's rush by the Congress that had cheered it a baker's dozen years earlier and awaiting the inevitable thirty-sixth state to ratify its demise.

Me, though, I was nice and safe up the river, protected on all sides by gray stone walls and armed men who, for the first time in my life, were on my side. My food was catered, on account of my bad stomach. I had my flowers and my birds. It wouldn'ta looked good for Lucky and Meyer and Frank to come visit me, but George Raft, big star that he was, showed up several times. What few women who worked in the prison went nuts, and once they'd figured out that he and I was friends, they were even nicer to me than before. I wasn't just a gangster; I was the pal of a *movie star*.

We never discussed my sister.

"There's a picture I might do," he said, "called *Each Dawn I Die,* with Cagney. I'm the bad guy." Georgie was always dithering over his roles, the dummy.

Cagney I liked. From time to time we'd met either in one of my clubs, like the Stork, or on my visits to Hollywood, where he always seemed to be imitating me in the picture shows. Born on the Lower East Side, he had the real mug's swagger. He was about my size, seven or eight years younger, not quite as good-looking but okay if you liked your hoodlums fake instead of real.

I tell you, I've lost track of all the movies that have featured me. I knew all the writers and producers back then, including Runyon and Mark Hellinger, so I wasn't too surprised when various versions of my own good self popped up on the screen. Offhand, I can think of Raft's imitation of me in *Scarface,* Cagney in *The Public Enemy,* Cagney again in *Blonde Crazy* and *Lady Killer,* although I never mashed no tomato's puss with a grapefruit, nor kicked one in the bum and thrown her down the stairs. My favorite was *Lady for a Day,* even though Warren William didn't look a thing like me, but since I'd let Runyon steal the story of Madame la Gimp and call me Dave the Dude, I figured I'd go along with it.

I almost drew the line when Hellinger and that one-eyed Walsh fella did *The Roaring Twenties,* where Cagney was so obviously a cross between me and Larry Fay that I thought about suing for breach or invasion of some-thing, but Shalleck told me to sit down and shut up, it wasn't every mug who got part of his life story up there on the screen. When Cagney got plugged at the end, it made me wince a little, though, since Larry Fay had gone out feet first in much the same manner in 1932, on New Year's Eve yet.

They let me out on July 3, 1933, one day before Independence Day. They gave me back my suit and my Panama, plus $51.52, which I'd earned while in stir. That included $17.52 for my labors with the flowers and the pigeons, twenty bucks for "rehabilitation" and the fourteen dollars I had in my pocket when I checked in. They offered me a new suit and a train ticket to New York, the way they do all the released birds, but I didn't need either one of them. "I got my own car," I said. "As for the suit, I wouldn't wear them rags if you paid me. Give 'em to some other mug."

The wagon was waiting outside, a brand-new shiny green Packard coupe that went well with my suit. Only problem was there was a horde of reporters clustered between me and the car. Flashbulbs popped, which usually enraged me, but this time I was actually glad the newspapermen were there, because I had something to say to them. First, though, I had to wait out a barrage of their dumb questions. I often wondered who was stupider, the reporters or the cops, and never could pick a winner. Still can't.

"How's it feel to be a free man?"

"Are you goin' back to the rackets?"

"Whaddya think about Repeal?"

Stuff like that.

"Boys," I said, "listen up and write this down."

You wanna get a pack of jackals like journalists quieted down, just tell them to listen up and write this down.

"I'm through with the rackets. I'm through with broads, beer and Broadway. I'm through bein' a punk."

"How old are ya, Owney?" shouted one jerk.

"Forty-one years old. It's time to start thinkin' about retirement, about goin' somewhere I can raise my flowers and my birds in peace and quiet."

"A changed man, huh?" said a yertz in a cheap hat and a bad suit.

That gave me an idea. "Changed man? You bet I am. Remember what you boys used to call me?"

"Owney the Killer!" they all shouted. Reporters find a story that works, they stick with it until the readers get sick of it.

"Well, now you'll be calling me Owney the Hermit. That's how changed I am." They loved that.

One of our new boys, Jim O'Connell, was the wheelman, a nice kid. Joe was in the back with Frenchy. "Everything jake?" I asked.

"Ain't like it was," said Frenchy, who'd put on weight. I think he was eatin' too good on my nickel. "Never is, is it?"

Joe Shalleck handed me my discharge papers. "You're still under aegis of the parole board until July 1, 1935, which means that legally you're not to leave the jurisdiction—"

"I got things to do," I reminded him.

"Correct, although legally—"

"Legally a million bucks ought to go a long way toward making my life easier. Is everybody paid?"

Shalleck nodded. "The bribe's been paid," said Frenchy, who never had much of an ear for subtlety.

"I don't like that word. It's like 'tax.' Let's call it . . . an investment. An investment in the Plan."

"You mean the Arrangement," corrected Shalleck.

"Whatever you wanna call it, just do it."

"We're working on it."

"Good." Joe shut up, which was a rare and wonderful occurrence. "Where'd we get the car?"

"I stashed the Doozy," said Frenchy. "Figured it'd be safer that way."

"Have it shipped down the Springs, quiet," I said. "Didja bring the map?"

Frenchy handed me a road map of the United States. I traced the route to Bubbles with my finger. "Fourteen hundred miles—"

"Thirteen hundred and ninety-three," said Frenchy.

"Thirteen hundred and ninety-three miles each way. Too bad it ain't closer, but if it was any closer, it wouldn't be no good to us. Bulletproof?"

I was referring to the Packard. From the front seat, O'Connell spoke up. "Take a tank to knock this baby over," he said.

"Where's the Dutchman?" There was an uneasy silence in the car. "Well, where the hell is he?"

"Gone fishing," said George.

"Somewhere upstate, in Jersey, who knows?" said Joe. "Good riddance to dead rubbish."

"Find him. We got some unfinished business."

Frenchy plunked out a big mitt, took the map from me and folded it up neatly. "Things ain't going too good for the Dutchman," he said.

"I'm all broke up about it."

"There's muttering he's cuttin' a deal for himself. State, feds, whatever it takes."

"That'll be the day. Dutch may be crazy but he ain't no canary."

"On the other hand," said Joe, "I have it on the highest authority, and I am talking the *highest* authority, just about the top of the line, and I mean all the way down the line, or up the line, whichever, from Pennsylvania Station to Washington, District of Columbia, that Dutch's still making noises about sending Bo Weinberg and Abe and Lulu to visit Thomas E. Dewey on his morning stop for coffee and doing unto him what Bo did unto the late Vincent Coll. But you didn't hear that from me."

"Not from an officer of the court," I agreed.

"Nor from Joseph Shalleck, private citizen, who has every hope and intention of living a long, happy and prosperous life and dying in his bed and not in custody somewhere at age oh I don't know, let's say ninety-two or thereabouts."

We passed through Yonkers and I thought about my wife, Loretta, and our little girl, not so little now, twenty-one years old, all grown up, and I wondered what had become of her. I wondered if Margaret ever thought of me, and if she did, what she thought of me.

Then we were driving down through Harlem toward the Cotton Club, and all at once a terrible wave swept over me as I realized that I was going to lose all this, my city, the only city I'd ever really known and certainly the only one

I loved. I loved her from her head to her toes, from the northernmost reaches of the Bronx, where Monk and Kelly had slugged it out, down to the tip of the Battery and across to Brooklyn, where so many of our associates lived, then up through Queens, past the laundry, and all the way out to the tip of the Island and across to the Jersey Shore, where so many of our rum cutters had sailed, during the glorious days of the Noble Experiment, when men like me made this country what it is today. I cursed the fate that was forcing me to leave it, and then I thanked the Good Lord above for allowing me to have thirty years here, including time spent behind bars, to live and work and realize my destiny. Still, it was a smart play and nobody ever said of Owney Madden that he didn't know a smart play when it came up and introduced itself.

A few days later the Packard and my own good self were through the new Holland Tunnel and then the long drive through Jersey, Pa., Ohio, Kentucky and Tennessee to Arkansas, down to Little Rock to stop in to pay my respects to the Governor and hand him a little token of our esteem, the first of many, and then over to Bubbles, Hot Springs, to see my sweetie, Agnes, and ask her to marry me. I thought she was going to faint dead away.

Agnes had been up to see me plenty in New York, and I always took her to the clubs, the speaks, anyplace glamorous, because she just ate that stuff up, like a kid gobbling an ice cream cone. It struck me during our courtship and later marriage that I could stash a good deal of cash on and about her person, in the form of bracelets, necklaces, rings and all manner of jewelry that dames swoon for, and did she ever swoon. Each time I gave her something she acted like she'd never seen anything like it, which in most cases she hadn't, but she'd take it, trembling, from my hands and then put it on or try it on or model it in some way that she thought might appeal to me, and whether it did or it didn't didn't really matter because we were both getting what we wanted out of our deal.

"When shall we be married, Owen dear?" she asked. She really did talk like that. All southern girls do, most of 'em anyway, particularly when they want something.

"I'll be fully discharged from parole in the summer of 1935," I told her. "Right after that."

"We'll live here of course." Here being 506 West Grand. Not far from the federal court building, where I knew I'd be spending some time, Arrangement or no Arrangement, and just down the road from Hot Springs High School, on which I'd be laying some charitable contributions, to establish my bona fides.

She'd been born in that house, which had belonged to her father, James Demby, the Postmaster. It was small, but had plenty of room for addition and expansion, and best of all it could be fixed up to accommodate my special needs. I put in a wing for myself, with plenty of avenues of escape if any of my old friends came calling in a bad mood. I also bombproofed the garage and put the mail slot there, in case any of my old friends sent me an explosive token or two. There was even a spot for my pigeon coop, and they say down here in Bubbles that every homing pigeon in town is descended from my flock.

I spent the next couple of years shuttling back and forth like this, closing down operations up North and setting them up down South. McLaughlin proved to be a most understanding Mayor, especially after Frenchy and I took him out for a drive one day and Frenchy stuck a gun in his ribs while I explained the facts of life to him. After that, everybody continued to kick back to Leo, and Leo kicked back to me; I gave Costello a piece of my action up North and Frank steered my clubs legit, just like we'd agreed. It was all part of the Arrangement.

Marty and his girl Kitty got married on the first of May 1934, but I had to miss the wedding on account of business. Which business I can relate quickly.

I found Branagan without much difficulty. He'd made it to retirement, pension, his little tin box full. I'd kept his palm greased through thick and thin, and the one good thing I can say about the former roundsman was that he was fairly cheap, drank no more than necessary to get himself plastered and had himself a nice flat on the Upper West Side. He was still chasing underage quim, which is what I found him with on the night I came to call and cash in his chips.

I shot him once, point-blank as he answered the doorbell, in his knickers just like the way I remembered him, only this time it wasn't Jenny Gluck, except that it was, if you get my meaning. Anyway, I didn't have no time for chitchat, this was just business, putting paid to an overdue account, and to his credit he never said a word, not when he opened the door, not when he recognized me even though my hat was pulled down low, not when the slug crashed through his forehead, right between the eyes, and he pitched backwards onto his Oriental carpet, the blood seeping out from the back of his dead head, and the girl—she really was a girl, not even close to a woman, even though we got older younger back then—not knowing whether to weep from sorrow or fear. I threw my coat around her and escorted her out the door, down the stairs and into my car and I took her home and never once asked her name.

Which reminded me that there was one thing about Branagan I never knew and that was his Christian name. If he even had one.

After a little friendly persuasion, Loretta gave me a Reno divorce, in August 1934. I was almost a free man.

Chapter

Sixty-Eight

"SO HERE'S THE DEAL, and this is the best deal we're gonna get, so my advice to you as your attorney-at-law, and you'd be well advised to take it, is to take it, which is: Whereas you, Owen Vincent Madden of Liverpool—"

"Leeds."

"Wherever, England, having been duly arrested in excess of one hundred times—"

"How many, exactly?"

"Who cares? and convicted once—well, two if you want to count the parole beef, which I personally don't—hereinafter known as the party of the first part, has been discharged from parole by the State of New York—"

"About time."

"And has duly authorized lawful counsel—"

"That's you?"

"Shut up and listen, in the person of Joseph Shalleck, Esquire, that's me, to petition the party of the second part, hereinafter referred to as the government of the United States of America—"

"Those rats—"

"Whatever, for redress of certain grievances, it is hereby concorded and agreed—"

"Very fancy."

"That, in return for certain assurances of personal safety and security, that the party of the first part—"

"That's me."

"Hereby undertakes and warrants the following—"

"What do they mean by 'certain'?"

"We're still working out some of the details, so the language is a little fuzzy."

"Go on."

"Hereby undertakes and warrants—"

"You said that already."

"To absent himself in perpetuity from the City of New York, including the Five Boroughs, as well as the Counties of Westchester, Rockland, Nassau and Suffolk, and the State of New Jersey."

"Did they throw in Poughkeepsie too?"

"I don't see nothing about that in here."

"What happens if I don't?"

"You'll be arrested and sent back to Arkansas."

"What happens if they don't?"

"Don't what?"

"Keep their part of the bargain."

"Nothing is what happens, what are you gonna do? Roosevelt's the president and you're not. Never can be, not being born American, and by the way you might want to think about becoming a citizen of the good old U.S. of A., after all this great land's done for you and besides it might come in handy one of these fine days, unless that is you don't care when your tushie gets put on a boat and shipped back to England or wherever as an undesirable alien, do you? And is hereby forbidden from owning any fiscal or fiduciary interests in or operating any business, whether legal or illegal, within said area, the current legality or illegality of which business is not affected by the Eighteenth or Twenty-first Amendments to the Constitution of the United States."

"What's that mean?"

"It means you can't brew beer no more."

"I wish they'd make up their minds."

"So do most people."

"That's it?"

"More or less."

"Did they put it in writing?"

"Not any writing that anybody's ever gonna read."

"That tells me something."

"You and me both. Agreed to this day, whatever day and date it is, Henry Morgenthau, Jr., Secretary of the Treasury and special adviser to President Franklin Delano Roosevelt."

"That rat."

"You already said that."

"Treasury never did like me. Where do I sign?"

"Right here." Joe handed me a pen and I scrawled my name.

"How can I trust them?"

"How can you not?"

"They ever find out what happened to Vannie Higgins?"

"Nobody saw nothing and Vannie ain't talkin'."

"That figures."

We shook hands. "When are you leaving?" Joe asked. The date was October 22, 1935.

"Coupla three days. Figure I'll be in Bubbles by the twenty-seventh or so."

"What's keepin' you?"

"Unfinished business."

"Don't dawdle."

"Don't worry."

"Write when you get a chance."

"Watch the papers, and I don't mean the funny papers."

Chapter

Sixty-Nine

I FOUND MY MOTHER back at the apartment at 440, sitting in her easy chair, listening to a program on her crystal set. Since my father's death, she had worn widow's weeds, I'd never seen her in anything but, a silent keening visible to every passerby, the subject of her grief obscure but personal. She had kept his picture displayed like the image of a saint in a roadside shrine, a holy relic minus the hank of hair or bit of bone, and all it needed was burning votive candles to make the devotion complete. The portrait picture she was even now packing away, laying it to rest carefully wrapped in the news of the day. She didn't so much as turn as she heard the key in the lock.

"Whaddya know, Ma?" I called out, alerting her to my presence. She kept wrapping, folding and wrapping, ever more tightly until if Da had still been breathing, he would have been smothered. "Whaddya say?"

I noticed she wasn't wearing black anymore. Her weeds had been tossed casually across the back of a chair, discarded, and instead she had managed to wriggle into some number that looked like it'd seen better days and many months and years too.

"Ma?" I said, sensing.

Methodically she finished what she was doing, which was wrapping up Pop but good and laying him to rest in the old steamer trunk she called her hope chest. I guess it was just about then that I realized I'd never seen that crate open, in all the long years we'd spent together, Ma and I. I'd never once been tempted to raise its heavy lid, with the big metal lock, never once been moved to discover what she had brought over from the Sod with her, what goods had survived the sea journeys, what was so important to her that she had sheltered it here, away from life's vagaries, safe and secure in her home.

She put the portrait into the chest and closed the lid as I came up behind her. "What's the occasion?" I said.

Ma took the nearest chair, smoothing her old skirts. "Owen," she acknowledged.

We looked at each other for a time.

"You've come to inform me of somethin'," she said at last. "Don't lie to me, boy, for sure won't I know, because you've been lyin' to me all your life."

"Never," I copped, "about anything important." This was important. We both knew it. "Where ya going, Ma?"

"Home," she said.

"Long way home."

She shook her head. "No it ain't. Home's right here." She gestured with her hands, old lady's hands, each of them sixty-five years old. Old people got older faster then. "Sometimes the longest journey you take is the one where you never have to leave. Because everyone else leaves you. And sure aren't you just as lonely as if you were the one who'd up and gone away, but worse, because they're all somewhere and you're left here alone, nowhere."

I had no idea what she was talking about. "So where you going, then?"

"It ain't where I'm goin'. It's where you're goin'. For goin' you are, unless I'm very much mistaken."

She had me there.

"Long ago, when I was nothin' more than a girl and dreamin' about the day I'd meet your father, I used to try to picture my life the way it would be henceforth. Most of the images that rattled around in me poor head were cutouts from the papers, things I'd heard at the *ceilis,* tales the silly geese in Lisdoonvarna told after spoonin' with lads who didn't know not a whit more than they did. I heard tell of journeys far and wide, to lands across the sea, not just Amerikay but Canada, Uruguay, New Zealand, Montserrat and I don't know where all else the Good Lord meant to disperse us.

"The one thing I did know is that once we was gone, we was gone. Nobody came back from them places. When they sailed away, they was as good as dead, and that's the way we treated 'em. When it came our time, we knew that's the way they'd treat us too. Didn't expect no more, didn't get it either. It was like a little death, the kind you have to suffer and pass through on the way to the next life. Sure, didn't we think it was as good as Heaven we was going to, no matter what heathen land we were bound for."

I couldn't tell if she'd been drinking or not. "I heard the stories, Ma. Belfast, Queenstown, Liverpool—"

"They wasn't just stories, Owen. They was life."

She turned away from me now and started wrapping again. This time it was the picture of May, her engagement picture, her of the Mona Lisa smile, looking into the future, and in that moment I knew just what she'd seen. She'd seen the same thing Monk had seen, lying there on his bed, nearly beaten to death. The same thing Da saw on the pier in Liverpool, half-blind and half-mad, gulping his last breath.

Nothing.

She shrouded May quicker than Da, opened up the lid and slipped her inside. "My daughter," she said, May's name having vanished along with her body.

There were two pictures left, mine and Marty's. I was wearing a fine suit and my fedora; Marty was hatless, his suit not so fine. "What about them?" I asked.

She sat back down, heavy with the weight of her years. "They stay. I used to think they was goin' places." She glanced up. "Get me a glass of tea, if you'd be so kind. In the kitchen."

A fat-bellied pot of tea snuggled in a warmer was sitting on the table, as usual. I poured a single glass and brought it in to her. Even though it was hot, she drank the tea down quickly. The sweat ran down her face, or maybe it was tears, but she didn't bother to wipe it away.

Instead, she wiped her lips and rose. "Time for my nap," she said. "Make fast the door on your way out, if you don't mind."

I stood there, watching her go off in her old youthful dress, seeing the girl she once was, the dancer, the beauty. She neither looked back nor said another word, a ghost on her way back to her private world.

I waited a decent interval and then opened the trunk. The smell of mothballs hit me square, and it took a few seconds for my eyes to penetrate the darkness within.

The picture of Da and the picture of May lay together, side by side at the bottom. Otherwise it was empty.

As empty as Da's lungs and Monk's head and Becker's conscience and May's future and my heart. I gazed hard into that emptiness and I was damned if I could see any more than she had.

Chapter

Seventy

THERE WAS ONE MORE PART of the Arrangement, and that involved Dutch. Dewey's pursuit of Public Enemy No. 1 had become a staple of the newspapers, which was another reason I hated the press. If a man's business wasn't his own business, then whose business was it? It was certainly none of the business of the newspaper lads, who were always poking their noses into places their noses didn't belong. I often found myself wishing, during this period, that we could do to them what the Big Fella had done to Jake Lingle—that is, shoot them in the head and leave their bodies on the sidewalk—because after all, they were no better than the rest of us. Didn't they all drink and have fluff on the side and steal from their employers and rat out guys—Hell, they made a living being rats—and switch to the side of whoever'd take care of 'em? Just as phony as goo-goos, reporters were, you ask me.

Still, Dutch courted 'em like a politician, and the deeper he got into trouble, the more interviews he gave. I'd seen this mistake before, and so had Dutch—it's what got Capone into trouble—but Dutch never learned nothing from nobody.

So we read about him in the papers nearly every day, how he beat the tax-evasion rap up in Malone by bribing the farmers and turning the tables on the feds. "I offered them one hundred thousand dollars to settle this thing when they were broke and people were talking revolution and they turned me down cold. I'm no gorilla. I never killed nobody nor caused nobody to be killed. They say I was a beer baron. So what? We got Repeal, ain't we? I gotta laugh when I read about a guy who gives the public a beer being called a public enemy. If that's the case—what do you call Roosevelt?" Dutch was always on the right side of the issues.

"I call him a dirty double-crossing sonofabitch," said Charlie Lucky. We were all up in Mr. Ross's suite at the Waldorf, waiting for Dutch—Charlie, Meyer, Frank, Lepke and his gorilla Shapiro, me.

"What was it Capone used to say?" asked Costello, tossing me the paper. " 'When I sell whiskey, it's called bootlegging. When my customers on the Gold Coast serve it, it's called hospitality.' "

"This Dewey stuff, this is much more serious," said Meyer. "The feds blew it. Dewey won't."

"What the hell's with that guy?" asked Costello. "Why don't he go back to Michigan, leave us all alone?"

"He wants to be Governor," said Charlie.

"He wants to be President," said Lansky.

"How many guys wanting to be President do we have to put up with?" I wondered. "How many Presidents does a country need, anyway? It's a damn shame when the pols can score cheap points off guys like us and then get elected for complaining instead of doing something."

"They're capable of anything," said Charlie. "They're fuckin' animals."

The buzzer sounded. Lucky mashed a button. "Tell Mr. Flegenheimer to come right up," he said. "Tell his associates Mr. Landau and Mr. Rosenkrantz to wait in the lobby."

The private elevator brought Dutch right to Lucky's door. "Come on in, Dutch," Charlie welcomed him. "You know all the boys."

Dutch threw his hat on the sofa. He was steaming. "This fuckin' Dewey, this sonofabitchin' bastard—"

"Let's save the pleasantries for later, Arthur," said Meyer, "and get right down to business, shall we?"

"Where's Mr. Weinberg?" inquired Charlie.

"Mr. Weinberg couldn't be with us today," replied Dutch. "He fell in with some bad companions, and he's doin' penance even as we speak."

"I heard he disagreed with something that ate him," said Gurrah Shapiro.

"You oughta know, Gurrah, you've fed enough mugs to the fishes over the years," snapped Dutch, who wasn't afraid of the likes of Gurrah Shapiro. "And they say the East River is dyin', Jesus what a crock."

Lepke, who wasn't any bigger than Dutch, moved forward belligerently. "You got no cause to be sore at Gurrah—" he began.

"Why don'tcha go fuck yourself, ya little yid?" barked Dutch, who was so proud of being German.

"Jesus," said Costello, "it's the War of the Jews all over again." Frank was referring to how Lansky had sent Waxey Gordon up the river with a timely and anonymous forwarding of some particularly incriminating documents, and the waxing of King Solomon, the Scotch-whisky monarch, up in Boston. Benny Siegel, Lepke, Curly Holtz, Shadows Kravits, Big Greenie Greenberg— all those tough Jews danced to little Lansky's tune.

Dutch sat down at the table like he owned the joint. Not a word or a glance between us, no recognition at all of the last time we saw each other. He was still the same old defiant Dutchman he'd always been, but I couldn't help but notice he was sagging a little.

"Pressure getting to you, Dutch?" I asked.

"That's what I came here to talk about," he said, brightening. "I got a way to fix things."

I knew Dutch Schultz well enough to know that he always perked up when he was contemplating murder, and sure enough, he was.

"We've staked out this sonofabitch Dewey and can you believe it this schmuck goes to work by the same route every day. He leaves his apartment at 1148 Fifth Avenue at eight each morning, then goes around the corner to a drugstore to have his coffee and use the pay phone. The fuckin' pay phone! Like he was a bookie or something. Apparently doesn't wanna wake the wife, Jesus they must have had some time in the sack the night before, huh? Maybe not. Anyway, he's there, in the fucking phone booth, a sitting fucking duck like Mad Dog Coll and we all remember what happened to him, right? He sips his coffee so he don't get his mustache wet and then his boys chauffeur him downtown."

"You sure you can get him?" asked Lepke, who'd cooled down. "I wouldn't mind seein' that putzhead go. But be sure you get 'em all. You know the old saying: no witnesses, no indictments."

Dutch waved his hand in the air dismissively. "Piece a cake. It's the Mad Mick all over again and Bo took care a him okay."

"But Bo ain't with us no more," reminded Charlie.

"Whattaya Charlie, questioning my professionalism? My judgment?" Dutch's voice was rising. "You think I need Bo for a job like this?"

"Settle down, Dutch," said Frank. "We're all friends here."

"You think my boys Abe and Lulu cannot take out a fucking *lawyer* and a couple of secretaries? You must have a pretty low opinion of me, Charlie, a goddamned pretty low opinion, you can say something like that to me. To Dutch Schultz."

Meyer walked over and put a hand on Dutch's shoulder. "Dutch," he said, "you can trust me. You and I are *lantsmen,* like Lepkeleh and Gurrah."

"I liked this whole thing better," said Dutch, "when the Jews were running the rackets and not the dagos—no offense, Charlie, Frank. What's happening to us, Meyer? We goin' soft, like the Irishers?"

That hurt.

"Maybe you oughta start spending more time in East New York, Brownsville, Ocean Hill," said Lepke. "There's plenty of tough kikes out there."

"But I'm here," said Dutch. "Hell, I ain't even supposed to be on this side of the river."

"Don't worry, we won't tell," said Costello.

"So it's agreed, then?" said Dutch, looking around the room. "Lepke, you and your pet monkey Shapiro agree with me, don't you? We get rid of Dewey, we get rid of a mighty big stone in our shoes. Because let me tell you, this guy will not stop with me. If he gets me, he'll come after you, Charlie, and you, Meyer, and you, Owney, and all of us, every last fucking one of us. He will not quit until he tromps over every one of our dead bodies on his way to Albany and then to Washington. He's a bad guy, and I am requesting your permission to take him out now, while it's easy."

"Just for the sake of argument," said Charlie, "what if we decline?"

I thought Dutch was going to start laughing. "You can't be serious, Charlie. You may be Italian but you're not stupid. You're—"

Dutch took a breath and started again. "I know you're trying to muscle in on my policy business, you and Meyer, and I understand that, even if I can't allow it. But that is something we can discuss like rational human beings, sit down, have dinner—"

"Just don't let Charlie get up to take a leak while you're eating," cracked Costello, and everybody laughed and maybe somewhere even Joe the Boss was laughing.

"—talk things over. Jesus, these politicians really piss me off. We work for them, we slug for them, we vote for them, we give them money and then they turn around and treat us like one of your two-buck hookers."

"I don't have any two-buck hookers, Dutch," said Charlie, real level.

"The point is, they don't respect us. This will not only get their attention—it'll get their fucking respect."

Nobody said anything for a while. Charlie looked both conniving and dubious. Lepke was obviously on Dutch's side and Gurrah did whatever Lepke wanted him to, but they were an entry, a team, so they only had one vote. Costello, I knew, would side with Lucky; he was the front man, and didn't need the bad publicity Dewey's assassination would entail. I was inclined to agree with Dutch; as far as I was concerned, whacking Dewey was the next best thing to whacking Roosevelt. Which left it up to Meyer.

"Mr. Schultz has made some very persuasive arguments, with the eloquence and tact for which he is so justly renowned," said Lansky. "Thank you, Arthur."

It took Dutch a beat or two to get the picture that he'd been dismissed, like a defendant the jury'd just found guilty. "That's it?" he said finally.

Charlie Lucky got up and pushed the elevator call button. "Thanks for stopping by, Dutch. You can go out through the underground garage and be back in Jersey in no time. Newark, I hear."

Dutch looked to Lansky for support. "Meyer, you said we were *lantsmen*. Well, maybe we are and maybe we aren't, 'cause I ain't no matzo ball like you. But where's Benny? Why is he out in Los Angeles banging B-movie actresses when he oughta be here, banging at our enemies? What kind of outfit are we runnin'?"

The little man gave a littler shrug. "Where shall we send our answer?"

I think Dutch must have sensed which way Meyer's mind was blowing. "Look at you. One foot still on the boat and already you think you're on Park Avenue."

"We *are* on Park Avenue," reminded Lansky.

Dutch shook his head in disgust. "In another two generations there won't be any more Jews in America, just a buncha yids in fancy clothes with phony names and fake English accents." I don't know why he looked at me when he said that, but he did.

"I got one last question," said Dutch. He seemed a little embarrassed. "You guys, you Catholics . . . Charlie, Frank, Owney . . . any of you ever . . . go to confession?" That was a question none of us expected. "You know all that Catholic jazz, confession, communion, extreme unction, the sacraments, the whole megillah."

Luciano shrugged off the query; his soul was long gone, if he ever had one.

"I ain't been to confession in I dunno how long," said Frank. "Too much like pleading guilty, you ask me."

"Here's why I'm asking," said Dutch. I'd never seen the great Dutchman like this, shuffling his feet in front of his pals like a little boy. "You all know I been through some tough times lately, what with the indictments, the acquittal, etc., and when I was seeing"—he shot me a quick sideways glance—"a certain lady, well, she got me to thinking that maybe it wasn't just luck, but something else, some*one* else. And that someone is Christ."

If I could have laughed out loud, I would have, and if I could have shot him, I would have.

"While I been lyin' low, I been studying," Dutch went on. "Catholicism. I'm thinkin' about converting." He paused. "Do they let Jews be Catholics?"

We all just stared at him, incredulous.

"I think so," said Costello. "I mean, they let Jesus. I don't think there's no laws against it." Frank looked at me, as if I was some kind of expert. "Why don't you ask Madden here? He still sticks his head in St. Mike's now and then, don't ya, Owney?"

I nodded, trying to avoid looking at Dutch. "Mostly funerals these days."

Dutch walked over and looked me square in the eye. He had some nerve, I'll give him that. "You ever go to Confession?"

"Only when I have to."

We looked at each other for a few moments and then Dutch turned and grabbed his hat. "I'm in the back room at the Palace Chop House in Newark," he said.

"We'll be in touch," said Lucky Luciano.

We were all silent until the elevator was well and truly on its way.

"Let's vote on Dewey," said Costello. He voted no. Lepke and Gurrah voted yes. So did I. Meyer voted no. That left it up to Charlie.

"Ixnay," he said. I wonder if Dewey ever knew how close he came to tasting Lulu's lead.

"And the Dutchman?" asked Lucky.

"I don't like Germans," said Meyer Lansky.

Chapter

Seventy-One

THE ONLY QUESTION was who should deliver the message. Meyer argued that whoever the messenger turned out to be, he should be Jewish, as a matter of respect.

Charlie and I and Frank disagreed. We were one gang now, working together. Cooperation was the future, and if we were going to cooperate, we might as well start at the most fundamental level of our operation. "That was the problem with Monk and Kelly, they couldn't cooperate," I said.

"About a little pissant thing like a stuss game," said Frank. "Who even knows how to play stuss today, 'cept a buncha old babushkas?"

"We have excellent messengers of all races," Charlie pointed out. "Irish, Italian, Jew, colored, Spanish, Polack, even a Welshman or two."

"It's important," said Frank, who was always thinking. "Important to show America that we can all work together for something more than our own good."

"Frank's right," I said. I felt myself getting a bit exercised, because I was about to say something I'd believed for a long time. All my resentment, at both the world I'd been born into and the world I found, suddenly bubbled up inside me. Then it all came pouring out, just like they say it does when you're dying, and there was nothing I could do to stop it.

The whole damn thing, from Somerset Street in Leeds to the factories of Wigan to the docks of Liverpool, my father taking that beating from Thomas Jefferson so we could get to America, only to find the selfsame bastards waiting for us on this side of the ocean that we thought we'd left behind. Little Fats Moore, knocking over my mother, and almost killing me, and even though I put paid to his arse, how he was still with me every breath I took.

The way they made our boys gonophs and our girls drabs; the way they worked us to death in the mines and the tunnels and on the streets and stole our money and our prettiest girls. The way they turned our own against us and turned 'em into cops and bulls, their nightsticks and their daysticks; their striped-pants lawyers and their prissy women in their summer dresses, so tempting and tantalizing but you could only look and not touch, paddy, unless you did what I did, took their law and turned it against them, twisted it, worked it over so that it didn't bear no resemblance to law at all, except maybe the law of the jungle.

And it was in that jungle, our jungle, that we had a chance. Let them decry us, scold us, remonstrate with us, send our own priests into our own neighborhoods to tell us what not to do. Give us our parades and hope like hell we'd go away; give us our drink to keep us drunk and then, once they'd got us hooked, take it away from us to turn us into criminals in our own houses. To put our pictures up in post offices, to tell American virgins that we were the Devil, come to turn them into whores and dope fiends when in fact it was them what was doing that very thing to us and ours. Which taught me early and often that whenever one of them opened his gob, you should believe the exact opposite, especially when he was tellin' ya how much he cared for you and how much good he was going to do for your people, if only you'd give the sonofabitch your vote and your money and your livelihood and, for good measure, your life.

All these things and more bubbled out of me like the waters in Hot Springs, came rushing down the hills of my soul like a torrent, a flood that would eventually wash away everything that stood before it, and might, just might, if I played my cards right, cleanse my soul.

"I'll take the message," I concluded.

"I thought he was your friend," said Charlie Lucky. "Despite that thing with your sister."

So they knew. They all knew, and didn't tell me. What are friends for?

"Who better to deliver the news?" I said.

"Let's say you get the message across," said Meyer. "Then what?"

"Then I leave. I'm getting out anyway, retiring—remember?—heading to the Springs to get married, settle down, run our businesses, make some money, maybe if I'm as lucky as you, Charlie, even die in my bed with my wife beside me."

"Mazel," wished Meyer.

"The question is: what are you going to do after I'm gone?"

I'm sure they'd never considered that. "Gurrah and I are going to take in *Porgy and Bess* on Broadway," said Lepke. I'd never known him to make a joke before.

"Or maybe Lunt and Fontanne in *The Taming of the Shrew*," said Shapiro, and that made two jokes I never expected. I guess the situation was funnier than I thought.

"It's all yours, Owney," said Charlie Lucky.

"No, Charlie," I replied. "It's all yours."

Chapter

Seventy-Two

THE PALACE WASN'T THAT GRAND. It was a former speak, on East Park Street across from the bus terminal in Newark, a town in a state I'd never much favored, despite having the Mayor, a couple of state senators and former Governor Silzer on my payroll. Newark in them days was basically Italian and Jewish, slowly turning colored, so none of us saw much of a future there, but it was a place we could do business in relative safety, and none more so than the Dutchman. I'm not sure why; maybe it reminded him of the Bronx.

I had the Bug case the joint that afternoon and he reported back. There was a long bar to the left and some tables across on the right, which led to a back dining room near a men's john. According to Jack Friedman, the bartender, the Dutchman and his circle sat in the back room, giving interviews, conducting business from the pay phone, dining, drinking, waiting. Because it was located in Jersey, Dewey couldn't touch the Palace or its occupants, and because it was on Longy Zwillman's turf, which was to say mine, Trenton left it alone. Abe Landau and Lulu Rosenkrantz even got themselves appointed deputy sheriffs of Essex County, so they could carry their heaters legally, wherever they went, and as for Dutch, what the hell did he care about the law at a time like this?

The time was a little after ten P.M. when our car glided up in front of the joint. We had a driver, name of Piggy, and two messengers, my Bug and another Jewboy named Mendy Weiss, whom Lepke had recommended.

"Got the telegrams?" I asked. As one, Bug and Mendy nodded. Bug had a .38-caliber revolver as his primary weapon, and a .45 backup; Mendy chose a shotgun for the evening's labor. "Lulu, the one with hair, will have a .45 or two and he's very quick. Abe will have a .45 as well. Berman has nothing but his noodle, so be sure you take care of that. Dutch usually has a .45 in his waistband, but that you let me worry about. Civilians?"

"Just Friedman, the barkeep," said Bug.

"Can we trust him?"

"How can we not?" said Workman.

We were right in front of the Palace now, and I eagled the hand-lettered sign in the window: "Closed for Private Party."

"I'll say," I said.

The only weak spot was Piggy, who looked a little skittish to me. "What's the matter, Piggy, never been a messenger boy before?"

"No, sir, Mr. Madden," he quivered.

"Don't worry, there's nothing to it. All you gotta do is sit here with the motor running until you see us come out. Then you drive like hell."

Piggy sweated and nodded. "Got it."

"Good. You don't, well, I gotta turn in a bad performance report to your employer. Capeesh?"

"Yes, sir, Mr. Madden."

I turned to the Bug. "Charlie, did you learn anything last time we were together?"

"And how."

"Tell Mr. Weiss."

"Don't be in a hurry but don't dawdle neither," said the Bug. "Don't let 'em say anything. Begging slows you down."

"Right," I said.

"Make each shot count. No showin' off."

"Good," I said to my prize pupil, the second coming of Johnny McArdle. "One last thing. Let Bug take out the gunners," I said to Mendy. "You handle Otto—"

"Aww—"

"Dutch you leave for me. No matter what happens, you leave him for me. Got it?"

"Got it," said Weiss, disappointed. This was the biggest hit of his life.

"Don't worry, Mendy," said Workman. "There'll be plenty of other chances."

"Thanks."

I patted the big Bug on the arm and could feel his muscle. "You're ready."

His big wide face broke into a grin that had more teeth than Eleanor Powell. "Gee, thanks, Mr. Madden."

I checked my own gun, Monk's gun, my last shot, whether fired in anger or during the course of business. There was one last bullet in the chamber, of which fact I didn't bother to inform my cohorts. Because after all these years of practice, either I was going to get this right or I wasn't. This was the test that Monk had been preparing me for, that all the time in the can was for, that all the bodies I'd caused to cease breathing, either directly or indirectly, were leading up to, stepping-stones, over which I was going to dance all the way to Arkansas and redemption.

"Let's go."

We stepped out into the night. Mid-autumn, cold enough for an overcoat, just barely.

I opened the door and let Bug and Mendy precede me. I saw Friedman already hitting the floor, the cloth he was wiping the bar with still damp and on the bar.

Nobody at the tables opposite. Closed for private party.

Bug striding forward like a boy who can't wait to take First Communion, reaching into his coat pocket, his hand on the butt of the .38, which was just swinging out now . . .

Mendy coming up with the shotgun . . .

Me, with Monk still in his holster, trailing both of them.

Abe and Lulu at one table, talking. Abbadabba at another, alone, totaling up sums. A third table, where somebody had been sitting, half-empty glass of beer on the table, the seat vacant for now.

If a man's life is measured in minutes, then his death gets cut fine into half-seconds. That's about how long it took for the three men in the room to say hello to their fate before the lead started to fly.

Bug sprayed the room, no questions asked or answered. Bang, bang, bang, bang, bang, bang—all six shots hit their mark before anybody knew what hit him. Then the .45 in his other spoke: *phut, phut, phut, phut.*

Ker-BLAM, Mendy's shotgun was heard from too.

Lulu featured us first, stood up, then went down, seven slugs in him already without so much as a how-do-you-do, but still whipping out his .45, trying to return fire, but unable, because he was hit from chest to belly, just like me so long ago, and I felt for Lulu, I really did, but it was too late for feelings now, and time only for settling accounts at the Big Register.

Abe was across from Abbadabba, his back turned slightly to the doorway, which let the Bug's first shot enter just below his shoulder and come out his neck, the second one shatter his upper arm and the third fracture his right wrist just as he was trying to get off a shot.

Otto tried to reason, to play the angles, to duck, but no luck. Mendy's second report caught him but good and put him on the ground, all 220 pounds of fat and brain and no muscle at all.

Maybe all of five seconds had elapsed and three men down.

No sign of Dutch. Monk stayed in my pants.

"For Christ's fucking sake," said Bug, reloading. "Where the hell is he?"

"Watch your language, boy," I said, heading into the only other room the Dutchman could be in. The men's room.

Which was where I found him, propping himself drunkenly up against the wall with his left arm while his right hand held his wiener, which was taking a leak. He was wearing his hat and his topcoat, which is the only time in my life I ever saw a mug wearing an overcoat in the pissoir. It was so funny, so dumb, that I almost laughed, except that this was no time for chuckles.

Even in his state, he must have heard something of the noise in the dining room, because at that moment he turned around, his dick still in his hand, shaking it onto his shoes.

"What is this, the Fourth of July?" he said.

"I brought your answer."

"Come and have a drink with me first," he said, trying to zip up and making a bad job of it. "You know how I hate to talk business on an empty stomach." He approached me with a sly camaraderie. "That fuckin' greaseball Luciano pinochled me pretty good, didn't he?"

I shot him once, right where Little Patsy's bullets had done their most damage, in the groin, the shot that had condemned me not to impotence but to childlessness, my first and only girl having been lost to me so many years before. The last bullet I would ever fire from Monk's revolver ripped a hole through the innards of Dutch Schultz, punched out his back and lodged in the tiles, shattered, its work and mine done.

He got this look of surprise and confusion in his eyes right then. I thought he might go for his .45, the one he always carried, but wouldn't you know it, on this evening he'd left it back at the hotel, the Robert Treat Hotel, just around the corner. The only time in recorded history that the Dutchman was without his gat, and he had to run into me.

But he didn't go down.

"Jesus, what did you do that for, all's I said was let's have a fuckin' drink." He pushed his way out of the john and into the dining room, his lifeblood trailing out in a mist behind him.

Abe, Lulu and Otto were all lying where they'd fallen, but if you can believe this, not a one of them was dead yet. There was blood everywhere, a real abattoir the likes of which I never seen before, all three of these tough Jews was either moanin' or movin'. In the meantime my lads were nowhere to be seen, and it was then I realized that I was the one who was dawdlin'. But I owed that to a friend.

Dutch stepped over Abbadabba's body like it wasn't there. "Where the hell's the bartender?" he said, tacking for his table. The mirror in the room had been shattered by two shots, and one of the pictures as well. The reflections were almost as crazy as the reality.

I never cease to be amazed by the things dying men do. Dutch plopped into his chair like he was about to order dinner after a hard day at the office, and looked up at me for the last time. "I thought we was friends," he said.

Then his head plunked forward onto the bloody table and he put his hands out like he was praying to Allah, because he sure as hell wasn't praying to Jehovah, or maybe he coulda been just another lush who'd had two or three or ten too many, when in fact he'd had just one too many, and who'd put his head down just for a minute, just to catch a few winks, just to catch his breath, just to collect his thoughts before going home to his wife and having to explain how he got in this condition, and no, that wasn't lipstick on his collar, it was blood, his blood, just look for yourself, put your hands into my wounds and feel for yourself.

I backed away, my empty gat in my hand, as useless now as Dutch's *Schwanstuck,* no backup, nothing. I knew the good busybodies of Newark would have already called the heat, and I was trying to make as graceful an exit as possible for a man of my age, which was forty-three years old, which still came as a surprise to Little Patsy in Hell I'm sure.

Then I did something, I admit to you frankly, that was pure sentiment. I wiped the fingerprints from the .38 and laid it down on the table next to the Dutchman, who was still moaning and muttering something. This gat had been out of circulation for so long, I reasoned, that even if the dumb Jersey cops put two and two together and matched the pieces of the slug in Dutch's gut or in the wall of the shitehouse to the heater, they'd be mystified how an ancient weapon like this could have killed a modern man like Arthur Flegenheimer on October 23, 1935, at the Palace Chop House, Sea Food, Beer on Draught, Dine and Dance, in Newark, New Jersey, Closed for Private Party.

This is why I have to laugh at crime reporters and scribblers and the movies and such, what happened next I'm talking about, because if you showed this in a moving picture or wrote this down in a novel, the audience would laugh and throw tomatoes at the screen or tear the pages out, because it could never happen in real life, except it did.

Otto Berman rolled over, moaning, clinging to a life that was doing its damnedest to escape him and was about to succeed.

Lulu Rosenkrantz, a bloody mess, was trying to stand up.

Abe Landau wasn't there.

I didn't want to turn my back on Lulu, but I sure wondered where the hell Abe was, so I was rotating my kopf back and forth like a dope at a tennis match when I hear more shots.

Abie had managed to make it to the street.

He had blood gouting out of a hole in his neck, an artery, so it was just a matter of time, but there wasn't any time, and he was firing with his right hand, even though there wasn't much left of it. This is what I mean by tough Jews, Abe Landau blasting away and my gunners in the car blasting back until a couple of more shots caught him and sent him flying into a trash can out by the curb, and this part was exactly like in the movies. Abe sat down hard in the can, which wobbled a bit and then tipped over into the gutter, and he rolled half in and half out, his gun hand in the street and his arse in the trash.

Only problem was my getaway car had gone away, leaving me there on the sidewalk without a firearm, a stiff in a can, and no way to get home.

I turned back to the Palace and can you believe it here comes Lulu, ventilated, and he's leaning up against the bar like the sousedest souse in the world and by God he's reaching into his pocket and taking out a quarter, a fucking quarter, pardon my French, and *getting change* from Friedman—I don't expect you to believe me now—and then staggering over to the pay phone near the front and plopping the nickel into the phone and having a conversation with somebody, the operator I suppose, a tough Jew who was also a cheap Jew, who didn't want to pay a quarter when he could have paid a nickel, which he did, and died doing so, the useless wire in his hand, hello Central get me Heaven.

I stepped back into the bar real quick, ready to kick Lulu to death if I had to, but I didn't have to perform this particular corporal act of mercy. "What did you see?" I asked Friedman, whose eyes were as wide as the nipples on a fifty-cent whore after she's earned her keep.

"Nothin'."

I looked at the twenty cents on the bar. "Keep the change."

I have to tell you I had no idea what I was going to do as I went back out into the street. Already I could hear distant sirens, fire or fuzz I couldn't tell, and thought about running for it, but decided not to, because what is more undignified than a middle-aged man in a fedora, fine suit, nice shoes and an overcoat from Saks running down the street like a teenage second-storey man?

Besides, what did it matter anymore? May was avenged, Lucky and Meyer had closed their deal, and the Syndicate would go on, no matter what happened to me. Frenchy had my clubs, Costello had the finances, Dutch had his answer, Agnes had her future and somewhere, wherever she was, Yonkers, Reno, wherever, Loretta had my name, and Margaret, whoever she was, had my heart. The heart that May took from me when she died, and gave back to me on that long ride to the boneyard.

I was glad Margaret had it, because where I was going, wherever I was going, I didn't need it anymore. Because the place where my heart belonged lay over the river, those lights, just across the water, and I wasn't going to ever get to call it home again.

Behind me, the show was over and the Palace was quiet, and the souls making ready to depart, wherever they were headed.

I saw the lights of a car, tearing around the corner: a wheelman and a shotgunner. There was no sense running. I put my hands up as a big mug got out of the passenger's side and took it all in.

"They musta done something wrong," said Big Frenchy DeMange.

"You can say that again, George."

"Come on, Owen. Time to go home."

He tossed his shotgun into the gutter. It bounced once and landed in Abe Landau's lap, where it belonged.

PART THREE

The 73rd and Last Chapter

April 24, 1965

I made Bubbles forty-eight hours later, the day after the Dutchman finally quit. Agnes and I were married on December 3, 1935. I was forty-three, she was thirty-four. We're still married.

Incredibly no one died in the Palace Chop House that night. They all made it to Newark City Hospital, and then one by one they checked out. First the magnificent brain of Otto Berman shut down just before three in the morning, then the lionhearted Landau followed him into eternity about four and a half hours later. Even with all that lead in him, Lulu managed to hang on until early in the morning of October 25, just about the time I was pulling into Hot Springs, my hands clean and my conscience clear. After all, I didn't kill nobody. The doctors failed to save them.

I heard later that Dutch had a few things to get off his chest before he went, which I guess is true of all of us who get more than a couple of seconds of reflection before the curtain falls. They got a stenographer into his room to take down what he was saying. It never ceases to amaze me that, at a time like this, the bulls will sit there and ask a man who's half-dead and out of his noodle the same dumb question: "Who shot you?" As if a mug like the Dutchman would tell them, because the real gangster's answer is always the same: "Nobody shot me."

I know.

"Please make it fast and furious . . . I will be checked and double-checked and please pull for me . . . Oh, I forgot I am plaintiff and not defendant . . . They are Englishmen and they are a type. I don't know who is best, they or us . . . A boy has never wept . . . nor dashed a thousand kim . . . Mother is the best bet, and don't let Satan draw you too fast." Poetry, if you ask me. The

Dutchman's last words were: "I want to pay, let them leave me alone," and he finally settled his account about eight-thirty in the evening.

But not before he got his wish to become Catholic. Father Cornelius McInerney baptized him and gave him the last rites bang-bang, one after another, snatching Arthur Flegenheimer from Satan's jaws once and for all. Most of us can look forward to quite a space between baptism and extreme unction, but the Dutchman got it all over within a couple of minutes. He was always efficient.

Since it was my Arrangement, I had him buried up at the Gate of Heaven cemetery in Yonkers, in hallowed ground and with a tallis around his shoulders. Talk about covering your bets. Dutch's grave is still there, not far from Larry Fay's. I wish I could be with them when my time comes, but Agnes won't hear of it, so I'm slated for planting in the family plot in Greenwood Cemetery down here. Among the Protestants, that's where you'll find me—quite a fate for a boy who lived his life among his peoples, the Catholics and the Jews.

Frenchy died in September of 1939 in his rooms at the Warwick Hotel, heart attack, what were the odds at his age. He'd just got back from the spread that "Mr. Fox" and Jane had in Florida and was going over some numbers when the odds caught up with him.

We gave him a Hell of a send-off, like in the old days, you woulda thought it was Chicago during the reign of the Big Fella, flowers, hearses, the works: six open cars chockablock with flowers, me in the third car, all the way from the Simons Funeral Parlor to Woodlawn Cemetery in the Bronx, way up, near the Yonkers line and Van Cortlandt Park, which some people called Vannie but I didn't. "You helped everybody," my arrangement said, "God will help you." At the funeral I met George's real wife and kids for the first time. He had a daughter, who wrote me for money later. I gave it to her.

I managed to get in and out of town without any trouble that time, but then that fat little goo-goo La Guardia called a press conference and solemnly swore to all the coyotes that if I so much as set a toenail in the great City of New York again, he'd have me arrested on the spot for vagrancy. Mr. Fusion: half-Jewish, half-Republican, and neither half a good half.

"Excuse me, Your Honor?" said one of the reporters. "Did you say for 'fragrancy'?" You see what I'd had to put up with all those years.

Arrested I was too, a whole bunch of times. You could argue that I wasn't quite keeping my half of the bargain, but then I didn't really expect the feds to keep theirs.

Mostly I visited the city to go to the fights, in which I still had plenty of interest and interests. My tomato can Carnera went all the way to the title, thanks to the fights we fixed, but like with most sad sacks, things went wrong for Carnera. He was in with Ernie Schaaf, a nice fighter, and clipped him with a light right, just the way he was told to, and Schaaf was being paid to take a dive anyway, but nobody had told us that Schaaf, who'd been smacked around pretty good by Maxie Baer in his previous bout, was concealing an injury—his head wasn't right—and so when the big Powder Puff tagged him, he fell down like he was shot.

"Nice act," said Frenchy, who was sitting beside me at the Garden, but I could see Schaaf's legs twitching, the sight I always hated, and then they fetched a stretcher and rushed him to Polyclinic, where the great Rothstein had expired, and where he lasted a couple of days in a coma and died. I sent Schaaf's family ten grand, anonymously, I felt so bad for the chump.

We put old Satchel Feet in with Baer for his next title defense, and the long and the short of it is I laid a couple of hundred grand on Maxie, no strings attached, and he put Primo on his can eleven times until finally the ref stopped what the papers the next day called the "Comedy Battle," and that was the end of Carnera. We shipped him home to Italy, where they say Mussolini stole all his money. Shalleck told me later that somebody wrote a book about it. All's I know is, don't blame me.

Maxie was a good-lookin' lad who liked dolls better than he liked training. Joe Gould decided to replace him with Jimmy Braddock, the Cinderella Man, a light-heavy moving up in class who decisioned Max in fifteen at the Garden on June 13, 1935, just before I left town. I won a bundle on that one and so did Maxie. "You know I never bet on anything unless it's a fight and I know what round I'm going down in," he told me. Smart fighter.

Braddock was my last champ. Prizefighters, like gangsters, don't last very long: the public gets bored easily, whether your map is on the cover of *Ring* magazine or hanging up in the post office. We wanted Jimmy to go out on top and the one who gave me the idea of how to do it was Mae West herself, who turned up in Bubbles, sitting plump and pretty in one of the suites at the Arlington. As luck would have it, Agnes was visiting a sick relative or something, and so I strolled across the street to spend some time with her. After we'd spent our time, she rolled over and said, "I got a favor to ask you."

She pulled her nightgown around her shoulders. It's funny that Mae was always sensitive about her figure, her being a big movie star and all. "There's this colored boy I been seein'."

"Yeah?"

"Pugilist. Well equipped for the title."

"I'll bet."

"Everybody's ducking him like it was the first of the month."

"You mean Louis. The Brown Bomber."

"I got other names for him." She turned back toward me, her nightdress splaying open, and I got an eyeful of two of the things I'd always admired about Mae and then we visited some more.

Then I picked up the phone and called Mike Jacobs, the promoter associated with the Twentieth Century Club, and made the deal for a title bout, Braddock-Louis. Braddock knew he didn't have a Chinaman's chance against a puncher like Joe Louis, but I softened the blow by telling him about the deal I'd made with Jacobs. Not only would he get his usual slice of the gate, but he'd also get ten percent of Jacobs's share of everything Louis would ever earn as a champion. That was a deal nobody could say no to.

I told Jimmy to make it look good, and he did. Chicago, June 22, 1937. He dropped Joe in the first round, put him down right on his brown backside, but Joe rallied as we all knew he would and took Jimmy out in the eighth, busted his nose, closed both his eyes. Jimmy had one more fight after that, a ten-round decision over Tommy Farr, and then retired. A hell of a mug.

I don't want you to get the impression that all the fights were fixed back then, just the ones that counted. Went up for the Marciano-Moore fight in September of 1955, forty-buck ringside seat at Yankee Stadium, courtesy of Al Weill, the champ's manager. Al wrote to me the week before the fight, with this prediction: "I figure this to be tough fight in the early rounds, but the Champ should come on strong in the middle and finish him in the later rounds." That Al was some kind of prognosticator, because sure enough Archie floored the champ early, but the Rock came back and took him out in the ninth. Marciano retired undefeated after that fight, two million bucks to the good. It was worth getting rousted to see that.

I bring this up because while you trust a fixed fight, you couldn't trust Washington, and those politocos who are always screaming about cleaning up the fight game wouldn't dare to apply the same dudgeon to themselves or their own rackets.

Take what happened to Lepke, fried at Sing Sing. Wouldn't ya know it, that fink Winchell was involved, got Lepkeleh to surrender to none other than that fairy Hoover, Edgar not Herbert, on the condition he got to dodge the Big Rap in New York State, but of course the feds double-crossed him.

That was in March of 1944. A Presidential election year, and guess who was still running for President?

Which pretty much explains this: Lepkeleh got a forty-eight-hour stay from my old friend Tom Dewey, now sitting pretty as Governor of New York, when he claimed to have information on various rackets that could reach all the way to the White House. I knew that meant all the way to "Clear it with Sidney" Hillman, chief of the Amalgamated Clothing Workers, which meant all the way to Roosevelt, and sure enough, they stayed Louis just long enough to find out everything he knew and then they fried him anyway.

The day Lepke died they also jacked up the juice for Louis Capone and Mendy Weiss, who went down not for the Dutchman hit but a whack job on some stoolie named Rosen. Charles the Bug got life and was let out last year after a mere twenty-two years in a Jersey stir. Like me, he got left behind when Piggy the Putz took off, and had to make his way back to New York, where they picked him up with blood all over his hands. He took it like a man. When it was clear the fix was in at his trial, he stood up, switched his plea from not guilty to *non vult* and told the judge: "I, Charles Workman, being of the opinion that any witness called in my defense will be intimidated and arrested by members of the District Attorney's office or police officials and not wishing members of my family and others to be subjected to humiliation on my account, do hereby request no witnesses in my defense except myself."

Deny, deny, deny—and when you can't deny any longer, when they got you dead to rights, attack the cops and the prosecutors. I was so proud of the Bug that I took care of his family for all the years he was in the slammer.

Three years after Dutch went down, Jimmy Hines got busted by Dewey for protecting the Dutchman's policy rackets. He was tried, convicted and sent to Sing Sing for four years. Everybody figured with his connections he'd soon be sprung, but Roosevelt let him dangle. That was the thanks Hines got from FDR, after all he done for him.

I was determined not to let that happen to me. One of the first things I did in Bubbles was buy the federal judge, and a good thing too because the feds didn't even wait a decade to welsh on me. They tried to deport me as an undesirable alien in 1943, just because I was still carrying my British passport. Luckily my pet judge was on hand to naturalize me PDQ, and when the Washington goons came down, I told 'em to go piss up a rope. All it cost me was a cool quarter of a million. For added protection, I moved the police chief, Ermey, in next door, just over the hedgerow. I even had him appoint me a reserve police officer, "reposing special confidence in the worth, ability and integrity of Owen Madden."

The neighborhood kids used to rumor that there was an underground tunnel between our houses, just in case a higher authority than the chief came calling. They also whispered that I was trainin' my pigeons to carry secret messages all the way to New York, to my gangster buddies, or maybe to Hollywood and George Raft, the big movie star, to avoid the prying eyes and ears of the FBI agent who set up housekeeping right across the street and never got a goddamned thing on me. I never told 'em otherwise.

My strategy in Bubbles was to make friends with everybody, whether I needed to or not, because you never knew. I bought all the uniforms and trophies for the Hot Springs High School sports teams and marching bands, anonymously of course, because for some reason, though the town was proud enough of my residence there, nobody seemed to want my name on anything, which was fine with me. What wasn't fine with me was when I bought a brand-new life-size statue of the BVM, complete with Lourdesian grotto, for St. Mary's Catholic Church, the one across the street from Ouachita Hospital, which gratefully accepted my gift so long as my moniker wasn't attached to it. A statue of Mary, in honor of . . .

My mother died in June of 1947. Marty, as usual, was the bearer of the bad news. He sent me a telegram, which arrived at the Hot Springs Western Union office at 11:39 A.M. Central Daylight Time, which was precisely sixteen minutes after he sent it from New York. "OWEN, MOTHER IS CRITICALLY ILL. BEST REGARDS TO YOU BOTH. MARTY."

By which, of course, he meant that she was already dead.

After I had Frank Costello make sure there wasn't going to be no trouble with the cops, Agnes and I drove up to New York for the funeral. It was at St. Mike's too, just like May's, and I shed a tear or two not only for Mary Agnes O'Neill Madden, the pride of the Burren, whose life was like her hope chest, which was to say empty, but for my sister, May, who never had a life, and for myself, who got the life I asked for, not to mention deserved.

That was my last official visit to a Catholic church, because Agnes was an adherent of the Christian Church, as they call it down here. I always thought I was a Christian, but she informed me I was just a Papist, which in Arkansas was a dirty word, like "nigger." Sure, from time to time I was able to sneak into a Mass or two, but I was fugitive enough without having to be on the lam at the altar as well.

Roosevelt finally kicked the bucket in Warm Springs, Georgia. Tom Pendergast's errand boy, Truman, more or less left me alone, although I almost had to face the Kefauver Committee, which convened in 1950 and '51, right on schedule, a generation after Judge Seabury and his mob. I would have had to testify, except that Fortune smiled on me the year before, when Tennessee Estes came down to the Springs for a little rest and relaxation.

To you Kefauver was Mr. Crime Buster and Vice Presidential Candidate, but to me he was just another cheap Washington hoodlum out for a good time. He arrived with a juggy babe, and I hosted them at one of my clubs, out of town where nobody would see him, together with a couple of local officials. Wouldn't you know it, as we were motoring back in my new Packard, the Doozies having gone under in '37, one of the politicos suffered a shock or seizure of some kind, don't ask me how it happened, so all of a sudden there was Mr. Crime Buster in a touring car with a blonde not his wife, my own good self—a gangster of some repute—and a fresh stiff.

"Don't worry, Senator," I told him. "I'll take care of everything." The stiff went to Ouachita Hospital, DOA, the blonde disappeared into a Kansas City whorehouse and the Senator trudged back to the Arlington Hotel with a plausible tale of an automotive breakdown. End of problem. End of my testimony. All my life, I never seen a hound like a Congressman, and that's God's honest truth.

The bum did drag poor Costello down to Washington, though. Frank refused to let the TV cameras show his phiz, and so all America saw of the Prime Minister of the Underworld was his hands, his shaking hands, and his dese-dem-and-dose voice, which more or less fixed the image of the goombah gangster in the public consciousness forever after.

As for Charlie Lucky, his luck finally ran out. Just as we'd said, Dewey trained his sights on the former Salvatore Lucania as soon as Dutch ate lead and forgot to digest it. The Special Prosecutor nailed Scarface Junior in '36 on a hooker beef—"extortion and direction of harlotry," you gotta love it, the revenge of the two-dollar hooker. Maybe even the revenge of Mary Frances Blackwell, although I didn't like to think about it.

I got a kick out of the fact that where does Charlie run while under indictment but to Bubbles, my Bubbles, checking in to the Arlington under one of his pseudonyms with a fleet of gunners and broads and asks me—me—to bail him out. After all he done for me. I told him yes, which was more or less true and more or less a lie, because I had one of my flunkies ring up the Gov and order him to a meeting. The normal course of business in Arkansas was I would tell the state's chief executive what to do and hand over a suitcase full of cash—never too much, fifty or sometimes a hundred grand, because we didn't want these rubes to get the wrong idea about the value of dough—and then he would get back in the unmarked car driven by the unmarked State Trooper and do what I told him.

At this particular meeting, I gave the Gov fifty grand, which Charlie thinks is to buy protection, but which in reality is to buy the presence of the Arkansas National Guard, which shows up and takes him into custody, gee I'm so sorry, and packs him off to the slammer for thirty to fifty in Siberia. Eventually they shipped Lucky back to wopland and I guess he got delusions of George Raft glamour or something, because he was at the Napoli airport a couple of years ago, strolling out to shake the mitt of some Hollywood producer, when he up and drops dead of a heart attack, right there on the tarmac. See Naples and die.

I got a kick out of what Dewey said about Hot Springs. "The whole crowd are a complete ring: the Chief of Police, the Chief of Detectives, the Mayor and the City Attorney." Well, sure, Tom—that's how you do it right.

As for me, I got Bubbles and Garland County running pretty much the way I liked it. I bought up or opened as many gambling clubs as I could manage—the Vapors, the Tower, the Belvedere and my headquarters, the Southern Club and Grill, which was tucked in next to the Medical Arts Building, one of the tallest in town; it reminded me of good old 440 West 34th. You shoulda seen the looks on their faces as one hero after another waltzed in the front door, magic names, like Costello and Lansky. Them Hot Springs hillbillies ate that stuff up, let me tell you.

I held court in the Southern Club every day, one of my Jack Russells by my side. As one died, I'd replaced him or her with another: Sissy, Thomas, Ginger, Blackie, Tammy. I never went anywhere without a dog; Paramount Theaters even gave my little Sissy a lifetime movie pass. Monk had his kits and his boids; I had my Jacks and my pigeons.

With Costello looking after my investments in New York, and Hot Springs ticking over nicely under Leo McLaughlin, Meyer and I went into business with our friend Batista down in Cuba, casinos and so forth. Meyer would shuttle back and forth between Lanskyland in Florida and Havana, while I would send my brother, Marty, there to look after my end of things. Marty liked the work; it helped him buy that farm of his in Virginia, the one he shared with Kitty. Marty was all the family I had left now, what with Ma and May gone and my daughter, my baby Margaret, not such a baby anymore, never really here, at least for me. The daughter to whom I've left the grand sum of One Dollar and No/100 in my Last Will and Testament, "whose exact address and married name I do not know, but who did live in Yonkers, New York."

Cuba turned out to be the thing that got Marty in dutch; no good deed goes unpunished, as they say. Back in December of 1930 I'd sent him over to Havana on business, and when he came back through Miami, he did what everybody else did, which was to say he was an American citizen, which he wasn't. So now here it is twenty-three years later and somebody in Washington says he entered the country illegally way back when and that, because of his priors, he was deportable on the grounds of moral turpitude. Unlike me, Social Security number 432–62–2509, Marty had never gotten around to fixing the citizenship thing, which meant that he didn't have the proper visa or some such, and given his rap sheet—a pathetic arrest record, not a patch on mine—he was ordered to return to England, the land of our birth.

That made me mad. Just like you don't choose your parents, you can't choose your siblings. They just happen at random, blind fate, turn of the card, spin of the wheel, all life 9 to 5 against. And yet there they are, squalling into the world, so I guess you can say we all beat the odds, for a while.

Marty and Kitty were living down at Somerset Farm in Charlottesville, Virginia, named after the street we were born on in Leeds, horses and cattle, but that came to naught, like everything else Marty tried, especially with the deportation proceedings looming, and so they sold it off in 1954 for $77,000 and moved back to Manhattan, to 27 West 96th Street, a nice building where I kept a couple of flats for emergency purposes. I didn't want to see my brother shipped out for Liverpool, the Madden family going in reverse, so I made a few phone calls and called in a few favors. What else were Senators good for?

The first bill to naturalize Marty, S. 3216, introduced on the Senate floor in March, crapped out, which meant my donation hadn't been high enough. It made me damn mad that these bastards were shaking me down for more, but there was nothing I could do about it. So Agnes and I made a handsome contribution to McClellan's reelection campaign, which was hand-delivered by one of my stooges in a nice tidy envelope to the Senator on July 10, 1954. "We decided this is more prudent than going to any Committee in HS as it seems every '2 bit' politician and newspaper writer tries to make capital with everything connected with our name," Agnes wrote in the note. I never put my name to anything I didn't have to.

The second bill, S. 541, introduced on January 18, 1955, was more like it. *"Be it enacted by the Senate and House of Representatives of the United States of America in Congress assembled,* That for the purposes of the immigration and nationality Act, Martin Aloysius Madden shall be held and considered to have been lawfully admitted to the United States for permanent residence as of the date of the enactment of this Act, upon payment of the required visa fee."

The bill was sponsored by Senator, former Governor, Herbert H. Lehman of New York, helped along by Senator McClellan, and was ratified by the full Senate on June 14. We listened hard to hear any objections from Dewey, but Albany was silent.

Things had come full circle: first the politicians owned the gangsters, then we owned them and then they became us. It was Tammany's last laugh, disguised as reform: the Tiger at a masquerade ball, wearing a goo-goo mask but still the same hungry beast beneath.

I got a nice telegram from Marty the next day: "DEAR BROTHER TRIED TO CALL YOU ALL MORNING AND NO ANSWER THE SENATE VOTED IN MY FAVOR ON MY BILL YESTERDAY AND IT PASSED EVERYTHING LOOKS VERY GOOD LOVE MARTY." Through the good offices of the Honorable W. F. Norrell of the Sixth District in Arkansas—he was from Monticello, Arkansas—it sailed through Francis E. Walter of Pennsylvania's Judiciary Subcommittee No. 1 (Immigration) in mid-July and passed the House on July 30, 1955, which meant that Marty was home free.

The New York law firm I hired, Cotton, Brenner and Wrigley, of 225 Broadway, prepared a handsome brief in support of S. 541. Testimonials from everyone who'd known my brother since we were pups—priests, rabbis and vicars. Kitty Madden. Cops and robbers, Sixty-seven pages of encomia, ending with this from the mouthpieces, dated March 2, 1954: "In our letter of yesterday, we inadvertently omitted to mention that the nearest relative living in this country of Mr. Martin A. Madden is his brother Owen Madden, who resides in Hot Springs, Arkansas. Respectfully Yours, COTTON, BRENNER & WRIGLEY."

You can't make this stuff up. Last billed in my most important appearance in my brother's life.

Marty died a few years later. Simons, where I was getting to be a regular, dressed him out and St. Mike's sent him into the hereafter. May, Ma and now Martin—four blocks from where we landed we were already a vanishing race, down to me and my little girl, wherever she was.

It seemed everybody was leaving me, or trying to. A punk named Vinnie the Chin took a shot at Costello right in the lobby of his apartment building on Central Park West, but Vinnie was a lousy shot and only grazed him. Frank and I knew Genovese was behind it, but unfortunately the botched hit led to an inquiry into our ownership of the Tropicana, which meant Frank had to do a little time. Vito took over Frank's business in his absence, which is to say my business, and that's how the Genovese "crime family" was born, even if Costello and I did all the heavy lifting.

Movie fellas kept pesterin' me about selling them the rights to my life story, as if they haven't already stolen it from me a dozen times. Mugs who were sportin' knee pants when I was running the rackets read the papers and get bright ideas: "Jutting brows over cold eyes, lean cheeks, aquiline nose, thick, tight lips, human TNT held in leash by an iron will—that's Owney Madden, Hell's Kitchen's 'Uncle Owney,' 'Owney the Killer,' 'Owney the Hermit' of Sing Sing, in his prime the terror man of mystery, richest and most politically influential racketeer of his day . . ." Swill like that.

W. P. Hendry of MGM wrote to me in 1943 that neither Clinton Anderson, the chief of police in Beverly Hills, nor the L.A. district attorney, Fred Howzer, would have any objection if I wanted to come and live in Beverly Hills—"provided, of course, no former business be transacted." I turned him down cold. Ten years later Metro came back to me in the person of one Art Cohn, who wanted to write a book about me. Gave him the air too. Jim Bishop had written me a month earlier, asking what my favorite prayer was. "It would be most helpful if it is a prayer of your own devising, your own words."

I guess this book's your answer, Jim.

And so I started to fade, like one of them old photographs. People that used to be so clear and so familiar that you didn't even bother to write their names on the backs turn into nameless ghosts, spirits of the past, the only power they have left to haunt.

It's funny how, at the end of your life, you finally start to think about the future, when it's too late to do you any good. The brightest kids in town like to hang out at the Southern, sitting in the front room, looking for swells and watching for gangsters, soaking up whatever they can. I always had time for 'em, and a word of advice or two, and once in a while a double sawbuck.

After the war I let Mayor McLaughlin go and replaced him with a bunch of GIs fresh back from the war, running on a reform ticket. This being Hot Springs, there was no Republican Party to speak of, so it was a Democratic reform ticket, which meant there would be plenty of Democrats and precious little reform. A trio of lawyers, Sid McMath, Clyde Brown and Nathan Schoenfeld, put up a slate of candidates county-wide, which included my own personal lawyer down here, Q. Byrum Hurst. Sid was the former southwestern Golden Gloves champ, which made me like him straight off. He ran for prosecuting attorney. They all won.

Naturally there was a great deal of flapdoodle about this bein' curtains for gambling in Hot Springs, etc., etc., but of course it wasn't. This was my kind of reform. Somebody asked Orval Faubus, the governor, why the state didn't shut down illegal gambling in Hot Springs and he said the state police were too busy directing traffic to interfere in local matters.

After eleven terms, Leo took it hard, but I wasn't in the mood to fool around, and so when he started kicking, I got him indicted on bribery charges, a nice touch. He did some time but he kept his mouth shut. Earl Ricks, who owned a Buick dealership with Raymond Clinton, became the new Mayor. That was in 1947.

Raymie's got a brother, Roger, who isn't much good for anything when he's drunk, which is often, but is a pretty good mechanic otherwise. He works on my cars. His wife, Virginia, a busty party-girl-turned-nurse, sometimes takes care of me whenever I need medical attention, so the Clintons have me coming and going. Virginia has a son I've taken a shine to, a bright kid named Billy who likes to hang out at the Southern Club with Byrum Hurst's kid. Maybe he'll learn something.

Later some zealous punk out to make a name for himself put Byrum on trial for income-tax-evasion shenanigans, but I testified that the income they claimed he was hiding was simply a loan from me, and no, I couldn't remember whether he'd paid me back yet, but I was sure he would. I loan money to lots of people, and some of 'em pay me back and some of 'em don't. Everybody knows that. He beat the rap.

One of the lawyers who handled his case wrote me a letter: "I am still enjoying the picture of you on the witness stand answering so well the questions I asked you relative to your background and your loans to Byrum, and I particularly remember the outstanding manner with which you handled yourself when cross-examined by the Government." That's me, still the master . . .

My friends down here gave me a testimonial dinner on St. Patrick's Day in 1958. Eddie Rogers and his Arlington Hotel Orchestra played my favorite songs: "Machushla," "Where the River Shannon Flows," and of course the best, "Danny Boy." I told them not to play "The Last Rose of Summer."

The papers say I'm sitting on four million dollars. That got the tax men all riled up, naturally, and the past couple of years they've been coming after me pretty vicious. Ever since they nailed the Big Fella, the green-eyeshade gang is feeling its oats. They want to know how I can report an income of less than ten grand a year when the word is that the Southern Club alone is pulling in thirty grand a month, but that's what the books show.

Cash is a different story. It's everywhere. Agnes stuffs it down coffee cans, slips it between book covers, wraps it up with rubber bands and hides it in the toilet tanks. Not to mention she wears it. A yellow gold heart-shaped brooch set with one hundred diamonds and one pear-shaped blue sapphire. A platinum diamond bracelet set with two square diamonds, fifty-four baguette diamonds and 244 brilliant-cut diamonds. A platinum diamond bracelet set with three marquise diamonds, thirty-six baguette diamonds and 340 round diamonds. You get the picture.

After I'm gone, after she's gone, nobody will ever find it. It's all taken care of. They say you can't take it with you, and maybe you can't, but you sure as hell can fix it so no dirty sonofabitch can take it away from you either.

So that's about it. I'm in this state now, this funny state that flashes me back to before I was even born, to where May wanted to go when she got to the other side, and where she is now, and where I'm going. Flashes me back to the Last Rose of Summer, which it's taken me all these many years to figure out all along what was growing in my own flat, my own 352, my own 440, my own flesh and blood and if that's a sin, then God damn me to Hell. You'd have done the same too.

I see my Da, lying on his back, not in the ring, but on the dock, fighting for breath, the breath You gave him and which You, the Boss, the Big Fella, the real *capo di tutti capi,* took away, for no reason, because You could.

I been in this damned Ouachita Hospital four days now, undershirt and pajama bottom my only inventory. Lying on my back, just like Da, just like I did so long ago at the Arbor, sucking in breaths with great difficulty, remembering, the pain intense, the clock ticking, and it must amuse You something fierce, something diabolical, only this time it's not a bull leaning over me, asking me Owney who done this thing, but a nurse or two, maybe a doctor, and they're all wearin' white, like the angels in heaven, or maybe all the saints.

The answer's still the same: I done it to myself.

They're leaning over me with that look on their face, that look I've seen once or twice, the look that says he ain't gonna make it, what a tough break, and do you have any last words?

I'm alone, which is the way we all go out. I can hear the voices, speaking through the solitude—the great Jack Johnson, who on the canvas in Havana embraced it; the great Dutch Schultz, on the deck in Newark, calling for the bill and begging for it.

I'm having trouble breathing. Emphysema, the doctors have been telling me. Cigarettes. Bullshite. Them bullets in me are acting up, and the ones that are gone are acting up worse. Each one with Little Patsy's name on it, every one reminding me of Leeds and Wigan and Liverpool and the time Fats cut the strings of my mother's purse. The time when I got my payback, when I conked him with the lead pipe; the time when he got my own wife, my Loretta, to lure me to the Arbor, so's he could take a shot at me. The time when I lured him with dear sweet Freda into Nash's, so's I could finish him off. And who would have thought that all these memories—especially now— could come flooding back to me, like the pigeon's blood, like Luigi's and Willie's and Vannie's blood, like Dutch's fedora, wobbling on that table, try- ing to decide which way to fall and coming right down in the middle, fifty- fifty, the jury still out.

I hope you're proud of me, Da. I wasn't a fighter like you, but I was a fighter just the same.

Not alone. Agnes is here, and Loretta, and I think that's Freda and Mar- garet Everdeane standing behind her, alongside my Mother, who's holding hands with Mary Frances. All the women of my life, the Marys and the Margarets and the Magdalenes, come to comfort me in my hour of need. To shepherd me.

All but one.

Dutch figured it out, delirious Dutch on his deathbed, with Monk's last slug in him, mother is always the best bet, Hoboe and Poboe I think mean the same thing, and you know what, Dutch, you almost got it right. If there's one thing we know, it's how to settle a tab and settle a score, no matter how long it takes.

We are Irishmen and we are a type and I know who is best.

A boy has ever wept. Tears and blood are the same thing.

My suit is pressed and ready, and my hat, the fedora I haven't worn since that day in 1935, and best of all my .38, Monk's .38, loaded again, a miracle, may all the saints be praised.

She's here, her face whole again, not a hair of her head out of place, radiant, smiling, happy . . . her hand extended.

I reach and rise.

The city, the river, the sky. Me, up high, duke of all I survey. Her hand in mine, looking out over our empire, and her head still intact, with her pretty face still shining and me with my guts and my spirit still in me, just the two of us holding hands, innocent as always, like when we were kids, looking out over all the world and knowing it was ours, and just waiting for the day when it would be, never to be separated again. Two holy ghosts starting over, stand- ing over 352, looking out, running now, into the darkness, rushing for the edge of the building—

We jump.

Not a dare or a dream but reality. Over the roofs of old New York, with the horses and the pushcarts and the dirt from the Seventh Avenue Subway spritzing everywhere, and the iceman and the coalman and the ragman and the boneman singing their songs, but we don't care because we're up above them now, beyond them, way up in the air, watching the Waldorf fall and the Empire State rise, watching the els tumble and the motorcars flock, sailing out over the Harbor, over the Bay, over the wide Ocean, over everything, until at last we can see, way off in the distance, the hills our Mother told us about, the grey limestone of the Slieve Elva and the green Bens and far off, the Mountains of Mourne, the Mountains of Home.

So please don't mourn for us, May and me, who didn't know no better, who didn't have a chance to know no better, for all of those who have gone before us in sin and sorrow, heathen or Christian, Jew or Gentile, the blessed and the damned, past and future to come, for we are all equal now and we don't need your sympathy, just your understanding.

May, we're flying. Just you and me and all the saints, forever and ever.

It doesn't hurt anymore.

So hold my hand.

And soar.

Acknowledgments

Spending seven years inside the mind and heart of one of American history's most ruthless, murderous, influential and altogether fascinating criminals is not a task undertaken lightly, nor without stout companionship. Among those who helped guide me on my journey were, in New York: Maureen Egen, Sara Ann Freed, Jay Cocks, Don Congdon, Susan Dempsey, Mari Ellen Goodspeed and the late John F. Kennedy, Jr.; in Hot Springs, Arkansas: Kathern Kinsey, Sandy Sutton, Q. Byrum Hurst, Sr., Chuck Cunning, Bobbie Jones McLane and the staff of the Garland County Historical Society; in Los Angeles: Daniel Melnick, Jeff Berg, Mark Glabman, Michael Nathanson, Greg Foster and Ken Atchity.

Special thanks to my wife, Kate, and our daughters, Alexandra and Clare, for indulging my enthusiasm for all things gangland these many years.

Finally, thanks to Owen Vincent Madden his own good self, at rest in Hot Springs nearly forty years, whose life and fate provide an object lesson for us all.

Lakeville, Connecticut
Summer 2002